PROLOGUE

L ife is not sacred. Not in Necropolis. But neither is death. Both serve a purpose, and here in Miss Wilkins' attic, death was a macabre obsession for the living. Petula Upwood, a necromancer, moved amongst the exhibitions, but she wasn't here to see the latest trends in taxidermy or the ancient ways to mummify the dead. She was here to catch a spirit let loose by a careless cleaner. Miss Wilkins had summoned her after two customers had been attacked and killed by the spirit. It had tried to possess their bodies. Without human flesh, the spirit was bound to the vessel it was trapped in and stuck here in the attic.

From its hiding place, the spirit wailed, trying to intimidate Petula. But she'd done this for too long to let the sound have any effect on her. Petula sometimes wondered at the habits of Necropolitans and their basic disregard for danger and hygiene. Tampering with the dead didn't come without a price. And this exhibition full of wonders was tempting fate. Not that this was an exception from the norm; the rest of the Necropolitans were as careless with the dead as Miss Wilkins.

All around her were not only dolls and charms containing evil spirits, but also rotting parts of some poor bastards whose families had donated them to be paraded here in the attic for a short moment of excitement.

Something crashed to Petula's right. She froze and turned around, ready to cast a protective incantation. But it wasn't the spirit. An orange tabby stared at her from the top of an empty exhibition stand. The cat had knocked down a pot, and fragments of pottery lay shattered at the foot of the stand. Around the broken pieces, white ash had spread. Petula grimaced at the bitter smell and hoped that whatever the substance was, it was tame and harmless for the living. But that was seldom the case.

"Who let you in here?" Petula asked.

The tabby tilted its head.

A black cat would have been more fitting in this environment and in Necropolis in general, but Petula had to admit the ginger cat looked cute with its big round eyes and fluffy mane.

"It's not safe," she said, not knowing if she expected the cat to reply. She hoped not. That would be a new level of bizarre even in the land of the undead.

The cat lost interest in Petula and turned its attention to licking its front paw.

"Oh, well. I guess I'd better take you out," Petula said, not understanding why she kept speaking to the cat.

She approached the tabby with caution, not wanting to spook the cat and be forced to give chase. That would be just perfect. Another reminder of what her career as a necromancer had amounted to: pest removal instead of using her full potential. But it was what it was. She had to resign herself to spirit control if she ever wanted to prove her talent. But she and the agency she worked for knew this was beneath her. She could do more. Real necromancy was about raising the dead.

The cat didn't seem to care about her approach. It sat on its post like the king of the valley, majestic and untouchable. But still, Petula crept forward with caution. It was a good thing she did, as behind the cat the air stirred.

PENNY FOR YOUR SOUL

K.A. Ashcomb

Glorious Mishaps Series

Liquid Hare Publishing

PENNY FOR YOUR SOUL

Published by Liquid Hare Publishing 2019

Riihimäki, Kanta-Häme, Finland

ISBN 978-952-69026-3-0 (Paperback)

ISBN 978-952-69026-4-7 (eBook)

Contact K.A. Ashcomb: k.a.ashcomb@gmail.com

Follow K.A. Ashcomb's blog: https://ashcombka.com

Cover Design by K.A. Ashcomb

Edited by Emily Nemchick

To my nephew
The scariest things in life define us, but you will never walk alone as
long as I am here

Also by K. A. Ashcomb

Worth of Luck
Penny for Your Soul

ACKNOWLEDGMENTS

A special thanking are needed for those who helped me to complete this book. Writing Penny for Your Soul and publishing it wouldn't have been possible without their support. Foremost, thank you for my husband, Henri, who carried me through the tough times and never let me give up, who is always pushing me to be the best version of myself. Special thanks to my beta readers who pointed out its weaknesses and strengths. Thank you, Emily Nemchick for editing, she scrutinized my text and made it better. And thank you for my friend Hanna who keeps me sane with our long walks in the woods.

PENNY FOR YOUR SOUL

Ever so slightly. The vibration was easily missed, but Petula sensed it before seeing the disturbance. She readied herself.

It wouldn't dare, she thought.

Petula tilted her head and waited, then saw the spirit becoming more solid. It screeched and surged towards the cat.

Of course, it had to be malicious. Petula had no other choice than to rush towards the cat as well. She snatched it into her arms, turning her back on the spirit. The undead lashed out, shredding the fabric of Petula's black wool coat. She let out an incantation as she held the soft cat close to her chest. Her words stunned the spirit. She slowly turned around to face it. A dark, faceless human-shaped spirit hung in the air. It flickered, but Petula's incantation held it present and in her control.

The thing had been trapped inside its vessel for so long that it had forgotten what it used to be. The only thing left was pure want.

The more recently dead usually hung on to their beliefs of what their bodies should look like and what their lives could be, but this creature didn't possess even half of that memory. Petula felt sad for it. Someone had done this to the spirit. They'd trapped it inside the vessel and prevented him or her from entering the afterlife.

The spirit screeched.

The cat clawed its way out of Petula's lap and made a run for it. She let it go.

The spirit screeched again.

It couldn't harm her, she was in control, but at least the theatrics would make anyone listening to them behind the attic door think there was a real struggle. A struggle to justify what she was about to do next. She would destroy the museum's showpiece and release the spirit from the mortal coil. It was the merciful thing to do, but Miss Wilkins wouldn't like it. But what Miss Wilkins didn't know wouldn't harm her. And if her actions ever came into the light of day, she would face the consequences from Miss Wilkins and the Necromantic Agency, her employers. What could they do? Kill her? They wouldn't dare.

1

RAISING THE DEAD IS A TRICKY BUSINESS

Amongst the thick leather-bound books scattered around him, a man worked at a pace to collect his belongings inside a doctor's bag. He pushed in stones, or, to be precise, crystals with drawn-on symbols. He worked methodically and carefully to get everything into the bag without invoking anything horrible from the darkness. His head wasn't in the right place to fight off monsters. In an ideal situation, he'd have more time to put his work-bag in order, but as it was, he was already running late. He'd forgotten tonight's appointment, and to make matters worse, his head felt groggy. Jeremiah was sure someone had slipped something into his drink at last night's poker game. He should be sober by now, but even as a new night crept in, he felt sick and thirsty. Jeremiah paused his packing.

Usually Jeremiah Black was nothing but self-confidence itself. His whole essence told him that he was the best necromancer there was. He could summon the dead back up just like that, even make them dance to his tune. His black silk shirt, long black leather jacket, and tight black trousers alone told the tale of his greatness, but now he found his gaunt legs tangled and his mind scattered.

Jeremiah flexed and squeezed his hands to stop them from shaking. A drink would help, but there was work to be done, so he shouldn't. Not with his new clients. They were the fastidious sort. But this shouldn't be that hard. He reached for the chest pocket of his jacket, where he kept his flask. He'd awoken the dead hundreds of times. So many times, in fact, he'd stopped counting. Half of the city was his to claim if he wanted it. A drink wouldn't do any harm. It would get his beat back on, quiet the whispers that chipped away his self-confidence. He took the flask out and took a sip. The first drink of tonight burned in his mouth.

One more item and he would be done with the packing.

Jeremiah put the flask back inside his jacket and plucked a small perfume bottle full of black liquid from the table. With the bottle, or vial, as he preferred to call it, he could do anything. It ensured that he was the best necromancer in the city. And tonight's job was important. He needed every piece of ammunition there was to take the edge off. He held the cold vial carefully between his fingers, moving it towards the bag. Jeremiah's shaking hands caused a tremor. He held the vial still and composed himself, wanting to take another sip from his flask.

A small creak echoed at the back of the room. Jeremiah shot a glance over his shoulder, but there was nothing out of the ordinary outside the gas lamp's circle. Just his study, full of bookshelves stacked with necromantic literature, ranging from silly fiction to the real deal, which altered the delicate balance between life and death. He swallowed and continued lowering the vial into the doctor's bag. One spill and everything would be doomed.

There was another creak; this time it came closer. It sounded like a floorboard being stepped on. He took a better hold of the perfume bottle and turned his head in the direction the noise had come from.

He saw a man standing between the bookshelves. Jeremiah bared his teeth, and said, "Come no closer, or I'll kill you."

The man made no move. Jeremiah was sure he could take him. He was no bigger than him. Even if he was, it wouldn't matter. One incantation from Jeremiah and the dead would tear the man apart.

"What do you want?" he barked.

No answer.

"There's nothing to steal here, and one spill from this and there's nothing left of you. No body, no soul, nothing." He peered at the man, not seeing far into the shadows the bookshelves cast. Anyway, Jeremiah was lying. The liquid didn't work that way. It could kill, true, but with a great effort on his part. And to be honest, it worked better for the undead. Jeremiah was sure the man in front of him was as alive as he. The man lacked the distinctive rotten smell of the dead.

"If I were you, I'd skip the wakening," the man said. He had a melancholic, melodic voice. Jeremiah was sure there was a hint of amusement in there.

"No one threatens me in my own home." Jeremiah spat the words out. The bottle between his fingers shook, but this time with rage rather than fear. The black liquid ocean shifted from side to side. A storm began to brew.

"It wasn't a threat; it was a friendly request," the man said, almost laughing out his words.

"Who do you think you are dealing with? Some common caster? I'm a certified necromancer. I'm *Jeremiah Black*. You made a big mistake stepping inside my home without permission."

"I know who you are, *Jeremiah Black*. And you look more like a poor excuse for a necromancer than the real deal with your dramatic dark clothes, charcoal-lined eyes, and cropped hair. And that top hat of yours with the skull and crossbones is a crime against fashion. I expected more from the greatest necromancer in the city, as you, Jeremiah, pronounce yourself to be," the man said.

And before Jeremiah could get a word out, the man was next to him, and he felt a punch to his left ribcage.

The stabbing sensation happened again, and again, feeling unreal and soft, as if it was happening to someone else. There was a haze, the kind of haze you get after drinking for several days straight, but the warm wetness spreading under his silk shirt felt real. Too real. Jeremiah put his hand to his side when the man stepped away from him.

He looked at his right hand, which was red. The bottle in his left hand dropped, but the man who'd attacked him caught it before it could smash against the floor. In an instant, the perfume bottle and its contents disappeared into the man's pocket.

Jeremiah collapsed to his knees and then crumpled onto the floor.

"You little fucker!" he let out, sounding winded.

Maroon-colored blood puddled all around him.

A knock sounded from the front door.

Jeremiah Black drew a deep breath in, trying to speak, but no words came out. He watched as the man walked away, unable to do anything as he slid out through a broken window.

There was another knock on the front door.

He tried to scream but couldn't.

And another knock.

Jeremiah stopped struggling and let go. He lay there motionless, frozen inside his own body, observing the world in sober alertness.

Not long after his killer slipped away, the front door was pushed open. Three men stepped in. Two of them were older gentlemen dressed in nice dark suits and top hats. The third one was similarly clothed, but he was a lot younger. He limped forward, leaning against his cane. He had been the one who contacted him.

"*Morris,*" Jeremiah said.

"Mr. Black?" the tall and thin one asked. He had a dry, sour face and silver hair.

"*I'm here,*" he said and stood up from his body, but he was pulled back inside.

"Oh no," another older man said when they got farther in from the door. The wrinkled lines around the man's mouth made a huge "O" shape. His soft belly rose as he took a heavy breath in and looked around.

The three men stepped closer, inspecting him. The younger man, Morris, crouched to touch Jeremiah's neck, trying to find a pulse. When he found none, he shook his head. Jeremiah tried to grasp him, to pull him closer and ask for help, but his hand didn't budge.

"How unfortunate," the tall man said, the one with charismatic wrinkles and dashing hair. He'd taken his top hat off.

Morris Reinhardt stood up and said, "Dead as a doornail." He prodded Jeremiah one more time with his good leg. Morris was his age and at least half the age of the two men around him. He was a banker with a sharp wit, and he was a wiz when it came to clauses and numbers. Jeremiah knew him. They ran in the same social circles. And despite the cane, women and men alike were charmed by Morris. Even Jeremiah found his sideburns, which came down from his short-styled cut, and his somewhat dreamy, mysterious eyes convincing. Convincing enough to let them drag him into waking up their friend. Not that he had minded. The pay was good.

"What're we going to do?" the man with the soft belly asked.

"*Now you wake me,*" Jeremiah said.

"We leave," the tall man replied.

"What about him?" Morris asked.

"Somebody else's problem," the tall man replied. "And we better leave before he attracts too much attention; we'll have to find someone else."

"What an inconvenience," Morris said.

"Yes," the tall man agreed and turned around.

Jeremiah watched Morris limp after the other men to the front door. He screamed after them, begging them not to leave him dead and alone. He begged them to send for a necromancer, but the three men didn't have his powers to see the dead. His screams went unheard. Of course, they knew he could be wakened; everyone in the city knew that. They just chose not to.

Before the front door closed behind the men, Jeremiah heard one of them, the tall one presumably, saying, "This is complete foolery. Doesn't he know we have a deadline to make?"

"It's not like he chose to die. He had quite a few stab wounds," Morris said.

"Yes, but he should know better. This is a lack of professionalism on his part."

"You can't—" the round man said.

The door closed behind them. Jeremiah was alone.

He struggled free from his body, mumbling incantations he knew when alive. When he was free, he looked towards where his killer had gone and then at the door. He chose the door.

◆

The three men stepped out of Jeremiah Black's apartment building into the night air. A coach waited for them at the front. It was an impressive-looking thing, polished black with golden ornaments. It could easily hold four people; two on each side. The view inside was blocked with thick crimson curtains.

The coach's driver held the door open for them. Morris Reinhardt let the two older men head inside the coach first. He watched as Wilbur, the owner of the vehicle, squeezed in before Ignatius, who once again looked like he'd sucked a lemon. Morris took a seat next to Wilbur, opposite to Ignatius. If he hadn't, he'd have received side glances and unsaid words from Ignatius. The man's ego was bigger than the whole city. Morris was sure that if Ignatius could, he alone would live in Necropolis and rule the undead. And the undead got to stay only if they promised not to make any loud noises, sudden movements, or think at all. Ignatius was always like that. Sour and dry. He got on Morris' nerves. But he had no choice but to continue associating with the man. Morris had to finish what he'd started.

"The man's death can't be a coincidence. Somebody knows we're trying to wake up Ira," he said as soon as his bottom hit the black leather seat.

"And they're trying to stop us," Wilbur added.

"Let them. There's nothing they can do about it now," Ignatius said.

"They already have," Morris replied. "What a mess."

"Do you think I didn't see the mess inside? The place was in shambles. Not a single book was in proper order, but that's only a minor obstacle," Ignatius said.

"I think Morris was talking about the mutilated body," Wilbur said. He fell silent when Ignatius glared at him. In Morris' opinion, Wilbur should grow a backbone. It was annoying as Kraken shit how the huge man let Ignatius boss him around with no good reason. Wilbur could stand on his own merits. He owned the third largest bank in the city. Of course, after his and Ira's. Ignatius didn't even come close to them, but he had connections. Ignatius had an aristocratic line like no other. He was as blue-blooded as they got. Almost purple.

"Why should I care about the body?" Ignatius snorted.

"You should care about Jeremiah Black if we want to wake Ira tonight," Morris said.

"I never liked the man. He was an arrogant little brat. Besides, we don't need him. Driver, take us to the corner of Stonemason Road and Little Ruddy Lane," Ignatius said to the driver, who was still holding the door open, waiting for instructions.

The man looked at Wilbur, waiting for confirmation. He was your average man when it came to his height and weight, but it would have been a blessing if the rest of his appearance had been average in any way. It was more like a crude joke at his expense. His face looked like someone had crunched it towards his nose. Morris felt sorry for the man.[1]

"A moment, Jeffrey," Wilbur said and looked at Ignatius, who was trying to find a better position on his seat. "What's over there?" he asked.

"The Necromantic Agency," Ignatius said. He took off his top hat and placed it next to him on the free seat, making Wilbur smooth his ginger hair, which in all appropriateness should have turned gray. It hadn't. The hair had stayed as ginger as the day he was born, making it an easy target for Ignatius' spite.

"Why are we going there?"

"My dear Wilbur, haven't you been listening? We need another necromancer tonight, and preferably in no less than..." Ignatius said, producing a pocket watch, "...an hour." He slammed the watch's lid shut and grunted.

Wilbur took a handkerchief out of his breast pocket and patted his forehead. "I hope there's someone to meet us at this hour."

"Of course there is. You wouldn't run a shop like that without having someone looking after it." Ignatius put the watch back in his pocket. The pocket watch was a

---

1   His pity was wasted on the driver, who didn't mind his looks. He thought they gave him character, something so many lacked nowadays. Like the gentlemen in front of him.

beautiful old thing with intricate gold adornments, an inheritance from his grandfather. Like him, Ignatius maintained the watch daily, seeing that its gears were running smoothly.

"True, true." Wilbur sank deeper into his seat.

"Sir?" the driver, Jeffrey, asked.

"You heard the man," Wilbur replied.

The driver shut the door, and soon they were on their way.

Morris leaned against his seat and watched the city go past. The city that never slept. The city that was in constant flux. The city built for the living and the dead. Morris loved observing the rhythm of the streets and the buildings. It soothed him, taking his mind off the uncomfortable silence between the two men, who were sulking away as always. He listened to the distinctive pattern of the wheels clicking against the cobblestones.

"Ten gold pieces, three silvers sterlings, and a copper," Wilbur said after a while.

"What?" Morris asked.

"That's the amount of my first transaction." Wilbur was right. That was exactly as much as he'd pried out of a dead man's fingers. It'd been one of those life-defining moments one rarely gets. It was the reason why Wilbur sat next to Morris and not some other bastard. That and the fact that Wilbur knew something's worth just by looking at it. He knew how many man-hours were put into the foundation of a building or a suit someone wore. He was that good. If someone said a number to him, it never left his needle-sharp brain. Never.

"And why would this information be important?" Ignatius asked.

"I never said it was important. I was just thinking aloud," Wilbur said.

"Don't. Or do you want me to start counting all the apples I received as a child and turned into profit?" Ignatius asked.

"I'm sure Wilbur didn't mean it like that. Small talk just makes the drive go faster," Morris said.

Ignatius snorted. "If you want to converse, then let's go over the fact that someone knows about us working together to get Worthwrite up. What do you say about that,

Wilbur?"

"I say you are jumping to conclusions. Someone might have targeted the necromancer over a debt or something else. I heard he was a money-squandering drunk," the man replied.

"Then we have nothing to worry about. His death is only a minor obstacle," Ignatius said.

"We could have called his death in," Morris said.

"And lose precious time? No, we won't get involved. The insufferable man's death must already be wreaking havoc. How many dead must he have raised over the years? They'll be dropping like flies across the city. That in itself could jeopardize everything we've been working towards. All our efforts wiped out because of some stupid debt. Let someone else find him," Ignatius said.

"I didn't even think about the fact that all of his clients would die as soon as he died, but you are right, we don't want to get in the middle of that," Morris said. He'd forgotten that when a necromancer wakes up a dead person, they lend them a tiny amount of their own life force to spark the soul back to its body. Then, if a necromancer dies, their subject dies, which leads some to argue that it's important to get them young[2]. Preferably someone fresh out of university. The University of Necropolis, to be precise. You could transfer possession from one necromancer to another, but it's risky. The soul could be lost, for example, and the undead would turn into a mindless zombie. No one wanted that. Not after the last plague of zombies, which nearly ruined the city.

"Of course I'm right," Ignatius said. "And we were never there. See to that. Both of you." Ignatius made the last point while looking at Morris.

Morris refused to engage. Ignatius constantly tested his ability to be agreeable. Always trying to infuriate him. The man had to be jealous of his age or something else just as absurd.

They sat through the rest of the ride in silence. The coach shook as it trundled through Necropolis under the full moonlit sky. Here and there a mist had crept into the city, hanging around the corners and above the rooftops.

Morris listened as the coach's wheels played a

---

2   The necromancer, not the deceased. That would be weird, and too much even for chronic worriers.

concerto, using the cobblestones as its keys. It wasn't a beautiful or complex piece, but it took his mind off tonight's task. Every time the key was out of tune, it made his leg twitch with pain. The coach stopping made it reach its crescendo.

"We are here, sir," the driver said as he opened the door.

Ignatius got out first, as if it was his coach. Morris followed close behind, and the two of them waited for Wilbur to ooze out of the tiny space. When he was out, standing next to Ignatius, they lifted their gazes in unison, watching the four-story-high building rising in front of them. Over the door frame was written in huge black letters: *The Necromantic Agency*. The frame glowed with a faint white light, making the letters even blacker.

"I don't care for them," Ignatius sniffed.

"Who?" Wilbur asked.

"Mrs. and Mr. Blacklead. Always so pompous. As if they are doing a great favor to the city just by existing. Ha. Before them, the city worked just fine. Better, if you ask me."

"I like the Blackleads. They are my clients," Wilbur said.

"Should have guessed you'd go with new money," Ignatius said and headed to the front door, not waiting for Wilbur's response. He yanked the door open and went in. Morris and Wilbur hurried after him.

"Welcome," a quiet voice greeted them from behind an L-shaped lobby counter. For a while, there was only the voice hanging in the air and no body belonging to it, forcing the three men to stare at a file cabinet behind the counter.

Ignatius harrumphed.

The room's poison-green wallpaper made Ignatius look sickly. The tiny lilies painted in lighter green didn't make the effect any nicer. Actually, they made it even more disturbing, if you asked Morris.

A head popped up behind the counter, presumably belonging to the voice. It was a tiny head with piercing eyes that seemed to look past them to the shadows that had followed them. The small man with the black eyes, bald head, and colorless face stood up to his full height, which was more than Morris had expected. There was a slight possibility that the night clerk was hovering.

Ignatius said, "We're looking for a necromancer to hire."

"Then you've come to the right place," the night clerk said.

"We need someone right now," Ignatius demanded.

Morris peered over the counter to see if the man was levitating. As soon as he did that, the man became much shorter.

"Ahem, that might be a problem. All our standby necromancers are out in the field, working. There's only me," the night clerk said, and smiled, revealing two sharp teeth.

"Then you'll do," Ignatius said.

"Sorry, sir?"

"Sorry what?"

"Sir, I'm not a necromancer. I'm just the receptionist."

"That doesn't erase the fact that we need a necromancer right now."

"I'm sorry, but that's quite impossible. You better come back tomorrow."

"Nothing is impossible. Give us a name and an address, and we'll do the rest."

"Sir, I can't really do that. Privacy is key in our agency."

"Then we have come to the right place. Wilbur, show him what we can offer."

"Me?" Wilbur said. It came out as a squeak, which echoed in the quiet lobby. The whole building was unnaturally silent, as if there was a rule in place forbidding noise; as if the tenants living over the agency knew there would be some horrible consequence for any frivolous clamor.[3]

"Yes, you," Ignatius said coldly.

Wilbur hesitated but stepped forward. He walked to the lobby counter and opened the bag of coins intended for Jeremiah Black. He began to count them out on the counter.

When he reached thirty pieces of silver, a smile spread across the receptionist's face.

"You want the best?" he asked.

Wilbur nodded and pushed the coins forward.

---

3   For a loud clock, it'd been a one-way trip to the bottom of Necropolis' sea, courtesy of Mr. Blacklead.

The receptionist said, "Just a second. I'll get the card for you." Then he disappeared under the lobby counter, leaving the three men to admire the view from the only window in the room. It led to a garden behind the building, full of necromantic flowers and herbs, making the room smell strongly of lavender. But now it was pitch dark, and the only thing they saw was a black window painted against the poison-green wall.

There was a quiet *tap-tap* of the index cards flapping against each other.

"Ah, here it is," the night clerk said, and his small, lifeless head rose up behind the counter. The night clerk held a white calling card between his fingers. Ignatius reached out and took the card, which had a hastily drawn star on it.

"Thank you," he said and walked out of the agency. Morris and Wilbur followed after him to find the new necromancer and wake up Ira Worthwrite. If you asked any of the men, they might confess in their weakest hour that the dead should stay buried.

2

NECROMANCERS COME IN ALL SHAPES AND SIZES AND WITH ATTITUDE

Petula Upwood looked outside through her apartment's window, glancing at the silver moon. It shimmered down across the neighborhood's rooftops. In the distance, she saw a dark figure, a werewolf, climb onto one of those looming roofs and howl. Petula shook her head, opened the window, and shouted, "Cut it out."

Someone else joined in after the first howl, and now their voices took over the night. Petula slammed the window shut and drew the curtains closed.

It was her last night in Necropolis, and she wasn't sure when she would get to practice again. She'd handed in her notice to the Necromantic Agency yesterday and was now a free agent with no license. The thought of not tinkering with her trade made Petula's jaw clench. She took a deep breath, and her jaw relaxed.

She took a candle from the small wooden desk next to the window and carried it with her, lighting her way so she could tiptoe around the book labyrinth she'd made this morning in her tiny apartment. She was going back home. Back to Leporidae Lop. Now she just needed to choose which books to take with her and which to leave behind, preferably before morning came. She'd left everything to the last moment, which if you asked her family, they would say was unlike her. Yet here she was, the small library of books she'd collected during her stay in Necropolis unpacked. Her love for old books, new books, all books was ridiculous. Half of the time, she couldn't even freely move inside her own apartment without stubbing her toe.

She'd lived here for eight years, renting the place without seeing it first. Its location right by the University of Necropolis and the main library had been her only criterion. Petula had fretted the first time she'd opened the door but found the place surprisingly livable. Okay, it was smaller than her room back at home, but she didn't mind as long as it was functional, decent, and rat free. The apartment was all of that, and it was austere except for her books.

Petula lowered the candle onto the nightstand. She took a book she'd started this morning and slipped into bed. She needed something to quiet down the arguments that urged her to stay and be a proper necromancer here in Necropolis and not become some quack on the wrong continent. Petula had been offered a position as an archivist at the Necromantic Council, or she could have stayed with the agency, but neither of those positions would have furthered her ambition to become a full-blown necromancer. They were both dead-end jobs. At least back at home, she could dabble. Not that she could ever wake the dead there. That was forbidden.

She glanced around the room and decided to postpone the packing until later. Petula still had tonight and tomorrow morning left. She took a sewn bookmark out of the book, laid it on her chest, and began to read. *The New Edition of Needlepoint Masterpieces* by Mildred Whither wasn't proper reading, but it helped her to arrange her thoughts in a neat pattern.

But this time the patterns didn't help her; her mind kept wandering. Back at home, her family waited for her. She was going to go to Leporidae Lop to open her own "necromantic" shop and consort with the spirits as she'd done at the agency. But she couldn't raise the dead. They, the Necromantic Council, wouldn't let her. Not outside Necropolis. Just spirit control. That was needless prohibition, as no citizen of Leporidae Lop would ever want to raise their family members. They were already hard enough to get rid of the first time around. But the Leporidae Lops would allow her to ease their dead relatives' journey to the afterlife. No one wanted any loose spirits hanging around, least of all those with strong opinions. But that was grunt work. Any head of organized religion could do that. Crit, any cult leader could do that. Maybe not as forcefully as a necromancer, but generally, a nice chat went a long way with the dead.

If she stayed here, there might come a chance for her to use all her skills under the council's rule. She'd be licensed and taxed heavily, but nevertheless she could wake up the dead. She'd hoped at least to bring one person back to life before going home, as what she did at the University didn't count. Waking up test subjects and sending them back to death wasn't real. Also, you could argue, not very ethical either.

At any rate, none of this mattered. She was sailing home tomorrow. That was that. Petula refocused on the words and patterns in the book, and they instantly drew her in. She didn't hear the howling anymore, or for that matter the sound of footsteps behind her door, along with the rest of the uncomfortable noises the world made. For a second, she was in a world that made sense, that had a clear purpose and structure. Petula snuggled in better, and if possible, a quiet purr came out of her throat.

She was beautiful when she read. At other times, not so much. Petula was a small woman with long, fragile, snow-white hair and grayish-blue eyes. Her appearance was due to all the experimentation she'd done at the University. Your mind stopped being frightened of the spirits and the undead, but your body never did. Petula's looks were somewhere between okay and all right, depending on the lighting and her mood, which was more often than not somewhat unappealing. Unless she was reading. Petula smiled as her eyes moved from word to word.

But nothing is ever simple. All the decisions, routes, and arguments in life have detours, twists, loops, jumps, disturbances...and if something goes according to plan, it's only natural for the brain to think, where is the *but?* And when a brain is on that path, it always finds the *but.* Or invents one.

Petula didn't have to invent a *but;* it came to her of its own accord. There was a violent knock on Petula's front door, making her heart race and her thoughts scramble. She jumped up from her bed and looked around. The awful noise was still coming, and it was more than clear that it came from her door. Actually, it'd been going on for a while now. Petula sent a curious look towards the door. It'd never been knocked on at this forsaken hour of the night. She'd come to Necropolis to study, leaving the rest of the funny business to others. Okay, she'd let Agatha into her apartment, but during the daytime, and only because of a joint assignment. It wasn't like she liked her.

Petula eyed the door. She took the candle from the nightstand and tiptoed around her books. Before opening it, she looked down at her white nightgown with its lacy ruffles. Not something she would wear publicly, but there was another urgent knock, and she decided the gifted nightgown would have to do. Not that she really cared what she wore. Never had, to her mother's and sister's annoyance.

Petula cracked the door open.

"Yes?" she asked.

There were three men outside her door. One tall and thin, one round, and one full of himself.

"Are you Petula Upwood?" the tall and thin one asked, judging her with his eyes. The man showed her an index card with her name on it.

Petula recognized the font and the style.

"Yes?" she asked again.

"You can't be the necromancer they recommended. You are—" the man said and was cut short by Petula slamming the door shut.

Petula's heart hammered as she listened to the arguing coming from behind her door.

There was another knock. This time it was gentler.

Petula opened the door and asked, "Yes?", sounding a bit spiteful. She'd be the first one to admit that.

"You are a necromancer, right?" This time the one who was full of himself asked.

"Y-e-s."

"We need you to come with us. We got your name from the Necromantic Agency and we..." He didn't finish his sentence as Petula shook her head.

"What is it now?" he asked.

"I don't work there anymore. I quit yesterday," she replied.

The man looked behind him to the two others, but said, "It doesn't matter as long as you're a necromancer and willing to be employed by us."

"It's tricky. I'm leaving, and the agency doesn't let those who aren't agency employees work in the city. You better contact the agency tomorrow to sort out your spirit infestation," Petula said.

The tall and thin one gritted his teeth. "They gave us your name. But if that's so, do you know anyone else we might ask?" he asked.

Petula shrugged. "No, not really," she added as a clarification.

"You can't be serious. You worked at the agency, and you say you know no one?" the tall and thin one asked.

"I work alone," Petula said as if that should explain everything. "What is this about?"

"We need to resurrect our friend in..." the full-of-himself one said and reached for his pocket watch. He flipped it open and said, "In two hours."

Petula shook her head, ignoring the pestering voice inside her head asking questions like, "Is this a test or invitation from the agency?" and "Who are these men?" and her favorite "Why is the tall and thin man squirming in front of me?" and saying instead, "Two hours isn't enough even if I came with you; you still have the problem that I'm leaving. You need someone else who is city-bound."

The problem with necromancy was that the resurrected, zombie, undead, or reborn was bound to the necromancer. It wasn't a must to be in the same city, but it was always better. A safer bet would be to turn the thing into a ghost straight away rather than go through the whole process of becoming undead. However, ghosts weren't yet legally recognized entities in the city. They had no claim to their former fortune or life in general as the more solid undead had. It was an understandable distinction made in the face of property laws. The living were already testy due to the solid undead and their habit of popping back up and taking jobs, inheritances, and pretty women or men as light night-time snacks.[4]

"We need someone straight away. You're coming with us," the tall and thin one said.

"And the agency sent you?"

"Yes, haven't we established that already?!" the man snapped.

"I want to see a written contract," she said.

"We don't have time for this nonsense. Get your things and...change into something more...necromantic," the man said, letting his eyes slide down Petula's white nightgown with all the ruffles and lace.

His gaze made Petula glance down at her clothes to check if she was still wearing them.

Yep, still on.

"I can give you the contract in the coach. So, are you coming?" the man asked.

"All right," she said, and added, "Give me a second."

Petula shut the door behind her. She hurried to get her clothes on. The kind the man had requested. It was stupid how an ensemble could make a difference, but the agency had insisted on her getting an outfit fitting for the part. She sniffed her black dress, which fell just below her knees. It smelled fresh enough. She put it on. To spite the agency, she'd bought the most sensible, long-lasting dress she could find. If a black dress can ever be dull, then this one was. It was the sort of dress you could pass on to your great-grandchildren, and they to their great-grandchildren.

Petula drew on tights and dragged her high leather boots on.[5] If you asked her, more important than clothes was her necromantic kit, which was already packed and waiting next to the exit. The only thing she had to do was decide what to take with her. And by what, she meant which book to

---

4   You could say necromancy was a nasty business, but the city thrived on it. There were powerful families who depended on the dead coming back. It gave them legal possession and control over businesses and wealth without taxation or any other form of hassle, keeping everything in the family. And, of course, it was always good if the original mastermind hung around in case of any future bright ideas.

5   Without heels, she insisted.

take. She never left the house without one. Never.

Petula grabbed a thick, dark-gray wool coat and took two books from her nightstand: the needlework book and a small black book full of ancient incantations that she'd found at a flea market. It was a rare book she hadn't even found in the University's catalog. She'd been saving it for a good day. A bad night would have to do. She put them in her doctor's bag.

When all was done, she smoothed and tied her hair in a ponytail, and then walked out of the door, hoping the three men were gone. No, they were still waiting for her.

Petula's heart skipped a beat. She knew there was something wrong, but she also knew this might be her only opportunity. She could always slip away unnoticed from the city tomorrow. Petula sighed and followed the men outside.

◆

Morris Reinhardt watched the new necromancer, Petula, shift her weight on the coach's bench next to Wilbur. He had a sickening feeling about tonight and about her. Everything had gone offbeat when Ignatius had been late, and then there was the murder. It bothered him. Who would go to such lengths to stop them waking Ira Worthwrite? Morris knew the man was one of the most hated and feared in Necropolis, but even he had a lawful right to a second life. The right to resurrection was secured by the constitution. And in the current economic downturn, it was downright rude if Ira stayed buried six feet under.

Morris saw Petula glance out of the window and shift her weight once again.

"You don't have to be scared of us," Morris said, wanting to touch her arm.

The necromancer narrowed her eyes and said with a superior voice, "Why would I be? The dead are always with me. One incantation from me and I can have you possessed."

Morris swallowed.

He heard Ignatius chuckle.

Morris couldn't quite laugh. A possession, even a short one, was horrific. He had the bad memories of a sixty-nine-year-old former champion boxer inside his head. If it hadn't been for his boarding school governess finding him lying next to a Ouija Board, then... He didn't even want to think about it. He'd been saved in time, before he lost his mind, and that was that. Except he sometimes heard the rhythm of leather being hit against leather. Shivers went down his back.

"No, I was wondering about the contract with the agency. Let me have it," Petula said.

"We don't have one," Ignatius said.

Petula stared at the man. She cleared her throat and said, "Even though I can't quite believe you broke in to steal my address, whatever your reason is, an unsanctioned awakening is out of the question. If the council finds out, we will all pay a hefty price. And I don't mean money."

She was right. Morris wasn't sure what the Necromantic Council's go-to punishment was, but he'd heard rumors. No one in the city went against them and their rule. Never. But they had a permit, so there was nothing to worry about.

"We have a legal right to resurrect Ira Worthwrite. The document is in here somewhere," Morris said, searching his pockets.

"You should be more careful with *his* name," Ignatius warned.

"It's not like she won't find out soon enough," Morris replied.

"Ignatius is right. The walls have eyes and ears. You can never be too careful, especially after you-know-what," Wilbur said.

"Here it is," Morris said and handed the legal document to Petula, not commenting on the fact that they sat in a moving vehicle and the two men were more paranoid than usual.

The three men followed Petula's eyes moving along the lines and frowning.

"So?" Ignatius asked.

"This is permission for *Jeremiah Black*," she said, spitting out the name. "The council doesn't like switches. You should get him." She handed back the document.

"Is there any way you can resurrect Ira? Jeremiah Black is unavailable, and you're our only hope," Morris said, putting the permit back inside his breast pocket.

"If there's a good reason why your *friend* is engaged elsewhere then the council might grant permission for the switch on the grounds of an emergency," she said and added, "But you will have to apply for another permit afterwards, and the council might still refuse. And your friend would be put down again."

"This is an emergency, and we've got good lawyers to battle with the council if necessary. And if I may add, your compensation will reflect the difficulty of this task," Morris said.

Wilbur winced.

"Okay," Petula said and reached for her doctor's bag, causing everyone in the coach to hold their breath. Morris instantly flashed back to his days at boarding school, seeing the governess' face.

"I'm just taking out my contract base," she said.

Still, Morris couldn't quite relax. He kept his shoulders tensed as he waited for her to take the contract out. As soon as she had it in her reach, Ignatius snatched the base from her.

"I'll take a look at it. This is my area of expertise," he said.

It wasn't. Morris knew contract law better than anyone. He'd spent years studying law at the University and was a dissertation away from his doctorate degree. Life had gotten in the way of completion. And what he meant by life was all the social gatherings he'd attended, and of course his father's death. Not that he had been that keen on that side of the law. It was just something that came naturally to him. Morris' mind was good at making clauses. The kind that went in loops and had holes.

He could take the contract away from Ignatius, but the man always got agitated when his hands were idle, and idle hands did the Devil's work. Or in Ignatius' case, the work of a neurotic man with a self-indulgent attitude, which was pretty much the same thing.

"I'd like the contract back," Petula said, saying her words as if "or" should follow the sentence.

"If we're the ones taking the heat from the council, then we'll be the ones to write it," Ignatius said, holding the contract tightly.

Morris expected her to snatch the document back.

She didn't. Instead, she reached for her bag and pulled out a thick red book, opened it, and began to read in the dimly lit coach. Someone had been clever enough to install oil lamps inside. That someone was the driver, Jeffrey Gilliam. The lamps cast haunting shadows across the necromancer's face, making her look sort of beautiful and calm. Calmer than he'd seen her until now. Morris never felt at peace around books. He often had the feeling he was missing out on something. That instead of reading, he should be out of the house, mingling.

The coach was filled with the rustle of paper and Ignatius' puffing.

Morris memorized the peculiar woman. There was something about her. Something he couldn't quite put his finger on, reminding him of someone he once knew.

"So, how long have you been a necromancer?" Wilbur asked.

Petula's features stiffened, and there was a sneer on her face.

"Long enough," she said, refusing to take her eyes off the book even when she'd clearly lost her spot.

"And you are quitting?" Wilbur asked.

Morris wanted to sink his head into his hands.

"No."

"No?"

The necromancer sighed and closed her book, making Wilbur excited. "I'm just moving."

"But—"

"Back home. That doesn't stop me being a necromancer." It kind of did. No one saw those outside Necropolis as necromancers. They were witches or something similarly demeaning. Necromancy took skill...and organization. Lots of it.

"If I may ask, where's home?" Morris looked into her eyes, searching for a connection, smiling.

She looked away through the windows but said, "Leporidae Lop."

"You're a long way from home," Morris said.

"If you say so."

"Isn't that the place that had that war two years ago?" Wilbur asked.

"Yes," Petula said. Morris was sure it was a warning

for Wilbur not to go any further.

"And you want to go there? Isn't it kind of dangerous?" Wilbur asked.

"Don't be daft. Of course, she's going to go back to her family," Morris interjected.

"Now, obviously, she'll stay," Ignatius said.

Petula gave the man a blank stare. "Not obvious for me," she said. "I agreed to help you, but I have to leave tomorrow. As your friend graciously said, my family is waiting for me."

"That's out of the question. You're staying," Ignatius said.

"There was an agreement before I left my house," Petula insisted.

"Situations change," Ignatius said.

"Then you better stop the coach and find someone else to do this for you in...five minutes. Or you can do this at the next full moon." She opened her book again and resumed reading, knowing full well the coach wouldn't stop moving. Ignatius attacked the contract in a frenzy.

She'd mastered sooner than most how to control Ignatius. Even Morris hadn't been able to handle Ignatius that way. The man bugged him, a second-generation immigrant, with his strict customs.

Again, there was silence and the gentle rustle of paper and Wilbur shifting his weight on the leather seat. After a while, Wilbur asked, "So what are you reading?"

The necromancer looked up from her book and put it aside.

"*Philosophiæ Naturalis Principia Necromantiae,*" she said. You could say she was lying, lying through her teeth. The red book was the needlepoint book. A long way from anything a necromancer should read. Not that it really mattered what she read, but perception is important, and even someone like Petula knew that. To people like Morris who played nice and were socially agreeable, appearance came before function and practicality. Despite the fact he liked to think about himself in the opposite way, deep down Morris would have thought less of her. So would Wilbur and Ignatius.

"Is it...informative?" Wilbur asked, searching for something to talk about.

"I'd hope so," she said and went back to reading.

"It must be important in your practice to read extensively and keep up with the times," Wilbur said.

"As is the case with everything," Morris interrupted, wishing to end the conversation.

"Yes, of course," Wilbur replied. "I wish I had time to read. With the bank, this thing we're doing, and my daughter giving birth, there seems to be no time to sit down."

"You are sitting down now," Petula said.

The man looked startled.

"Life is easier if you get past your own nonsense," Petula said and flipped the book open once again.

Morris watched Wilbur swallow his words and open and close his mouth without letting out a sound.

"Here," Ignatius said and interrupted them. He offered the contract back to Petula just as the coach stopped moving. He even chuckled as he watched the two other men. You could say he was the kind of man who appreciated honesty more than the usual social dance people did around others. But bluntness is and would surely always be out of fashion, no matter how much someone like Petula or Ignatius tried.

The necromancer took the contract and read it. She took her time, forcing Morris to listen to his own suppressed breathing and a quiet *tick-tock*.

"So?" Ignatius asked when Petula flipped the contract over again.

"This is like selling my soul to you," she said.

"With a generous pay. And you'd get to leave after we've acquired a third party to take your position." Ignatius wasn't lying. The pay was generous. With it, Petula would have enough money to set up her own shop back in Leporidae Lop.

"This doesn't leave me time to pack."

"Hire someone to do that. After this you'll have money to do that and whatever else you like. But you can only go back to your home country when you pass the duty on to someone else," Ignatius said and handed a fountain pen to her.

"You know the transfer is difficult and dangerous not only to the undead but also to me," Petula said, refusing to take the pen.

"You should have said something at the beginning if

you're not up to the task. We could have gone with a better necromancer. I'm not offering you a penny more."

"Give me that pen," she snapped.

"We also require your complete discretion. If you mention to anyone where you've been and what you've done, I'll not only come after the full amount, I'll also make sure you don't have enough reputation left to work in this city or anywhere else," Ignatius said.

"Ignatius!" Morris rebuked.

"What? Discretion is part of any standard contract."

"You don't have to sign. We can take you back home," Morris said. He leaned forward to wait for the necromancer to hand the contract to him. She didn't do what he wanted.

She said, "Before I sign anything, I want a guarantee that states I'm to be paid tonight and that even if something were to fail, I can leave on my booked voyage to Leporidae Lop."

"We can compensate the cost if..." Ignatius said.

"There's no if; I'm not staying. I've already ended my lease, there won't be another ship for months, and my family is waiting for me. And you don't need me to stay here. I'll wake up your friend, go home to pack, do the transfer ritual tomorrow at noon, at exactly twelve o'clock, and then leave with my ship at four pm. It has to be that way," Petula said. Her words cut the air.

"You're going to do a ritual at noon?" Wilbur asked.

"What does it matter what time I do the ritual?"

"Are you even a necromancer? All rituals are done at midnight," Ignatius replied before Wilbur could.

"Superstition. I could have woken your friend at nine am. It doesn't matter," she said.

"But a full moon and..." Wilbur said.

"I know what I'm doing. I'm one of the best necromancers in the city. Either you agree with me, or I walk out of the coach." Petula stated it as a matter of fact, leaving no doubt about what would happen if she wasn't pleased.

"That's not—" Ignatius said.

Morris interrupted them. "Enough. Add what she wants into the contract and be done with it, or else we'll be arguing here until tomorrow, and all this'll be meaningless."

Ignatius groaned but took the contract back

forcefully and began to amend it. He soon handed her the contract and let Petula go over it one more time.

"This is not a proper way to conduct business negotiations," he muttered.

3

KILLING LEAVES A BAD TASTE BEHIND

H e hurried down the stairs, almost twisting his ankle. He muffled his curses and listened to the three men heading over with the new necromancer. Herbert Ringworm had hoped the woman would say no, but as always, the world and people in it disappointed him. He couldn't help but wonder why everything insisted on being Kraken shit. He didn't have that basic trust that the world and the future would be all right. The only thing he knew was this heavy, choking hate at his own existence.

"*I'm sorry. I never meant to lose our love,*" a voice whispered in his ear. He looked around, but he saw no one. Herbert massaged his head, sure he was losing his mind.

"*This hurts,*" the voice said again.

"What do you want from me?" he whispered back. "Isn't this enough?"

But there was no answer, just the absence of the voice and the beat of the crippled man's cane coming closer. Herbert turned around and rushed out of the stairway to the outside world. He moved too carelessly, causing the driver to look towards him, following his every movement with his gaze. Herbert cursed. He slowed his pace and walked away from the building and the coach with purpose. The driver kept his eyes on him, forcing Herbert to hide behind the corner of the two-story-high building he'd just left, a building like any other in the neighborhood. Herbert counted to ten and then glanced around the corner. He saw the driver help the three men and a smallish woman inside the coach.

She would be easy. Not that he enjoyed killing. Taking Jeremiah's life had left a bad taste in his mouth, even though the pompous asshole had deserved it. Jeremiah had been about to wake up Ona's murderer, and he couldn't let that happen. He would do the same to anyone who got in his way. Ira Worthwrite had to stay dead.

Herbert watched the driver go to his seat and coax the two horses into motion. If they went past him, he could jump on the coach and finish this once and for all, taking out not only the necromancer but the men as well. Damn the consequences.

Herbert pushed against the building's wall, waiting.

The roof of the University of Necropolis rose over the neighborhood's buildings. The old castle was grotesque with its dark towers, a drawbridge, and monstrous statues. Herbert knew almost every building and their figures in the city by heart. He'd have welcomed imagination with their aesthetics. But everything was done in the same Gothic style, and that was thanks to the late architect and sculptor Johan Engel, whose theory of art could be summed up with one sentence: "Anything dark goes." All the sculptors in the city mimicked him. Herbert had tried to do something different when he'd studied to become a sculptor, but he'd failed. He hadn't been able to compromise with his taste and go with the flow. When he'd tried to make something light and gods forbid something whimsical, they'd kicked him out of the University. Of course, they'd said it was due to the infringement with Ona, but that was a lie. They all knew that. Being a sculptor would have been a lucrative profession in a city full of megalomaniacs; now he barely scraped by.

Herbert was sure he saw a dark figure, most likely a werewolf, scurry across the rooftops. Soon a howl followed. He pushed the noise out of his consciousness and listened for if the coach was coming. It wasn't. That would have been too perfect. It didn't matter; he knew where they were going, and he had a trick that would get him there before them.

Herbert took off running.

He ran fast for a man of his size, not being a tall man. He was an average man, but not average in any other aspect than height. One could say he was a testament to the human body. He'd pushed his body to its limits with strength and agility. However, it was not enough to outmatch horses. He didn't need his lean, tight body for that. He knew the city better than anyone. Herbert had a habit of climbing everything he saw. At the end of the street, in the opposite direction than the coach had gone, Herbert latched on to a building's wall and climbed up. He joined the world of squirrels, birds, and werewolves.

Herbert knew if he was swift enough, he would get there before the coach, which had to navigate the zigzagging streets of Necropolis. Streets that had been built without deliberation. Necropolis had grown from a camp and its cemetery to a sprawling city unnaturally fast. It wasn't more than two hundred years old, and already it was one of the biggest metropolises in the world. They built Necropolis around the dead right from the beginning. At first as a hunting ground for the living to gain prestige and riches, and then as a city evolving around the undead in various ways, catering to their needs. You could say the dead had won.

As soon as Herbert's feet hit the rooftop, the pressure of the voice disappeared. He felt calm and almost free, his purpose buoying him up. It was the same feeling he always got when he was up here above life. There were no problems, no rows, no future here. Everything seemed unimportant. The city. People. Even the Town Hall, which he could see from up here, seemed irrelevant. Around the Town Hall buzzed all those who decided the destinies of men like him. Not one of the men and women in fancy clothes, the stiffs with gleaming, dead eyes, or the pack of ghouls waiting for their meeting to start looked like someone who had his best interests at heart. He hated the Town Hall and the people in it, except maybe Dow, Dow Spurgeon.

He shook off the image and continued running over the rooftops. Whatever disasters occurred beneath his feet held no true interest to him. He pushed his feet to their limits and leaped across to another roof. His feet slipped on the slick tiles, but he caught himself with his right hand before he fell off. Herbert swung the other hand onto the metal railing and secured his hold. With one careless-looking movement, he drew himself back up. He jumped to his feet and continued running, softening his knees and balancing his soles to stop himself from slipping a second time. The edge of another roof waited for him. He took the jump without thinking and arrived on the other building with ease. Whenever he stopped to think, it always got him into trouble with Ona and with everyone and everything. Too many thoughts complicated things.

He scurried through five districts of buildings, avoiding the other lifeforms on the rooftops. It was always tricky with werewolves. They were a curious bunch, aggressive and with an acute sense of smell. One of those breeds who made their decisions with their mauling teeth. Herbert had nothing against werewolves. Some of his best friends were werewolves. Still, it was best to avoid their company on nights like this, when astronomical objects were messing with their destinies.

Before Herbert reached the cemetery grounds, he had to go down to street level and move across the main avenue of the banking district. Coming down was always like the end of a sugar rush. He felt nauseated and full of regrets. He had two more blocks to go, and to be there on time, he had no other choice. Herbert climbed down. What they didn't tell you was that the climbing up was the easier part, but when you climbed down you fought against the nasty habits of gravity. But he managed. He carefully stepped down into an alleyway.

Herbert glanced around the main street, which swarmed with people. The money never slept in the city. It was always in constant flux, moving from one dead hand to another. Herbert saw no one who would pay too much attention to him, only the usual crowd: the desperate, the rich, the lucky, the cursed, the contented, the feared. He moved past them, hunching his shoulders and merging into the mass.

Next to the opposite bank, there was a one-man-wide alleyway. He slipped in when he was sure no one was watching. Generally, no one did. In cities like Necropolis, people tended not to care about others, keeping to themselves, and definitely not intervening with any crime in progress. Not even a daylight murder would make them stop. Not their problem, not that they even saw it. Shield the mind. Blind the eyes.

Then there were those whose job it was to watch: the law officers, gods, and gargoyles. If the city was wise enough, they could turn the latter into their private surveillance system, but for some reason, the argument for privacy, who's watching the watchers, and the fear of abused power won. No one understood why. But someone whose job it was to watch shouted as soon as Herbert's hands touched the painted windowsill of the bank.

"Stop in the name of the Law!"

Herbert cursed but didn't stop. He latched his hands better and pulled himself up.

The officer followed him to the street and jumped up and down to reach the same windowsill he had touched a moment ago.

Herbert pushed upwards, hearing the officer curse underneath him. He glanced down. The woman was on the first windowsill and hadn't gotten farther than that. He left the officer behind, slipping across the roof and continuing his journey, knowing she wouldn't catch him. No one ever did.

The two remaining blocks were easy. The buildings were huddled together, and there was no inconvenient height difference. He could already see the cemetery. It stood there held together by black iron fences, swallowed by mist. Old trees pushed out of the cemetery, shadowing the first gravestones. The cemetery at Old Lich St. was a huge park in the heart of the city. All the prominent and ancient families were and would be buried there.

To his misery, the coach had gotten there before him. It was parked in front of the main gates. But he couldn't see anyone. They must have gone in already. He descended via the nearest building, sneaking into the cemetery, assuring no one took any notice of him and checking the officer who'd pursued him hadn't magically appeared. There was no one there. The street in front of the cemetery was abandoned.

You could easily assume in Necropolis that the cemeteries were the main attraction, and that people spent their leisure time there, but that wasn't the case.

Necropolitans were more interested in money than visiting their dead relatives who hadn't been wise enough to get back up and join in the game. And if they paid a visit, the dead went on and on about how a newcomer had moved to the grave next to them and was making a racket. So...

Herbert walked across the street. Despite his careful approach, someone did notice him: a gargoyle. But it wasn't part of any shadowy surveillance force and didn't find humans that interesting. It continued fending off evil forces who tried to break in from other dimensions.

Near the coach, it was dead quiet, and the mist kept oozing out of the graveyard gates. Herbert listened for a while to make sure he wasn't walking into the group before he was ready. Necromancers had tricks up their sleeves. He pushed his hand into his jacket pocket to take his knife out. His fingers touched the glass bottle he'd taken from Jeremiah. Nasty tricks. He took the knife out. It still had dried blood on its curved blade.

The longish knife was designed to penetrate anyone's chest. It wasn't enchanted or in any way magical. Its efficiency came from its form and the handler's agility. The blade had been designed so that the hook underneath the handle ripped open the wound to maximize the damage done as the blade came out. Its sole purpose was to wreak as much havoc as it could, but if you asked the knife, it'd have liked to be used for things like carving wood or maybe peeling fruit. Apples especially.

Herbert advanced past the coach. He stepped in through the gates, which bore a plaque reading *Old Rainy Meadow Cemetery*. It was almost impossible to see far inside the grounds, as the mist was thick and nearly tangible. He could see the groundskeeper's shed, but not the necromancer or the men. Herbert moved past the first tree and didn't get farther than that. A hand landed on his shoulder. The driver stood behind him; he'd been waiting for him. Herbert swung the blade with his right hand, shifting his weight to his left foot to face the man. However, he was too slow. The driver blocked his attack and jumped back before the blade slit open his throat.

Herbert gritted his teeth.

"*Please,*" the voice said, but he didn't hear it.

He faced the driver, who'd taken a step back.

The man lowered his weight and watched Herbert's eyes instead of the knife.

"May I?" he asked, pointing at his hat.

Herbert nodded, watching the man, who was an adult-size version of a Leprechaun, take off his overcoat and fold it on the lawn. Finally, the man put his hat on top of the pile and rolled his sleeves up. He lifted his hands into a relaxed position in front of his chest.

Herbert took a step to his left and watched for how the man would react. He stood his ground, still watching Herbert. The driver was someone who took a defensive stance in any fight, forcing the opponent to make the first move—and the first mistake. Herbert didn't mind. He would not let the man intimidate him into failing. He was fast and knew how to use that to his advantage. He tipped his weight to his left foot, leaped, and pushed his knife hand forward, forcing it into the man's chest. But it didn't even scrape the driver, who pushed his weight forward and seized Herbert's knife hand. The man slammed his free fist into Hebert's side. The driver tried to struggle free of the knife, but Herbert was faster. He took hold of the man's wrist and took a step back, making him lose his balance, then he twisted his wrist, causing the man to let go. Herbert didn't wait for a reaction. He jerked his knee against the man's chest. But the driver wasn't born yesterday. He slammed his hands against the knee and pushed Herbert away at the same time, making Herbert search for his footing.

Herbert took a step back and looked at the man, who was gasping for air. Herbert wasn't even close to being tired. He leaped forward a second time, aiming for the man's chest. This time the knife sank in. He pushed the blade deeper and twisted it. The driver looked at him with a frozen expression of bewilderment and hurt. Herbert pushed the man away, sliding the blade out at the same time. The driver fell on the ground, gasping for more air. Blood poured out of the gaping chest wound.

Herbert didn't wait. He took the man by his arms and dragged him farther away from the path to the cemetery. The driver didn't struggle. It'd take a few more minutes for him to die, but until then Herbert was free to do what he wanted. He lowered the man behind a tree a gravestone away from the main walkway. He looked around to see if anyone had witnessed their exchange. No one had.[6]

Herbert left the man against the tree and went back to his clothes. It'd be too late to interrupt the ritual, but he'd get them later. Herbert put on the driver's overcoat and finished his transformation by pushing the man's hat deep onto his head.

---

6 Except the mist that liked to hang around the Old Rainy Meadow Cemetery, but it wouldn't say anything. Not that anyone would listen to it if it tried. Whenever it tried to communicate with humans, for some odd reason they got scared and ran away.

4

EXCUSE ME, COULD YOU TIE A BELL TO YOUR LOOSE UNDEAD?

A t the Town Hall, away from all the confusion, Minta Stopford sat behind her office desk, writing in her notebook. She'd fortified her desk with government papers, newspapers, and protective runes. They shielded her from the office door and any distractions that came from there. In her line of work, she gained enemies daily. In Necropolis, you couldn't be too careful as the Mayor. "Mayor" might not be the most accurate word to describe her, as Necropolis was more than just a city. She was a president or a despot and had been for almost thirty years now. Minta was also a necromancer. The most powerful of them, despite what Jeremiah Black had wanted to think. But power fades, and Minta knew that.[7] One day someone would challenge her, and it'd be the end of her claim to the throne and, for that matter, the end of her life. That was how it was done. That's what she'd done. Minta had earned her place by

---

7   And absolute power corrupts absolutely; she knew that too.

killing the former tyrant. Back then everyone had been pleased with her for getting rid of that awful man with a penchant for torture, ritualistic murders, and loud parties, but now things were different. There was this thing called the economy, and it was making people discontent. And it was making Minta desperate.

She glanced over the pile on her desk. No one had come in. But she was sure she'd heard footsteps. Minta lowered her head back down and sat more comfortably on her chair. Once the room had been a bedroom in her manor, but when she'd killed Oliver the Great,[8] she'd moved the center of political power here and moved her home out to another manor. Okay, she spent most of her nights on the office's sofa, listening to the tree branches scraping the windows. She was sure they wanted to get in and tear the house apart. That was always a possibility in Necropolis. And she wasn't sure if she disagreed with their motives. The Town Hall had become a dark old place with twisted intentions, and sometimes she'd go so far as to claim there was not a single ounce of rationality left in the building or its legislators. Everyone had gone mad for money.

Minta had killed Oliver here in this same room. His blood had splattered across the floor when she'd turned the man's own guarding spirit against him. The spirit had torn the man apart, leaving his head intact as proof of the deed. Even after she'd washed the gore away, she still saw his mutilated body. It'd been the shortest fight she'd ever had, and kind of a disappointment. She'd expected more from the necromancer, drunk or not. Back then, she'd have given anything for a real challenge. A real test of her skills as a hunter and as a necromancer. Now she couldn't care less. Not about fighting or about anything else really.

All she could think about was writing her memoir and steering the city as her duties dictated. Duties she'd imposed on herself. Upon stepping into power, she'd written the Constitution anew, winning friends and alienating parts of the city. She'd introduced a more egalitarian method of decision making: a council of men and women formed from the living and the dead. Minta was beginning to regret that. Being a sole ruler would have made it easier to act against the

---

8   The former ruler and an imbecile.

economy.

Economy, ha, what a thing. Even the philosophers didn't agree with what it was all about. They collected different theories and argued amongst themselves while the economy went on and on, doing what it did. Minta wrote her thoughts down in the notebook. Someday someone would want to write about her, and she had her heart set on having the history written as she wanted.

Minta felt odd, as if there was a presence. She didn't look up. She continued writing down her words, but said aloud, "What is it, Dow?"

"Good evening, madam," Dow Spurgeon said. Dow was a small man, and not pleasing to look at. His face and body were something someone might describe as having character if they were trying to be polite. Minta would call him ugly, but not to the man's face. He didn't deserve that. Dow had odd brown eyes; they looked almost yellowish, but most thought it was the light playing tricks on them. He had a sharp, hooked nose and a stern gaze that burrowed deep into your soul.

"Evening, Dow," she said. Dow was her secretary, and much more. Sometimes Minta thought that he ruled the city instead of her. She'd be happy to hand the power to him, but you had to be a necromancer to rule Necropolis.

"I have tonight's newspaper," he said.

Minta groaned.

"I think you have to see it, madam."

"Give it here then," Minta said, putting down her pencil and the notebook.

Dow handed her the paper, and she instantly saw what he wanted her to see. It was there on the front page.

"I thought they had to give notice before organizing a protest?"

"Oh, but they did."

"Hmm?"

"I think they have someone sympathetic to their cause working at the registry office. The notice was processed instantly but buried in a heap of files. It never got to us in time, but everything is legal."

"Ah," Minta said. "And it's tonight?"

"Yes, madam."

Minta studied the picture of Ernest Shivers on the

front page. The fifty-year-old man with a huge mustache, soft belly, and round spectacles didn't look like a man to inspire protest. It was a young man's game. But he'd been in the right place at the right time. He'd become a figurehead for the discontent through a similar picture in the paper, but then he'd been holding his apprentice on his lap, who'd hanged himself after the man had to let him go. The boy was found too late to be turned. A tragedy. But there was not much she could do to change it. It was the man's honest face that compelled others to act, to say: "Enough."

"What do they want me to do?" she asked.

"You appear too weak, letting bankers and business owners walk all over you and do as they please," Dow said. He wasn't a man to sugar coat anything. Minta liked that about him. She'd always liked Dow.

"I'm doing the best I can, but it's not like I'm the only one sitting on the council, and there's a process," Minta said.

Dow coughed. "Yes, but you know you could act. You are the sole ruler of Necropolis," he said.

"We're not going back to tyranny," Minta said. Yes, it was still an option in the constitution. She'd rather save it as a last resort for when the Apocalypse came.

"As you wish, madam," Dow said.

"We better show our faces at the meeting," she said.

"That will be easily arranged. They are coming here," he replied.

"Hmm," Minta said, leaning against the table and glancing at her notebook. "Anything else?" she asked.

"No, madam," he said. The way he said it sounded like there was more, but nothing he was willing to disclose. And Minta wished he could cut all the madam, mayor, sir business. They'd known each other for over thirty-seven years now. But she knew such gestures made Dow happy.

"Then I better get going to the council meeting," Minta sighed.

"Yes," Dow said. "I'll leave you to get ready."

"Keep me posted," Minta said before Dow slipped out of the room. He could be too silent for his own good. He kept spooking the Town Hall's staff and the council members. Then he wondered why people flinched around him. Even after all the times she'd told him to be more accommodating to people's needs and weaknesses, he never was. Minta sometimes thought it was all deliberate. That as long as she played along, Dow got to do as he pleased.

When Dow left Minta alone, she smoothed her hand across her short hair absentmindedly. She'd gotten used to keeping it cut when she worked overseas as a monster hunter for the Necropolis' Foreign Aid. Fleas and other parasites were easier to manage with shorter hair. Not that those mattered any longer; she could take better care of her hygiene now she no longer had to stay in poor camping conditions or spend long days tracking some poor beast through a rainforest. Her hair had kept its thickness and natural color. It was as dark as the blackest cat you could find. It looked beautiful against her dark complexion, which had kept some of its youthfulness. When she'd been young, Minta had been quite a beauty with her tall build and fierce face. Not an ounce of that charisma was lost now.

Minta took her notebook and slipped it inside the pocket of her leather jacket. Then she took her government papers, those relevant for tonight's meeting, and headed out of the door. She took one last glance at her former bedroom. There, behind the desk on the wall, was mounted her spear. It'd served her so well in the past. It was too bad she couldn't take it with her to the council meeting. Maybe with it, she could get some respect. The council had gotten too used to her mild, mediating manner.

It wasn't a long walk through the Town Hall's corridors to the auditorium. She had to descend from the upstairs to the first floor. The auditorium would be there, right in the middle of it all. It was a huge circular room that dominated the building. First, she had to sneak past all the ministry offices and hope no one pulled her in. She shifted onto the balls of her feet to stop her high heels clicking against the white marble floor.

She gave a polite nod and encouraging smile to each member of staff, clerk, or council member she saw. That small combined gesture said to the recipient: "I see you, you're real, but please let me pass." Such a simple gesture often saved her from an unnecessary conversation.

Minta's politeness and genuine interest towards anyone she came across, from the common people to the heads of other states, had gained her respect and goodwill.

She even made sure to greet and smile at the maintenance staff. They made things run smoothly inside the grotesque building with too many statues of gargoyles and gods, and beasts of all flavors. Minta hadn't wanted those symbols in her home, but they'd come with the relocation of power, as for some peculiar reason they seemed to comfort the Necropolitans. She'd never understood the logic behind the statues. First, they sent people like her overseas to fight against the monsters, and then they immortalized them with marble and bronze and worshipped them. The paintings weren't that much better. On the walls hung the former rulers, the necromancers, with tormented expressions. She guessed people had to remember their history, both the good and the bad.

Minta almost got down the stairs without being disturbed, trying to ready herself for the battle to come. But a moment of uninterrupted preparation would have been too much to ask for.

"Mayor Stopford," a rasping voice said.

Minta knew that voice and couldn't believe that she'd let someone sneak up behind her. The proper term would be shamble behind her, but that sounded like something she should have heard.

"Good evening, Mrs. Maybury." Minta turned around to greet the undead woman.

"Good evening to you too," Mrs. Maybury said.

"Are you joining us tonight?" It was a stupid question, as Mrs. Maybury was always there. Altogether, she was a horrible woman. Minta wanted nothing more than to get rid of her, sometimes hoping for her to rot. The woman had a knack for testing her politeness and civility. She'd never met anyone like Mrs. Maybury; nobody else was as unreasonable and infuriating. She always detested anything Minta brought to the table. Actually, the horrible undead woman detested everything said inside the auditorium and most likely outside of it. She was one of those people who had nothing good in their lives and thus made sure others didn't either.

"Of course I am; how could you even ask." Mrs. Maybury spat out the words and in the process lost one of her teeth. It flew past Minta's shoulder and landed on the floor, making a sharp high note.

Minta counted to ten, reminding herself that kindness and compassion were more useful than dominance and spite. She even made sure she pretended not to notice the tooth flying past her. When you gave someone an opportunity to maintain their dignity and save face, they would repay that back in kindness. However, that might not apply to Mrs. Maybury.

"Good. Never mind me, I was just wondering aloud," she said.

Mrs. Maybury snorted.

Minta counted to ten again. "Let me escort you to the auditorium," she said.

"You think I'm too senile and can't manage on my own. I might be twenty-five years older than you, but my brain is in far better shape."

"Of course it is, Mrs. Maybury. I was just—"

"You were just what? Wishing that I wouldn't show up? That my embalming oils finally gave up?"

Minta gritted her teeth. "Goodness, no. I've always valued you as a council member and couldn't bear to lose your wisdom in common matters, Mrs. Maybury."

"Ha, common matters? Am I no use for anything other than seeing that the trash gets picked up and the colors of the drapery are the latest fashion?" she asked and slouched past Minta.

"Not at all. Common matters like our joint interest in a good life."

"Oh, that. What's so good about life?"

"Nothing at all," Minta replied and regretted her words as soon as they left her lips.

"Damn straight," Mrs. Maybury said.

Minta chose not to respond or even mutter a word under her breath. The undead had an acute sense of hearing, to everyone's dislike.

The rest of the journey to the auditorium passed in awkward silence. Minta, out of politeness, tried to come up with something to say but always swallowed the words before she let them out. Mrs. Maybury didn't seem to feel any better. She moaned and complained as she walked along with her. You could say the woman liked to battle with Minta but not to mingle with her.

Minta wished she could go back to her hunting days,

so she could be out there wrestling rabid werewolves instead of politicians.

The auditorium was a huge room. It was circular, and in the middle of it was a huge round table surrounded with chairs. Around the table were the audience seats. You could easily fit fifty people in there, but the seats were seldom filled. People found politics uninteresting as long as what politicians decided didn't interfere with their lives. Lately, as the economy wasn't doing so well on its own, there'd been two or three viewers for their sittings. Mostly reporters, and never painting their actions in a good light. At least not Minta's.

Minta and Mrs. Maybury were the first two to arrive, as always.

Minta chose her chair. It wasn't a special chair. It didn't differ from any other chair in the room, but nevertheless, it was her chair. She always sat in it, giving her the best view around the room and more importantly of the doorway and the windows, so no one could sneak up on her. She lowered her papers onto the desk and waited for the others to come and Mrs. Maybury to take her seat. The woman always chose the one opposite Minta.

"How are your sons?" Minta asked when she couldn't take the awkwardness anymore.

"Fine," Mrs. Maybury said.

"Good to hear. The business is doing well?" she asked.

"What is it to you?"

One...two...three Krakens...four...

"The work your sons do is vital to our city. It can't be easy to provide the necessary products at times like these," Minta said.

For a short moment, Mrs. Maybury seemed to relax. Minta wasn't sure if she detected a smile. You never could tell with the undead. Taxidermy, embalming, and other ways to keep them life-like and prevent rotting took their toll on some of their expressions.[9]

"They are managing...but...not if you continue with this charade. We need to act now!" Mrs. Maybury said.

"You're right. We need to act upon the situation, but

---

9   Or it could be an affliction of being undead that they lacked emotions, but saying such a thing was prejudicial. Especially when the other side could easily crack your skull open and eat your brain.

in due time and after deliberation," Minta said. She was never one to advocate for swift action. When you gave issues time, they solved themselves. If you had to intervene, at least you knew what you were doing instead of going in blind and thrashing about.

Mrs. Maybury looked at the Mayor. She was recharging herself for another round. She had that expression on her face that told Minta she was searching for an insult in the previous statement. Minta knew the woman thought she hated her, but that wasn't true. Hate was such a strong word to use with anyone. Minta would rather not agitate Mrs. Maybury. It would be a long two hours if she got her all stirred up.

The impending verbal assault was interrupted by the arriving council members. Minta stood up and greeted everyone.

◆

A thick mist liked to hang around the Old Rainy Meadow cemetery. It was summoned there every night by the dead, who argued its presence was necessary for the place to have the right ambiance. Without the massive vision-blocking wall of moisture so concentrated it made movement feel like swimming in a swamp, the cemetery would be just another park. Also, creating ambiance was as good of a purpose for existence as, say, breeding, and the mist liked the cemetery. It was never dull. There was always someone creeping around, doing things they shouldn't. Last night a group of grave robbers had come ill-equipped. A few of them had gotten away alive, but the rest had ended up as light midnight snacks. Their bones still lay somewhere on the grounds. The groundskeeper hadn't gotten that far in tidying up the place. There was too much to do with the littering adventurers, annoying necromantic students, and bothersome weeds.

The mist and the dead observed as a group of one woman and three men proceeded in, waiting to see if an intervention was needed. They had to, as the groundskeeper had moved inside his shed as soon as it became clear he wouldn't get home before night fell. He huddled there, unsuccessfully blocking the noises coming from outside with two pillows tied around his head.

A narrow path squirmed between the graves and tombstones.

"Show me the way," Petula said.

The crippled man offered her his hand.

She stared at it and waited for him to withdraw it. He eventually did, turning his back on her and moving away.

Petula followed the three men, minding her step. However, following the men turned out to be difficult, as the mist tried to swallow her short frame whole. She kept up the pace, occasionally stomping on Morris' heels. When she left any more space between him and her, she could barely see the man. She listened to the echoes of their steps and searched for their faint shadows. In the distance came a moan and a shuffling sound. She felt the hairs on the back of her neck rise. That shouldn't happen; she'd been prepared for this. But sometimes imagination got the better of her. Petula squeezed the handle of her bag and searched for the men but found only mist. The sound of their steps was close, but the mist distorted them.

She wasn't sure if they had gone left or right, or maybe they had gone straight. Petula stopped and examined the narrow path dividing into three ways.

"Where are you?" she asked. Her voice scraped her throat.

No reply.

"I'm afraid I'm lost. Where did you go?" she said. "Right or left?"

A shuffling sound came from her right. She turned her head in the direction, seeing only a dark shape amongst the white mist. This was nothing like the wakenings she'd done at the University. A loose, uncontrolled undead would be all she needed right now. She formed an incantation, ready to spit it out at any moment.

Petula tilted her head and waited for the zombie to get closer.

Before she knew it, a hand came out of the mist and grabbed her, fastening around her arm. Petula let out the incantation.

If it'd been an undead, it would have submitted to her will, but it was the smug man, Morris Reinhardt. He softened his touch.

"What was that?" he asked.

"Nothing," Petula said.

"Are you sure?" he asked.

"As sure as I can be," she said.

"Then follow me. We are almost there," he replied. Behind the man, Petula thought she saw a spirit. A man in a top hat. But when she looked more closely, it was gone.

Petula let the man guide her by her arm. His touch stayed soft but persistent. He moved forward with the same shuffling noise she'd heard earlier.

The mist continued distorting the surroundings, but now everything seemed less sinister. The man's closeness reassured her, which she hated. Petula tightened her grip on the bag's handle, turning her knuckles white.

As promised, it was a short walk to the grave with a huge man-sized headstone, red rose bush, and freshly dug ground. The two other men already stood around the unopened grave. Petula lowered her doctor's bag onto the foot of the mound. She couldn't believe they'd forgotten the most basic element of the ritual. She needed the body. Before she could open her mouth and protest, she found a shovel thrust into her hand.

"You can't be serious?" she asked.

"I'm an old man," Ignatius Vaughn said.

"My bad back," Wilbur Sumner said.

"My lame leg," Morris Reinhardt added.

"You could have gotten someone else to do this beforehand."

"We forgot, and now it's too late to get anyone else. You better get cracking," Ignatius said.

Petula tried to suppress her initial thoughts of swinging the shovel against the man's face in favor of a more pleasant way of seeing things. Think about the money, think about what you get to do, she reminded herself. She'd never cared about money. All she wanted to do was point out their idiocy. She didn't. She heard her mother's voice, scolding her. *"Young girl, you can't say to someone that they're an idiot, imbecile, cretin, or a numskull. And if you dare to utter those words aloud, I'll take the dictionary away from you along with the rest of your books. Can't you see, you won't make friends if you don't know how to play nice with others."*

Ha. She would start playing nice as soon as people

stopped being morons.

"If I dig open the grave, there won't be much time left for me to wake up your friend," she cautioned without releasing all her inner venom.

The men shrugged. The only one who seemed nervous was Wilbur. Petula got the distinct feeling that was exactly the point. On some primal level, they needed their friend to stay buried.

She readied herself, squinted her eyes, and peered at Ira Worthwrite's name written in beautiful gold lettering on the gray stone. Petula wrinkled her nose. It only dawned on her now that her first real awakening was going to be the head of the Worthwrite Bank of Necropolis Ltd, the biggest bank in the city. They said he was an unpleasant man.

Petula set the shovel to lean against the tombstone next to Ira's, took off her wool coat, lowered it to the stone, and retrieved the shovel. She worked the ground, pushing the shovel time after time against the soil, perfecting a pyramid-shaped mound next to her. She mumbled an incantation to aid the process. The soil moved of its own accord. If she hadn't, she'd still be digging six hours from now. The incantation used the dead life-force around her. It was your standard first-year stuff. All necromancers knew it.

The men shifted their weight from one foot to another, groaning as she took her time. Ignatius glanced at his pocket watch and tapped it to show her the time. Petula cursed under her breath. This wakening was a half-assed job, and she hated to be part of it. One would think waking up a friend, let alone a man like Worthwrite, would be done with forethought and rigorous planning. It seemed she was wrong, that even powerful men and their companies were prone to errors. Something to do with decision making and no one daring to object, she guessed.

Petula wiped her forehead to stop the sweat running into her eyes. She made matters worse, covering her forehead with a thick layer of cemetery soil, making her want to slam the shovel onto the ground and storm out.

"You shouldn't do that; it'll bring bad luck," Wilbur said.

"What?" Petula snapped. Her heart was beating fast.

"Playing with the soil of the dead like that," he said, oblivious to Petula's tone.

"An occupational hazard." Petula hissed the words out.

"It must be, but still, you should show some respect for the dead," Wilbur said.

Petula gripped the shovel harder and stared back at Wilbur.

Wilbur looked away.

"No time to chitchat," Ignatius said. "We have to get Ira up in half an hour. If you keep standing there, we won't have time to do the ritual."

Morris leaned against his cane and acted as if he wasn't part of the conversation.

"Then you might lend a helping hand," she said.

That got them to shut up. Petula knew these kinds of gentlemen back at home. They were too fancy to get their hands dirty, but not noble enough not to get their hands bloody. It took her another fifteen minutes to bare the coffin. Petula jumped down, not expecting help from the others, and pushed open the lid. Inside the coffin lay an unpleasant-looking man on a white silk cushion, looking remarkably peaceful. In fact, so peaceful that Petula was sure it'd be better to leave him to his slumber.

Ira Worthwrite had decomposed to the point where his skin had lost all, shall we say, glow. And no one could say Ira had been the most handsome man when alive, but now... half of Ira's face was rotten and eaten by little vermin despite the heavy amounts of embalming oils. Without them, the body would have turned from green to red. Its blood should be decomposing and the organs accumulating gas, but it wasn't. The taxidermist had done a remarkable job of enchanting his lively appearance and speeding up the process of decomposition so he was past the bloating stage and could be awakened after a week, before the teeth and nails fell out. That normally took several weeks, but with some, the process started sooner. The undead weren't happy about the loss of hair when they woke up. You couldn't blame them. They also had beauty standards. But while the taxidermist had done an excellent job, someone else had messed up with Ira's process[10].

---

10   Most likely the one who'd sealed him into his coffin. The one with a grudge. The one whose loan application had been rejected by the Worthwrite Bank of Necropolis Ltd. And all he, Sam, had wanted to be was an actor, and not one undertaker amongst the many.

His face shouldn't be so bad. Entropy had found a way into the coffin. Ira's eyes had sunk deeper into his skull. His abdomen had turned inward, making his rib cage poke out. All the symmetry from his face and body was gone. And they say symmetry goes a long way. It even gives an unfair advantage to those less...pretty.

Getting the decomposition just right was one of the reasons the dead were awakened after a week. The rest was due to old customs that died hard. And there was no reason to bury Ira in the ground except that this was how it was done in Necropolis. You could say it was more fun that way. Like a scavenger hunt, except with rotting bodies and angry spirits.

The man was nothing Petula hadn't seen before. Taxidermy was part of her training. All necromancers took the courses, even when they didn't specialize in it. She looped her hands around him and inched the man up from the coffin. Something oozed out of his side onto her black dress, something wet and sticky. Petula refused to look down and continued moving him to the firmer ground. A maggot crawled inside her sleeve. She clasped her hands tighter around the man. It wouldn't look good if a necromancer was afraid of maggots and other critters. She dragged Ira up. Her heels sank into the freshly dug ground, and she fell backwards, Ira toppling on top of her.

"Critting Kraken shit from the bottomless sea," she said, and then she remembered she wasn't alone and coughed.

"Do you need any help?" Morris asked.

"I'll manage," she said. She would not let anyone swoop in at the last second to save her from a splinter when she'd just slain a dragon, rescued a village, and was about to marry the princess. Petula pushed Ira off her and stood up. When she got up, she refused to look down her dress and see the mess she'd created. It doesn't matter, she said to herself. It mattered. If she had one weakness, it was that she hated germs and dirt. She'd been a fussy kid when sitting outside playing with others. She'd rather be inside reading, but her mother had insisted that outside air would do her good. Ha.

Petula took Ira by his armpits and arranged him into a more dignified position on the ground.

"All right, let's do this," Petula said.

"Here?" Ignatius asked.

"Why not?" Petula stated.

"But there's a perfectly fine mausoleum on the grounds just for this."

"I don't doubt that, but I thought we were in a hurry? It would take me more minutes we don't have to drag him there," she said, knowing full well she wouldn't get any help. All this had already taken her forty-five minutes, and if they wanted their friend to be awakened at midnight like they usually did, they'd only got fifteen minutes left.

Ignatius groaned. "Then you better do it here," he said with a sigh of disappointment.[11]

Petula wondered how these men could have survived this long with their preferred avoidance of reality, their great disregard for people, and also their lack of physical strength. It was probably something to do with mastering the rules and being dick enough to exploit them. Soon that wouldn't matter. She could be back in her bed with a good book. She walked next to Ira's head and lowered her palms against the man.

"What are you doing?" Ignatius asked.

"Preparing to wake him up," she said.

"Shouldn't you start by lighting candles and drawing symbols around him?"

"Nah, I'm good."

"But—"

"Words are enough," she said. They were. All the trinkets, candles, and other showy stuff were reserved for those who didn't possess the raw talent she did. The only thing she needed was her voice. Trinkets, vials of unspeakable things, and the dark clothes only slowed her down. All that mattered was her. She could do this bare naked if needed, but she preferred not to. Too witchy for her liking. Most necromancers could do this without the thingamajigs if only they trusted themselves. Necromancy was about your inner voice.

"But—"

"You should leave this part to me. I know what I'm doing."

"I guess," Ignatius said. He muttered under his breath, "But this isn't the right way."

---

11 He'd wanted to sneak into Worthwrite's mausoleum, as Ira never let him in there. There were rumors of hidden treasures, banned symbols, and eye-opening revelations.

Petula ignored him and began her threnody for Ira to show respect before bringing him back to life. She'd read from a passage in the olden days that they used criers[12] at funerals to ease the mourners' sorrow. This was the same but for the dead. To help him mourn the life he'd lost and lessen the trouble of coming back. It basically started the whole thing off on the right foot.

She took a deep breath in and half sang, half spoke her words. "Superingero, gnascor Worthwrite. Superingero, gnascor Worthwrite Ira. Superingero, gnascor Ira Worthwrite!"

Her words made the body jerk. Its back twisted into an arch. The three men held their breath. Then the body collapsed back onto the freshly dug ground. It lay motionless. Ignatius snorted. "You need the candles," he said.

Petula pretended she didn't hear him. The old dead bastard was playing hard to get. If he thought she'd make a fuss, he had another think coming.

"Superingero, gnascor Worthwrite. Superingero, gnascor Worthwrite Ira. Superingero, gnascor Ira Worthwrite..." she continued, repeating it five times.

The body jerked upright with a violent surge. Then it opened its lifeless eyes. They glowed.

"You are late," Ira Worthwrite said. Then he coughed, as his mouth was unused to speaking, thinking the air pushing from his lungs should aid the process. It didn't. Everything came from the spirit. The body was just a vessel to move his consciousness around, making it easier to claim his earthly possessions again.

And they weren't late, they were just on time in a way you can only be on time at the last minute.

"Who's this?" Ira said and squinted his dead eyes at Petula before the others clawed back their dignity and protested.

"I'm Petula Upwood, and I'm the one who woke you," she said, knowing that if she gave the others permission to speak for her, that'd be the case forever.

Ira looked past her to the others and said with a tight, angry voice, "Where's the one I said to contact?"

"He's dead, sir," Ignatius said.

---

12   Usually women.

"Dead? Which one of you morons let that happen?" Ira asked.

There came a silence. You know the kind of silence; when you can hear people turning in their graves. Also, the kind of silence where someone, Petula for example, is plotting a beheading for not being told about Jeremiah's death.

Ignatius' lips curled into a snarl, and his eyes narrowed. "Someone got to him before we did," he said.

"How?" Ira asked and pushed himself up from the ground.

Petula offered her hand to the undead man, who swayed back and forth as his body relearned the basics. Morris rushed to aid him, but Petula was closer. Ira gave the man a warning stare and took Petula's hand to steady himself. His touch felt like, you know, dead skin: leathery and cold, like a hairless bat. "So, you are the one who I'm stuck with," Ira said and released Petula when he was sure his estranged feet were once again part of him.

She nodded.

"We don't—" Ignatius said.

Ira lifted his hand, and the man swallowed the rest of his words. Ira familiarized himself with Petula, letting his eyes wander around her body.

"Makeup would do you good," Ira said.

Petula opened her mouth but never got her words out. Ira had already turned his attention back to the men.

"I see everything goes awry when I'm not there. We better get going and see what mess you have created," he said.

"Sir, there's one thing about Miss Upwood—" Morris said.

"You can tell me that in the coach. I assume you brought one," Ira said.

"We took mine," Wilbur said.

"Then just give me a moment," Ira said and lowered himself back into his coffin.

Petula walked to her coat and took it.

"Thank you," she whispered to the grave's owner. She'd learned throughout her life that it helped to be kind to the dead, solid or not. Spirits had always been there with her. Following her. Ever since she could remember. She put on the coat. There was a slight tremble in her hands. She was still elated by the surge of power that'd gone through her to him.

She could feel the connection. If she wanted, she could grope for the man's mind and push him, but it was forbidden. Free will. Still, this was a feeling like no other, better than commanding spirits. This was what she was meant to do. This was who she was.

Ira got up from the grave. He'd taken two golden coins out of the coffin. He pocketed them.

"I'm ready. Lead the way, Wilbur," he said.

Home or not? Petula thought.

5

I'D RATHER NOT HAVE MY VEINS
PUNCTURED

erbert Ringworm and the necromancer rode outside
in the night air. The air was barely breathable, as the
whole Necropolis stank, like huge cities do, of
sewage, humans, and cruelty. They'd left the
cemetery only a moment ago and now rode between the old
houses with guarding gargoyles, ornamental railings, and
French balconies, whatever those were. The houses reeked of
old money. It was only natural, being so close to the banking
district—or soul-sucking exploitation district, as Herbert liked
to think of it. This place gave him the shivers, to put it
mildly. To put it more accurately, this place made his inner
rage flare up. He only had to make the horses obey him for
three blocks, and then he could leave all this behind, the
entire parasite-infested, good-for-nothing city.

He'd choked when Ira and the rest of them had
approached the coach; seeing that man after all this time had
made Ona's death even more real. He should have struck him
down there and then, but...he hadn't. He'd failed Ona, again.

But to his fortune, the bankers had forced the necromancer to ride outside with him, giving him the chance he needed to redeem himself. Not that the woman had objected. What she'd objected to was being taken to Ira's bank instead of straight home.

There was this heavy, oppressive atmosphere between them. Her silence made Herbert tense. He watched the horses' heads bob up and down as they pulled the coach along the cobblestone street. The hilt of his knife banged against his hip. He waited for the right moment, as the necromancer was different. She was alert and rigid, unlike the drunk and overconfident Jeremiah had been. She observed her surroundings and made a note of his every movement. But she couldn't be faster than the werewolves he wrestled in the ring. Then again, she was a necromancer, and she didn't need to be fast like Herbert. She only had to say one word, and his fate was sealed.

Herbert reached inside his jacket, but at the same time, the woman made her move. She reached for her bag. Herbert tensed up. He found his trusted knife and readied himself to react.

The necromancer pulled out a red book. He couldn't quite relax. You didn't know with her sort what dangers they hid inside texts.

But it was time he finished this once and for all. What did he care if he died or not as long as Ira died too?

"Do you mind if I read?" the necromancer asked, surprising him.

"*It hurts,*" the voice said.

"I..." he started but finished with a grunt. The voice made everything in him ache.

The necromancer glanced past him, shook her head, and turned her attention to the book she'd taken out. She mumbled something Herbert couldn't hear. Maybe protection of some sort?

The necromancer was about the same size as his Ona. She smelled the same, something sweet and spicy at the same time, with a slight whiff of formaldehyde, soil, and rotting flesh. Herbert squeezed the hilt of his knife. He couldn't quite let go. He hurried the horses onward.

"Do you mind if I use a light?" she asked and turned to face him. Her silver-blue eyes seemed to peer into his soul and steal something from it, but he had to be imagining that.

"No," he said. All this talking was distracting him. It even made him move his hand from the knife to the reins.

The necromancer whispered something he couldn't quite understand. It sounded like a command. A moment later, a light surged out from the nearby trees. He knew what it was and was about to cast a protective chant to get rid of the pest[13], but the woman said, "Don't, I need it."

His hand reached for the knife, but her curious eyes stopped him from going further.

"You can't be serious?" he asked instead.

"I can handle it. It's just for a short moment. Everything will be fine."

"Aren't the street lights enough?"

Someone had already lit the lampposts. They cast a soft yellowish light.

"Not for reading," she said. "And I can control it."

He nodded.

The summoned will-o'-the-wisp came closer, hovering above the necromancer's head. She opened the red book and slid her gaze over the text. Herbert let his eyes wander over the pages. The text was written in small print, but he could see the patterns drawn on the paper. They looked like a game of Tic-Tac-Toe. Groups of dots moving on a grid. He wasn't sure what spells they were, but they looked powerful. They seemed to entrap her. Ona used to be like that, to be so immersed within her own world she forgot all about him. When that happened, he knew not to disturb her or she would lose her concentration. He'd found nothing to occupy his mind that way, say maybe Ona herself. When he was with her, he could only see her, but she laughed at him whenever he mentioned that she was his sole passion. That's nonsense, and it doesn't count, she would say, and shrug it off. Herbert guessed it was a lie; his art had always made hours and days go by, but not while he was with her.

Herbert turned his attention back to the horses, steering them around a corner. Until now, the street had been empty of other travelers. But now he had to navigate the coach through the busy Old Willy Wrangler's Street, where all the money got made. This wasn't the first time he had been

---

13   Yes, he knew the simple ones too; everyone in Necropolis did.

behind the reins, but he'd never been a natural with objects as big as horses. Something about them made him nervous. He wondered how the driver managed to do this for a living. Or had. He grimaced.

Herbert glanced over at the necromancer. The wisp flickered over the woman, casting nasty shadows on her face, distorting her.

This had gone on long enough. He should never have got lost in his own thoughts. Action, that was what he was made for. He knew there was only one outcome, and there was no escaping it. Herbert could already see the Worthwrite Bank of Necropolis Ltd. Behind it, there was a back alley. When they got there, he'd stop this nonsense.

"Do you think we're masters of our own fate?" the necromancer asked without taking her eyes off the book.

"What?" he replied and pulled the coach back to make room for the oncoming traffic. A large carriage full of people rocked by. There was nothing merry about the passengers; their faces were long, and they looked like someone had gathered them and was moving them into a poorhouse. There were several such places in the city where the not-so-well-to-do were huddled to work for their upkeep. These were not those people. That carriage had left the district two hours ago. These were men and women who cleaned and worked in the banks. The so-called day-shift, getting home to have five hours of shut-eye and then hurrying back here.

"That our actions are ours. That we control what happens," the necromancer stated. She laid the book on her lap and looked at him. Those eyes of hers.

He reached for his knife.

"I've been thinking, if we lived in a perfect world, we'd have more say about our destiny. There wouldn't be things like chance, luck, chaos, harm, or greed, or even hurt. But we don't live in a perfect world, so we can't truly control our destiny. The only thing I think we can control is our reactions," she said before he acted.

"Why—?" Herbert asked.

"Why am I asking?"

"Y-es," he said. He wasn't sure where this was going.

"I was just wondering about my own choices. Tomorrow, I'm meant to take a ship and travel back home to be with my family, but today or tonight I was offered a chance to be what I am. Before that, my life had been decided. I had a clear picture of where I was heading and what I was going to become."

"Why are you telling me this?" he asked. He made the coach turn into the alley leading behind the bank.

"Because of..." She paused to think. "I was wondering what you believed in."

"If you say our reactions are the only things that matter, then everything depends on how you react now," he said.

"Exactly, but sometimes you can't decide what you should do. Would you choose a life of death and violence or a life without excitement but with a greater commitment to the well-being of others?"

"I..." he said.

"Not that easy. But then again, I can't complain; I have the option to decide. Not many do. But either way, I won't let myself end up in a ditch with my belly cut open," she said.

The voice wailed next to his ear.

The will-o'-the-wisp flickered rapidly.

"I thought as much," she said. "But before you take out that knife you have been so obviously fiddling with all this time, think what kind of future you'll form for you and her."

He divided his attention between the necromancer, managing the coach, and the voice screaming into his ear. Herbert let go of the reins and reached for his knife. He drew it out, readying himself to stab.

The necromancer said, "Occupo." Before he could react, the knife was tugged into the book and yanked out of his hand.

The book hovered in the air, the wisp wrapped around it. If a ball made of soul light could look unhappy, this one did.

"Whatever your reasons are, I don't care. But I'm not willing to die for them," the necromancer said. "And before you make another foolish attempt, think."

He didn't get to decide; the four men pushed out of the coach.

"Jeffrey, why didn't you open the door?" Wilbur's voice came from underneath them. Herbert watched, bemused, as his knife and the book with the wisp floated into the necromancer's bag.

The necromancer took the interruption as a cue to put distance and Wilbur between her and him, taking her bag with her.

"What has gotten into you? You stopped us this far from the bank?" Wilbur continued.

"One of the horses was limping," the necromancer said.

Herbert grunted.

"Still," Wilbur said, not finishing his sentence. He had that look on his face that said he'd rather not take the twelve steps necessary to get to the bank's back door.

"Oh well, you better mind the horses and wait here. This won't take long," Wilbur said, looking at Herbert, who'd lowered his head. The man frowned but forgot what he was thinking when Ignatius let out a loud sigh behind him.

Herbert wasn't sure what was going on. Why had the necromancer helped him? But he took advantage of the turn of events. He nodded to the man and turned his attention to the horses while he made his way down from the seat. Without glancing towards Herbert, they left him alone, walking to the bank's back door. The necromancer was the only one who peeked over her shoulder, but he was sure she did that to see if he was coming up behind them.

The last thing he heard was Ira saying, "Things better be in motion already. Or have you messed up everything while I was gone?"

"Everything has gone according to plan," Morris said.

"Don't worry. After tonight, we'll hear confirmation, and then we can start the process."

"And the bill?!" Ira asked.

"Almost done," Morris said.

"You should be finished with it by now," Ira complained.

"I'll finish it tonight," Morris said; his words sounded pleasant but annoyed. You know, the tight words said between a smile.

"And the city?" Ira asked.

"There'll be a protest at dawn to stop the workers getting to work. Or so I've heard," Ignatius said.

Ira chuckled.

Whatever they said next came out too muffled for Herbert to hear.

Herbert waited for a moment longer to be sure they were gone. That none of them would return through the door. He looked around to see if anyone was looking at him. He found no one with enough intelligence. Okay, there was a cat sitting on a trashcan, stalking rats. Who are we to judge the intelligence of animals? Herbert took off the heavy wool overcoat. He laid it on the driver's seat along with the hat. When he was done, he took off at a run towards the bank's wall and leaped to the first ledge. Herbert pushed his feet against the wall and pulled himself up. Once there, he climbed higher and higher, navigating towards Ira's office. He knew where it was. One of the office's windows was loose, and if he shimmied it, it would come open. What he would do when he got there, he wasn't sure.

Herbert's muscles were sore after the scuffle with the driver. He paused to hang with one hand, giving the other a rest. When he was sure his arms would hold, he grabbed the edge of a rain gutter, and after that he didn't stop. Herbert had to know what they said and did inside that office. Ira's words were more important.

Underneath him he heard someone say, "Stop."

The voice sounded familiar, but Herbert ignored it and pushed up. There was nothing they could do to him. Not here and not on this building. It took enormous skill to get even to the first ledge. But he had to admit that the owner of the voice irritated him.

◆

Somewhere else, away from the cold, misty night air, Bertha Chaplain, the leader of the Union of the Undead, moved through her house with a light step. She was setting up for a party. Bertha was going all in with this one, having invited every member of the Union. They'd arrive soon. Right after the boring old council meeting. Bertha moaned as she traipsed up and down the stairs and supervised her staff. She complained about every missed detail. She found more than a few skewed nameplates, and the black and white rose arrangement hadn't been cut to an equal height. If she'd been a man, that wouldn't have mattered. Her wife or a member of her staff would have gotten the blame. But as a woman, they would crucify her. Having been in politics all her life, having won battles with and against Oliver the Great, and having sacrificed her own life, her ability to rule would come down to flowers. Funny how the good old world worked.

Bertha Chaplain was an undead. Had been for seventeen years now. She'd died in her prime, at the age of fifty-seven. After her death, she'd restored her face to almost living-like through a massive amount of taxidermy. The only thing that was missing was the glow of flowing blood. Everything else about her was perfect. Her manners, her temper, her looks, her posture, and her you-know-what. There was nothing out of place. Okay, her long chestnut-colored hair looked odd against her greenish-gray complexion, but there were those who found that attractive.

However, none of that should matter in a perfect world, but in this one there were two types of female politicians: those who looked like they'd walked there from a beauty pageant, and those who looked like a mother. A mother willing to whack your bottom. She chose to be the first kind, as she didn't care for spanking.

Tonight wasn't only about the Union's social hierarchy. She had an agenda. Whenever she had one of those, it was always to screw someone over, but this time she was sure it was for the good of everyone. Herself included.

Bertha moved to the kitchen and watched the food being prepared. It would have been nice to have an appetite again. Bertha pictured all the lavish dinners she'd had back when she was alive, and her mouth didn't even water. Fish had been her favorite, with a little bit of salt, the right amount of lemon, and a dash of pepper. Served with roasted beetroot spiced with thyme. Just perfection; and afterwards, a dessert rich with vanilla and served with berry sauce and nothing could ruin that day. It was the only thing she missed about being alive. Now her perfect white kitchen was as alien to her as a beating heart.

"Agatha, come here," Bertha shouted.

Soon her assistant rushed to her.

"Yesshh?"

"Did you order the veal?"

"Yeshh."

"Why would you do that?"

"For our guestshh," she said.

Agatha was Bertha's assistant and more. She was beautiful in that special way that made her look frail and a bit unintelligent. A person's initial thoughts upon seeing her were usually "poor, pretty girl." The trouble was that when she opened her mouth, it blew away the previous thoughts. Not because she used fake vampire fangs, which were sharp and realistic, but because out of her mouth came opinions, and strong ones. Or at least that used to be the case before she started working for Bertha Chaplain. Now she looked beaten, tired, and phlegmatic. Her dyed black hair didn't fit. It made her look ill and haunted.

"Who would eat that? And what are they making?" Bertha said, looking at the cooks.

"Pas—"

"I can see what they're making, that wasn't a question. Our guests are all going to be of the dead variety, and none of them will eat this," she said, gliding her hand over the readied food.

"Oh," Agatha said.

"Yes, oh. Take care of this and find me real meat to serve," she said.

"Oh," Agatha said again.

Agatha turned her attention to the food. "You won't be needed tonighthh. You can take all the food withhh you," she said, nodding to the cooks.

The cooks were relieved. They hurried to take everything with them and ran out of the house before they became something to be served.

When they were finally alone, the huge kitchen island stood between the two of them, with the evidence of Agatha's mistake lying on top of it. She should have known better, but as always, she'd mixed up what kind of soiree this was. She should have learned by now to check her calendar. Not that it'd do any good. One thing Bertha Chaplain was lousy at was writing. Her letters were formed in a hurry, and they arced without any logic.

"Oh," Agatha said. "They...never mind. I better get the servingshhh from the market." She took a black velvet cape with a red silk lining off a hook next to the back door.

"You're not going anywhere tonight. Send someone else," Bertha said.

"Sshuure, who do you suggesthh?"

"Well, you better come back, and fast. Be careful, won't you?" Bertha asked.

"Alwayshh," Agatha said.

"I'd be happier if you took someone with you, one of the boys."

"I'll be fine on my own," Agatha said, revealing her teeth. They could open a tin can. "It'sh only the marketh plache."

"It's just that—" Bertha said.

"I know, I'll be exshtra careful."

"Good."

Agatha left, and soon Bertha stepped out of the kitchen holding a sharp knife in her hands. She headed back to the dining room to attack the roses. They still weren't the right size. It took her the whole evening to make the house presentable, and the whole time she strained for any odd sensations in her body or mind, to see if Agatha was all right. There was the usual numbness and the occasional tickling of her parasites, but otherwise, everything was hunky-dory.

She sent the servants away when the house looked okay enough. Bertha kept tidying up the place, occasionally popping into the window to see if Agatha was coming back. It shouldn't take this long to get sufficient food. She peered out between the lace curtains Agatha had made. It'd gotten pitch dark outside, and there wouldn't be enough time to prepare food if she insisted on stalling.

Bertha drew the curtains shut and headed upstairs to change into something decent. She had her black-and-white lace dress waiting for her there. But she needed Agatha to help her get into it. There were too many holes in the dress, which had proved dangerous over the years.

Bertha took the dress out of her closet anyway, looking at it the way women do when they believe that a simple dress can solve all their problems.

Bertha lifted the dress, and already her dead fingers tangled in the lace, getting stuck as she tried to get them free. She should have burned the old thing years ago, but she looked so stunning in it, even more so now she'd taken out unnecessary ribs.

Where was that silly girl? Doing only Kraken knows what.

Bertha sat down to wait, staring at the wall. She began to formulate her plan for what to say tonight and how to act. She formed a mental image of how everything would go with the other Union members. How to drive her points through and how to assert her power. It was always touch and go with some members. Many of them thought they could do the job better; for example, Mrs. Maybury. The woman could be a pain in the ass. Always in a sour mood, always nitpicking about tiny details, always the prophet of doom. Altogether a horrific woman. She wasn't even the worst. The others could be just as tedious. Always undermining her authority. The most obnoxious bunch of undead she'd ever seen, and she'd invited them to her home with open arms. But tonight she'd introduce her plan, Bertha Chaplain's plan, and history would be hers.

Bertha stood up and shuffled down the stairs to see if she'd missed Agatha coming back. There was no sign of her anywhere in the house. What could you do when you couldn't rely upon your own necromancer, who knew better than to leave her silly errands until a night like this. She'd been her necromancer for three years now, after taking over possession from the previous one, who'd gotten too ill to carry on.

It was no use moping around. She'd make sure the girl got an earful later. Now she needed to get into the dress and find a light night-time snack for her guests.

6

AS GOOD A PLAN AS ANY OTHER

Ira Worthwrite felt alive as he walked inside the building that made the city pulse. Being away for a week had made him turn in his grave. Nigel, his assistant, had come once a day to read him the relevant papers, keeping him in the loop. But it wasn't the same as being here. When he shut his eyes, he heard all the coins clinking together, all the paper rustling as money poured into this magnificent building. All his employees worked hard for that, and sometimes it felt like magic how they made money multiply. All Algor's rhythms in place.[14]

Despite the advantages, which he didn't understand fully, his passion lay in creative accounting. With it, he'd been able to turn loans into assets and assets into loans. How

---

14 Algor was an ex-employee of his, a genius really. He'd come up with a way to quantify everything so the human problem could be solved with numbers. Then he'd gone and connected his rhythms to the glowing skulls tied to the esoteric realm of the dead to tap into the full calculative power of nature. That'd changed everything. Now the whole banking system was full of skulls, and Ira couldn't imagine it being done any other way.

the process truly happened was a mystery no one could make sense of. If anyone ever solved it, the universe would stop working, as the universe was fueled by nonsense, or at least the humans in it were. The duality of the accounting nevertheless made money float through this house and stick in his pockets.

Ira hummed as he led the three men and the necromancer through the hidden corridors inside his bank's walls. When he commissioned the building, he'd made sure there was always an escape route in and out of the bank. And he shouldn't be seen with the men, as the rules dictated that they were mortal enemies. A glimpse of them together would fuel wild speculations, causing sheer panic. At first he'd opposed the idea Morris had brought to his attention: that together they had more power than anyone in the world. That instead of fighting against each other, they could control the economic situation not only here in Necropolis but overseas. Now he saw how logical it was.

"Sir, we need to address the issue of the necromancer," Morris said. The man slowly moved his cane up the stairs. There would be a steep climb to the top floor.

"What issue? There's no issue. She's here with us, and the details of the contract will hold," Ira said. "You should be more worried about the half-finished proposal. Is it with you?" he asked.

"No," Morris said.

"Actually, there are two issues we need to talk about —" the necromancer said.

Ira waved his hand, dismissing her. "And they'll be dealt with in due time. I'm more interested in what happened in the week I was away," he said. Yes, Nigel had kept him up to date, but he knew nothing about what'd happened between Ignatius, Wilbur, and Morris. For all Ira knew, they could have forgotten his little black book and divided all the winnings between the three of them.

"What do you want to know?" Ignatius asked, not sounding pleased.

Ira would later squeeze out of him whatever was the matter. "What have you been up to?" he asked.

"What we planned to do," Ignatius said, glancing at the necromancer. "Our part, at least," Ignatius added. "Your sudden death left your bank unaccounted for, which was a big hole. It slowed things down."

Ira groaned.

"Nevertheless, the city is one push away from chaos," Morris reassured him, as always trying to defuse the situation. Ira never cared for that side of him.

Wilbur was the only one who refused to engage in the conversation. He chose to be quiet. It irritated Ira how Wilbur could disappear into his own head, and he'd bet that the man was thinking about his family. No one should or could be so obsessed with their home life. A sensible man stayed away, keeping himself busy by perfecting his own trade.

"Yes, like Morris said, the economy has taken a darker turn and is almost ready to be built anew from the ground up. Yesterday they announced the factory making coaches will shut down. Which means two hundred people will lose their jobs," Ignatius said. He glared at Morris and then shot a quick glance at the necromancer, who'd become unusually quiet.

There was something here he'd missed. Morris had tried to warn him about the necromancer. Could they have been stupid enough to hire her without a contract?

"And the Town Hall?" Ira asked, vexed by the situation.

"In turmoil. Minta Stopford will have her hands full after tonight's protest. They're already questioning her inability to lead and be tough on the rule breakers. Tabloids are saying she's on the side of the bankers, letting them have their big bonuses at everyone's expense. They're demanding her head on a spike. You should have seen yesterday's caricature. It made me spit out my morning tea," Morris said.

"You are forgetting the political parties and their lack of support. And there's this new guy. He preaches about the needs of the common man. People are saying he should run for office. They listen to him," Ignatius said.

"Who's he?"

"Nobody," Morris said.

"Someone who we should get to know," Ignatius interjected.

"Won't matter after we get things going, and he isn't a necromancer, so there isn't much he can do unless we change the constitution," Morris said.

"There's a thought," Ira snorted.

Wilbur stopped climbing. "Isn't anything sacred with you guys? The constitution is off limits. I won't cross that line," he said.

"And Mrs. Chaplain?" Ira asked, ignoring Wilbur. He was so easy to ignore. He let them.

"On board," Morris replied.

"Good," Ira said.

"I'm not so sure about that. You said she wavered last time you met with her," Ignatius said.

Morris took a long step to catch up with Ira, putting all his weight on the cane. "It was about the details, not about the plan," he said.

"Make sure she comes around. There's no backing out now," Ira commanded.

"As far as I gathered, she's on board as long as her name will be on the proposal. It's the rest of the Union that needs convincing," Morris said. He now stood next to the undead man.

"Anything else I should know?" Ira asked, turning to meet them.

"About the—" Morris said.

"If you're going to finish that sentence with 'necromancer,' I don't want to hear it. We'll take care of that up in my office," Ira said. He didn't need bad news. Not now. Not when he had got his life back and while trying to piece together how they'd screwed him. He hadn't yet found out how the others had cut him out of the profits, but he was sure Morris and Ignatius had something up their sleeves. He would make Wilbur squeal.

"We should really talk about *her*," Ignatius said and looked at Petula.

Ira frowned. Yes, the new necromancer was a hindrance. Jeremiah Black had been vetted thoroughly despite his drinking problem.

"You did secure a contract with her?"

He saw Petula instinctively reaching for her chest pocket; whatever else she was thinking hid behind her stoic face. He'd have expected her to show terror or dismay, but no. Her silence was disconcerting.

"Of course I did, but a lot of good that'll do us. A contract is a contract, and she can still damage us. And she insists on leaving Necropolis," Ignatius said.

"What!? That's out of the question. She isn't going anywhere. She's my lifeline." Ira twisted his mouth into an angry moan, revealing a row of rotten teeth mixed with sores. His eyes bulged out, and if this was any other kind of situation, everyone around him would have fled. He would have fled if it wasn't his own body making the expression.

The moment passed. Ira went back to his usual expression, which could only be described as restless hatred.

Morris, who was standing closest to Ira, straightened his top hat and said, "In our defense, we didn't know that, and we had to act quickly after Mister Black's death."

"In your defense!? You have to be kidding me. I don't give a rat's ass if the necromancer died or not. What I care about is that you didn't take the possibility into account. You should have had a backup, someone better than...a girl."

"I would object—" Petula said.

"Object all you want. This has got nothing to do with you. So shut up. I'll deal with you later," Ira snapped and took more forceful steps up the stairs.

"It was just that there was so much to do with all the other preparations to press through the law and make the situation ideal, and then there's Wilbur's daughter giving birth, and—" Morris said.

"You're saying I'm in this mess because Wilbur's daughter gave birth? You can't seriously mean that."

"No, it's just that..."

"Yes, you better not finish your sentence. Let's go," he said and turned around to face the stairs. He resumed his climb. The others tiptoed behind him. Ira muttered under his breath, "I doubt any of you were needed at the birth. None of you should be let anywhere near a pregnant woman, let alone an infant."

"She *is going to* give birth," Wilbur muttered under his breath. "Anytime now. I really should be at home."

Ira heard the man, but he refused to comment. He was already on thin ice, what with him being silent all the time, brooding, and letting the two other men mess things up. He'd expected more from Wilbur, who he'd known the longest. Ira had always considered the man to be his friend. For Kraken's sake, the man had been in his daughter's naming ceremony, and he'd been at his.

As they headed upwards, Ira got more irritated, and not because he was getting tired. Wilbur's muttering, Morris' moaning, Ignatius' fast heartbeat, and the necromancer's footsteps throbbed against his skull. All of them sounded like they were dying. Some more than others. He took off his shoes and left them there on the secret passage's steps. He couldn't fathom why he'd ever thought them necessary. They made walking that much harder.

The stairs finally ended in a wall. Ira pushed a panel, and it turned out to be a door that opened into his office. More than anything he wanted to be left alone to go over the papers that must have accumulated on his desk, but no, he had to endure these morons for an hour or two longer until they sorted out the necromancer mess and went over the details for tonight and tomorrow. There was no reason to prolong their plans. Ignatius had been right, to his annoyance. His death had already taken a toll on getting the timing right.

Back in the good old days when he was alive, the wall between the secret passage and his office had always caused him great distress. He'd been forced to ram against it. Now the panel opened with ease. Ira marveled at his own hands. He flexed his fingers open and shut. His joy was short-lived as the others joined him at the top of the stairs.

"If you want them to work better, I would suggest using a taxidermist. They can do wonders nowadays," Petula said.

Ira stopped moving his fingers, unsure if the woman had said that as a power play or to be helpful.

He said, "I'm sure that's something one must do, but for now this is enough." He let her and the rest of them in. The office was his home. He had gone with the traditional style. Everything was massive and made from dark wood and leather. Nigel had made sure during his absence that everything was the way he liked. If he put his finger against the baseboard and wiped it, there wouldn't be a single speck of dust. And on his huge table, which took up most of the room, he would find every single file needing his attention put in its appropriate folder by Nigel. He only had to sit behind the desk to start his work. "Now take a seat and try not to be in the way."

The necromancer squinted her eyes, and for some

reason, it disturbed Ira. Usually, he didn't care what other people thought or felt, but now there was an extra throbbing inside him. He wasn't quite sure how it'd gotten in there.

"Show me her contract!" he said and headed to his desk.

Petula smiled.

The smiling didn't help. Even more emotions and demands bubbled inside him. This was getting ridiculous. Ira collapsed behind his desk on his chair, and the usual effect of power, clarity, and determination didn't come.

"Why are you stalling? Give that contract to me, and now," he said.

Ignatius hurried past the others to give the contract to Ira, taking it out of his jacket pocket. When he'd given the contract to him, the man took his pocket watch out with shaking hands and fiddled with it, lingering near Ira.

The necromancer took a seat, as asked. She sat opposite the desk and readied herself for negotiations. Ira glanced over the contract and made eye contact with the necromancer. He hoped she would appear nervous, but she had a relaxed way about her. A book materialized from her bag and she became disinterested in her surroundings.

"She knows a breach of contract comes with a hefty price. And I have to say, once again, we had no other choice; it was now or at the next full moon a month later," Ignatius said. He spun the dial, adjusting the watch using the huge grandfather clock on Ira's wall.[15]

"Put that away," Ira said and slammed his fist on the table. There was a loud cracking sound. He lifted his hand up, and it hung loosely from his wrist. Everything below the wrist yo-yoed when he moved his arm. He shook it a couple more times and frowned.

Ignatius staggered.

The necromancer laid the book on her lap and said, "Let me." She reached over the table. Ira instinctively retracted his hand, but she persisted. She seized his arm and tugged it towards her. When Petula had secured a hold, she pushed the hand into the wrist. There was another cracking sound. With one hand, she held the arm, and with the other,

---

15   Actually, Ignatius was wrong. A full moon wasn't necessary to wake the dead, despite what the majority in the city thought, including most of the necromancers. It took a special sort of mind to go against the unwritten rules.

she tore a piece of her dress' hem and tied it around his hand. Everyone looked at her, dazed, when she returned to her seat and opened her book again.

"Mrs..." Ira glanced through the contract. "Mrs. Upwood, will you hold to the deal?" Ira asked.

"It's miss," she said without taking her eyes off the book.

"At your age?"

"Y-e-s," she said.

"What's wrong with you?" he blurted without thinking.

Morris rolled his eyes, and Wilbur coughed. Ira still didn't catch the drift. What Ignatius was thinking or doing had little to no bearing on events. It was better left unsaid.

"Everything," she said. "And you'll find out all my flaws if you don't soon find another necromancer to take my place as discussed."

"Is this true?" Ira asked, turning his attention to the men.

Ignatius looked around, trying to find an escape route. Wilbur squealed, and Morris shifted his weight from his good leg to his bad one.

"You mean to say that instead of concentrating on what we've been planning for a decade, I'm stuck finding a new necromancer because the one I got is...?" he asked after it became obvious the others would remain silent.

"Leaving," Petula said.

"...leaving, and I have to trust wholeheartedly that she will keep her mouth shut. Out of the question! She's going nowhere!"

"You can't exactly keep me here," Petula said, and her voice rose high. The same sensation Ira had had earlier came back. "As is written in the contract, you have to get another necromancer to take my place by tomorrow at noon."

"You—" Ira said, but the necromancer pushed herself to her feet and tucked the book under her armpit.

Ira's jaw dropped open. He pushed it back into place. "Would you be so kind as to let me confer with my associates?" he asked.

"Sure, but then someone will take me home. I need to pack," she said. Ira was sure he detected a slight hesitation. Maybe there was a way in?

"Yes, of course. Morris, take her to the other room," Ira said, pointing to the doors opening into an annex.

Morris offered his hand to Petula. She walked past it to the doors, opened them, and disappeared into the office's annex. It was a library of some sort, with shelves full of the bank's history, law books, records, and other miscellaneous things Ira had acquired during his life. There was an armchair and a table, and nothing more.

Ira waited for Morris and the necromancer to leave them alone. As soon as the door closed behind them, he shredded the contract.

"This is invalid, and you must do everything in your power to keep that girl here. Do you hear me?" he said.

"But," Ignatius said.

"I'm not risking my second life with some transfer."

"But," Ignatius tried again.

"That's that. Now, we have more important things to discuss," he said and pushed the shreds of paper into his desk drawer and shut it. There, now it was done, and he didn't have to think about it.

"But she still has a copy. You destroyed not only her rights but yours as well, protecting you as an independent agent from her."

"Don't worry, we'll get the contract back from her. In the meantime, one of you has to take responsibility for her, for example Wilbur. You can do it, you have daughters," Ira said.

"No, not me," Wilbur said, shaking his head. "She creeps me out. Let Ignatius or Morris do it. They can handle her better. I'd be too soft and all that." Wilbur pulled his handkerchief out of his pocket and wiped his forehead.

"For Pete's sake, you can't be that wimpy," Ira snapped.

He wasn't if you saw him running his bank, but Wilbur always argued that it was different, as banking was about money. Wilbur was like a truffle dog when it came to gold. He could smell it miles away.

"Anyway, it's settled. Morris will do it," Ira said.

"He won't like it."

"We voted on it. Three against one; it's a democratic vote, and it counts. And who knows what might come from that. It's time he settles. Having him running around is risky."

"Now, to business," Ira said.
"Shouldn't we get Morris?" Wilbur asked.
"No."

◆

Morris Reinhardt listened to the leaves of Petula's book turning. The noise made him grimace every time. As soon as they'd gotten into the room, she'd sat down and opened that book of hers. He wondered what was in it to make her so fascinated.

"*Philosophiæ Natu...*" he began and abandoned trying to get the book's name right. "What's it about?" he asked instead.

All he got was a glance. She went back to reading.

He couldn't understand how anyone could live without the need for social interaction. The thought of being stuck in the same room as her and not saying a word made him confused.

"I..." he said, but cut his words short.

Morris started several other conversations, never letting them out. He walked to the window, glancing out, hoping that there was something he could offer as a point of interest to the necromancer. But there was just the Necropolis skyline.

He let his thoughts wander to the final draft of the law proposal. His hand itched, and Morris scratched it as he went over the clauses he had to put in the proposal to create loopholes to be exploited at a later date. You needed loopholes. They were like a safety net. Morris was good at technicalities. His mind had been built that way. That same mind had come up with all of this. He'd seen that the constant rising of new banks undercutting their fees jeopardized his father's bank. Also, he'd foreseen that the notes they wrote with the false promise of gold backing would eventually collapse the whole city. Which was exactly what had happened. You could only continue for so long until the lies caught up with you. All the banks in the city were in trouble. His was on firmer ground, but the rogue banks would topple his if he let them. What Morris and the rest of them were trying to do was a natural step to protect their livelihood and the city itself. Some might argue against that, but he wouldn't. So what if their actions to strengthen the monitoring created a monopoly? It would bring stability and continuity at the same time. It was better for everyone. It wasn't like he'd abuse the position. Yes, with regulations they could run all the other banks into the ground and share the profits between the four of them, but that wasn't a sustainable plan. There had to be a little competition. It kept them honest. He and the others wouldn't sit on the finance committee that would control money sources and prices. They would put politicians there. So everything was fine.

Morris turned away from the window to face the necromancer once again, but she barely noticed him. She looked serene with her book on her lap, despite her dress being covered with dried-up bits of Ira. He couldn't understand how she could be so calm about what she'd done at the cemetery. Morris opened his mouth to say something but thought it best not to. He left the window and paced around the room despite the prosthesis pressing uncomfortably after the long day. He'd had it since his youth. The prosthesis and the pain had grown to be a part of him. The only thing he hoped was that someday someone with enough innovation would provide one without all the straps that pressed hard against his leg and hip. He'd tried to do without it, but often enough, people looked at his leg instead of him and made excuses to flee. With a wooden leg, they could at least pretend. And some were horrendous towards him despite the prosthesis. Then again, some were born nasty, brutish, and full of pride, and he left them to their own doom. Ira was one of those people, but he wasn't petty about things like appearance. The man looked past flaws to see the value of people and used them for his own personal gain. But Morris thought he understood Ira, and they got along well. Though he liked Wilbur the most.

Morris went back to the window. He leaned against his cane and fiddled with the joint of the handle. If he opened it, he could draw out a sword hidden inside. It was made from the finest steel around. Forged carefully with different carbon concentrations by the best blacksmith in the city. When he'd gotten the sword, he'd made sure he knew how to use it. He'd been part of the University's fencing team, composed purely of law students.[16] Morris flashed a smile, remembering the good days. He'd won every single match.

Before becoming a banker or studying law, he'd wasted his youth drawing seashells, trying to find meaning there. Then he'd seen his father's bookkeeping and its beauty, and it'd decided his future along with his father dying and leaving behind a DNR order: Do Not Resurrect. Some chose that path. Those who believed nothing would change the second time around. People were always people. He respected his father's choice and might follow his lead. Now he had to make sure their family legacy lived on.

"I'm sorry that we dragged you into this," Morris said, watching his reflection in the window. He straightened the collar of his shirt and wished he'd gotten a haircut.

In the reflection, he saw the necromancer look up. He expected her to go back to reading, but she said, "I came with you of my own free will."

He turned to face her. "Yes, but we didn't exactly give you a choice."

She sighed.

He wasn't sure how he'd offended her. He—all of them—seemed to do that time and again. But she wasn't finished.

She said, "There's always a choice. If someone says otherwise, then he or she's a fool. I'm no fool, and I won't blame my own actions upon others."

Morris was surprised to hear more than the usual grunt. He was unsure what to say next, but his lawyer instincts took over. "But the blame is always on the instigator."

"That might be. But I'd rather take responsibility for my own actions."

"That's an admission of guilt."

"And what is it that I'm guilty of, if I may ask?"

Morris spluttered.

She shut the book.

Morris felt as if something was lodged in his throat.

"What is it that you're doing here?" Petula asked.

He swallowed and waited until he could get his words

---

16   Which ensured they won all their matches outside the strip as well.

out. "Do you really want to know?"

She said nothing for a while, just looking at him, stripping him naked, and then gazing past him to the window. "I guess...I don't."

"I think that's better, if you want to go home," he said.

"Hm," she replied.

He smiled at her.

She turned back to her book and hesitated.

"None of this should have gone this way," he said. "Everything went downhill when he died. Do you want to know how he died?"

Petula shrugged.

"He choked on an apple. Can you believe that? Man of his caliber. A man with a city full of enemies, and he dies because of an apple. It's a wonder he's even here. I was sure someone would steal his body when it was in the ground," he said.

She gave a faint smile.

"Am I boring you? I guess you want to go home. You know what, I'll take you home. You've gone beyond the call of duty, and you must be tired after all you did," he said. He was half right. Petula was feeling tired, but that was her mind predicting the future. Her body was alive and vibrant. More than it'd ever been. Petula wanted to go out and raise the whole cemetery, and then... And then she wasn't sure what to do next with her army of undead. Her body hadn't gotten that far with the planning. That might be because her mind wasn't in on the plan. It was still fixated on the future, picturing a nice hot bath with a good book. If Morris had known, he could have given Ira the ammunition to keep her in Necropolis.

"Yes...I better go home," she said half-heartedly and stood up.

Before Morris could make a move to accompany her out of the room, there came loud arguing outside the annex. The sort of noise that never amounted to anything good. The sort of noise that made Petula squeeze her book.

"We better see what's going on," Morris said. "Let me go out first," he added.

Petula gave a slight nod and pushed her book inside her jacket pocket. She crouched to pick up her bag and followed Morris to the door. Morris paused before opening the door. It wasn't as if he cared for arguing either, but he had no other choice than to go ahead.

They found an officer of the law going around Ira's office, peering out of the windows.

Ira followed after her, shouting, "You can't be here. This is an invasion of privacy!"

"Sir, I need you to calm down. I'm in pursuit of a criminal. He has been spotted climbing the bank's walls, and when last I saw him, he was heading this way," the officer said. She added when Ira continued looking angry, "Sir, this is important. In the name of the law, I had to pursue."

"I'll have your badge if you don't leave now," Ira cautioned.

"Sir, under section four-b two hundred seventy-nine, I have the right to do anything to stop a crime in process," the officer said and peered out of the window again.

"Not inside my bank. This is private property. You can't just barge in," Ira said, reaching for the officer's arm to drag her out.

She gave Ira one warning look from under her overly large helmet. Her look seemed to say, "*If you lay a finger on me, I'll arrest you for assaulting an officer of the law, and don't for a moment think your status will protect you.*" The red-haired officer with freckles and big eyes was tall and awkward-looking, and might appear to be someone Ira could easily take. But that would be a mistake. Yes, some might call her lanky and gawky, but she wasn't one of those people. The officer herself looked past her rosebud mouth and overly large uniform, calling herself tough, resilient, and sharp. She'd wrestled and fought all her life, protecting the weak against men like Ira who thought they owned the world just because they knew how to bully others.

Ira withdrew his hand.

"I'm sorry, sir, she...I couldn't stop her," another lanky fellow with a head too big for the rest of his body said. He'd followed the officer in. He was Nigel Kneebone, Ira's assistant.

"I want your name," Ira spat out, ignoring Nigel.

"Hortensia Caster, sir," the officer said and pushed the window open.

"I'll have you thrown out of the force. I know Mr. Cuddy personally, and he won't like this when he hears what you have done," Ira said. "What are you doing? Get down instantly!"

Hortensia Caster was also one of those people who didn't let obstacles discourage her.

"Come here this instant! Don't make me come after you!" she shouted, not to Ira but to the intruder she saw on the roof. She was also one of those people who upheld the law to the letter, or at least as far as sensible morals took her. It was farther than most. She pushed herself through the open window. The last thing they saw of her was her size seven boots disappearing out the window. The room could hear her shouting, "Officer in pursuit." They couldn't understand who she yelled that to, but she repeated it several times.

"I'm sorry, sir, she pushed through," Nigel said.

"Through the security? Through the whole bank?" Ira asked.

"Yes, I'm sorry, sir. I'll fire everyone who let her pass," Nigel said.

"See to that."

"I'll pack my things and be on my way, sir," Nigel said.

"We don't have to be that drastic," Ira said, refusing to meet Nigel's eyes.

"No, sir?"

"Not this time. But see that she won't be coming back this way again and that Mr. Cuddy knows what his subordinates are doing. Running around like that is a disgrace," Ira said.

"Yes, sir," Nigel said. He walked to the window, pushed it shut, and locked it. "And sir?"

"Yes, Nigel?"

"I'm sorry that I didn't know you had come in," he said.

"That's all right, Nigel. Now check whether that godawful woman is off my roof and find out who she was pursuing and why," Ira said.

"Yes, sir," Nigel said and left the room.

"Things have gotten out of hand. Morris, what do you have to say for yourself?" Ira asked. There was no mistaking his venom. The man was even more spiteful now as an undead than when he was alive. Someone would pay for all the misgivings.

It wasn't going to be him. Morris lifted his head up and said, "I promised to take Miss Upwood home. We are leaving."

7

YOU SPEAK TO IT AS IF IT WAS A... PERSON!

nside the circular Town Hall auditorium, everyone had equal standing, or at least there was the possibility of equal standing. However, the small things always seemed to come between people, not to mention height. That was humans for you: always calculating, categorizing, and judging. You couldn't take that out of them. It might be due to something called pattern recognition, which had snuck in to aid survival and hunting at some point. Suddenly, the chaotic flight of birds had a pattern, the fractal kind, and you had a belly full of meat. And if observed closely, the council members pouring into the auditorium had a pattern, the fractal kind. But only an acute eye caught that, and Minta had such an eye. She greeted all of them with a dignified nod and separated the weak from the herd.

The men and women's degree of decomposition varied a lot, not counting those with extra hair and some with pointy fangs, and the rest not so easily categorized.

When the doors closed behind the last of them,

Minta banged the gavel she produced from her loose black leather jacket. The gavel glinted in the bright light the full moon cast through the windows. Its white, polished bone felt cold against Minta's long fingers. The banging silenced the auditorium and made the council members and one visitor settle in their seats. Tonight they had an extra pair of eyes watching them. A newspaper man, R. Porter, leaned against his seat and took a notebook out, turning his attention to Minta.

"Good evening everyone," Minta said, smiling. "Tonight's docket is short. We have to decide where the new cemetery will be located and whether we accept the new taxidermist shop's building permit."

This should be a quick and simple meeting, unlike the one they had last night. It'd turned into a full-blown battle. The matters had all morphed into one, changing from undead workforce, to banking, to bailouts, to bonuses, to immigrants, occasionally going back to the subject at hand, which was about funding a proper sewage system along with water supply network, but it quickly went back to sharing insults, and the matter had been moved to a later date to be solved. They hadn't even managed to have the usual nay and yea vote at the end of the meeting. It was lucky that the reporter had chosen cemeteries over sewers or last night's war between the Union of the Undead and the Necro Democratic Alliance would be front-page news. And she'd be out of her office, or worse, declaring a state of emergency and bringing back her rule of tyranny. Not that last night's outburst differed from any other night. It'd been like this the past year.

It was this economy thing again. More and more, Minta felt like it was out to get her. The constant arguing about what constituted communal troubles and what fell within the personal realm made her head hurt. No one seemed to agree on anything. Already her declaration was causing a stir, and she saw battle lines forming. She could easily command or kill the dead inside the room and do something nasty to the living, but it wouldn't be very democratic of her. She held the belief that democracy should be spread and cultivated at every possible turn. She was a firm believer in freedom, whatever that meant. The philosophers didn't seem to agree on whether there was such a concept as freedom or free will, or whether humans or variants thereof could even be free. If you asked Minta, philosophers tended to make things harder for themselves than necessary. But if it kept them happy, who was she to argue.

"First on the docket is the new cemetery grounds to meet our growing need. There have been several out-of-city compounds proposed, meaning we would have to acquire the lands and..." Minta said, not even finishing her sentence before the room exploded. The council members began to argue amongst themselves. Yesterday's bad feelings still hung in the air. Even the ghouls, who were normally deadly calm, got excited and jumped up and down in their seats. They were the kind of dead no one liked. The Union of the Undead had to take them in, as they were technically dead. There'd been an argument about whether the ghouls should be thought of as evil spirits, but the argument had been dropped quickly when the first ghoul bared his teeth.

Minta banged the gavel. She saw the reporter writing down everything, pages turning faster than Minta liked. She felt a headache building.

One of the ghouls made a disappointed gurgle.

One thing had to be said for the ghouls: they seemed to be able to sense the pulse of society. Minta glanced towards Cruxh, the leader of the pack. He sat there with a calm, composed demeanor and waited for the chaos to die around him. The silly bugger wore a stylish suit, making him the best-dressed person in the auditorium.

Minta banged the gavel again. This time it worked its magic, and the room fell silent.

She opened her mouth, but Mrs. Maybury interrupted her by saying, "We really should be concentrating on the already existing cemeteries. There's no point in wasting money on a new one when the old ones would be perfectly fine if they had more care." The impudent woman swept a few other town council members with her. They nodded and murmured in agreement.

"We have already gone over the fact that there isn't enough space for the dead in our ever-growing city. The cemeteries are full. We need to decide what proposal we accept. This is a voting matter," Minta said. She'd lost count of how many times they'd had this same argument. There were so many old customs surrounding the cemeteries that to arrange them efficiently would require someone with a mastery of quantum physics.[17] Families kept their plots ready for future need, and the occupied graves could never be reused, as the dead had rights beyond eternity, or until their formaldehyde-covered bodies decomposed completely. No one in the city was willing to let go of the old superstition that the dead had to be buried before they were awakened. Everyone knew they'd come back half-there and with a craving for human flesh otherwise.

"But there's a perfectly simple solution for that too. We close our borders and don't let any new people in." Mrs. Maybury's eyes shone in triumph.

This one got more support.

"Yeah, we don't need stinky foreigners taking jobs away from good lads and gals of our own. Mrs. Maybury is right, let's close the borders," one of the living council members said, and got the stink-eye from some of his party members.

Oh, good gods, not this again, Minta thought. This same argument came up with any problem they faced. It'd even come up when they had discussed painting the Town Hall's benches. Minta wasn't sure how it'd come up, but it'd come up anyway. Her headache was getting worse.

Mrs. Maybury grinned, and she locked her gaze with Minta's as if she'd won some battle Minta hadn't signed up for. A maggot rolled off Mrs. Maybury's ear and dropped onto the table. It almost got away, but a ghoul's talon reached for it, and it disappeared.

"And what's this about raising taxes on the undead? That's heinous persecution if I ever saw it," Mrs. Maybury said.

"Yeah, what's with that?" someone joined in.

Minta hated straw-men. "We can talk about that at the next meeting, when it is on the agenda. Right now, we should get back to the location issue," Minta said. She couldn't keep the weariness out of her voice.

"Yeah, but she's right! We work and work, and our hard-earned money is taken away, and in this economy," an undead man yelled.

Taxation wasn't a problem for those who weren't that solid. Ghosts and spirits and whatnot lived solely from their

---

17 Whatever that was.

minds. But the more solid undead needed money. Their repair costs were insane.

The last statement got a rise out of the Necro Democratic Alliance, who saw taxation as a way to balance the living and undead workforce. If the undead weren't taxed, the city's business owners would move to employing only the undead, and where would that leave the living, eh?

Again, an argument broke out.

Minta wondered if she should bang the gavel at all or wait to see who was the last man or woman standing. Most likely it would be Mrs. Maybury.

She banged the gavel.

"Silence!" she said, hating her own harsh voice, but the others didn't leave her any other choice.

It took a few more bangs and demands until they finally complied.

"In the face of the law, we either vote on the location collectively, or I'll be forced to make a choice on behalf of the city as I see fit," she said. Minta was losing her temper. She'd had it with both parties and with the city. Until now she'd been playing nice, but what had that gotten her? Respect, yes, but a reputation as a pushover.

"You can't—" Mrs. Maybury began.

"The location of the cemetery has to be settled tonight. We have far more important subjects we need to decide by the end of this week. So, what do you want me to do?" she asked.

Mrs. Maybury's face began to twitch. "But, what I mean is that... I mean..." she said.

"The matter is closed, Mrs. Maybury. I appreciate your input, but I'll choose the location. Now, to the next order of business," Minta said, seeing the reporter smile at her. There was no need to guess what the headline would be tomorrow, but at least she'd made a decision. Yet, why was she feeling lousy?

The nervous tic in Mrs. Maybury's face continued dancing.

"Are you all right?" Minta asked.

Mrs. Maybury wailed, causing her face to twitch more. "What's happening? It doesn't normally do this!"

Minta wasn't sure if this was theatrics to get attention or something else. She said, "You need to rest." She stood up.

Three overly helpful ghouls got to Mrs. Maybury before her.

"Weeh can helph," a ghoul said.

"Yesh, weh helph ourh fellowh partyh memberh," another one of the ghouls said.

Minta sat back down. "Thank you," she said.

Mrs. Maybury didn't seem convinced. The ghouls took her by both of her arms and carried her out of the auditorium. Minta heard Mrs. Maybury wail, and after a short while she wailed again. She was sure she heard a munching sound coming from the hallway.

Should she go and see if everything was all right or continue the meeting? She was more inclined to the latter, but a moral duty insisted on the former.

Oh, from the bottomless sea with it, she thought and walked out of the room. Not caring about others and learning to mute that inner guidance system would be an easier way to live a life, but Minta wasn't blessed with ignorance. That had always been her problem, making her a great and lousy fighter. She'd been able to find compassion even for the monsters, saving a few of them during her hunter years, Dow being one of them. Then again, she'd killed her fair share. Only those who had a great disregard for others' lives and freedoms. She'd been an efficient killer. No fancy moves, just a quick killing blow and on she went. In her glory days, she had taken part in vanquishing a cult that controlled the city by the sea.

Minta headed out of the auditorium and found the ghouls circling Mrs. Maybury. They were launching attacks against her, taking bites from here and there. Mrs. Maybury tried to defend herself by clawing them, but she was too slow for the corpse eaters. This was nature for you. Minta felt her spear between her fingers. The pressure, its weight, the wood, and there was that desire to throw.

Instead, she said, "Stop that, right now!"

It had the same effect as the spear on her wall. The ghouls turned their attention towards her, and they had a predatory glint in their eyes, calculating if they could take her. Minta pushed her shoulders back, widened her stance, but kept her arms open at her sides to pacify the ghouls. She didn't want an unnecessary fight.

The ghouls bared their teeth and let out high-pitched

howls.

Minta narrowed her eyes.

The ghouls put their hands behind their backs in unison and smiled angelic smiles. Their faces looked peaceful, if that was even possible for ghouls. Still, there it was. It must have been the maggot that pushed them over the edge. Why else would they do this?

In the background, Mrs. Maybury continued wailing and trying to reach the ghouls. Every time she almost touched them, the ghouls shuffled their feet farther away from her, still looking at Minta and smiling.

"Mrs. Maybury, are you all right?" Minta asked.

"Of course I'm not... I... I...those monsters!"

Two things happened at once. More people began to pour out of the auditorium to see what the commotion was about, and Minta opened her mouth to demand the ghouls let Mrs. Maybury pass. The ghouls looked at each other, then at Minta and the rest of the people. They let out the same howls from earlier, which rang in the hallways.

Mrs. Maybury wailed also.

This was not the night Minta had planned. Too loud, for starters.

One of the ghouls curled its lips and yelped. The others joined in, and in that instant, they ran towards the crowd of council members, who stiffened at the sight of greenish-white, lifeless flesh with a mouth full of sharp teeth coming at them. But the ghouls just ran past.

"What are you doing?" Mrs. Maybury shouted. "Catch them!" When no one did anything, she raised her voice higher and as demanding as it could get. "Catch them! I want justice."

Despite the council members' initial reluctance to get involved with any nasty business that had nothing to do with them, they came down on the side of getting away from Mrs. Maybury and took off running. They went after the ghouls. Soon it turned into a competition between the Necro Democratic Alliance and the Union of the Undead. There was some taunting and cheering going on. It became a very high-spirited effort.

Minta preferred to trust her own eyes when it came to believing things. Now she wished she didn't. She couldn't quite believe what was happening. There they went, she and

Mrs. Maybury watching their receding backs. Mrs. Maybury had strange powers.

"Madam, if I may be blunt, I am afraid there is no catching them if they do not want to be caught. This situation requires the finesse of diplomacy or the cunning use of a trap to ensure the justice you are after," a ghoul next to Minta said, startling both her and Mrs. Maybury. He or it, depending whom you asked, had come silently to their side, making Minta's heart race, and from the look of it, making Mrs. Maybury's dead heart do funny things too.

"Another one!" Mrs. Maybury wailed. "Seize it!"

"That is quite unnecessary. I assure you, I have only good intentions towards you. I sympathize with the horrors you have endured," the ghoul said.

Mrs. Maybury stood there, her dried dead muscles hanging loosely from her bones. All over her body were small bite marks, making her look pitiful.

"Mister Cruuuxhs," Minta said.

"Cruxh," he said, or it sounded a lot like Cruxh. It was more like a rumble coming from inside his mouth through teeth that were chewing nuts and bolts.

"Yes," she said and didn't even try to repeat the name after him. The ghoul bothered Minta. He insisted on acting and dressing as humans did, or more to the point, better than humans did. Someone had tailored the clothes to his small, hunched figure, ill-shaped arms, and legs. To top it all, he was always so polite and correct.

"What do you have in mind, sir?" Minta asked.

"You speak to it as if it was a...person!" Mrs. Maybury said.

Minta took a deep breath in and said, "Mrs. Maybury, he was nowhere near you when the attack happened, and on this occasion, he happens to be right. If you want your justice, we need to do more than running after the ghouls unprepared."

"I..." Mrs. Maybury said.

"I offer my full services," Cruxh said and bowed.

The woman's eyes widened in horror.

"I don't think that's necessary," Minta said. "We have a fine police force who are happy to assist with the matter."

"If I may interrupt," Cruxh said. "I have a clear idea where they are heading, as I know which den they are from. I can talk them into coming with me and surrendering to your fine officers of the law. Would that help?"

"See, it's one of them!"

Cruxh stood there, saying nothing to defend himself.

"That's enough, Mrs. Maybury. We better go to my office and sort out this mess." Minta knew for a fact that these two had been in the same political party for years now, and yet the woman acted like this was the first time she had set eyes on him.

"But—" Mrs. Maybury said.

Minta spoke over her and said, "Tonight's meeting is over. This takes priority. We'll continue where we left off at a later date." She said this not to the two standing next to her but to R. Porter, who'd snuck up beside them and was immortalizing the moment.

"Mr. Porter I assume you'll send your article to be reviewed by my staff before publication as a courtesy," Minta said.

"Of course, that's what custom dictates. You'll have it by the end of tonight," R. Porter said. He sounded cheery, which was so unlike the pessimist he usually was. The imp-like man was an old-school reporter, or used to be, until the politics changed. Now, the handsome man with a square jaw and a full head of hair looked like yesterday's news. He'd let his suit wrinkle, there were two dark rings under his eyes, and his hair was greasy and badly cut.

"Thank you. I appreciate that. Now, if you don't mind, I and Mrs. Maybury and Cruxhssh will leave to sort out this unfortunate incident," Minta said.

"By all means. Don't mind me."

8

DO LIKE I WANT OR ELSE!

etula Upwood should never have left the comfort of her own house. She'd complicated her life with unnecessary action. As had the police officer. She could have had a pleasant shift if she'd just looked away and shouted, "all is well." Or the driver on the roof who'd scurried past the annex window. He made his life more than complicated. Petula had to ask herself what she'd been thinking to end up inside this madhouse.[18] She watched as the officer followed after the driver or whoever he was. The man who'd changed between here and the cemetery. She wondered if she had made a mistake not outing him. He could be useful, but dangerous. Petula turned her attention back to the bankers when she heard her name mentioned.

"No, you aren't taking her anywhere. That's the last thing you will do. If there's some lunatic out there killing necromancers and spying on my roof, then Miss Upwood stays close by," Ira said.

"Miss Upwood is going home, thank you. I don't

---

18   Or the biggest bank in the city, as others called it.

need you or anyone else to protect me. This has nothing to do with me," Petula said. She had her own ways to keep herself safe. She'd managed to stay alive thus far in a city where you could say death lurks behind every corner. And there was the will-o'-the-wisp in her bag and the protective symbols she'd tattooed on her skin.

"Out of the question. Your life is too valuable," Ira said.

"As it has always been," Petula said and narrowed her eyes.

Ira opened his mouth and closed it without letting out a sound.

She heard Morris chuckle, making her want to say something spiteful. Like, "*What are you laughing at? You are nothing but a glorified lackey.*" But instead, she took a crack at Ira.

"I demand to be paid my dues and taken home by Mr. Reinhardt, as *he* helpfully suggested." Petula was getting tired of all this. There was no need for her necromantic skills, and being around people irritated her. She tugged Ira's mind to make sure he'd meet her halfway. It was not technically forbidden, but if Ira noticed it, he could sue her. She didn't care at this point. Petula's mother always said her irritation knew no bounds. Occasionally Petula agreed with her.

"I..." Ira said.

The three men looked at Ira in disbelief. Morris stopped chuckling and shifted his attention from Ira to Petula.

"Nigel!" Ira shouted.

Nigel pushed the door open with inhuman speed, looking the spitting image of readiness. Ira had to have done something horrible to mold Nigel into being so obedient. But the truth was, he hadn't. Nigel had trampled over others to get into this position. This was as close as one could get to royalty in Necropolis, and Nigel was dead set on serving anyone with greatness. He had even changed his name from Larry Evans to Nigel Kneebone to give himself the right mental attitude to serve someone like Ira Worthwrite. To be truthful, Ira didn't care for the name. Nigel was a perfectly fine name, and a lot better than Larry, but Kneebone? Anyway, none of this meant he lacked the ability to think for himself or lacked aspirations. He had so many thoughts throughout the day, along with opportunities to put them in motion, that he felt satisfied. It was more than any other person in the room could say.

"Sir?" Nigel asked.

"Get me the key to the vault," Ira said.

"Sir?"

"Just do it," Ira commanded.

"Yes, sir," Nigel said and headed out of the door. Nigel had hidden the vault key from Ira. On Ira's request, of course. The last time he'd gone into the vault there'd been a slight possibility of madness taking over. There was something about the way the gold glinted in the gaslight that did funny things to your head. If Nigel hadn't been with Ira, Ira would most likely be curled on top of the gold, dreaming fiery dreams.

"I'm willing to pay you, but I have to request you come home with me," Ira said.

Petula coughed.

"We'll send someone to pack your things, if that suits you?" Ira added. Petula heard his thoughts. Actually, not heard, more like sensed them. He was genuinely scared for her and for his life. Jeremiah's death and the officer had shocked him.

"Yes, if I must." Avoiding packing suited her. She pictured Nigel going over her sensible underwear and cursing.

"Then it's settled," Ira said.

"There's still the fact we need to find a necromancer to replace her," Morris said.

The unwelcome words lingered in the room. You would think Morris, who was usually good at reading people, would know how to pick a moment, but no. He had to go and add fuel to the fire. In his defense, the day had stretched longer than he had expected. Longer than anyone had expected.

But Petula wasn't drained. She was a night owl. Before shutting her eyes, she'd have thought of at least five new ways to improve her trade. Not spells exactly, but commands. She did her best thinking[19] when others slept. Sometimes she hung between sleep and waking to get the most out of her consciousness. Here, between apathy and

---

19   And packing.

frustration, she knew what lever to pull.

"I have a name for you. She's good, and you can trust her not to botch the transition. I've worked with her before," she said.

"I'd rather get my own. Thank you, but no," Ira said.

"It'd tie your and Bertha Chaplain's fates together," Petula said. She saw she'd struck the right chord.

"Who?" Ira asked.

"Agatha Wicks," Petula replied.

"And who's that?"

"You know, the one that always hangs around Mrs. Chaplain and wears those fake fangs," Morris said.

"She does?" Petula said. She hadn't meant to say that aloud.

"Yes. How exactly do you know her?" Morris asked.

Petula couldn't believe Agatha had stooped so low. Then again, Agatha had always been childish and easily swept up by gimmickry. She liked to be admired. Still, Petula felt disappointed. More than she cared to admit.

"We studied together and have passed possession from one to the other before," Petula said, embellishing the truth somewhat. Yes, they'd studied together, and yes, they'd passed possession, but it was just an animated raccoon.

"Is she any good?" Ira asked.

Not as good as I am, she wanted to say. "Yes. She has to be, otherwise Bertha Chaplain wouldn't have retained her before her necromancer's death and before Agatha's graduation," Petula said instead. There was a sting in her heart. Agatha wasn't as good as Petula, and Bertha Chaplain had walked straight past her as if she wasn't even there. Everyone talked about how lucky Agatha was the whole semester. It'd pissed Petula off, a lot.

Nigel stepped into the room before Ira had time to reply. "I have the key, sir. Do you want me to accompany you into the vault?" he asked. He held the key close to his chest, not wanting to let go. It'd be easy to think of it as golden, but you would be mistaken. It was bad enough to use a key to get into the vault, but to make it from gold would be the same as inviting Calamity—that one entity in the world that made sure all the bad that could happen happened, especially for the good people.

"No, I and Miss Upwood will manage on our own.

You three get me that Wicks woman," Ira said. "And bring her to my house."

"Morris can do that. I have things to do," Wilbur replied.

"No, three of you. I want to see you before day's end."

"But—"

Ira had already turned around and marched to Nigel, snatched the key, and motioned Petula to follow.

"Come along," he said at the doorway when she made no move.

"Don't worry, I'll be there soon," Morris said and reached for her.

Petula looked at his hand on her arm and lifted her gaze to meet his. He let go. She left him there without saying a word. She heard laughter behind her. If she'd been a kid, she'd have gone stiff and screamed from the bottom of her lungs, but those days were gone. Imbeciles, she thought and hurried after Ira.

◆

Herbert Ringworm hurried across Worthwrite Bank's metal roof, followed by the police officer. He didn't like this new evolution of the city's finest. They weren't supposed to run on rooftops, especially not shouting so loudly. The officer insisted on pursuing him. He came to the edge of the building. The next bank's rooftop wasn't far. He only had to leap. But Herbert heard yelling behind him, a different sort from earlier. He glanced over his shoulder and saw that the officer had slipped. She hung on to the railing and tried to move her legs to secure a better position. Herbert hesitated. He looked at the other roof and then glanced back at the officer. He took a step closer to the edge and shut his eyes. Herbert heard the officer's legs scuffling against the railing. If she continued swinging them around in such a fashion, she would wear herself out and fall.

Herbert opened his eyes and turned around.

"*What about me?*" the voice asked.

Herbert froze. He watched the officer as she hung by her right hand.

"*Why her?*" the voice asked.

"This is not about you. She'll die," Herbert insisted.

The voice greeted him with silence.

Herbert ignored the voice and made his way to the officer, but before he got to her, four men clambered onto the roof from a nearby window. Two of them ran to aid the officer, and the other two scanned the roof for him. Herbert flattened himself against the nearest chimney and waited. He listened to the noises they made getting the officer back up. The commotion muffled any other sounds. Herbert dropped to his knees and began to crawl to the edge. He wasn't going to take chances, and brute force was out of the question. He had to get to Dow; what he'd heard inside the bank was enough to turn the man against Ira. Maybe this time he'd believe him.

Dow had to help him with the necromancer. Herbert could still see her looking over her book at him past Morris, and she'd said nothing. She would help them; he was sure of it. And Dow could make sure there was a legal way.

Behind him, the men had gotten the officer up, and they were actively searching for him. They hadn't yet seen Herbert. He went over the edge and descended down the bank's wall, occasionally glancing up to see if they'd spotted him. Whenever a guard came close to the edge, he pressed himself against the rough brick wall or hid on a window ledge. On a dark night like this, with a heavy mist, it was almost impossible to see past your own feet, let alone spot a man in dark clothes. But Herbert didn't take any chances. He moved slowly. His legs shook when his feet hit the ground. He was sure they would give in at any moment. He tasted blood in his mouth. Herbert steadied himself against the bin in the alleyway, getting his breath back before heading to the Town Hall.

Dow would see him. The man owed him that much. None of this would be happening if Dow had listened to him a week ago and sent Ira to jail. The man wouldn't be a rotting corpse, and Herbert wouldn't have had to kill Jeremiah or the driver to get justice for Ona. He'd never killed anyone before tonight. He'd mangled several men to the point that there was almost no coming back, but as far as he knew none of them had died. At least not by his hand. And the werewolves, he'd incapacitated them in the ring, but kill, no. Dow couldn't ignore him this time.

Ona didn't have to die.

Herbert put his full weight back on his feet, releasing his grip on the bin. They would hold. For now, however, he would have to use the streets to get to the Town Hall. Luckily it wasn't too far from here. The city planners had stuck the important buildings near each other, as if they had a mutual destruction pact or as if a black vortex would appear between them if they were too far apart and swallow the city whole.

Herbert left the alleyway. He didn't run. It would draw too much attention, and to be honest, he wasn't sure if he could. He passed a man who was putting up posters all over the street. Herbert glanced over his shoulder at one of the posters the man had already put up. It was a call to action for tonight's protest. The man was cutting it close. As far as Herbert knew, the protest should be in a couple of hours. Next to the poster, there was a we-need-you banner with a man's picture attached to it. Underneath the image read "*For the real people!*" Herbert was sure there were no real people in the city. All fakes or wannabe fakes. He wasn't interested.

He continued down the street. Herbert stepped aside and nodded as the Cult of Kraken worshippers passed him by. They were a long way from home. Herbert hoped they were here to storm the money district and turn things around, but as far as he knew, the church was all about soul-saving and not about doing the right thing. He'd always been sympathetic towards the sea monster. It was a fitting god for the city. But he couldn't be bothered with the cult and its church. It wasn't because he lacked belief. He knew the god to exist. He just wasn't that into rituals and groups. They complicated things. Every now and then he tossed a coin into the sea to pay his respects, but he wasn't sure what use the sea god had for gold. It wasn't as if it needed cash for clothes, watches, or ships. Kraken had other means to get them.

Herbert continued on when they were gone. He had a way to make Dow listen to him. He knew his secret. Herbert had saved the man from public shame. Herbert fought at the illegal underground werewolf fighting league. Humans against the beast. Not a pretty sight. If you weren't careful enough, you could get yourself killed. He used a sensory deprivation powder against the werewolves. Anything to take the edge off the beasts was considered fair game. He made sure no one knew what exact mixture he used, making him one of the securest bets in the ring. Almost every night some newbie died. They came in full of bluster and got pulverized in the first round. That always got the crowd roaring. There was a match tonight, but he hadn't been back there ever since... He couldn't. It didn't feel the same. Then it'd been a perfect escape from home, not having to stay in and build things no one wanted. Now, it felt like a waste of his time. He should have known better. He should have been dancing the night away with Ona, making her spin and tipping her over to give her a kiss. On those nights, everything had been perfect. Her pressed against him so close he could smell her skin mixed with her perfume while the music played on.

Herbert drew his jacket tighter around him. The cold air was making his bruises ache. He continued making his way to the Town Hall. The buildings on Old Willy Wrangler's Street had been slathered with the call-to-action posters. The man had been busier than Herbert thought. This was the closest the banking district would get to the people's voice. The place had nothing to do with democracy, even though it held enormous power over the city. Herbert liked this look. But already building managers had instructed their subordinates to tear down the abominable declarations.

The Town Hall rose high at the end of the street, where the swamp used to be. No one sensible built a house in a place like that. But there it was, surrounded by huge weeping willows, shielding the place from the world. There was no sign of the ghouls or the rest of the council members. Out of habit, he circled behind the building to slip in through a window. He could use the front door, but that didn't seem right.

He found the window he always used as his entry point. He pushed his knife between the double window and made the latch pop. Herbert shimmied it. Then he carefully drew the windows open, making sure the swollen frames didn't shriek. These sorts of windows always confused him. They welcomed men and—why not—women like him to break in and do whatever occurred to their twisted minds. A back door to the promised land.

He closed the windows behind him. Next he had to get to the basement without being noticed. Dow's office was there, but so were the kitchen and the staff. He could walk in as if he belonged in these halls or sneak in, trailing after the staff and hiding behind the statues. Both had their advantages. What he chose always depended on his mood, and tonight he wanted privacy. He walked down the stairs as if he belonged there.

A kitchen maid passed by, but she barely looked towards him. She was too absorbed in carrying a heavy sack of flour, cursing as she went.

Herbert knocked on Dow's door. It was the nearest door to the basement stairs to the left. After a long while, it opened, and Herbert stepped in. At first, he thought there was no one in the room to welcome him, but before he could turn around, a familiar voice asked behind his back,

"To what do I owe the pleasure?"

Herbert spun around. The short, wrinkled man pushed the door shut and watched him expectantly.

"I need to talk to you," Herbert said.

"Do you? You do, don't you?" Dow asked. His serious face somehow looked like it was smiling and mocking Herbert.

"This is important, Dow. I wouldn't have come if it wasn't. It's not like..." He let his words trail off; some things were better left unsaid.

"Hm," Dow said, and stepped past him. The man walked to his desk, which was the only distinctive feature in the room. The only other thing in there was a dog bed next to the desk, but Herbert had never seen a dog with the man. If there was a dog, it was one huge, scary one, from the look of the bed.

Dow followed Herbert's gaze. He said, "Don't worry, it's just the two of us.

"What is this about?" Dow asked.

"This is about Ir—" Herbert said, not getting to finish his sentence.

"Not this again. Didn't I forbid you to go near the man and his grave?" Dow asked.

Herbert used all his willpower not to hit the man. Who was he to forbid him?

"He isn't dead anymore. You have to understand, he's a monster. He's playing games with our lives, dressed in his fancy outfits, disguising his intentions with false manners. You know as well as I do that he's nothing but a predator, and no lights will keep him away. No laws will stop him. You have to help me with him. You know this as well as I do."

"Tsk-tsk." Dow sucked his teeth. "You are being melodramatic, as always."

Herbert was wrong in one respect: Ira didn't disguise his true nature in any way. He didn't have to. The laws and the atmosphere of the city, which valued bankers more than anyone else, let him do whatever he pleased.

"This isn't just my crazed fantasy..." Herbert said. He was on the brink of hitting the man. "I heard him plotting against your boss, trying to get her out of the office." He had to believe that the only place for Ira Worthwrite was behind bars. He'd heard Ira and the others talking about a law proposal Morris was preparing, and they'd push it through. Somehow, it'd end up undercutting Minta's leadership. He hadn't quite understood the details, or how Morris could ruin it all, but it was not his job to understand. It was already noteworthy that the four biggest bankers in the city were meeting behind closed doors.

"Hm," Dow said.

"I'm not just any old fellow with a petty grudge. This is a real threat. Maybe it's better if I see the Mayor?" Herbert's voice got high and tight when Dow looked at Herbert as if he was ready to dismiss him.

Dow shook his head. "In what universe do you think I will let you see Miss Stopford?"[20]

---

20 Dow was a man who believed in multiple universes, or rather he was sure there had to be alternative paths to all decisions made. Somewhere, there was another Dow who had a better life than he; he wasn't quite sure what that life might consist of, but the other Dow had to know the secret of what would make a man like him happy, or content, at least. Dow didn't quite believe in the pursuit of happiness. It seemed like too fleeting and annoyingly hard an equation to combine with life. But he was sure that in none of the universes out there would he let a man like Herbert Ringworm see Miss Stopford without an excellent explanation.

9

GLOOMY THOUGHTS INSIDE A BANK

he city of Necropolis was built in an intriguing pattern. The buildings, the roads, and the marketplaces, along with everything else, were placed there to tame the chaos of life into manageable pieces. Somewhere beyond the walls of the Worthwrite Bank of Necropolis Ltd, people made patterns by following predefined rules. Rules few understood or saw, but rules nevertheless. Pedestrians trailed after each other, thinking they as individuals were walking to their own destinies, but instead, they followed an example laid out in front of them. If someone could harness those patterns under the surface of human consciousness, they'd be powerful and rich.

Morris thought he understood people, he thought he knew how to speculate with his knowledge, and he thought that made him a great banker. He'd been on top of the game until Algor quantified those rhythms for all to see. But Morris was sure those rhythms in his skulls lacked the rudimentary understanding of people, that they were weak compared to Morris' instincts—those instincts his father had taught him. His father, A. P. Reinhardt, was the most beloved and revered man in the city in his time. He'd gone against Oliver the Great and built the city as he had envisioned it to be: a place for everyone. His father had thought they should give loans to all, that it was the little man, the working-class fellow, who shaped the city with dreams. On his deathbed, his father had been proud that every single loan he'd given was paid in full. He died knowing he'd made a difference, and he'd done all that without taking a cut, without taking bonuses. He'd devoted his life to reading and education and gave away the fortune he had inadvertently accrued to the Necropolis Library and the Raisin's School of Education. He was proud that he as an immigrant had done all this, built a strong community around his bank. Morris sometimes feared he'd ruin that legacy, that the common man wasn't enough at this level of the game.

"What does he think we are?" Wilbur groaned when they made their way down the secret passage.

"You know perfectly well what he thinks of us," Ignatius said, sounding disinterested.

"I'm no one's servant," Wilbur said.

Morris wondered what the necromancer, Petula, had thought about his leg. Had she seen it wasn't real? His cane was a giveaway, but still, someone might think it was a normal stiff leg and not a useless, broken, good-for-nothing stump. He felt the heat spread over his face. A cripple, a fool, someone to be used and pitied.

Morris groaned.

"What?" Wilbur asked.

"Oh, nothing," Morris said.

"You agree with him then? That we should run around the city and look for this Agatha girl?" Wilbur asked.

"There's no point in agreeing or disagreeing. The fact is that we'll do it despite what we think," Morris said.

"But couldn't I just pop out and be back soon? Just to check if everything is all right?" Wilbur asked.

"He'd know," Ignatius replied.

Wilbur moaned.

"Stop complaining," Ignatius said.

"What's the harm? I'll drop you off wherever you want to go and come and collect you soon after. It's not like all of us are needed to convince that Wicks girl. Morris can handle it," Wilbur said. Morris suspected that not knowing if his daughter was doing well and if his future grandchild had survived was killing him.

"What on earth are you talking about?" Ignatius said.

"This is taking too long. I have my duties at home."

Ignatius said nothing. He walked down the stairs. Morris could hear his breathing.

"Why not?" Morris said eventually.

"Out of the question!" Ignatius snapped.

"We really don't need him. He can join us at the Worthwrite mansion," Morris continued, despite the looks Ignatius was giving him.

"Both of you are as bad as each other. You think he'll be soft because of her? Don't think for a second that the man will be lenient to us because he showed humanity towards the necromancer. If you think about it, she's above us all, even Ira." After a dramatic pause, Ignatius continued, "We better find that Wicks woman and see to it that she's on our side. That woman there is on no one's side. So, we need everyone there, even you, Mr. Sumner."

Wilbur sulked for the rest of the journey down the stairs.

Morris hobbled behind them, thinking gloomy thoughts. So did Ignatius and Wilbur. Ira had more than money and esteem to hold over them. He had his little black book and all their dark deeds in it. They had the usual quiet moment of contemplating doom and what that might be like.

They reached the bottom of the stairs. Morris clumsily pushed the secret panel open, and the outside world welcomed them with the backstreet's medley of rotten smells. Any sane person would turn around and spend the night inside the bank rather than lumber around the streets of Necropolis. There was something sinister in the air.

The coach was still there where they'd left it. Morris limped to it, and the others walked behind him. There had been too many stairs for his and their liking. Ira should install something to ease the travel. Maybe put a ghost in a machine to ferry people around. The three men stopped next to the coach to wait for the driver to emerge from his seat to let them in. They waited there for the better part of a prolonged minute. At the same time, they complained loudly. When it became painfully clear that the driver would not show up, Ignatius and Wilbur turned to look at Morris expectantly. Unfortunately, he knew what that look entailed.

Morris did as they asked and took those five long steps and peered up at the driver's seat. He found the coat and hat laid on the seat. He pulled the thick coat closer and saw the dark blood in its lining. Morris frowned and showed it to the two other men.

"It appears there has been a mishap," Morris said.

"That can't be!" Wilbur said and rushed to see if there was a body.

"He's not there," Morris said.

"Ignatius, see if he's inside," Wilbur cried.

Ignatius stepped closer to the coach and for a moment stared at the handle as if he'd never seen such a thing before and couldn't understand how it functioned. Eventually, he planted his hand on it and drew the door open. He poked his head inside and then withdrew it. Ignatius shook his head.

"He isn't here," he said.

"Are you sure?" Wilbur asked.

"Unless he is a master of the dark arts, yes."

"We need to alert the—" Wilbur began.

"We're not alerting anyone. Least of all that silly little girl who paraded into Ira's office," Ignatius said.

"But someone has taken Jeffrey," Wilbur said.

"You can do that tomorrow. Right now, we need to find the necromancer and free Ira from Petula's clutches before she owns the bank," Ignatius said.

Morris laughed.

Wilbur shot a glance towards him and silenced Morris.

"Now, if you don't mind, we should be on our way, young Reinhardt," Ignatius said. Ignatius stepped into the coach, not waiting for a response. Wilbur followed him in, and they left Morris on his own.

Morris looked at the coach, then at the nervous horses, and then to the steps leading to the driver's seat. All the gods in the netherworld, he thought and curled his fingers around the railing next to the steps. He dragged himself up, taking his time and planning his every move. He heard complaining coming from inside the coach, but he ignored it. When he got to the seat, he took hold of the reins and wasn't sure what to do with them, or with the horses.

Morris held the leather reins, and he shook them. Nothing happened. He could feel Ignatius' judging eyes. Morris pulled the reins and jiggled them up and down with force. The horses took two steps forward but stopped when Morris let the reins hang loose. He repeated the first action, but his movements were too soft. One of the horses just looked at him, and Morris was sure it raised an eyebrow.

"Why can't you move? I bet there's a pack of werewolves somewhere, waiting for an easy dinner," he said.

The horse looked away and did nothing.

"You piece of..." he said and waved his hands again. This time the horses moved, not from any command Morris had made, but out of pity. The horses would like the usual man to come back. It was bad enough that wolves, ghouls, demons, and the rest of them constantly lurked around, but now they had to let a buffoon lead them.

Morris took off his top hat, lifted the driver's hat, and pushed the dark blue hat with a huge rim onto his head. It felt warmer than his. This was something a man could do, to watch the streets pass by, use his own hands, and not be called a math wizard or a law wizard or any of those names. Despite the fact that when a clause hit the right note, and a new melody was composed, he heard it, he saw it, and he could almost taste it. It tasted like metal.

Morris steered the coach around the corner, emerging onto the main street. He pulled the hat down further to avoid being seen by anyone who might recognize him.

While Morris mulled over his future, a pack of ghouls ran past the bank and between the horses' legs, causing the horses to kick and the coach to shake. The ghouls let out a series of high-pitched yelps, making the horses stomp their feet in the hope of getting at least one of the bastards. Morris pulled the reins without effect. He took the whip next to his seat and let it sing. It made things worse. The horses dashed uncontrollably forward. Morris fought for control, but it was a losing battle. The horses went where they wanted to go, and that was as far away as possible from the ghouls.

◆

Petula Upwood followed Ira down the stairs, which were

covered with thick green fabric, leading downstairs to the bank floor. Petula had never understood why they first acquired expensive marble floors and then hid them under hideous carpets. Waste of money and time, which bankers should know all about. From the walls, serious-looking men and women looked down upon them. The too-realistic paintings gave her the creeps more than any monster or ghost could. Petula wasn't sure if they were Ira's ancestors or others who'd found banking to be just as intriguing, but it didn't matter; the effect was the same. They were put there to make her feel small and irrelevant. She refused to feel either of those.

"You know, Morris means well. You should stay; that's rare," Ira said.

Petula pretended she didn't hear him. Instead, she continued looking around. She'd never been inside the Worthwrite bank. Her money was invested in a smaller one, against her father's advice. She was starting to see the downside. Banking wasn't about money or the economy. It was about things that started or ended with social.

When they got downstairs, the heart of Worthwrite bank opened up in front of her. There, hidden inside the magnificent building made from marble, mahogany, and brass, everything pulsed. Nothing slept. The bank tellers, loan officers, customers, errand boys, and speculators moved amongst the glowing skulls, whose light ranged from blood red to electric blue. At the closest counter to them, a skeleton was talking to a cashier.

"Mr. Stiffleg, your balance is three gold pieces and five silver coins," the cashier said to the skeleton.

"But I'm sure I had seven silver coins more," the skeleton rattled.

"The skull doesn't lie, Mr. Stiffleg," she said with a tight voice.

"But—"

"The skull is connected to your bank vault, and the balance is as it says," the cashier continued in the same tight voice, as if she dealt with situations like this all day long. "Maybe we should order you a balance book, as I mentioned last time."

"I have a perfect memory," Mr. Stiffleg said.

"As you say. Is there any other way I may be of

assistance today?"

"I would like to put in a penny," Mr. Stiffleg said.

The cashier, Rose Pettyshare, took an ivory pen and a form from under her counter.

Petula and Ira stepped past the desk.

"I made all this. My father started overseas trading with antiques and gold, but I turned the business into a real bank with international branches. This bank here in Necropolis is the heart of our business," Ira said. All this had made the relationship between Ira and his father complicated. One might even call it spiteful.

The place was impressive, Petula couldn't deny that. She just didn't care for all the showiness. She watched as a woman with a well-formed figure walked towards them past a brass figure of Ira, who had been given a soul-piercing expression. Beside the woman trotted two small black dogs with pricked ears and soft fur. They reminded her a lot of something called a Schipperke.

"You know, after this place opened, even my idiotic brothers had to acknowledge that I knew what I was doing," Ira said and waved his hand at the woman.[21]

"Are you talking about your brothers again?" the woman asked. The two dogs who were loyal, fearless, and at the moment very keen on Ira's legs, sat next to her.

"Kitty," Ira said.

"You should forget your brothers and be more worried about your sister," Mrs. Worthwrite, or Kitty, as Ira liked to call her, said.

"Leave her out of this."

"She didn't have to marry that wretched philanthropist man. Good for nothing, and taking your sister with him on the wrong path." Ira's sister lived next to them, but they rarely saw each other, even though Ira and Iris had been inseparable all their lives until recent years.

"We can't do anything about it, so let it be."

Mrs. Worthwrite puffed. "And who's this?"

---

21 Ira had made his brothers work for him. They had no other choice, or else he'd have ruined them. They gained gold and wealth overseas and brought it back to his vaults to be sold forward with a profit. Then he turned the money into real assets like embalming and skull factories. The math inside the skulls was worth more than gold and more than humans. Ira felt proud that he'd made this and not his bright brothers, who their father had loved more.

"She's my necromancer," Ira said and bent to pet the dogs, who were unsure what the creature in front of them was. It looked and acted like their former master, who they'd sort of liked, but the thing smelled wrong and looked more like something they buried in their backyard. When the dogs didn't look their usual friendly selves, Ira drew back his hand and stood up.

"Her?" Kitty asked. She leaned forward to inspect Petula.

Petula felt like the woman expected her to curtsy. She stared back at the towering figure. Mrs. Worthwrite, Kitty, was impressive. Petula had to give her that. She was taller than Ira even without her colossal hat. She had a strong body, which she'd enchanted with a dark brown fur coat. Petula could see why Ira had chosen her. The woman had that superior way about her, and to be honest, she was a beauty, with her round soft cheeks and big eyes. The only problem was that now she narrowed those same eyes and judged Petula as fast as she could.

"How unfortunate," Mrs. Worthwrite eventually said. "But I guess she's better than you being dead. I heard what happened to Mr. Black, and I had to come."

"I'm fine," Ira said. One of the dogs had stood up and was sniffing his leg. To bite, or not to bite, that's the question.

"Come here this instant, Bella," Kitty said.

The dog went back to sit next to her.

"Then we better take her along," Mrs. Worthwrite said.

"After we have visited the vault," Ira said.

That caused an argument. Not a loud one, but enough for Petula to want to tune out. She let her gaze wander around the bank, wondering if she should just leave and forget about being paid. It'd be easier.

All around them were busy people going about their business with a master-of-the-world attitude. She knew the best bankers in the city worked here and made sure to hit their goals at any cost. When they passed Ira, they corrected their posture to look sharp. At the nearby stall, a woman swept pink slips under her desk and hoped Mr. Worthwrite didn't see what she was doing. Petula looked at the one visible slip under the table and saw numbers and percentages written on it. She couldn't make head or tail of them, but if she had known something about banking and the general mood in here, she could have guessed the woman was hiding risks. The woman took another pink slip in her hand and wrote on it feverishly. Then she fed it to the skull on her table, and its eyes glowed in the faint pink light. The slip slipped under the table, and the woman took another note and began the process again.

Petula opened her mouth and then closed it. There was no point trying to intervene. Even if she had, Ira couldn't have done anything for the pink slip lady. Banks were highly hierarchical. Only through proper protocols could he have interacted with the woman, and most likely her manager should be present and someone from HR. Before any of that could have happened, memos would have been flowing back and forth throughout the bank, and some of them would have gotten lost and found and then lost again. Also, he would have to contact someone from the risk assessment department to go over the pink slips and see if she'd done any damage and so on. All too complicated to get involved in, especially in a bank with hundreds of employees and thousands and thousands of transactions going on daily, needing an army of clerks to manage. Anyway, Ira was too busy planning to swallow smaller banks and form one megabank under his name to notice.

At the next stall over from the pink slip lady, another woman chatted to a client. She sold business loans, but that was not all she did. The woman sold insurances over the loans, and insurances over the insurances, and proposed more loans. What she did was like tiny little hexes that kept delivering. All wonderful and legal. No one at the bank understood the contracts she made; neither did the customers. To them, the promise of minimizing their risks was enough. What they later knew was that money from their vault magically disappeared into the bank's vault and sat there waiting for a catastrophe to occur.

Ira finished the argument by reaching for Mrs. Worthwrite's hand. She flinched when her husband tried to touch her. Petula could see her itching to pull away. Marriages were difficult. Death complicated them even more. There was a whole new branch of lawyers specializing in marital affairs after death. Most divorced, but when there was a great fortune involved, it wasn't an option. Ira and Kitty would most likely be stuck with each other for the rest of eternity, or until one of them rotted away. Petula found the whole Necropolis effect quite disturbing.

"Then we better get going to the vault," Mrs. Worthwrite said, her voice full of venom.

10

RELATIONSHIPS MAY CAUSE ANIMOSITY

nside the Town Hall, the place where equality and reason governed, or should govern, Minta, Mrs. Maybury, and Cruxh made their way to Minta's office. The undead woman sulked and shot angry side glances towards the ghoul, which in a way was altogether reasonable. Her body still bore the marks of the attack. And even if you argued that she'd somehow caused it, that she'd agitated the ghouls, there was no excuse for what had happened. There was this thing called the integrity of the body. Mrs. Maybury was a respectable woman with three boys who ran her late husband's shop, supporting their ma as best they could. Minta was sure that, after all these years, she still mourned the loss of her husband every day. After fifteen years, if she was correct. The woman deserved better than this.

"I want them hanged," Mrs. Maybury said, after listening to their footsteps echo in the halls.

The Minister of Defense and Security stepped out from a nearby room but turned inhumanly quickly, darting back inside and locking the door behind him. He was almost sure the hanging didn't apply to the minister himself, but he wasn't taking any chances.

"Indubitably," Minta replied. "I'll address all the issues when we get to my office."

"I'd rather go home."

"We better play it safe. They've tasted your flesh and marked you as prey. The best thing for you is to stay inside these walls and amongst friends. We'll send someone to take word to your sons to arrange an escort home or to a taxidermist, but in the meantime, we will come up with a solution," Minta said. Her mind kept wandering to the matter of how to catch the ghouls. The best option would be to use Mrs. Maybury as bait, but Minta couldn't quite see the woman agreeing to step inside a man-sized trap and sit there nicely.

Was it wrong to feel this happy? Not of course about Mrs. Maybury's accident, but about feeling like herself after such a long time. Someone once said to her that to lose oneself is a tragedy, and to stop valuing oneself is a silent death. For the last few years, those words had echoed within her every day.

Mrs. Maybury moaned. "If I must."

Cruxh stepped closer to the women. "All this is a travesty. I cannot fathom what got into them. Justice must be delivered," he said, startling both Minta and Mrs. Maybury. Somehow they had forgotten the polite ghoul trailing after them.

"A travesty? I would call this more than a travesty! Do you see me? How can I show my face ever again in these halls?" Mrs. Maybury asked.

Cruxh shrunk a couple of inches, which was a lot for his short frame. He went from dwarf-size to gnome-size with one angered glance.

"I assure you, no one thinks less of you. All this is the fault of my fellow creatures, and they should never have been sitting on the council to begin with."

"I never wanted you in the party in the first place, not you or your fellows, as you put it."

Now, Cruxh was trying to shrink to the size of a flowerpot.

"I'm sure you did," Minta said. The way she said it made the unwary ministers and staff flee to the other halls, hide behind statues, and cower inside their offices, away from the sight of Minta and her companions. This was one of those nights they better not be seen or heard. Good, there was plenty to do, like dusting and alphabetizing the office filing cabinets. Not that Minta had been unpleasant or rude, but when you knew Mrs. Maybury, her words had sounded like a declaration of war.

Minta kept smiling a pleasant smile while they made their way to her office. When they got there, she held the door open and motioned the two others to go inside. Not as easy as it may sound. There was a silent fight over who would go in last. Cruxh tried to be polite and let Mrs. Maybury step in first, and Mrs. Maybury wanted no ghoulish condescension, so she insisted Cruxh go in ahead. There was also the thing about the last man stepping in having the power. Minta was planning for it to be her.

"Step in, Mrs. Maybury," Minta said, trying to keep the smile on her face. Mrs. Maybury was testing her nerves more tonight than ever before.

"Yes, I better, as the senior member of the party," Mrs. Maybury said and walked into the office as if she owned it. Minta saw her measuring the room, judging every inch. She realized this was the first time she'd let the woman in there. It felt like she'd broken some protective barrier, as if she'd invited her to come in anytime she wanted to, like a vampire.

"What are you going to do?! I bet you can find them in one of our cemeteries. Those horrible little beasts. How can we ever again feel that our dead are safe? Miss Stopford, I demand you do something or, or I will!" Minta hadn't even shut the door behind them before Mrs. Maybury exploded. She searched for the farthest place to sit from the ghoul, who kept his calm and sat down on the couch next to the window. The only seats left were Minta's chair and two benches opposite her desk. Mrs. Maybury's eyes drifted to Minta's seat, making Minta wonder if the woman was that impudent. She was.

But before Mrs. Maybury made a move to storm to the chair, Minta said, "Take a seat, Mrs. Maybury," and showed her own chair to the woman.

Mrs. Maybury gulped but went for the seat anyway. She sat down. They could barely see her over all the papers, books, files, and trinkets on Minta's desk. A carpenter had made the chair for Minta's tall frame. The woman reached for the books on the desk and stacked them underneath her. Soon her head rose higher.

Minta wanted to ask if Mrs. Maybury felt better now, but she didn't. She went to sit on a bench opposite the desk and turned her back on the undead.

"Where can we find the ghouls?" Minta asked.

Cruxh coughed and looked bashful, which was a very confusing look for a ghoul.

"The thing is," he said.

"He's not going to tell us!" Mrs. Maybury shrieked. "We should have marked and cataloged them a long time ago."

"My dear Mrs. Maybury, I sometimes wonder where you get all your ideas. That mind of yours must work in a superior way," Minta said.

"It does. And it demands you do something."

Cruxh stood up and walked to the undead woman. Mrs. Maybury backed away on her seat, and Minta had an urge to jump up and reach for her spear. Minta stayed where she was, and Mrs. Maybury continued sinking.

"I mean no harm to you, madam. I am eternally at your service, and I promise to restore your honor," Cruxh said and knelt down in front of the undead woman. "May, I?" he asked, indicating the woman's hand.

Minta held her breath.

As did Mrs. Maybury. She obeyed from pure shock. She held out her hand to the ghoul, who gave it a light peck with the remnants of his tight blue lips.

Cruxh let go of the hand and stood up. "I will personally lead the expedition to catch those who did this to you. They will be judged in the court of law."

Minta coughed.

"If that suits you, Miss Mayor," Cruxh said.

"I'm afraid we need an officer of the law to go after them."

"They won't be any use. I know where the ghouls went, and I know how to make them come along. And it is my moral duty to protect Mrs. Maybury's honor."

"Yes, that might be. But I can't send you alone," Minta said.

"Then send me with someone who has the stamina to match mine and who has the authority you seek."

No human could match the stamina he asked for. Maybe some undead might, but to send an undead into a den of ghouls was risky at best.

"Hmm. Maybe you are right," Minta said.

"I know I am."

"If you don't mind waiting here, I have to speak to Dow," Minta said.

"You can't leave me with...it," Mrs. Maybury said, feeling confused.

"Do you, Miss Mayor, happen to own a pair of cuffs?"

Minta's right eyebrow rose up.

"So you can lock me to the couch."

"A couch?" Mrs. Maybury asked.

"I don't have any cuffs at hand," she said and glanced at her hunting spear on the wall. "And I don't want us to tie you to anything. You might need to protect her in case they come back."

Doubtful, Cruxh started to say, but drew back his words.

"You seriously plan to leave me with it?"

"You can trust Cruxh, and I do need to fetch Dow for you to get your justice."

"If you have to..." Mrs. Maybury let her words trail off.

Everyone knew about Dow, even though the man liked to be thought of as invisible. They knew if there was someone in the city who could fix any situation, it was him. They also knew that for some twisted, awful reason, he was loyal to Minta. Indubitably.

Minta got up from her chair and made her way to the door.

"Look after her," Minta said before she stepped out of the office.

The night was going badly. She'd even let the reporter get away. Only the gods knew what tomorrow would bring. There would be an outcry, which would cause an avalanche of events, if the reporter showed the attack in a bad light. It would be another weapon to be used against her. She was already dancing on thin ice, despite her mayoral position being for life. There was something working against her. Most likely it was Bertha Chaplain. Or who knew, it could be Frederick Kilborn, the leader of the Necro Democratic Alliance, but he usually landed direct blows. She could not imagine either of the political party leaders running Necropolis. It took more guts than they had. Luckily, both lacked necromantic abilities. However, it didn't mean they couldn't find one. She had to get the ghouls tonight. They had to be taken publicly to jail. She took longer steps.

Minta made her way down to the basement. She'd proposed moving Dow's office next to hers many times, but he kept refusing. He liked his den under the stairs. Away from the hassle, as he put it. He also reasoned that his disfigured body caused uneasiness, so it was better if he stayed away.

Minta gave a smile to a kitchen maid coming up the stairs. She was holding a tray, and from the look of it, it was going to the Minister of Education. A man with a bottomless belly.

"Good evening, Ann," Minta said. She liked the girl; always punctual, always kind. She was a bit naive though.

"Ma'am," she said and curtsied. The tray didn't even tremble.

"Is everything all right?" Minta asked.

"Everything is fine."

"And Shirley?" Shirley was the cook. There was no one else like her in the city. She knew how to make food taste mouthwatering. It was a good thing Minta didn't know what went into the cooking. She would have been appalled at how much butter, sugar, and salt one could put into a dish.

"She's fine."

"Good."

Minta made a move to leave, but Ann stopped her.

"Ma'am, may I ask a question?"

"Always," Minta replied.

"You know the protest at dawn?"

Minta nodded. She wasn't sure where this was going.

"Would it be all right if I went?" Ann asked.

"If you think it's important, then of course you can," Minta replied.

"It's just that my ma and papa and my brothers are not doing so well, and I thought I should do my part to help them. I know what they say about you ain't true. I know that you're kind and here to help even the little guy, but..."

"I understand, Ann. Don't worry about it. You have to do what is right for your family," Minta said and laid her hand on Ann's arm.

"Thank you, ma'am."

"Don't mention it."

The maid hurried past her, smiling.

Minta sighed and made her way to Dow's door. She began to knock but heard Dow arguing with someone. She hesitated, but when she heard her name mentioned, she opened the door and stepped in, making the two men freeze.

"What about me?" she asked.

◆

Necropolis is filled with love, like any other city. There's brotherly love, which goes beyond blood, there's love for parents, children, even for neighbors, self-love with tendencies to be constructive or destructive, but most relevant in the room was the notion of romantic love, riddled with faulty concepts and idealistic expectations. Petula listened to the diminishing love between Ira and Kitty Worthwrite as they made their way to the vault. She could hear in the silence each of them trying to understand what Ira's death meant to them.

Then there were the two black dogs trailing after them. They could be considered as having love for their master, but then again obedience and dependence could be misinterpreted as love.

When the silence grew too great, Ira asked, "Have you ever considered working in a bank? I bet you have a brain fit for details."

"No, I'm happy with what I do," Petula replied and glanced over her shoulder. She was sure she heard someone whisper her name.

"I'm sure I could find you a great managerial position in the bank. Something with all the perks and none of the responsibilities. What do you say?"

"When you put it like that, it's tempting, but...no, thank you." She turned her attention back to Ira.

Ira just smiled back at her.

Kitty glared at him.

They walked past the open front doors. The sickly, fruity smell of the city seeped inside the bank. At first, when Petula had settled in Necropolis, she'd found it hard to be outside, or for that matter inside. Everything smelled as if something had died. It was unlike the fresh air of industrialized Leporidae Lop or the manure of her family's sheep farms. But within a week she'd gotten used to it; during that time, she'd been a little queasy. Her classmates had attributed it to her small frame. They had all been complete morons.

"Someone shut that door," Kitty snapped and pulled her furs tighter around her.

The doorman forced the doors shut, pushing out Lady Meagre, who hadn't even gotten through the doorway.

Kitty walked past the two without noticing them. Not that Kitty was evil or inconsiderate. She was just used to getting her way, and somewhere down the line, she stopped noticing other people and what they needed. That was what'd happened to her and Ira. They saw their relationship as a function for a cause. A cause that seemed to rise higher with every year that passed. Somewhere inside them, that something special that had kindled their love still hid underneath all the issues that had to be dealt with.

It'd be easy to think Ira and Kitty had an arranged marriage or a marriage of convenience, but that couldn't be farther from the truth. Ira's family had opposed his marriage to Kitty, a woman ten years younger than him and with radical political ideas in her head and actions under her belt. She had a master's degree in Political Science and Economics and had been the first woman from her family to gain an education. She'd had aspirations, but then Ira happened, and their firstborn son came along. Kitty's family hadn't been that happy either.[22] Ira's crude manners, his temper, and his reputation made him less than a gentleman, and Kitty's family came from a long line of aristocrats. They were sure a proper man should be a gentleman, with some leniency as to what sport he played and how he occupied his time, but manners and habits of speech were not negotiable. Ira had always been a few cards short of gentlemanly behavior.

---

22   And no, Kitty's name was not short for Catherine. Kitty had always been Kitty and would always be in every way.

All that hung in the air between them. If Petula cared for other beings, she'd have said a kind word, but she didn't. She'd always found the whole love thing, romantic or otherwise, peculiar and confusing. The only thing she cared about was knowledge, and right now, getting her money, changing into clothes with less goo on them, having a lie-down, and while she was at it, deciding what to do with her life.

They walked to the bank's farthest left corner, behind the last bank counter. There were heavy iron gates decorated with vines, leaves, and other symbols of power and bad taste. Petula thought it would have been more sensible to hide the vault behind a supply closet or something similarly inconspicuous, but apparently not. The bankers' reasoning continued to perplex her, as if they'd lost an important part of their logical mind and let it run free doing Kraken knows what when it came to showing their status.

Petula took the book out of her pocket and drummed her fingers against it. Soon she opened it out of habit and trailed after them, using Ira as her mental anchor. She'd never done needlepoint in her life. She had the theoretical knowledge and was a master of the craft, but she had no practice. She was sure her fingers would obey. They'd obeyed her thus far. It was just that she never had the time. Maybe on her way back home, or if she stayed, she would finally use what she'd learned.

Just when she was getting to the good part, she sensed a look, which told Petula that she should put the book down or all the demons from the netherworld, or presumably inside Kitty's head, would break loose. Petula had gotten used to that sensation. It was a somewhat harsher version of her mother's attitude towards Petula and her obsession with books and where her mother thought it appropriate to read. It was also the same expression her mother had made whenever the subject of marriage or even finding a partner came up. Those things were usually avoidable by lifting the book higher so her face would be out of view. That small action almost always caused a massive amount of rage to build up inside her mother.[23] Petula judged that would be the case with Kitty as well. She was right. The woman gasped for

---

23 To be precise, just the right amount to make her unable to form any words.

breath and searched for a perfect word to attack with, but when you were so far gone with rage, there were never any perfect words.

"You—" Kitty started.

Petula ignored her, as she'd done whenever her mother had brought up the subject of marriage, her future, or what women of her age should do and shouldn't do. Petula didn't hate her mother. She loved her, and she wasn't the monster she sometimes made her out to be. Her mother was a perfectly lovely woman, and wise, but she had a blind spot when it came to her oldest child. Petula seemed unable to do anything right, unlike her younger sister. Not that she minded. She had her father.

Kitty made small squeaking noises, and finally, she asked, "Whose girl is she? Whose girl are you?" She turned her full attention to Petula, who had a great urge to disappear. Back at the University, they'd taught her how to handle ghosts, zombies, demons, and other monsters associated with death and dying, but they never taught her how to deal with the mothers, wives, and girlfriends of the deceased, let alone with their counterparts.[24]

Petula pushed her shoulders back to gather her dignity. "That isn't something you should concern yourself about. The more important question is my knowledge of the arts of necromancy and if I'm a professional or not. And I'm a master of what I do and entitled to respect, appreciation, and my payment for waking up your husband." Petula stared Kitty down.

"You are a rude little thing!" Kitty said.

"Not everything in the world revolves around you. I want to be paid and get back home," Petula said.

"Ira! You cannot let her speak like that!"

"Calm down, darling—" Ira began. He shouldn't have.

"Calm down?! I'm calm. What I need you to do is put her in her place. No servant talks that way!"

"Ha," Petula said.

"Ladies, ladies," Ira said and didn't get much farther.

"This has nothing to do with our gender! This is about disrespect," Kitty said.

Sadly, Petula had to agree.

---

24   Men were as bad as women.

"And you can't let her leave. Think what happened to Kitty Hogwood and her husband."

"Don't worry, nothing of the sort will happen here," Ira said.

"Excuse me, but that wasn't what we agreed to," Petula said.

"Let's talk in the vault," Ira said, lowering his voice.

"Everyone will hear us from here." He was right. Their voices echoed from the hollow staircase up to the bank floor. Especially to the nearby bank tellers' ears, who tried to serve their customers but couldn't help but squirm.

Kitty tried to stare Petula down.

Petula didn't flinch.

Ira reached out to touch Kitty. The woman's expression turned from agitation to horror, then to disgust, then back to horror, and then settled into a blank expression when Ira finally touched her.

Deep down, if Petula truly searched, she felt sorry for Kitty. The usual vows, *in sickness and in health, until death do us part*, worked poorly in Necropolis. Not that those vows were easy to keep even without the after-death part, but still, Kitty's life had to be in turmoil.

Ira guided his wife down the stairs. Petula wished there had been a course on marital affairs back at the University, then maybe she would know how to defuse the situation. Then again, she was leaving tomorrow, and Ira and Kitty would be Agatha's problem. Petula smiled. She opened her book once again and followed after the couple, carefully taking one step at a time.

11

VALUE OF HUMAN LIFE IN PENNIES

Life has a funny way of throwing things at you, like obstacles, curveballs, and ghouls. Yet the old saying about lemons and lemonade didn't come into Morris' mind as he held on to the reins for dear life. He kept his eyes closed as the horses, along with the coach, dashed uncontrollably forward through the busy Old Willy Wrangler's Street. People jumped out of their way, screaming as they went. A few drivers chauffeuring businessmen zigzagged around the horses and into the oncoming traffic. Morris[25] left behind a wake of near misses, two or three collisions,[26] and one major incident where an undead man lost half of his torso when Ira Worthwrite's statue outside the bank landed on him. Tomorrow there'd be a lawsuit waiting for Ira on his desk for leaving his things scattered around in a public place.

    Morris heard shouting coming from inside the coach,

---

25 You couldn't really blame him.

26 Depending on how you looked at things.

but he couldn't do anything about it. He'd opened his eyes and watched as the city moved past him. People yelled curses after them. Luckily, the horses moved fast and erratically enough that the curses didn't catch up. His body shook and bounced up and down on the seat. The only thing keeping him from flying off was his hold on the reins. All the slamming against the seat caused pain to shoot down his leg. He took a tighter hold on the reins and pulled back as hard as he could. To his surprise, it worked. The horses calmed down. The coach had by then traveled through the entire street and left the banking district. Unfortunately, it had also taken them in the opposite direction from Bertha Chaplain's house, which was beyond the cemetery on the seashore.

The horses slowed to a complete halt and waited for the next command. They'd have to wait for a long time, because Morris was fighting to get his breath back and keep his heart from jumping out and doing a tap dance on the ground before running off with the ghouls.

"What are you playing at, kid?!" Ignatius asked as he pushed out of the coach. He looked disheveled and angry. His gray hair was messy, his coat was wrinkled, and he squeezed his top hat as if he was about to use it against Morris.

"Just a scare. Everything is fine now," Morris said. He himself didn't believe a word coming out of his mouth. The short, uncontrollable gallop through the city made him re-evaluate his life. He wasn't entirely sure if he was doing the right thing being involved with all this, not forgetting the fact that he'd gotten the ball rolling. It was just that maybe his father had been right, that banking itself wasn't the cause. It was just another tool to be used to advance the city and its inhabitants. You could say his father thought of it as a service. Not a free service, of course, but a service nevertheless. Now the money itself had become the goal, forgetting all about creating, building, nurturing, and passion. How could he have forgotten passion? He once felt passion for structures found in nature. Take the flight pattern of a moth; he could have spent days studying it. Morris wanted to say all this aloud, but he couldn't. Neither Ignatius nor Wilbur would understand him; both men had despised his father.

"Start explaining!" Ignatius said.

Wilbur came out. His face looked sickly. "Stop

shouting. I'm sick and tired of you shouting all the time," Wilbur said calmly.

"He nearly killed us!" Ignatius said.

"Kill you? You are as dead as the next undead," Wilbur sneered. Some color had come back into his face, and he looked sharper and more alert than he'd done the whole night.

"You're talking nonsense. See, Morris, what you did? You made Wilbur bang his head and lose his mind," Ignatius said and turned his back on the man.

"I haven't lost my mind. I see things clearer than before, and I hate you and Ira bossing me around. *Poor old fat Wilbur. Let's make him dance to our will, let's keep shouting at him to make us feel better about the mistakes we made and not him.* I don't make mistakes. It has always been you and your stubborn, arrogant nature. Because of you, we arrived late to pick up Jeremiah Black; because of you, we are in this mess; and because of you, Jeffrey might be dead in a ditch. It was never my fault and never Morris' fault. So stop shouting; you're not helping anyone," Wilbur said, brushing past Ignatius to the horses. He stroked them and searched for cuts and bruises.

Ignatius chose to ignore Wilbur. "So?" he asked, maybe in a slightly weaker voice.

"A pack of ghouls ran past the horses, agitating them," Morris said.

"You should have been more careful. Anyway, we better get going to find *her.* Wilbur, come back inside," Ignatius said in a careful tone.

"I'm going home. I need to organize a search party for Jeffrey and..." He let his words trail off. There was no point stating the same fact that he'd repeated several times tonight.

Ignatius opened his mouth but then closed it. "Have it your way," he said after careful thought. "You better get back in though."

Wilbur did as asked after he made sure the horses were fine. They were.

When the two men were back inside, Morris adjusted his stump, took hold of the reins, and motioned the horses onward. This time they obeyed him without hesitation. Wilbur's place was on the other side of the city. Everything was more luscious and greener there. But first, they had to go through the market district, which was chaotic and crowded. He liked the place, except for the children who hung around the Moorland Market, mocking him and his cane. As an adult, he knew he shouldn't care, but still, those potty mouths got to him.

It was just as well the ride gave him time to think. If his instincts had been right, he'd have to change everything. But he had to do it without destroying his father's bank, meaning he couldn't abruptly stop associating with the three others. He had to work from the inside to change the industry, and maybe make a few bucks while he was at it. He knew where he'd hidden the loopholes. But before that, he had to get Wilbur home, find Agatha Wicks, maybe have a word with Petula, and then go home to alter the proposal. A monetary committee acting under his guidelines might change the city's economics for the better. But he'd make an enemy out of Ira. He could live with that.

The houses got smaller, huddled together, and more ominous the farther they went from the banking district. They'd arrived in the part of the city where the middle class lived. Once those same houses had belonged to the immigrants and less fortunate, but the ever-expanding population had pushed them away from the city center. Now the place was an artistic neighborhood, full of up-and-coming folks who dreamed of making it big time. Morris sometimes visited the place to see if he could find anything pleasing to his eyes. He'd bought a painting or two based on a friend's recommendations but regretted them as soon as he'd taken them home. They didn't seem to speak to him like, say, a leaf did, or the steps at the Library did. Nevertheless, he'd doubled the value of those paintings while keeping them in crates.

He was sure one of the houses on his right was where he'd bought a painting. But all the houses looked the same, and he could be mistaken. He made the horses turn right at the corner, which would take them past the marketplace and to Wilbur's estate.

The Moorland Market was a place like no other in the city. He heard it before he saw it. The place was full of a cacophony of noises, some delightful and others less so. You could buy any product there, from human bodies to plums, or any service you might think of, from assassins to lovers to taxidermists. It was a place that never slept. Even when they closed it at three in the morning to be opened again in four hours, there was always someone hanging around, willing to exchange services for money. It wasn't only the vendors that attracted people there. It was the pleasure and fun the place promised, with sweet apples, intoxicating drinks, and wonders hidden behind curtains.

Morris hoped the streets weren't too crowded and that the horses would obey him long enough to get them past quickly.

At the next corner, the square leading up to the covered marketplace opened up. Right away Morris was hit with the smell of spices, human sweat, and the grease from baked goods. It wasn't only the smells that overloaded his senses. The place was packed tonight. Everyone was doing their shopping before the five AM. protest happened. Morris had to pull the horses to a halt and wait for another coach to pass them. He let his gaze wander over the market. The place was full of humans at their best. They moved around, twiddled this and that, moved on, heckled, ate, drank, followed others, played music, and painted pictures. And that was without the preachers and fortunetellers who took care of the souls of the visitors. If he had talent enough, this was the picture of the city he would want to paint. Here in the chaos was humanity.

When the road was clear, he urged the horses left to circle the square. They wouldn't be going under the glass-covered street with geometrical brown, blue, and yellow tiles. They'd turn into one of the side alleys before it. In the meantime, Morris listened to the haunting violin solo coming from nearby. It almost got buried under all the other noises, but it spoke to his soul, drawing him in.

He was almost too enchanted by the violinist to notice Agatha Wicks waving at him. She balanced a man-sized carpet against a coach. He yanked the reins, causing the horses to dig their hooves into the ground and causing Ignatius and Wilbur to fly off their seats. He got off the coach as fast as he could before the woman had an opportunity to go back to ignoring him and disappear into the crowd. He made his way to her, brushing past people, having to shove a few aside. Morris didn't care about the fact that he heard Ignatius shouting after him.

"Good evening, Miss Wicks," Morris said and spooked the necromancer, who dropped the carpet next to the coach. It slumped down heavily like a sack of potatoes.

"Mr. Reinhardthh," Agatha said when she recovered. Her lips bulged a little. "I thoughthh ithh wash you."

Morris had forgotten how tall she was and how agreeable she looked.

"How have you been?" he asked.

"Finehh, and youhh?" Agatha replied.

"Perfectly well. One might say lucky, as you are the one I was looking for, and here you are," Morris said and gave her a smile.

A warm smile spread across Agatha's face. "I washh?"

"Yes," Morris said. "Do you happen to know Petula Upwood?" he asked.

Before Agatha had time to answer, Ignatius stormed over, and Wilbur wasn't too far behind.

"What are you doing?" the man asked. "You can chat to women on your own time."

"Forgive me, my dear Miss Wicks. Let me introduce my associates. This here is Ignatius Vaughn, and here is Wilbur Sumner," Morris said and motioned with his hand at the two men who had joined them.

"Is this the Wicks woman the necromancer kept mentioning?" Ignatius asked.

Behind him, Wilbur sighed.

"Yeshh, I'm Agatha Wickshh and you're...wait forh a shhecond," Agatha said. She took out her teeth and pushed them inside her purse. She smacked her lips three times and then said, "Your associate was just telling me how he'd been ever so lucky to find me here."

"Splendid, then everything is settled, and you're coming with us," Ignatius said.

"I'm afraid we haven't gotten that far. Let me talk to her alone," Morris said.

"Okay, but you better deliver," Ignatius replied.

Morris nodded. The two men left him and Agatha alone.

◆

You can calculate the value of human life as parts, as a whole, and before and after death in money, or so some say. Others think the value of human life can never be measured in worth, that human life is valuable in and of itself and should never be mixed with bankers, insurance agents, or lawyers. Bertha Chaplain knew how much her body was worth to her as itself and to others in numbers. To some, her body was costing money, and to others, she was a source of money.

There'd been those who'd wanted to get rid of her. It wasn't like she'd died of natural causes the last time around. Her mortician had found poison in her body when they'd prepared her for the awakening. She never found out who'd done it, but she had her suspicions. Few liked a living person running the Union of the Undead. But they'd been wrong about death slowing her down. It'd fueled her even more. Still, she was afraid of letting Agatha Wicks go out on her own. She knew the necromancer's body and mind were worth more even than hers. But the silly girl insisted that she should have freedoms. At first, Bertha had restricted her movements outside the house, but the necromancer had grown restless and downright destructive. Her spirit had seeped into Bertha. She had to release the girl from being housebound. Her mood had lifted, but still, she sulked around. The way she sucked air between her teeth when she was bored made Bertha's skin crawl.

She could spend nights and days thinking of ways to entertain the necromancer, and none of them would work. Agatha had grown weary of balls, operas, theater, fancy dinners out, and everything else Bertha had financed.

Oh well, Bertha thought and lowered the curtains. It was better if she concentrated on the night at hand. The guests would be there soon.

Bertha shuffled back upstairs. It became obvious she couldn't put on her perfect dress that always impressed everyone, even the stiffs. She had to put on the second-best thing, and that was her red v-neck dress, which looked amazing against her lifeless, greenish complexion. The red thing she could manage on her own, but it wouldn't solve the problem of what to serve if Agatha didn't come home in time. She needed flesh for the undead to win them over to her side. There was nothing like fresh blood to get things rolling. Could she serve one of her servants? There was the old fool lurking around the house, pretending to be her butler. His meat might be too dry, and she had already sent him to his room. What he did inside there, she didn't want to know. The only thing she knew was that the smells coming from the place weren't for the faint-hearted. Bertha kept him on the payroll out of sentimentality. Then there was the odd jobs boy who popped in now and then, but someone might miss him. It'd be easier if they had a maid, but Agatha insisted on fixing her own dinner, against her better nature. Thus they had only employed a cleaning lady, who came once a day to tidy up the place, but she had already left. It had to be some poor bastard off the streets, whose skeleton Agatha would help her hide later.

She opened the door leading to her room and walked to her wardrobe, which was taller than her and wide enough to contain clothes for all occasions. When she'd been alive, she'd liked to dress posh and keep everyone on their toes with her apparel, but now she did it out of habit and out of the power it brought, without having the same rush she'd had back then. The wardrobe itself was a gift from her lover. Contrary to everyone's belief, she never married. She'd had a series of dalliances, even with the late Oliver the Great, but she'd never committed.

She drew the wardrobe open and took out the red dress. She laid it on the canopy bed. It looked stunning against the white silk cover. Bertha got out of her clothes and kicked them under the bed. She squeezed into the red piece. Her dead flesh pushed against her bones. She looked at her reflection in the mirror, feeling satisfied. Bertha didn't linger long in the bedroom. She had no use for it. As an undead, she did not need sleep, or the other sort of lie-down. Bertha never got the mind-body connection back. Some undead did. Some faked it. Bertha didn't. She had always had one goal in life, and that was to rise to and stay in power. Ever since she had sold matches in the streets as a kid, she knew one day she'd be the one walking past her with contempt. One day she'd change the Constitution so that there was no need to be a necromancer to be the Mayor. This proposal Morris had brought to her attention was one way to achieve that. In a day or two, they'd hail her as the savior of the economy and question Minta's role as Mayor. But such a day wouldn't come if she didn't get tonight right.

Where was the foolish girl? If only Agatha was

stronger, maybe she could use her to put pressure on Minta.

Bertha went back downstairs and moved into her hallway. All this parading up and down was getting to her. She should never have commissioned a house with two stories. From the look of it, she should have bought a slaughterhouse. Then there wouldn't be all this worrying about what to serve. She drew open her front door and swung her head from right to left in search of someone, preferably Agatha. The salty sea air whipped against her face. That was another reason she should never have bought the place. It was always draughty and cold, and the wind never stopped howling. But a house with a sea view had seemed like a reasonable investment. She didn't even want to look at the outer walls and see how the paint was already chipping off. She kept her eyes scanning for anyone who might pass by. No one did. The wind was especially bad tonight, keeping people away from the shoreline.

Bertha slammed the door shut.

It infuriated her that all her plans were being ruined by the tiny, unimportant details. It wasn't like the undead needed to fuel their bodies with eating, which had become more like a symbolic act. A communion.

There was only one option, and that was to go back up the stairs, again.

When upstairs, she walked up to the butler's door, took a deep and concentrated pause, and knocked.

"Yes?" The word came out in a low, careful tone.

"It's me, Bertha. Edgard, open the door," she said.

"What do you want?" he asked.

Bertha heard the shuffling of feet and tools being put down. Or at least she guessed it to be something heavy and metallic.

Soon the door cracked open. Edgard's round bald head peered out.

"How may I serve you?" the man asked.

Bertha lifted herself onto her toes and peered over the man's head to see what he hid in his room. It was too dark. She lowered back down and said, "I need a body."

"How do you propose I acquire one, madam?" Edgard asked.

"Don't play coy with me. We have known each other for years now. Do you think I don't know what you have hidden in that room of yours? Do you think I can't smell it? It's your business what you do in there, but I need a body to serve for the guests. I wouldn't be asking if this wasn't an emergency."

"Can't the miss help you?" Edgard asked.

"She's out. The gods only know where, and the guests will arrive soon."

Edgard sighed. He opened the door and said, "Then you better come in and help me."

There between the bed and wardrobe, the man had built a laboratory. There were jars with human body parts, all sorts of chemical bottles, saws, medical equipment, and tubes going down to a metallic table where a naked female body lay. Next to the table was an apparatus of a type that Bertha had never seen before. It hummed in a low tone.

"I was in the process of draining her out," Edgard said. "I need to put her organs back in and stitch her stomach together. Then you can have her."

Bertha was at a loss for words. She kept swirling her head around, trying to take everything in. She barely registered what Edgard had said. Bertha nodded along and counted how many hearts she could find inside the glass jars. She was sure there were five hearts, not counting the one in the metallic dish next to the body.

"Wha—what are you doing?" she asked when the initial bewilderment wore off.

He glanced over his shoulder at her, searching for the meaning behind her words.

"Do you want to know?" he asked.

Bertha hesitated, but then she nodded.

"I'm trying to wake her up without the need to resort to necromancy," he said.

The man sounded cautious when he said it. Bertha could understand why. Going against necromancy was like going against the gods. You didn't do that if you didn't want to get burned.

"Hm," she said.

"I'm sorry, madam. I'll pack my things first thing in the morning and be on my way," he said.

"I didn't mean that. I was thinking. Why haven't you told me this sooner?" she asked.

"It never occurred to me," he said.

"I could have helped you. Given you money and time!"

"You would have?"

"Of course! But now we better get the body ready, and we can talk about this tomorrow."

"Thank you, madam."

"As I have said, call me Bertha."

"Bertha."

She helped the man as best she could, but her help was useless. His stubby little fingers worked faster than she thought possible as he stuffed the intestines into the body and sewed the gaping hole in the woman's stomach together.

They carried the woman downstairs to the dining room and laid her on the table. She would have to do. Going about it the old way might be more novel than serving her in bite-size pieces. Maybe she would start a trend and stop the false pretense that the food undead ate wasn't made from voluntary human donations. Bertha hoped the woman's body was just that; that her family had sold her to be reused. She didn't dare to ask.

The man made a move to leave her alone.

"Before you go," Bertha said, "I want to ask why you're doing this."

"Doing what, ma—Miss Bertha?" he asked.

"Trying to wake her up without necromancy."

"There has to be another way. I'm sure of it," he said, sounding excited, sounding like if she let him go on, it would take the whole night and the next day before the man stopped.

"Good," she said before he could say anything else. "I'll set up funds to see you can go on, but you better not say a word about this to Agatha."

"No, we wouldn't want to upset the miss."

"No, we wouldn't. And thank you, Edgard. Take the necessary money out of the petty cash for however much it cost to acquire her."

Edgard nodded and left her alone with the body in the dining room.

What a pity for such a young woman to die, Bertha thought. But at least she had their dinner now, and the woman had briefly aided the progress of science. Bertha wondered if the girl's spirit hung around her body. It would be a shame if she started haunting the house. There were already too many people living in a house of this size, with only two stories and three bedrooms, attic, kitchen, dining hall, library, and the drawing room. Three people, the ghost of her former lover, and whatever demons haunted Agatha made the place too crowded. Tomorrow she would send for an exorcist, Maggie Ravenheart, to come in and have a look around. She was the best in the city. She was also Bertha's taxidermist. The woman could work real miracles with a needle and thread.

There came a knock at her front door.

Holy Kraken, Bertha thought and hurried to greet her guests, who were in high spirits after chasing down ghouls through Necropolis.

12

THE DESPICABLE NATURE OF OTHER PEOPLE

ontrary to general belief, a banker's greatest tool is understanding emotions and people, and not the glowing skulls with Algor's rhythms in them. Ira Worthwrite knew people. He knew what their fears and hopes were, what motivated them, and what made them tick, and he knew all about emotions and their power. That didn't mean Ira had to be pleasant. He just had to know what levers to pull. He sensed the tension between Mrs. Worthwrite and the necromancer. Ira was beginning to like Petula. She wasn't a wimpy kid with too much power in her hands. Anyone who could hold their own with Kitty was someone to watch out for. He'd give her the money she was due, but he wouldn't let her go. It was too dangerous now, as he'd torn up the contract. Sometimes his theatrics and temper got the better of him. This time it'd been Ignatius' fault.

Ira glanced over his shoulder. The necromancer had opened her book again and was somehow walking down the stairs without stumbling. His wife was glaring at the other woman, clearly looking for a way to start a new argument. There seemed to be so many things nowadays that rubbed Kitty the wrong way. That hadn't always been the case. She'd always been headstrong and, if he was honest, arrogant, but underneath all that, she had something that sparkled. When she laughed, she lit up the whole room. Bella and Lugosa, the two dogs who trailed after Kitty, were the only ones who kept her mood somewhat jovial nowadays. Whatever thorn he'd inflicted on her, he should remove it.

Ira turned his attention back to the stairs. They were well lit by the gas lamps he'd installed. He'd made sure there were no dark corners for anyone to hide in. The other thing he'd done was to employ gargoyles. He'd hidden them throughout the building. Ira knew without looking that one observed them from the ceiling. The only trouble with gargoyles was that they didn't intervene. They only watched and reported back painfully accurate details if asked. He'd even installed one at the cashier counter. None of the employees knew it was there. But he had obviously failed to install one on the rooftop. He would ask Nigel to employ one more.

"Why are you indulging her?" Kitty finally asked.

"Who?" Ira replied and thanked Kraken for the fact they were already well under the bank and there was no one to hear their screams. Except the gargoyle.

"Her," Kitty said, trying to engage the necromancer. The tone and stare didn't work on Petula; the woman kept the book between her and Kitty, using it as a shield.

"She deserves her pay," Ira said.

"Yes, but on our terms. She'll marry one of our boys. Maybe Bernard. That's how the Mores did it. They got their daughter to marry that, that, what was his name. Anyway, they kept it in their family. And you know as well as I do that they're doing fine. He even got their grandma to come back as a spirit. You know what she's like."

Ira counted to ten, waiting for the necromancer to explode. She didn't. She ignored them.

Ira would not let her marry Bernard. The man was an imbecile. She deserved more than to be married to one of his boys. Kitty had pampered them too much. Maybe one of his younger brothers. At least they had something going on between their ears and knew how to pay for their own upkeep. Yet he wouldn't wish either of his brothers on her. One was a loudmouth and the other as tedious as a welcome mat. If she had to marry someone, it had to be Morris, as he had agreed with Ignatius and Wilbur. But it'd be a waste of a good woman. She could be so much more.

"No one will marry anyone," he said.

Petula let out a quiet snort. Kitty didn't hear it, or else she'd have torn the necromancer's head off. Yes, he was liking the woman more and more. They'd have to find her a comfortable position. If she wasn't willing to work in the bank or marry Morris, maybe something else might tickle her pride. He wasn't sure what made her tick other than books. Unfortunately, he had nothing to do with books, and her desires couldn't be that simple. She couldn't solely live for reading. That was... Ira didn't know what that was. It was at least a waste of a life. But if she loved them so much, maybe he could buy the Necropolis Library and hand it to her. Petula could replace that awful Nosferatu working there, then she'd never leave the city. She'd be safely locked away from harm. Ira wondered how one went about buying a public library as he took the key from his pocket and put it in the iron gate that led up to the hall where the vault was. He might write it off as a charitable action.

"Are you sure you want to leave? There's no need for that Wicks woman. Working for me could be profitable," Ira said. He pushed the gate open, letting them into the hall. Bertha Chaplain's assistant was an intriguing possibility, but he rather liked Petula.

"Wicks woman? One of the prominent Wickses?" Kitty asked. She stepped into the hall, Petula trailing after them, still keeping her eyes on the book.

"Yes, Agatha Wicks. Bertha Chaplain's assistant," Ira replied and waited for the necromancer to interrupt them. She didn't.

"She's passing her possession to her?"

"That was the original plan, yes."

"It's a good plan. You can't go wrong with the Wickses. You know what they say about them."

"I know." They said that a Wicks came to Necropolis with the original boat, that they were the first necromancers to settle here. The Wickses were more royalty than the royalty itself.

"You should have contacted her to begin with, so you wouldn't have to pay one sum to *her* and another to Miss Wicks and who knows who else," Kitty said.

"The events weren't exactly in my hands."

"They should have been."

There was no point arguing with her, and it wasn't as if she'd been there to aid the process of him being awakened. As soon as they'd gotten married, she'd pronounced that she wanted nothing to do with his resurrection. The whole sordid affair gave her the creeps. He was to see that everything went according to plan but not to involve her. Ira was sure it had something to do with her father's failed attempt, but none of it mattered.

Ira shut the iron gate behind them. Opposite them, the circular vault door was embedded in a long wall. It was the only thing in the hallway, and behind the door, the city's heart was stored. Ira slipped the key back into his pocket and walked to the door. He didn't need the key any longer. The only way to open the vault was to get through the set of combination padlocks. Six, to be precise. He'd arranged the letter combinations so they made no sense. Not, at least, to anyone else but him.

Ira turned his back on Kitty and Petula and took the first lock between his fingers. He swirled the brass letter rings back and forth until they satisfied him. The first lock opened. Soon the second and the third followed suit. The last three were difficult, as he had to hunch down to open them. His body didn't work the way it should straight out of the grave. He needed a spot of taxidermy. The miracle that kept the undead stitched and oiled and the city open around the clock. But now every bone and dried tendon moaned. His body could shamble after anything with full force, bite through flesh with ease, but going up and down was nightmarish. Still, he got to the locks and opened them. He even got up without severing a muscle, but with a constant groan. However, as he pushed all his weight onto his feet, one of his toes came free. There was a loud click. Ira looked down at his feet, at his severed toe. Before he could bend to pick it up, Bella launched at it and took it between her teeth.

"Could you?" Ira asked.

Kitty puffed but pulled the dog into her lap and wrestled the toe loose.

"Keep it until I get to a taxidermist," he said and turned to the vault door. Ira dragged it open and was again surprised by how easy the action was. He usually had to fight the heavy door open.

He heard his wife mutter behind him, "She stinks. You stink. Nothing is the way it should be. What a horrible night! I could be at Lace's anniversary dinner or even home doing anything but this."

Ira chose not to say anything. When he'd gotten the door fully open, it dropped from its hinges, collapsing against the wall. At that same moment, he heard Kitty shout, "Those little monsters! They're robbing us!"

"What?!" Ira shouted and hurried in to see what his wife saw. He expected to find the vault's contents missing and all the lockers open, but there was a pack of ghouls frozen, staring back at them. One of them was holding a floor tile. They looked out of place in the huge vault with lockers from floor to ceiling.

"Catch them!" Kitty let out.

The ghouls screamed high-pitched screams, and the one holding the tile dropped it on the floor.

"Do something!" Kitty said, prompting her husband to rush into the vault to seize the ghouls. The ghouls ran in different directions, leaving Ira unsure who to follow.

"Not you, fool. The necromancer!"

"Mm," Petula said and lowered the book.

"Do something!" Kitty screamed.

"Ghouls are not my area of expertise, I'm afraid," Petula replied.

"I knew you were incompetent the moment I saw you," Kitty snapped.

"I wouldn't call myself incompetent," Petula said and lifted the book back to her eye level.

Ira had stopped moving, still deciding who to seize. One had dived into the hole. Another one had rushed behind him. Ira wasn't sure if he'd run past Kitty and Petula, whose conversation he was barely following. All he cared about was catching the thieves. The third one had hidden behind the table where the clients could lay their safety deposit boxes. Ira advanced towards the table.

"Then do something," he heard his wife say. He'd never heard such a plea in her voice.

"You need a demonologist. I know many think ghouls are evil spirits and fall under a necromancer's jurisdiction, but that would be a mistake. Scholars have never conclusively proved what ghouls are, but I can say with confidence they are not undead, spirits, or any form of being whose soul I can control. If I were you, I'd call the guards," Petula said.

"You are useless," Kitty snapped.

"All right, I'll see what I can do," Petula said. "But I mean it, you better call the guards."

Kitty turned around and headed to the gate.

Ira had advanced to the table. He launched himself at the ghoul, who dived with ease to his right and jumped into the hole. He turned around to dash after the ghoul as fast as his dead feet could go, only to stop and see another ghoul leaping at Petula, who'd stepped in. An overwhelming fear washed over him. Every fiber of his being needed to protect Petula.

"Watch out!" he shouted.

Instead of seeing the ghoul tearing the necromancer's throat open, the ghoul froze in place after Petula lifted her book in the air.

"You can choose: either I hit you with my book or my bag," Petula said. She still kept her back to the ghoul.

"Missr, I have nothingr againstr your, Ir justr wantr tor gor homer," the ghoul said.

"Why didn't you say that in the first place?" Petula asked and lowered her book.

"Itr wash allrr therr screamingr thatr scaredr merh," the ghoul replied.

"I know what you mean," Petula said. "You better go then."

"Thankrr missr."

The ghoul ran past Petula and went through the hole. Before it could drag the floor tile back into place, Ira stomped his feet on its claw. The ghoul yelped and drew its claw back in. Ira peered into the hole but didn't see the ghoul. He saw nothing but a pitch-black chute.

The necromancer stepped up to the rim of the hole and followed Ira's gaze.

"Why did you let it go?" Ira asked.

"What did you want me to do? Wrestle with it?"

"You could have done something!"

"I might have, but that would only have agitated the ghoul."

Ira glared at Petula.

"You can't let them get away with this!" Kitty screamed at the door. Bella and Lugosa wagged their tails behind her. Mrs. Worthwrite had come back, as the gate to the outside world was locked, and the only creature behind it had been the gargoyle, who found Kitty mildly interesting, but not interesting enough to move. The two dogs of hers were another matter. "Those, those..." Kitty tried to match an insult to the ghouls' despicable nature, but there was no lower position in Necropolis than a corpse-eating monster. Though those same monsters came in handy when you needed your chimneys cleaned.

"Never! I'm going after them!" Ira said and lowered himself to the floor.

"I'd advise against it, sir," Petula said.

"Advising me about my own business? Who do you think you are?" Ira asked, but didn't wait for a reply. He went down the hole, which was a deep drop, judging by his echoing moan.

◆

There are those moments in life that define the path ahead, and often enough it's hard to separate those seemingly small decisions from the major ones. Standing in Dow's office was one of those moments; Herbert wasn't sure how it would turn out. He stood there being scrutinized by the Mayor herself. Herbert had to give it to the woman, she had an impressive way about her. She was more than half a foot taller than he. Now he understood how the woman had risen from a soldier's rank to running the city. And even more so, he understood why it took four bankers to go against her. Underneath her pleasantness and openness, an iron will seeped out.

"Dow, would you be so kind as to introduce me to your new friend?" the Mayor asked. She extended her hand to Herbert. "I'm Minta Stopford."

Dow looked at Herbert and hesitated. "This is Herbert Ringworm. He is an old associate of mine," the man said.

Herbert reached for the woman's hand and shook it. She had a firm grip.

"I'm pleased to meet you, Mr. Ringworm," Minta said. "How may I assist you?"

Dow shook his head, but Herbert ignored him. "It's not how you can assist me, it's how I can help you, Mrs. Mayor. I'm here to warn you," he said.

The little man drummed his fingers against his desk. Herbert was sure he looked displeased, which was Dow's equivalent of angry. Even when Herbert outmatched the smallish man's strength, Dow held himself like he could kill anyone just with the snap of his fingers. Most people in Necropolis believed he could. Many aristocrats and politicians and even citizens had reoccurring nightmares about Dow hunting them down. Not Herbert though.

"Warn me about what?" Minta asked, keeping her voice soft.

"About Ira Worthwrite. He's planning an attack against you," he said, irritated that his voice didn't match hers. His words came out tense and angry.

"He is?" Minta asked. Her question didn't sound serious, and Herbert knew that he should have chosen his words better. That he'd sounded childish.

Lazy, worthless shit, he thought, and not for the first time.

"Mr. Ringworm overheard Mr. Worthwrite speak ill of you, but as we both know, this is nothing new. I saw no reason to alarm you," Dow said.

Minta turned to face Herbert, and he instantly saw that she was going to shrug him off.

"This isn't anything you can take lightly," he said. "It's not only Ira who's against you. Morris Reinhardt, Ignatius Vaughn, and Wilbur Sumner were there with him, along with his new necromancer, and they mentioned Bertha Chaplain." There was still tension in his voice. He couldn't help it.

"They are working together?" Minta asked.

This time he'd got her. She looked wide awake, and not as open and relaxed as before. To someone else, the slight change in her posture might have meant nothing, but he had a trained eye, and he could tell the Mayor was highly stressed.

"Dow, did you know about this?" Minta asked.

The man looked from Herbert to Minta. "No-o, but I know Jeremiah Black is dead, and all the prominent members of the city under his possession are now dropping dead," Dow said, squinting his ugly eyes at Herbert.

A warning? Herbert couldn't care less about his warnings. What Dow was doing was, at best, fishing. If he knew he'd killed the man, he couldn't act on the information, not when he had to confess to the Mayor how they'd met each other.

"If I have this right, the situation is this: tonight there'll be a protest against me, a plot is put in motion to remove me from my position, there was a murder that took out half the city's elite, and Mrs. Maybury was just attacked by ghouls, and if she doesn't get justice, she'll raise Kraken itself to bring havoc into the city. Did I miss something?" Minta recounted.

Herbert was glad he'd caused only one out of four. Maybe it would be a major event that would shake Necropolis, but good riddance to all those who were gone because of him. To tell the truth, yes, there were a lot of dead men and women who'd stopped working when their ties had been severed with Jeremiah, but not as many as you might think. Jeremiah's drinking had hindered his career early on. Also, many thought it wasn't a good thing to put all their eggs in the same basket case. Of course, there might be some serious ramifications if the deceased's relatives weren't agile enough to seize the mindless zombies before they took to the streets. But in general, if they did, Necropolitans were quick to neutralize a threat against their body parts. One could say they had an aversion to becoming snacks.

"An attack?" Dow asked.

Herbert was sure the man's voice wheezed.

"Yes, Mrs. Maybury was attacked by a group of ghouls at the Town Hall meeting," Minta said.

"That is bad. You need to send someone to retrieve the ghouls before the city gets wind of this," Dow replied.

"Which is the reason I'm here. I was coming to retrieve you. Mrs. Maybury is waiting for me in my office with Mr. Cruxh."

"Was that wise?" Dow asked.

"There was no other choice."

Herbert couldn't follow. He'd had enough. This had got nothing to do with Ira and his buddies. The Mayor and Dow couldn't be so ignorant as to what was the real threat here.

"You haven't answered my question," Herbert said.

"What might that question be?" Dow asked.

The little man was getting to him. He was always annoying, but now he was trying to derail him. "About Ira and what you'll do about it. If they start a nasty campaign against you, you'll be ruined."

"Is he right, Dow?" Minta asked.

"He could be," Dow said. He sent another one of his glances towards Herbert, which was meant to silence him.

Herbert didn't give a rat's ass about his warnings. He was going to see this through and finally get justice for Ona. That was the thing with rich and powerful men: they thought they could get away with anything, and they did, but sometimes there were men like him who didn't stand silent and watch from the sidelines as the world went to pieces.

"You have to put the man behind bars. He's dangerous, and he'll do whatever he wants if you don't stop him now," he said.

"And why is this so important to you, Mr. Ringworm?" Minta asked.

"Does it matter? Or is this just a game to you? One way to protect him and the other bankers, as they say in the newspapers. I thought you were someone with integrity. Someone with the courage to do what is right—"

"That is enough," Dow said. He stood up behind his desk, but that was unnecessary; his voice was enough to silence the room.

"No, Dow, let him speak," Minta said.

"He's a murderer and a madman. Isn't that enough of a reason? Don't you want justice?" Herbert asked when he had composed himself. Dow was close to having his secret revealed.

"Yes, I want justice, but Ira is not an easy man to catch. Nothing he has done has been strictly illegal. But if your information about him working with the other bank heads and with Bertha is correct, then that can be thought of as distorting the competition and attempting to build a monopoly, and we have strict laws against monopolies. But that has to be proved, or it's just a rumor, and he'll walk away scot-free. If and when we do get the information, Ira will face justice. But I need this ghoul attack to be handled to Mrs. Maybury's satisfaction now or I won't be here to help you, Mr. Ringworm. So, if you could be so kind and leave me to talk to Dow?" Minta asked.

"I'll help you," Herbert said. "I can handle myself with any creature. Point me where they are, and I'll bring them to you."

"I..." Minta began. "That's not how these things go. There's a—"

"You think some police officer can handle himself with ghouls? Give me a break. You need someone more experienced. Someone like me," Herbert said. He couldn't believe he was saying this, but he was. He'd do anything to make Ona happy again.

"And you can handle yourself with ghouls?" Minta asked. She sounded somewhat amused, but not so much that she'd say no.

"If I may interrupt, I don't think this is a good idea," Dow said.

"I'm sorry, Mr. Ringworm, I have to agree with Dow. I can't let you get involved."

"What other options do you have?"

There was no answer. They all waited for someone to say something. Herbert knew he should push for the Mayor to see his side of things. She'd sounded more lenient than her words led them to believe. She needed a miracle to get her out of this mess, and if Herbert could find the right words, he could make her see that he was that miracle. That they could be helpful for each other.

"Mr. Ringworm, who is the new necromancer you mentioned earlier?" Dow asked after a while.

"What?" Herbert asked.

"Who awakened Mr. Worthwrite?" Dow repeated his question.

"What does that have to do with anything?" Herbert asked, but when Dow raised his eyebrow, he added, "I think she was called Miss Upwood or something."

"Aah," Dow said.

"Dow?" Minta asked.

"Just thinking aloud," Dow replied. He massaged his

left-hand fingers against each other, deep in thought. Then he said, "Ma'am, maybe you should let Mr. Ringworm help you. If there is anyone in the city who can hunt and trap ghouls, it is him. I can get him and Cruxh the proper paperwork to legally bring the ghouls back for Mrs. Maybury to get her justice."

Herbert wasn't sure why the man was toying with him, but he'd be a fool if he didn't take all the help he could get. Maybe the man finally saw his obligations towards him, but he was doubtful. Dow had no loyalty towards anyone else but himself and the Mayor.

"Are you sure?" Minta asked.

Before Dow said anything, Hebert answered, "Miss Mayor, I'll promise to serve you as best I can, and I will bring the ghouls back here if it's the last thing I do."

"Hm," Minta said. "Dow?"

"The man is right. We need more than your basic police officers to retrieve them. Of course, there is the monster hunter force, but their jurisdiction is out of Necropolis' compounds. Also, if you get them involved in the city politics, everyone will think you are using them as your own special force, and there will be outrage from the special community, from the werewolves, vampires, and the rest," Dow said. "And in the meantime, I will find out all I can about Mr. Worthwrite and his associates and their plans. Leave this all to me. By tomorrow, the city will be as good as new, and all the problems you mentioned will have gone away."

"I guess this is settled then," Minta said, not sounding too pleased, yet somewhat relieved.

"I will bring you the proper paperwork for Cruxh and Herbert when they are done. It won't take long," Dow said. He opened one of his desk drawers and took a letter set out.

"Then you better follow me," Minta said, looking at Herbert. She held the door open for them to leave Dow alone in his office with his weird dog bed. That dog bed alone was reason enough to leave with Minta without asking too many questions about the man's change of heart.

As soon as he stepped away from Dow's unusual charm, the voice said, "*Please.*"

Minta coughed.

13

IF ONLY UNDEAD COULD BLUSH

orris' luck was turning. He'd found Agatha without lifting a finger. Most would think it'd been gods intervening into their lives, but not Morris. Life was full of weird coincidences, like a picture dropping from the wall when you spoke ill of the person. Or dreaming about a major catastrophe the night before and then hearing about how zombies had wiped out an island outside Necropolis. Or winning the lottery. It was a small chance, but a chance nevertheless. It didn't mean gods or the universe had a plan for you. Chaos and coincidences, that was what finding Agatha felt like. If you asked the gods, they would say it'd been them. But they liked to take credit for everything, even the creation of the Universe, which according to the cosmos came into existence with a bang.

There was something in how Agatha held herself that made Morris forget what he was doing there. The woman made him think of how it was a shame that humans were made to die. Until now, the fact hadn't bothered him. It'd seemed more like something to look forward to.

"Miss Wicks, about Petula Upwood. You know her?" Morris asked.

"Oh yes, we went to school together. I hope she's doing fine," Agatha said.

"Yes, perfectly fine, but she, we, need another necromancer to assist us, and she suggested you, as you've worked together successfully before," Morris said.

"She said that?"

"Yes, in her own words," Morris said. In a way, she had. Hadn't she? Maybe not putting too much emphasis on successful, but at least the word "good" had been mentioned.

A group of men walked past them. They looked drunk and cheerful. Despite their current state, Morris saw them observing him and the necromancer. Morris shifted his weight, moving his balance away from the cane and correcting his posture.

"I'm sorry. This must seem odd to you, me being forward and seeking you out like this," Morris said.

Agatha frowned. "Mr. Reinhardt, I'm not sure what this is all about, but I don't mind you being forward, as I should already be back at my mistress' house. So, say what you need to say."

Morris gave her a friendly smile, which didn't disarm the woman as intended. This horrid night must have skewed his usual charm. Normally women were putty in his hands, and Agatha shouldn't be an exception. Or the other necromancer had put a curse on him, putting him off his game. Then again, necromancers might be a different breed altogether.

"Hearing me out will only take a moment of your time, and I assure you that Mrs. Chaplain would approve of you helping us out, as we are her close acquaintances."

"Then you better help me get her goods on my coach, and you have that time to say your piece," Agatha said. She turned and bent to lift up the rolled mat, which had tumbled against the coach.

Morris followed her example, letting his cane rest against the coach. He squatted down to pick up the bulky mat. There was discomfort in his bad leg when he pushed himself straight, taking the full weight of the load.

"Petula suggested you'd take over possession from her following tonight's awakening. Would that interest you?" he puffed. He stepped more to his left as Agatha guided the package closer to the coach's door. Whatever was wrapped inside the mat swayed between them, weighing as much as an ox. Or, to be accurate, weighing as much as an ox's hind leg, which was the mass of your average male.

"I wouldn't mind helping Petula out, but I'll have to get permission from my mistress before I take on any other clients," Agatha said.

"Yes, of course," Morris said, sounding less winded. "We could pop into her place and ask."

"Oh, I was thinking like tomorrow, earliest," Agatha replied.

"This has to happen tonight. Miss Upwood is leaving Necropolis tomorrow."

"She is? I always thought she'd stay. She liked being a necromancer so much," Agatha said.

"She's going back to her family."

"Oh, that makes sense. But tonight?" Agatha asked.

"Yes, we wouldn't ask if this wasn't an emergency. We had to do an impromptu awakening."

"I guess I could always ask my mistress," Agatha said. She left an unsaid "but" hanging in the air.

"I'm sure she'll agree. As I said before, this is beneficial for all of us," Morris said, and together they pushed the mat onto the coach's floor. It rolled open, and a head lolled out. Morris found himself staring into Jeffrey Gilliam's dead eyes.

He gasped for breath, looking at the man with disbelief. His mouth must have hung open, or something else gave away his astonishment, as Agatha asked, "Mr. Reinhardt, what is wrong?"

"That's Mr. Gilliam," he said and frowned.

"Gilliam?" Agatha asked next to him, peering inside the coach. She'd stepped aside to let him do the final push.

"Yes, that's Wilbur's missing driver," Morris said. He took hold of the mat and opened it more, but the mat was tightly wrapped around the man's body. He'd have to get in the coach and wrangle it open to see better, but he was sure he saw blood on it. "Where did you find him?"

"I bought him at the market booth where they sell roadkills and other recycled meats. You know, that's an ecological way to buy meat. I don't believe in the processed stuff."

"But that's Jeffrey."

"I'm sorry, but I'm not sure what you mean," Agatha said.

"He was just with us a moment ago, before he went missing. He's not roadkill or ecological meat. Jeffrey is Wilbur's driver." Morris felt like someone was messing with him. This was beyond crude.

"You keep saying that, but—" Agatha said.

"He shouldn't be in your coach. Someone killed him," Morris interrupted her.

"Oh, that's horrible," Agatha said.

"It is," Morris said. He wasn't sure what to do or say next. He looked at Agatha and then back at Jeffrey. "I think I better talk to the man who sold him to you. Will you guide me there?" Morris asked and shut the coach door; watching the man's dull, dead eyes disturbed him.

"I should be heading back to my mistress. The guests must have already arrived, and she has nothing to serve, and then the whole night will be ruined, and that's because of me. I got the dates mixed up. I thought this was another kind of party. Not a party for the undead, who definitely won't eat veal, and—" Agatha said and stopped. She blinked her eyes, taking in all that had happened and what she'd said.

Morris wanted to draw a deep breath in on her behalf. He wasn't sure what she'd said, but he'd heard "mistress" and "definitely won't eat veal." He could understand her agitation. Talking to Bertha was alarming enough in a social context, let alone working for her.

"Wait here by the coach. I'll get my associates to go to Mrs. Chaplain's house and explain why you can't come back straight away. She'll understand when it comes from them," he said.

"Miss," Agatha said.

"What?"

"Miss Chaplain. She never married."

"Er... I didn't know that... But anyway, wait here while I explain the situation to my associates."

"Okay," Agatha said. She took her teeth out of her purse and pushed them back into her mouth when Morris began walking. He heard sucking.

Morris made his way back to the coach. He heard a

murmur coming from inside. At least he didn't hear arguing. Morris often wondered how Wilbur had the stomach to spend all his time with Ignatius. Whenever he saw one, the other wasn't too far behind. He opened the door and for a moment shut his eyes to push away the emerging doubt. The night was getting weirder, or you could say the morning was getting weirder, as dawn was fast on its way.

"Are we going? Where is she?" Ignatius asked as soon as the door opened.

"Not quite yet," Morris said.

"Then what?"

"There has been an incident, and I need to take Agatha to talk to her meat vendor," Morris said.

"You are babbling nonsense." Ignatius didn't look pleased. Not that he ever did.

"What is it, Morris? Is Miss Wicks all right? Will she help us?" Wilbur asked.

"She's fine, and she might help us, but before she can there's one thing we need to sort out. I'm afraid there was a body wrapped inside her mat, and it was your driver, Wilbur," Morris said.

"Jeffrey?" Wilbur asked. His voice wavered.

"Yes, he's dead. Someone sold him to Agatha, and if you let me handle this, I'll find out who and why," Morris said.

"This doesn't make sense. It can't be him. You have to be mistaken," Wilbur said.

"I'm afraid it is, but I'm not sure why or how he got inside Agatha's mat. I'll find out, if you let me. But I have to ask you to go to Miss Chaplain's house and explain why Agatha is engaged at the moment. We'll join you shortly," Morris said.

Wilbur stood up, making the coach rock. Morris' leg, resting on the step, waved along with the motion.

"Sit down," Ignatius snapped.

"No, I need to see him myself. I can't just go sit in Mrs. Chaplain's house and do nothing."

"Yes, you can. We are already wasting time with this nonsense."

"Ignatius," Morris warned him.

"All right. Have it your way," the man said.

"Wilbur, Ignatius is right. Not about wasting time,

but it's better if you don't see. Agatha and I will talk to the meat vendor and meet up with you as soon as we make sense of this. I promise, his death will be noted, and justice will be served."

"Okay," Wilbur said and slumped back down. He looked beside himself. His face had gone pale, and he looked confused. "If you think it's better, then it has to be." Wilbur took out his handkerchief and patted his forehead.

"We'll follow you as soon as we can," Morris said and took hold of the door to shut it.

Ignatius stopped him by pushing his hand against the door. "Who will take us?"

"Eh," Morris said. He hadn't thought that far.

"For Kraken's sake. I can drive my own coach," Wilbur said and stood up. The coach rocked again.

"Are you sure?" Morris asked.

Wilbur stepped through the door, forcing Morris to move aside.

"Do you think I want to be stuck in there with that insufferable man after what he said?" Wilbur asked when he'd pushed the coach door shut.

Morris was sure Ignatius could hear them. "I guess not. But are you sure you can handle it?"

"I've been around a lot longer than you. I used to know my way around horses and women. I wasn't always a family man. Let me tell you, you better find a wife and soon, or else you'll get kicked in your private parts, the way you're going, and that's not fun. Believe me. You don't want Ira or Ignatius to find you one."

"I will," Morris said, unsure what the man was babbling about and what any of this had got to do with Ira or Ignatius.

"Before you go," Wilbur said. "I only said that because you are a decent man. I've always thought that about you, despite your taste for partying and ladies. I was never made for that sort of life. Those dalliances in my youth were good for then, but home and family means more to me than anything else. Don't make the same mistakes as Ignatius did. Ending up alone and bitter is not a way for a man to live his life." He landed his hand on Morris' shoulder and squeezed it.

"Thank you," Morris said, still unsure what the man

was going on about. He left him. The thought of ending up like Ignatius repulsed him. And Wilbur was wrong. He was nothing like Ignatius. He wasn't a control freak who opened and closed his house door three times before entering or exiting, and he wasn't rude or bitter. No, he wasn't, but Morris was wrong in one respect. Ignatius had had the same taste for life as Morris did back in the day, but things had changed when his obsessive symptoms from childhood returned in his late thirties. No one knew what'd triggered the change, except Ignatius, but he wasn't one to disclose his heart. But when Morris saw Agatha waiting for him, sucking her teeth, he shook Wilbur's comparison away, not wanting to think about the spiteful old man.

◆

Minta guided Herbert to her office. There was this what-is-one-supposed-to-say-in-this-kind-of-situation silence between them. You know, your clever brain won't come up with anything decent to say even when you bombard it again and again with questions. And when someone, at last, speaks up, the rest will respond with nervous laughter, making everyone even more uncomfortable. And at the end of the night, when you are lying on your bed alone, rethinking the day, you finally have that epiphany about what to say, but by then it's too late.

Before Minta knew how to conduct herself, before she'd become the Mayor, she'd have chosen to stay silent. But now she knew there had to be a release to the oppressive pressure. She had to be the one to release it, to make the man feel at ease with her, despite not being so sure about him. There were occasions when it was best to leave the first words to someone else. On those occasions, the conversation was a power play, trying to make the other slip and let them ramble on and on until a satisfactory conclusion was met, but this was not such an occasion. They needed to trust each other if they were to work together, and the only way to achieve that was through true interest towards him. The trouble was, what kind of question or observation would make him open up? Sometimes Minta wished she'd been born with the natural talent to be social, but she hadn't. *Six Steps to Win Friends and*

Twelve Ways to Influence People had changed her life. Not a title she would have chosen.

"Mr. Ringworm, or may I call you Herbert?" Minta asked.

"Herbert is fine," he replied.

The kitchen maid, Ann, passed them, but this time a footman accompanied her. She blushed when she saw Minta and Herbert. She and the footman hurried their steps, holding back repressed laughter, which bubbled out of their lips as soon as they were around the corner.

"New love, what a thing," Minta said.

"I guess so."

Minta's heels clicked against the floor. She knew without having to concentrate that the man made no noise as he walked. His clothes didn't rustle. He didn't stomp his feet. He walked without his head popping from side to side. She'd been like that. She decided to test whether her hunch was right.

"I don't know many who can handle themselves with werewolves."

"That's because most people think you need to be more agile and stronger than them, but that's a mistake," Herbert said.

Minta wanted to jump in to finish his sentence, but she waited.

Herbert didn't disappoint. He said with a livelier voice, "They are animals when they are in their wolf-form, despite what their legal status says. You better play against their instincts if you want to survive. But I'm sure you know this."

She smiled. "I've had my dalliances with them, but never one on one, and never without something longer than my hand," Minta said. Her purpose had never been to kill. Like the man had said, werewolves had legal status in the city and beyond its borders. They were human beings with a monthly affliction. "What I gather is that you handle yourself differently."

The man looked at Minta, measuring her reaction. After a while, he said, "The point is not to harm. The point is to survive. Some use weapons and traps, and that's okay, as there's always the possibility of the werewolf biting your head off. But where's the fun in that?"

Ha, she'd known that the man was a wrestler. Minta was sure she'd seen him in the ring. Dow didn't know she knew about his habits or that she herself had seen several fights. It was the monster hunter force that'd started the underground fighting scene, and she was still in contact with her old troop. But the matches were condemnable. The Mayor in her hated them and would shut them down if she could, but the huntress in her knew you couldn't weed violence out of society.

"Someone might argue that nothing about it's fun," she said. She wondered if the man's past was the reason why Dow had a sudden change of heart. Minta had wanted to decline the offer, and still did, but she trusted Dow even with her life.

"They'd be right. But when you can't do anything else, you better do what gives you money to put food on the table," Herbert said. He reached to open the door to let Minta into her own office.

She let him. Minta wasn't sure what she would find there. Maybe a half-eaten Mrs. Maybury or a ghoul curled into a ball, wailing in the corner, which was more likely when taking Mrs. Maybury into consideration. Minta braced herself for what she was about to see and entered her office.

What she found there was even more disturbing than she could have imagined.

Cruxh sat next to Mrs. Maybury, and there was a smile on the woman's face. They looked shocked and caught when Minta and Herbert stepped in. Minta was sure that if an undead could blush, Mrs. Maybury would have glowed bright red. Minta fought to get her words out. Mrs. Maybury and Cruxh sat frozen in their positions an inch away from each other. Cruxh's hand hung in the air as if he'd hastily withdrawn it from the councilwoman's arm. There was an awkward pause as everybody in the room wished time could be rewound, or at least that there'd been a knock on the door.

Minta coughed, and then said, "Mr. Cruxh, I found Mr. Ringworm to assist you. He's, as you asked, someone capable of tracking down the ghouls and bringing them to justice." Her words released the room from its spell. Cruxh inched away from Mrs. Maybury, keeping a grin on his face. The grin could be a mask of "*nothing to see here*" or "*yes, I just did that.*" Minta didn't want to know which it was.

It didn't take long for Mrs. Maybury to recover from the initial shock of being caught with her pants down, or at least caught with her guard down, which was the same thing for the woman.

She said, "That scrawny kid?!"

Minta wouldn't call Herbert scrawny, but then again, she knew better than Mrs. Maybury what functional muscles looked like. They weren't huge and bulging, requiring their own carriage to be hauled around. Herbert's were lean and fast.

"Yes, him," the Mayor said and offered no other explanation. Not because she couldn't explain, but because the scene between the ghoul and the undead had rendered her speechless. Such a union might be harmful for the Town Hall in the long run. Not because of their different state of decomposition, but because it wasn't wise to date where you worked. There would be tears, and Minta wasn't keen on hearing a ghoul wail.

"You say *that's* going to defend my honor?" Mrs. Maybury said. Gone were the softness and vulnerability. Her eyes narrowed. There was even an attempt to sneer, but her facial muscles didn't comply.

Cruxh stood up and put distance between him and the undead.

He said, "Mrs. Maybury, I will help him. You have nothing to worry about. We will restore your honor." His words softened the expression on the woman's face. It still didn't make her appear pleasant.

"I'd rather work alone," Herbert said.

"What do you have to hide?" Mrs. Maybury asked and turned her full attention to Herbert. The man wavered. Before anyone could answer, she said, "I do have to insist Cruxh goes with him. At least he's on my side."

Minta smiled. She admired the other woman. She knew how to use selective memory to her advantage. But Minta was glad of the woman's change of heart. They needed Cruxh.

"Mrs. Maybury is right, we need both of your expertise if you're going to bring the ghouls back here, unharmed, before morning."

The undead woman opened her mouth, but Cruxh interrupted her. "It is my pleasure to assist you, Mister

Ringworm," Cruxh said and offered his hand to Herbert.

The man hesitated. He looked at the huge claw with long nails and blackened fingers.

Minta coughed.

Herbert gave the ghoul his hand.

"Mr. Ringworm, together we will fetch the attackers. You can count on my loyal support," Cruxh said, and he lowered his head and bowed.

Herbert said nothing. The ghoul lifted his head and peered into his eyes.

Herbert took a step back.

"I'm glad you find it possible to work together. This is of the utmost importance. You two better wait here for Dow to bring you the necessary papers to arrest the ghouls, and then you should be on your way to their lair. In the meantime, I'll take Mrs. Maybury home," Minta said.

Actually, she didn't know if there was a lair or not. She'd never thought about where the ghouls lived. They seemed to be hanging around every corner in the city, doing odd jobs. This shouldn't be. She should have been paying attention, not ignoring the ghouls like the rest of the city did.

"Where's—" Minta said.

"I'm not leaving. That's out of the question. I want to be part of restoring my honor," Mrs. Maybury said.

"You can't exactly follow them into the ghouls' lair," Minta said.

"Why not? I'm able to handle myself," the woman said.

"There's no question about that, but they've marked you as their prey. It would be too dangerous," Minta said.

"Is that true?" Mrs. Maybury asked and turned to meet Cruxh's eyes.

Cruxh shuffled his feet and looked at the woman. "If their itch for undead meat has taken over, there is a possibility that I might not be able to protect you. I think it's better if I and Mr. Ringworm take this journey alone and persuade the ghouls to come with us."

"Persuade?" Herbert asked.

"Yes, persuade. Or what did you have in mind?" Cruxh asked.

"I'm not entering a lair full of ghouls without an army or armed with traps and weapons," Herbert said.

His words stunned Cruxh.

Before a conflict could start, Minta said, "I'm certain what Mr. Ringworm means is that you should go prepared and respect the rights of both Mrs. Maybury and the ghouls." She looked at Herbert and pursed her lips.

"Yes, I meant we go prepared," Herbert said.

The ghoul beamed. He looked deep into Herbert's eyes. Minta couldn't even imagine what went on inside the ghoul's head. She always found Cruxh's eagerness disturbing. There was something in his eyes that made the receiver think they should live up to his expectations and do the right and difficult thing or the eyes would be disappointed. People with such talent were generally ostracized. Not because they were bad people, or ghouls; quite the opposite, actually. It was because people felt uncomfortable and inferior around them.

"Are you sure you won't need me to come with you?" Mrs. Maybury asked.

"In an ideal situation, you'd go with them to be a witness," Minta said. Back in her monster hunting days, she'd have used the word bait. "But I can't let you go with them, Mrs. Maybury. You are too valuable alive and here."

"Alice," Mrs. Maybury said.

"What?" Minta asked.

"Call me Alice," Mrs. Maybury said.

Minta flinched.

"Alice," Minta said and let the name hang in the air. "It'd make it easier to use you as a witness to draw the ghouls out, but that's something I'm not willing to do. Like I said earlier, you should go home and leave the matter to the two of them."

"The Mayor is right. It would be too dangerous," Cruxh said.

"Then I'm going with you. If my coming along gives you a better chance, then it's settled. You can use me as a witness if Miss Stopford sees that as a wise course of action. I won't sit idle while you go out there and risk your life," Mrs. Maybury, or Alice, as she wanted to be called, said. She didn't seem to see anyone else in the room except Cruxh.

Minta opened her mouth, closed it, and opened it again. She said, "If you think it necessary, then who am I to say no." Who was she to stand in the way of the woman's happiness? Or destruction?

"Then we better get going!" Mrs. Maybury said and marched out of Minta's office.

Cruxh rushed after her, nodding to the others in apology.

"Wait," he wailed. "My dear Mrs. Maybury, it is not that simple, and we have to wait for the papers."

"It doesn't work that way, you know it as well as I do," Herbert said.

"No, not exactly. But you will be there to make sure everything goes accordingly. I'm counting on you. We both need this. We both know what's at stake," Minta said. She truly hoped that Herbert was as good as Dow seemed to think, or as the man himself thought.

"I'll get the ghouls," he said.

"You better."

"Shall I wait for Dow outside?"

"If you wish," Minta said. "And Herbert?"

"Yes?"

"I need you to keep an eye on those two."

"Okay," he said and left her alone.

Minta took her notebook and pen from the desk. It was a shame that a young man like Herbert carried the dead with him. The spirit who trailed after the man was the worst kind. Sometimes spirits lost their minds, so that there was nothing left but need and want, and there was no way to quiet that thirst. If and when he got back, she'd help the spirit pass over or it'd consume the man. She opened the notebook and wrote down the date and time.

14

FREEFALL OF HELP

Petula knew people acted foolishly, but she'd never seen anyone who people would consider to be rational disregard common sense so badly as to follow a group of ghouls into the abyss. Not when you were a corpse. The trouble with the undead was that they stopped fearing for their lives and found their after-death stamina unbeatable. Such arrogance was amplified in Ira, who had enough ego to share with the whole city. But she'd expected more from the man. For Kraken's sake, the man had built a huge banking empire. But maybe she had to finally acknowledge that success had nothing to do with rationality and logic; that luck and background had a greater role to play than anyone would like to say.

"You have to help him!" Kitty said next to her. She heard someone else say those words, but instead of "him" the voice said "me," pushing past the usual protective aura she'd put around her to quiet the needs of the dead. She looked around and only saw the woman, who'd been unnaturally quiet.

"What do you want me to do?" Petula asked. The dogs at the woman's feet tilted their heads and locked their black eyes on to her. Bella and Lugosa confirmed Petula's belief that there was a lot to be said for cats. Cats saw the spirit world and would definitely tell her who'd been lurking behind her all night. She had her suspicions, however.

"You have to go after him! It's your duty." The word "duty" echoed in the vault. It wasn't a pretty sound.

Petula had grown up with women like Kitty who knew nothing about life. They expected everything to be handed to them. They thought what they said was the truth, and if someone insisted on thinking otherwise, they were rude and irrelevant. Petula's mother wasn't like Kitty per se, but she'd collected a flock of women and men around her who acted the same. The concentrated power of *them* always made Petula wish she had the power of witches. The power to curse.

"It was your husband's free choice to pursue the ghouls. This has nothing to do with me and my relationship with him." Petula said every word slowly to let them sink in.

"Ha, we'll see," Kitty said, a smug smile on her face.

Petula opened her book.

"You know, he has the key," Kitty said as soon as Petula had found her spot.

"Key?" Petula asked. She had a sinking feeling that there'd been a reason for the woman's smugness. Petula was even surer that the two dogs were chuckling, but that would be impossible.

"To the gate leading out of here. You can wait here with me until someone notices we haven't come back or you can go after my husband. It's your choice," Kitty said, and there was no doubt about her smugness now.

Petula lowered the book and looked at Kitty and then at the hole, then she glanced out of the vault's door to the locked gate. She hadn't been paying attention. She should have.

"I can help you," Kitty said.

"How?" Petula said, and promptly found out what Kitty meant by "help." The woman pushed her into the hole. Petula could try to latch her fingers around the edge before she went down, but that'd mean she either had to let go of her needlework book or her necromantic kit. She wasn't willing to part with either.

"You fiendish woman. If I get out of here, I'll see to it that your soul won't rest..." Petula shouted, and swallowed the rest of her words as a gush of air whipped against her. This was a good thing, as it was normally customary to shout things like: "Oh, my gods, don't let me die!" Or even better: "Why me?" Then again, Petula had always known gods and silly questions had nothing to do with death. It was your body running out of time. Instead, she concentrated all her efforts on looking for Ira underneath her, hoping the man was intact enough to catch her before she plummeted to her death.

But the sound of Petula's body smacking against the ground never came. Ira's arms moved up and down with force as he caught her. His body had gone into protective mode.

"I'll kill your wife!" Petula said, lying in the man's arms. In books, women often craved moments like this; Petula knew that. She'd always found those rescue scenes silly. Now, after experiencing it outside the pages, she could testify that it was as inane as she'd thought, despite the palpitations of her heart. She knew how to distinguish the rush of adrenaline from love.

"Get in line," Ira said, and let her down onto the ground.

The two of them stood in a cave. The only light coming in was through the hole in the ceiling. The drop from the vault was surprisingly short. A ghoul could easily leap from the ground, latch on to the soil underneath the opening, and climb back up. For the human and the undead, escaping through the opening would have required cooperation from Kitty, but she was gone. She was back at the gate, arguing with the gargoyle, with lousy results.

There are occasions when you find yourself in a black abyss, but such occasions are better experienced alone, without a banker looming over your shoulder. Petula found Ira's closeness disturbing, despite him being technically her creation. Considering where they had got her, there was a lot to be said against free will and original thought.

"Where are we?" she asked. She could see a tunnel leading out, but beyond that everything was a mystery.

"I'm not sure," Ira said.

"Are you intact?" Petula asked.

Ira was silent.

A weaker person might find not seeing and hearing anything paralyzing, but Petula had experienced worse. She'd let her classmates bury her alive in a coffin as an experiment. It hadn't gone that great, as her classmates had forgotten her, either by accident or on purpose. She was more prone to believing the latter. She'd shown them how to rise back from the dead. Petula did now what she'd done then. She concentrated on the moment at hand, not fearing the future or blaming the past.

"Not quite. I think my right leg broke in the fall. It doesn't hurt, but I'm not sure if I can put my full weight on it. Catching you made it worse," Ira said, after checking his systems.

"Let me see." Petula crouched down next to the undead. She opened her kit and let the will-o'-the-wisp out of her bag.

The creature screeched, yet hovered over Petula's head.

The light of the will-o'-the-wisp was enough for Petula to see the leg. Ira was right. The fall had twisted his knee joint out of its socket. His tattered flesh prevented it from sliding off. The knee joint needed metallic plates to keep it intact.

"I have to push it back in. It might pop out again if you make any sudden movements or put too much pressure on it."

"Do what you can," Ira said; he sounded uninterested.

Petula followed his gaze and saw what he was looking at. The light had illuminated a carved relief on the cave's wall, which continued out through the tunnel. There were square-looking ghouls, humans, and wildlife on it. It was exquisite. There were symbols underneath the picture in a language Petula couldn't understand. She popped the knee back into place and stood up.

"That's something," she said.

"You could say that—and all this is mine," Ira said.

The more time Petula spent with Ira, the more obvious it was that the man's self-indulgence knew no bounds. Though, this was nearing the level of absurdity.

"We better head back up," she said, wanting to add: "*before you get us killed.*"

"No, we are going down the tunnel and bringing the

thieves to justice."

Petula entertained the thought of taking Ira under her control, making him her meat-puppet, as was intended when humans first experimented with necromancy. The only trouble was that it was illegal. If Ira noticed, she'd not only lose her necromantic license, she'd be jailed.

"I don't think they took anything."

"Of course they took my gold," Ira said.

"All the lockers in the vault were intact, and I didn't see them carrying anything with them. Leave the matter be. It's foolhardy to go after them with just two of us," Petula replied.

"You can hide rubies, emeralds, diamonds, and gold inside the lining of a coat. It has been done several times. I've done that very thing in my youth. Believe me, when there are uninvited guests inside a vault, they aren't there to have a nice Sunday stroll. No one steals from me," Ira griped.

When Petula said nothing, Ira added, "And I have you with me."

She snorted. "What do you want me to do? Hit them with my book?"

"It worked fine in the vault. They were scared of that," he said and nodded towards the red book tucked underneath Petula's armpit.

Petula laughed. It was a hollow, superior laugh.

"This?" she asked and took the red book in her hand and waved it in front of the man. "This is a book about needlework. This can't harm anyone or anything. It might have surprised the ghoul in the vault, but this can't even beat a human into obedience, let alone a ghoul."

Ira bared his teeth. He said, "You are still a necromancer."

"Yes, but like I said to your horrid wife, that doesn't do any good with ghouls. They are not undead like you are. You need a priest or demon hunter."

"But—"

"Here, have this if it makes you feel better," Petula said and handed the book to the man.

Ira opened the book and read aloud, "*New Edition of Needlepoint Masterpieces by Mildred Whither. Third edition.*"

Petula glanced at the book, already missing it.

"Of course, those morons had to hire a second-grade

necromancer who thinks needle and thread are more important than being powerful," Ira said. He shuffled into the tunnel. Soon Petula couldn't see him anymore, but she heard his murmuring.

She looked back at the way they'd come and then at the tunnel, moving her eyes along the continuous relief as far as she could. She listened to the background noises of the place. There was a quiet whisper of air and life somewhere deeper within. Petula hurried after the man; he had her book, after all.

◆

Jeremiah Black had tried all night to push past the necromancer's barrier. He was sure she'd seen glimpses of him every so often, but she'd refused to engage despite knowing the dead gravitated towards her. It was her moral duty to help and not to shy away from her skills. Not that he hadn't done the same, but he'd been too busy to address such matters, as he was keeping the undead alive. She had no excuse. All she did was read.

"You have to help me!" he screamed.

She glanced towards him, but once again, she didn't react. She'd heard him. He was sure of that. So there was hope. "My body is still fresh enough. Leave this and be the necromancer you know you can be. What you're doing is what a servant does and nothing to do with the powers an independent practitioner has. I'll pay you anything you want, but you have to come with me, now," he pleaded.

She looked past him over her shoulder to the vault door. He saw her biting her lip.

"It's the best offer you'll get tonight. And I won't even demand that you stay. I can pay for your voyage home. To Leporidae Lop," he said. "It's safer that way, anyway," he added.

Even if the necromancer had intended to reply, she had no time. The other woman in the vault pushed the necromancer down the hole.

He wailed and surged towards the woman, slamming against her back. He went through without sticking. The woman turned on her heels, and the two dogs followed behind as she made her way towards the gate they'd come through, leaving him staring into the abyss.

At first, he worried the necromancer had died, but he could sense her. She shone like the sun, or like a duck amongst the swans. But the thought of going after her repelled him. There was something he couldn't quite understand keeping him away. Jeremiah tried to follow her down the hole several times, but every time he made a move, his whole essence screamed danger. The air smelled of something. Something he didn't like. Not dead and dying. That he'd gotten used to, and it wasn't as if he could actually smell anything, lacking the usual parts for the job, but there it still was, the odd, pungent aura.

Jeremiah hesitated, but he was forced to leave the hole and the necromancer behind. He had to find another way. He'd follow the woman and her dogs. She looked like someone who got things done, to say the least. Jeremiah took a crack at the gate, trying to make it move from its hinges. It didn't budge. He hadn't quite tapped into his inner poltergeist, despite all the screaming. Emotional outbursts were just a normal side-effect of the confusion of being in limbo. He was forced to listen to the woman persuade, threaten, bribe, and bore the gargoyle to death to open the gate. He did that longer than he cared to admit. Jeremiah eventually had to accept he'd have to approach the gargoyle if he wanted to get the woman out. The gargoyle didn't even bat an eyelash when it saw him. And it saw him. Gargoyles saw the dead along with all the other dimensions concurrently present. Their ability to see everything was why you could call them inanimate. But Jeremiah had all the time in the world to get the gargoyle's attention and make it understand that it would be healthier for it if the woman passed swiftly.[27]

◆

Bertha Chaplain had been waiting for an opportunity to write herself into the history books for a long time. Of course, with the help of the bankers, but she'd have the last word. The people would remember her forever as the woman who saved

---

27 The gargoyle had already gathered that much. It was only letting the thought of moving settle in, which wasn't helped by Jeremiah's and the woman's constant jabbering.

Necropolis. Also, if everything went as it should, she'd be there, enjoying history being made. Maybe at some point, she'd be able to transfer her consciousness into a younger body.

Bertha glanced at herself in the mirror over the dresser in the hallway before opening the front door. All her body parts, including her fabulous hair, were in their rightful place, as they should be. She took wax and a bottle of formaldehyde out of the dresser drawer and coated her hair and face. When she was satisfied, she went to the door and drew it open, giving a pleasant smile to her guests.

"Good evening," she said.

William Cockerham stood on her front steps. He gave a polite nod and said, "Blessings to this house."

"Do come in," Bertha said, stepping out of the man's way.

Soon after, the rest of the members arrived. She smiled at their surprise that she was opening her own front door. To the last members, she said with ease,

"This meeting is being conducted with great discretion. Now, step in before anyone sees you." She led them into her drawing room, where the rest of the members waited.

The Union of the Undead jumped eagerly into the charade. The thought of secrecy made them feel special and important. Bertha found it amusing how they kept whispering and acting as if they were part of some great plot. She was sure someone mentioned deploying his agents as soon as they got home, and there was even a rumor going around that acquiring a cat[28] would make a huge difference.

Bertha positioned herself in the center of the room so everyone could see her. She watched the party members and couldn't help but notice a few of them were missing. She frowned but continued along with the plan.

"My dear friends," Bertha said. "We've gathered tonight to discuss our party's future. But before we get into the details, I've prepared dinner for you to enjoy. So, would you be so kind as to join me in the dining room and take the seats reserved for you?"

Everyone followed her.

---

28   Preferably a long-haired white cat with blue eyes.

The dining room had been painted white. It had a long table and a fireplace without a fire. She'd lit candles all around the room, and the silver moon shone in through the high windows, straight onto the offering laid on the table. Some of the guests moaned when they saw their meal.

Bertha saw that everyone took their rightful places. It was important, as she had to separate those who had a habit of mutiny. At first, Martha Coffin had tried to sit close to her friends, but Bertha had taken her by her arm and guided her to sit next to her own seat. All the way there, she chatted pleasantly. Martha wasn't the worst of them. That was Mrs. Maybury, but she didn't see her anywhere. Bertha detested the woman, but she needed her to be on her side. The woman could twist anyone's arm to get her way. Maybe she'd stayed behind to pester the Mayor. A pleasant quirk of hers.

"Does anyone happen to know where Mrs. Maybury is?" Bertha asked, sitting down at the head of the table. She needed everyone who had enough power to swing the votes to be here.

The party members murmured.

"One of you has to speak up."

Martha cleared her throat and said, "Ghouls attacked her at the Town Hall meeting."

"How horrific," Bertha said, trying to sound genuine. But she couldn't help but think she'd finally gotten rid of her.

She took a moment too long to think about what the woman's absence might mean. When she noticed her long pause, she hurried to add, "Is she all right?"

"I don't know. We don't know... There was this terrific chase, and then the NDA[29] guys went and beat us and..."

All the party members burst into talk in unison in high, cheerful tones. There was even a smattering of laughter.

"Hm," Bertha said. She couldn't make head or tail of what was going on. She half-listened to what was said as she tapped her finger on the table. It was her cue to Agatha to bring in the dinner. She remembered a few moments later that the silly girl wasn't there to rescue her from this discord, and that the food was already laid out.

---

29   Necro Democratic Alliance

"Thank you, everyone! First thing tomorrow, I'll visit Mrs. Maybury to make sure she's all right and insist that she let me help with this sordid affair," Bertha said, raising her voice to silence the others.

There were still three more empty seats, which irritated Bertha.

"And what about George Astrid and Lacy Astrid? Were they attacked as well? And Cruxh?" She said the last name in a low, careful tone.

The chatter died. No one hurried to answer her.

Bertha waited a moment longer for someone to say something, anything, to get this over with, but still, they refused.

"What is it?" she asked.

No reply.

"If there has been a series of attacks against Union members, I need to know. It's unacceptable. Someone needs to speak up," Bertha said.

William Cockerham coughed.

"My dear William, what is it?" she asked, trying to sound pleasant, but failing. Besides Martha and Mrs. Maybury, William was one of the ones who was always trying to undercut her authority. He'd been the one who introduced ghouls into the Union. Finally, she could hold that decision against the man. Bertha grinned.

"We aren't sure what happened to Mr. and Mrs. Astrid, but I promise I'll find out. But Cruxh stayed behind to help the Mayor with the attack," he said.[30]

"The Mayor helped the ghouls to attack?" Bertha asked, stunned.

William laughed. A few of the other members followed his example. Some because Cruxh made them uncomfortable and others because the thought of Minta commanding an army of ghouls was something out of their nightmares.

"Now you're deliberately misunderstanding the whole thing. Mr. Cruxh is a polite young man who saw it as his

---

30 At this precise moment, Mr. and Mrs. Astrid were roaming the streets of Necropolis in search of something to bite into. Luckily for the citizens, they lived in a secluded housing area with high walls. Everyone knew zombies couldn't climb. Though they knew how to open doors thanks to something called muscle memory.

duty to mitigate Mrs. Maybury's agony by offering his help."

To call Cruxh a young man was absurd. Cruxh was older than anyone in the room, even though most of them were stiffs from another era. Cruxh was twice the age William was, but to him, he would always be that intelligent young man who he saved from a career of street sweeping by bringing him into politics.

Bertha wanted to reply that if she'd got everything right, Mrs. Maybury was attacked by a group of ghouls, and the men and women in the room had done nothing about it except have a nice evening stroll then head home to dress up fancy and come here and leave a ghoul to deal with the aftermath. If she didn't need them on her side, she'd call them a bunch of morons, but instead, she said, "Yes, Mr. Cruxh always seems to do the right thing. We're so lucky to have him around. If you, William, would be a dear and check on the Astrids, I'd be ever so grateful. It seems like we can do nothing about the attack for now, and we already have a Union member aiding the Mayor, so I don't see why we can't get on with tonight's agenda. But before we do that, I want you to enjoy the feast." Bertha waved her hand over the corpse.

Everyone went still, not knowing what to say. You simply didn't serve a whole body. Usually, they were sliced into thin servings and presented with parsley on a fancy dinner plate to make the affair, you know, tasteful. The guests looked at Bertha and then at the body. Martha let out a pent-up giggle. Her jaw snapped open, and saliva dripped from the corner of her mouth.

"Excuse me," she said.

"How old-fashioned!" another member of the Union said.

"Then dig in," Bertha said, finding her own unrefined words horrible. "*Dig in*," who says that?

No one cared about her unfortunate choice of words. They launched at the corpse, biting into the flesh.

The whole scene made Bertha hungry, but at the same time, she found it too horrific. The eating was too...too animalistic... No, maybe too common. Bertha looked away.

She forced herself to face her fellow Union members, who seemed happy. Now was the perfect time to say her piece.

"Why I asked you to come here... Don't stop eating

on my account," Bertha said. "You may have noticed that our city is in financial ruins and..." A string of flesh hung between Martha's teeth as she looked at Bertha with eager eyes. An old memory in her body wanted to convulse. She continued, "And I have to say, our beloved leader isn't up to the task of lifting us out of the rot. It's our duty to do something about it. That's why the citizens elected us. And I feel that if the matter is left alone, there won't be a city left when the bankers drive us into the ground with free racketeering and reckless money lending—"

"Ha, hogwash," William said, wiping the side of his mouth. William Cockerham was an aristocrat. His family was one of the oldest families in the city. His grandfather's father had been a powerful necromancer, and so had his father, but dear William hadn't followed in their footsteps. Instead, in his past life he had been in the business of importing and exporting trinkets and charms. If Bertha was correct, his daughter still did that, while William had retired and turned his mind to politics. William was one of those undead who was well preserved. He would almost look alive, if it wasn't for the dullness of his eyes.

Bertha smiled. "Then, my dear William, what do you think is happening?"

"Just your normal economic turmoil. It'll pass, as other situations have passed. I've seen these things many times. You need to let the markets do what they do and winnow out those not fit to handle their affairs."

"That means good people and undead will be ruined by the freefall of the economy. We can't let that happen," Bertha said.

"We can. We are all responsible for our actions and should bear the ramifications of them," William replied.

"Not when you are hunted by the most ruthless people and trapped in perpetual purgatory with cunning words and small print," she said without missing a beat.

There were mixed feelings around the table. Most of the guests had stopped eating by now and weren't sure what the two of them were arguing about. They watched Bertha's and William's match without comprehending the rules. They waited, ready to take sides with whoever won.

"Ruthless? No, they are men who know their professions and are there to aid our economy. Without them, how would a Tom, Dick, or Harry or even Sally ever get their ideas off the ground?" William asked.

"You are wrong. Monitored banking can secure a more stable economy, giving us control over what's happening in our own city. Now, anarchy is running us into the ground. We have to stop it. Or haven't you looked out of your window and seen how people are hunted down and murdered in our current situation?"

"Aren't we being a little over-dramatic?" William asked. It didn't get the response he intended. No one laughed. He said, "Yes, there'll be casualties, but less so than with what you propose. The control you're after won't remove future turmoil or make things better. The free market is a better way to balance the system than through regulations. Regulations with which only the rich and the big can compete."

"I'd argue otherwise; a financial committee tied to our Town Hall is a more secure way to ensure the well-being and happiness of all of our citizens."

"Why not remove gold while you're at it," William hissed.

"Yes, why not? It's inconvenient and unstable. With money regulated by the government, there's more money in circulation and more to give to others. It'll advantage our society. Who knows, maybe it'll even aid the University researchers in stopping the process of decay?"

That got a rise out of the others. The rotten faces around the table would like nothing more than a miracle cure for entropy.

"This is scandalous, and you are a moron to believe a committee can be our savior. It'll be our final doom. I won't accept this," William said, jumping up from his seat.

"Sit back down!" Bertha said.

William sat down.

"I'm a firm believer in hearing both sides of the argument, and I'm a firm believer in democracy. So don't storm out like you always do," Bertha said. From the look on the man's face, she'd won this round. "We'll decide this together. I'm just here to share the solution I've been thinking over for a long time, and I want a fair discussion about it. To see if it's something all of us can present together in a Town Hall meeting and to the people. They need to see their leaders doing something about their misery," Bertha said, smiling and moving her eyes from member to member. She was sure she was winning them over, even Martha, who often sided with William. The woman had wiped off the string of flesh and offered her full attention to Bertha.

"I think we all have to vote with our conscience when the time comes," William said. "And you haven't exactly come to us first, or does my memory serve me wrong? I recall seeing your comments on an article in the *Necropolis Heritage* about controlled monetary affairs."

"We are a union, and we vote as one. And as to the second matter, I can't help if people are curious about finding solutions to our problems and asking what I think is the best way about it. I've only talked at length about the concepts with the University's economics professor."

"I'll never accept a government-controlled financial committee into this city," William said.

Bertha massaged her hands out of habit. "It will be an important entity for our economy, which needs enlightened men on its board to see it's run properly. I'd reconsider your position," Bertha said. "And what do you think?" she said, letting her gaze glide over the rest of the members.

"What would such an entity do?" Martha asked.

"Ruin everything," William snapped before Bertha had time to answer.

"Regulate and control, for starters. We can see the markets are running as they should be. No wild goose chases that could bring our system down. It'll stabilize our society."

"Ha, stabilize it for who, I ask," William said.

"For all of us," Bertha said.

"With loose money?"

"Yes, with it and the rest. Don't you see, by the power of the committee, we politicians can create money and see it's used wisely. It's us in power, not anyone else. Us saying what's all right and what's not to the bankers. It's a new political entity with the power to regulate the laws and rules. That's what we need, and even you, William, can't argue against that."

"There has to be another way."

"None where we have a say in the matter; of course, speaking on behalf of our voters. But this doesn't have to be decided now. We have time to think it over. I wanted to bring it to your attention. You can make up your own mind, and then we can work together to form a plan."

"I still think gold and a free market is a more stable system."

"And this situation we are in now, is it stable? All of us have friends and relatives who have been destroyed by it. But enough arguing. We're repeating ourselves. Let's enjoy the rest of the meal and have a laugh."

Bertha made sure William didn't get a single word out of his mouth. "More meat?" she asked.

15

POWER AND DOMINANCE GO
TOGETHER LIKE PUDDING AND RICE

erbert waited for Dow outside the Mayor's office. He hated waiting, as he was beginning to doubt his decisions. Again, he was struggling with too much time left for thinking. Nothing good came out of it. In the distance, he heard the ghoul's and the undead's loud talking. He tuned it out, not caring about what had gotten them riled up. He knew he should pay attention, but instead, he focused on a minister or some other big shot passing him by, most likely with her assistant. They glanced towards him, and he felt an urge to hide.

"Good night," he said.

The minister looked at the Mayor's door and then at him. The woman nodded to Herbert.

He held her gaze, reminding himself of his master's words: "*You belong where you think you belong.*" This was no different from the ring. The rules might differ, but the game was the same. The game of power and dominance. Be the master of the situation but don't force the situation; that was another one of his master's sayings. Sometimes he thought it was nonsense, other times he swore that his master's approach to life worked.

The woman averted her gaze and hurried away with her assistant. Herbert went back to waiting.

"*Please, it's so cold,*" Ona said.

He tensed his leg muscles. The thing with Ona was that he should probably ignore her. Not play into her fantasies. Especially if she continued lying. There was no coldness where the dead were. There was no hurt. There was nothing but time, space, and that moment. But he had to answer. He couldn't let her suffer alone.

He whispered, "Where were you?"

"*Here, but it hurts,*" Ona said.

Again with the lies, but this was the first time she'd answered back.

"I'm trying," he said.

He waited for another response, but there was only the quiet murmur of the minister. Ona's pressure was still there, feeling like a solace of sorts.

Herbert let his gaze wander around the Town Hall corridors. Seeing all the statues of monsters made him wonder why there couldn't be some softness and light. Why did the city and its inhabitants have to be bred in darkness and the macabre? But if he looked carefully past the grotesque, he was surprised to find lightness. No other buildings in the city had white marble floors, and certainly not against white walls. This was almost rebellious. Definitely not designed by Johan Engel or Lilith Nutterbird, who'd done most of the important buildings in the city. Lilith had been the one to design the Library, the Royal Opera House, and the Clock Tower, and had built the University along with Johan Engel. The place was too hauntingly romantic for the two architects.

He didn't get any further with his thoughts; Dow interrupted him. Herbert had barely noticed the man walk up to him. Only when he was an arm's reach away did the man's presence jolt him awake.

"Dow," Herbert said, gritting his teeth.

"I have the legal documents for you and Mr. Cruxh," Dow said. "These are all you need to arrest the ghouls."

Dow handed over both the warrant for an arrest and

the document stating Herbert's position as an officer of the law. Herbert took them without saying a word. Without commenting on the smug expression on the man's face.

Herbert glanced over the watermarked documents with legal seals and bearing his name. His body relaxed. The papers would open doors for him and even save him if he needed a get-me-out-of-jail card. He pushed them inside his pocket next to Jeremiah's bottle. He'd forgotten he still had the mystery liquid with him.

"What about Cruxh's papers?" Herbert asked.

"I better hand them to him myself. Is he inside?" Dow asked.

"No, I think he's outside waiting with the undead woman," Herbert said.

"Aah. Then we better head there to meet them. Would the undead woman be Mrs. Maybury?" Dow asked.

"I think so."

They left the office behind and walked downstairs. Dow had this polite, controlled way about him. He kept his hand behind his back as he walked, making him look priest-like with his long black coat and calm but superior composure and an expression that said that even if Herbert insisted the world was about to come to an end or that he'd found a talking dog, nothing would surprise him.

Outside, they found the ghoul and the undead woman standing in uncomfortable silence a few feet apart. The ghoul's eager eyes greeted them before Herbert or Dow could decipher the situation. Herbert hated ghouls. They were unpredictable. And his new partner was more dangerous than the others. He smiled.

Dow stopped Herbert in the doorway before they joined the others. He coughed and said, "A word before you join them."

If he thought they were far away enough for the undead and the ghoul not to hear him, he thought wrong. When you're not restricted by the limitations of a live human body, any physical activity is more about your imagination than boundaries. For example, Cruxh, or any ghoul for that matter, could easily hear what the whole city did and said, but who cared to hear the discord of life? Who would have time for that? It'd require an artificial intelligence system with the capacity to process copious information at the same time and make conscious conclusions from it. Anybody with such a birth defect would probably go insane.

"I'm officially your boss now, and your loyalties and life lie with me," Dow said. "I need you to play by the book. No rash choices. Do we understand each other?"

"And Ira?" Herbert asked, looking out at the looming city under the full moon. Sometimes he thought the city itself was sentient, gifted with dramatic tendencies. It was always raining, cold, damp, gloomy, dark, and melancholic, and there was no end to the list. But tonight, it looked even more sinister than usual. More so now, as Herbert knew he was heading into a lair full of ghouls.

"Leave him to me," Dow said.

"Then we have an understanding," Herbert replied.

"Are we leaving now?" Mrs. Maybury interrupted them, glancing at Dow.

"Mrs. Maybury," Dow said, nodding to the woman and moving from the Town Hall steps towards her and the ghoul. Herbert followed him.

"You can leave as soon as I give Mr. Cruxh his papers," Dow said.

"Then go ahead," she replied.

Herbert was sure Dow clenched his teeth tighter together than usual, but he could be mistaken. But if he wasn't, maybe he should have allied himself with Mrs. Maybury. She looked like a woman with the power to take down Ira. There were no words to describe her. Herbert's own mother had been flowery and well-intentioned even in her disapproval. When she'd disowned him, she'd said it was for his own good, that he needed to learn to appreciate what it meant to stand by his actions. He'd have preferred Mrs. Maybury's frankness.

Dow moved to offer Cruxh the legal papers.

"An officer of the law?" Herbert heard the ghoul ask.

"Yes, you have been deputized to have the authority to seize the ghouls and bring them to face justice," Dow answered.

The ghoul straightened his humped back and beamed. Herbert made a note that Cruxh's glow rubbed Dow the wrong way. He was glad that there was someone else who didn't appreciate the mockery the ghoul made every time he opened his mouth.

"Thank you," Cruxh said and bowed his head.

"Good luck," Dow said and left them alone. As he moved back inside the Town Hall, he gave Herbert a look that was meant to put him in his place. It would take more than a look to discourage him from getting justice for Ona by any means necessary.

"What now?" Mrs. Maybury asked.

"Now we get weapons," Herbert said.

"But—" Cruxh said.

"We'll take my coach." Mrs. Maybury interrupted the ghoul. "Where are we heading?" she asked.

Cruxh opened his mouth, but the undead woman silenced him.

"Hallows Street," Herbert said.

"Where's that?" she asked.

"At the Mess," Herbert said.

"And where's that?" Mrs. Maybury asked when they reached her coach.

"It's in the bad part of the city, madam," her driver replied when they neared the coach, keeping the door open for them.

"Then we'll go there."

They left behind the Town Hall, which was moderately busy at this time of night. The city and its government never slept. They had a duty to hear all the petitions the citizens had, ranging from world peace to more serious issues.

◆

Minta sat in her office. She massaged her temples. Herbert, Mrs. Maybury—or Alice, as she wanted to be called—and Cruxh had left a moment ago. Her leadership was turning into a farce. She could always retire and leave the city to Ira and see what he made of it. This position was nothing but compromise after compromise on things like how to educate children (for free or not), how to handle the poor (use them as cheap labor or not), and what to do with the sick and elderly (push them into the sea or stash them in an old folks' home and lose the key). Now, as she thought about all the compromises she'd made and how pointless they were, she was reminded that she had wanted to learn how to paint for as long as she could remember.

Then there was the possibility that what Mr. Ringworm had said was false, and she only had Mrs. Maybury's issue and the protest to deal with, and Jeremiah's murder. She'd forgotten all about the last one. Dow would have to find out who did it so she could sentence them to serve in one of the city's labor camps.

The city didn't seem to lack prisons of all sorts. There were the labor camps, poor houses, institutions for the criminally insane where all the mad professors got sent, and then there were the common prisons where you put the wrongdoers who didn't fit into the places with fancy names. You could find a prison in almost every district, but still, there wasn't enough room for all the convicted.

Minta scribbled her first sentence in her notebook under today's date. If this was going to be the last chapter of her memoir, she had to get this right. People had to know the reason for her actions. Often enough, her actions were a reaction to the events, and other times, there was a coherent idea behind her policies. Like the one she'd started with: to make the city livable for all, despite their state of decay, sex, or their inner animal. But noble causes were easier to uphold from the sidelines, when you didn't need to think where and to whom the pennies went. Again, it was the economy thing making trouble. People had different, funny ideas of what belonged to whom, and certainly of what they and others deserved.

She drummed her fingers against the book, unable to write her plans down.

Suddenly she felt chilly, her arms going into goosebumps.

"Dow," she said before there was a knock on her open office door. She looked at her secretary past the documents and newspapers.

"Ma'am, may I come in?" Dow asked, lingering in the doorway.

"By all means. Are they gone?" Minta asked, more testily than she'd meant to. After all this time, she thought she'd have learned not to fear tomorrow, but now she found herself fretting not only about the future headlines but the day itself.

"Yes, with all the legal permits. I had to give Mr.

Ringworm more authority than I would have cared to," Dow said and moved in without making a sound.

Minta watched the heels of his feet, which barely touched the floor. One thing had always troubled her about the man: he never seemed to age. Not at all during the thirty-seven years they'd spent together. He looked the same and acted the same.

"The man bothers you?" Minta asked.

"He is a loose cannon, ma'am. I would have preferred to send someone else with them."

"Then why did you agree with him?"

"There wasn't time, and he was the best available. He is the best man to go after the ghouls. He was right about that. No law officer could match his abilities."

"Hm, I hope you're right about him. We need Mrs. Maybury to come back in one piece. Have you sent someone to check his claims?" she asked.

"Several someones."

"Won't you sit down?" Minta stated. The man stood there anticipating the end of the conversation, always in a hurry to get back to whatever he did.

"Ma'am, I'd rather not," Dow said.

Minta let her posture sag down. "How many times have I told you, Minta is fine," she said and scratched her head with her pen.

"I will sit," he said.

"Is that the only concession you're willing to make?"

"Ma'am," he said, a pained look on his face that was unbecoming in a man of his charisma. Dow walked to the couch and sat down as stiffly as he'd stood. Outside, the branches scratched against the window. When Minta looked at them, they stopped their attempt to break in. One day she'd catch them red-handed.

"We need to come up with a way to stop Ira," she said, still looking outside.

"How do you want to do that? We don't exactly know what he is planning," Dow said. He was using a different tone. He came alive in these kinds of moments. Gods forbid she ever let the man loose on his own.

"Don't we? I thought we knew. He has formed a coalition with Bertha and the other bankers, Vaughn, Sumner, and Reinhardt. It's such a shame to hear about young

Reinhardt. I always had such a good working relationship with his father. But sentiment won't help us against them. Do we know when they're planning their *attack*?" Minta asked. It felt absurd to use such a word. Attack was something you did with physical force, not with political maneuvers. When had the military slang snuck into the discussion of the common good?

"No, I don't think we do. But judging by Mr. Ringworm's urgency and by the fact that Mr. Worthwrite is alive again, they will make their intentions clear soon, and most likely publicly. Sooner than we would like."

"Tomorrow?"

"Maybe."

"Then we beat them at their own game," Minta said, and this time it was her who felt alive.

"How?"

"We form our own coalition of experts." Minta had been thinking of involving the bankers and other professionals for a while now. The current economic situation was due to reckless money lending overheating the system. And that was not all. What she'd gathered was that the bankers had been doing creative bookkeeping, which contorted the truth of their assets. It would only take one bubble bursting to bring the whole Necropolis down to its knees. One bankruptcy, taking away jobs and salaries. Minta had thought she had more time to come up with a new reform to fix everything, but she'd been naive to think so.

"Are you sure you want to intervene in that way?" Dow asked.

"What other choice do I have?"

"We could always make the threat obsolete," Dow said.

"You know my answer to that."

"Yes, ma'am," he said, looking disappointed.

"I'm afraid we have to go with a group of experts."

"Shall I set up a meeting?"

"Yes, do that."

"When? And who do you have in mind?"

"Tonight, before the protest. I need to have something to give to the people; either the bankers' cooperation or their heads."

Dow smirked. A rare treat. There was something

wicked about how his lips curled up. He stood up and said, "I'll set up the meeting here as soon as you give me their names."

"I guess we have to include Frederick Kilborn, two bankers, anyone with enough collateral and a somewhat good reputation, and bring me one of those buggers from the University. Someone who thinks they've figured out what the economy is. Get them...and before you go, ask that newspaper man here as well."

Dow's lips tightened. "Who would that be, ma'am?"

"R. Porter; who else?"

"Is that wise, ma'am? From what I have gathered, he works for the newspaper owned by Mr. Worthwrite's holding company. He is not someone I would call independent or impartial, or for that matter a reporter," Dow said.

"Even more reason to ask him. He used to be one of the greatest. I'm sure that astute, award-winning mind of his knows a good story when it sees one."

"If I must," Dow said.

"One more thing before you go. Find me Ira and his associates. I want to meet them here as well after I've had time to chat with my experts," Minta said. She hated playing silly games and prolonging the inevitable. With either outcome, this would be resolved tonight.

"Do you want me to arrest them?" Dow asked.

"No, give them an invitation they can't refuse."

"And what about Miss Chaplain?" Dow asked.

"Yes, I almost forgot all about her."

"She has to be dealt with. She has been gunning for your position ever since you got here."

"Yes, she has, but she can't do anything with that necromancer of hers. Bright girl, but not imaginative enough. We can deal with her later. She's harmless," Minta said.

"She should have gone with the other one," Dow said.

"Which one?"

"Someone else with less show and more talent."

"That's always the case with Bertha. The exterior means more than the substance. Should I be worried?"

"There is always a need to be cautious. I'll set up a meeting for you and Miss Chaplain tomorrow."

"Do that."

"Ma'am," Dow replied and left her alone with her thoughts. Back in the good old days in the monster hunter force, her thoughts had been about how to arrange her men and traps to catch beasts. What she did now wasn't that different; only the tools differed. Instead of barking orders like in the force, where her troops had been taught early on that she was their god, their father, their mother, sister, brother, lover, and their worst enemy, she had to use honey. But bankers had all the honey they could eat, with the ulcer to prove it.

Minta sketched her plan into her notebook. It was supposed to be a speech, or more like a push for an argument, but her hand drew trenches, fences, traps, and even herself and Dow in their positions. The Town Hall was perfect for modern urban warfare. Easy places to corner the enemy and block their exits, but enough exits for her and Dow to make their retreat if necessary. When Minta had covered all her bases, she frowned. She ripped the paper out of the notebook and crumpled it. She tossed the speech into the wastebasket next to her table. Rather than trenches, she needed carrot and stick. In times like these, she understood despotism better than she cared to. She only had to turn over the whole economy by convincing a bunch of squabbling bankers to unite their forces for the common good. Laughably easy.

"Constant growth," Minta snorted.

Minta lost her train of thought. She had to start all over again, planning the whole evening with her experts and the bankers. She glanced one more time out of the window, looking at the branches. How she wished she could be the one in Herbert's place, tracking down the ghouls. There was nothing like the thrill of a hunt. Nowadays, she had to admit, the only hunting she did was with pen and paper. Still, they had proved to be mightier than her spear. Even so, she would rather use a spear than clauses on the politicians and bankers, or anyone else willing to hurt the city, which she'd gradually turned from an asylum into a work-in-progress.

16

I THINK THIS CARCASS IS ALIVE

etula followed the soft scuffling sounds Ira's feet made. She was torn between rushing after her book and memorizing the relief. The ghoul and human figures on the wall acted out a play. Petula needed to understand what it was about. She'd never seen the language written underneath. How could she have missed the fact that ghouls had their own composed syntax? This made the ghouls even more puzzling.

She'd written a paper about the possession of the demonic soul and its uses for necromancy. The conclusion had been null, and so had been the interest towards the paper, despite it being published in the *Necromantic Journal* and getting high marks. Not even the demonologists had wanted to touch the subject. The lines between the two disciplines should never be blurred.

"I need to see," Petula said aloud.

The will-o'-the-wisp, which hovered over her right shoulder, surged closer to the relief. Its light illuminated part of it. Petula leaned forward and let her eyes wander over the symbols. They didn't look like any alphabet she'd ever seen. Not even the ones in the ancient books in the University's rare books library, which no one except the faculty leaders should know about. It'd been sadly easy to find the secret passages and the other wonders her superiors had hidden from her and her fellow students. In the spirit of the tradition the professors had established, she'd told no one what she'd learned in those passages, but they'd given her an advantage not only over the other students but also the teachers. Half of whom had seemed as if they knew nothing of the higher arts of necromancy. Petula stopped herself from reaching for the symbols and tainting them with her touch.

In the distance, she heard Ira's footsteps. She looked at the relief and then towards the way Ira had gone. She wavered. Petula took in the symbols one more time before heading after the man. He had her book.

Petula followed the tunnel, listening to Ira. The will-o'-the-wisp hovered over her, showing light, but casting nasty shadows and making the sound more distorted with its humming. She reminded herself that she was the big bad wolf here. She had the knife, the wisp, and her words. At a cross-section, she strengthened her and Ira's connection to get a sense of where the man had gone. He was nearer than she thought. Lost, most probably. She could force him to come to her, but Ira had been right. They had to follow where the tunnels led. There was no going back the way they came. She hated Ira being right. She knew it was silly to care about who was right, as they were in a deep mess, but she was always the one who had the last word. Had been since her childhood, to her parents' dislike.

With the last turn she made, she saw Ira's silhouette against the end of the tunnel, where a faint light dawned. Petula opened her bag and forced the will-o'-the-wisp back in. The spirit let out a shriek. She expected Ira to shoot a glance behind him, but whatever he was looking at was too mesmerizing for him to care. When she got to Ira, he stood on a ledge, peering down.

"You took your time," he said without turning to greet her.

"Had other things on my mind," she replied, noting that Ira clutched her book in his right hand.

"What do you make of this?" he asked, nodding

towards the ledge.

Petula took a step closer. She wasn't that convinced about heights. Even less now, after taking the fall. She left a few feet between her and the edge, trying to see what had caught Ira's attention. They stood watching a huge cave opening up. Its ceiling seemed to reach for the skies. Or actually, it reached just underneath the floor of the Cult of Kraken's Church, which was the highest point in Necropolis.[31] But the vanishing ceiling wasn't what held Ira's or Petula's interest. It was the city opening up at the bottom of the cave floor. The lively city glowed in soft blue light.

The ghouls who they'd followed here climbed down a set of narrow, steep steps at the edge of the cliff. Petula had to lift her head up to stop her body from swaying. She hated heights. No, that wasn't the right word. Hate indicated fear, and she didn't fear anything; she just didn't get along with heights. That was it.

"I saw them coming here," Ira said.

Petula wondered what "here" was. She saw stone buildings and ghouls zigzagging between them. Somehow, she'd expected to find a cave with bats hanging from the ceiling and bones and bodies stacked around huddled ghouls. Of course, they had cities, houses, culture.[32]

Petula let her eyes wander around the city. The place looked better than Necropolis, but there was something peculiar about it that she couldn't put her finger on. If Herbert had been there with her, he'd have known what that odd sensation was. He could sum it up with one word: elated. As Petula had never been that good a friend with anything gleeful, she found both the city and the emotions disturbing.

"Isn't that something," Ira said.

"That's one way to put it. Can I have my book back now?"

---

31 You could say that religions had this weird obsession with heights. Something to do with wanting to overlook the city, or maybe something to do with wanting to be looked at. The Cult of Kraken had almost lost its advantageous spot to the Library, but they'd gotten to the Zoning Committee before the Head Librarian. There'd been cake involved, wrapped with sweet words and a hint of eternal damnation.

32 But where there was free time, dreaming, or the ability to think, there were also complications.

"Oh, yes," Ira said, handing back the red book, disinterested. He looked down at the ghouls and the city as if he was ready to plunge in.

Petula took the book, clutching it hard. "We better leave," she said. She wasn't sure of her own words. One part of her wanted to go down there to see what this was all about, but the stronger part of her that'd always made her unable to join in, commit to others, and take risks urged her to get away from here as fast as she could and hurry back home to her books. If she didn't, then her life might change. She wasn't that keen on change.

"No. We're going after them," Ira said and took a step closer to the ledge, where the stairs were cut into the rock.

"You have to believe me. They couldn't have taken anything. At least not anything worth following them down here just the two of us," Petula said.

"This is not about that anymore. Can't you see all the real estate down there? I'd be a fool to ignore the potential this place has, and the fact is that they entered here through my vault. We go down," he said.

"I'm not going down those stairs," Petula said.

"What choice do you have? You can go back to the tunnels and find what exactly? Or you can come with me, and at least we can ask for a way out if nothing else comes of this," Ira stated.

If Petula had had any doubts before about how the man had been able to build his banking empire, she had none anymore. Some people had the gift of instantly seeing the advantages and disadvantages of any given choice and planning their moves ahead of time, and Ira was one of those people. He knew how to seize the moment.

Ira peered over the edge. Petula didn't have to; she'd seen enough to know there was a straight seventy-five-foot drop. She was only wrong by five feet. She'd miscalculated due to her distaste for heights. Otherwise, she'd have been able to give the correct answer. Petula had gotten good at measuring everything and anything. She knew how many windows there were from her apartment to the University. She knew how many square feet the University was, including all the secret passages. She knew it wasn't silly for Ira to ask her to be part of his bank, but her mind did the calculations automatically. Sometimes she wished she had an approachable and friendly personality. But no. Now her mind had evaluated how much strength there was in her arms and knew the stairs were a deathtrap.

"I'm not going down those stairs. One slip and we'll die," she said.

"I can carry you down," Ira said. Something you wouldn't expect to come out of the banker's mouth.

Petula did. The need to take risks oozed out of him. Thus far, his gambles had paid off. Time would catch up.

"Not with your broken knee," Petula replied.

"I'm not leaving empty-handed. We have to get down somehow," Ira said. He turned to face the city once again, searching for another way down.

Petula sensed the desperation in his consciousness. She understood it. Even she had to wrestle with her desire to go into the ghoul city and have a look around and maybe find someone willing to explain to her what ghouls were. Now, as she thought about it, it was weird how little anyone on the ground level knew about their existence. As if it was almost deliberate.

"There were other tunnels," she said and pressed her fingers tightly against the needlepoint book.

The undead hesitated.

"Let's go," he eventually said.

"Down or to the tunnels?" she asked.

"Back to the tunnels," Ira said and walked past her. He mumbled as he retreated from the faint glow of the city. Petula ignored his words. They were not flattering. Not to her or to him. Petula had gotten used to the fact she often strained other people's nerves. Ira was surprisingly accommodating of her habit of saying no to everything. In the past, that'd infuriated her always cheery and friendly and open-natured sister, who took Petula's sulking inside the house as an insult against everything she believed in. There'd been a few major wars between her and Larissa, which had required both their mother and father to negotiate a truce. Petula was glad her younger sister had found someone else to torment: her husband. She'd had a couple of years of pester-free time.

Petula opened her bag, letting the wisp out. She followed the banker, knowing that if anything happened to her, Larissa would be the first one to come here and give hell to anyone who'd hurt her older sister.

◆

Necropolis' marketplace was a place where everything and anything got sold and bought. It was one of the major attractions out-of-towners came to see. Many of them went home robbed and humiliated, but happily toting bags full of junk. The illogical conclusion was the key to the merriment. Both the vendor and the tourist went their separate ways thinking they'd gained something to be content about. Occasionally, it was the seller who found that they'd drawn the short straw, finding the coins gained funny enough to cry. And the tourists, they were happy in that moment when they haggled and pocketed the item. Back at home, the treasures they'd bought turned into shabby old things. All part of the conundrum of being abroad.

Neither Morris, nor for that matter Agatha, had to worry about deceptive, glittering items. They had one objective, and that was to find out who'd sold Jeffrey, Wilbur's driver, as roadkill. Agatha guided Morris past the booths and people. Along the way from the coach to here, she'd picked up a sense of indignation. She'd spoken to herself and to Morris, if he cared to listen, about social injustice, about the sanctity of life, and about clear food chains. She wouldn't let her madam poison her body with just any food. Who knew how ethically the man was killed. Morris had found out the whole debacle went against her morals on so many levels that it left her in a numb stage of rage. Morris nodded and tried to keep up with her, opting not to comment on anything. Her storming encouraged people to make room for them. Morris found the whole business of murder like any other day, or night in this case, in Necropolis. The city had been founded on killing and death. Not that it was ever nice when those two things happened to someone you knew.

"Someone needs to do something. This marketplace should be regulated better. Is there an inspector? I'm sure there should be," Agatha said. She'd taken her teeth out in the midpoint of her ramble. Morris didn't get a word out before Agatha added, "That someone has to be me. I need to do something about this. I'll see Bertha takes this to the Town Hall."

And then she noticed Morris smiling, and she blushed.

"Oh, I'm sorry. I sometimes get caught up..." Agatha said, searching for the last word. Her posture shrunk, and the spunk of her earlier statements lost its salience.

Morris continued smiling. "No need to apologize. You have every right to be angry. They shouldn't have sold him as they did. It's against the law," he said. It had to be. Technically, it wasn't. "Finders keepers, losers weepers" might not be written in any law book, but neither was it forbidden. "*So pick a penny, keep it, pick a corpse, eat it*" was as good as any other motto Necropolitans lived by.

Agatha slowed her steps, letting Morris come beside her. "What are you going to do when we get there?" Agatha asked.

"We're going to talk to the meat vendor and see where we go from there," Morris said, and added when he realized he hadn't gotten the message through, "By we, I mean you and me."

"I do hope there's a sensible explanation," Agatha said. Her voice sounded weak, making Morris think there were two women trapped inside her body: one molded by Bertha and one that'd caused the earlier avalanche of opinions.

"So do I, but a senseless answer is more likely, as what happened to the poor man was vile. To be served as a piece of veal," Morris said.

"I'm sorry," Agatha automatically said.

"You have nothing to feel sorry about. You did nothing wrong, and it's I who should apologize to you. Not only for causing you distress in this hunt for answers but for delaying your journey back to Miss Chaplain," Morris said. He had a hard time accepting the words Miss and Chaplain together. It didn't seem right. Not for a woman who'd been around decades before he'd been born, and he himself was already past marriageable age. It would horrify his mother to hear that he was a bachelor. She'd loved children and had expected him to carry on their family name. She'd been proud to move here from the old country and to marry his father. Morris was sure they'd been happy despite their rigid marriage, which he only later understood as a sign of real love. In his youth, he'd thought true love was passionate. That there had to be lust and at least kissing, not only side glances and unsaid words. He'd been sure there was someone more real and better for his mother than his father. On his father's deathbed, it dawned on him that his father had never remarried after his mother's death from common fever. That his heart had gone with her to the grave. Morris had been twelve when she died. Twelve and angry, to be precise.

Agatha gave a faint smile, which came behind concern and disbelief. "We will be there soon. The place is just behind these stalls," she said when they passed a vendor selling sugar apples.

Morris could already see the place. A wagon had been parked next to a booth where a man was hanging dead squirrels to dangle from the roof. Next to him, a woman worked on mending a patch of leather, which from the look of it had come off a deer. Behind them were other carcasses, and two of them were human. Yesterday Morris had thought nothing of it, but in the new light of things, the place was macabre.

"Is that the booth?" he asked.

"Yeah. Mr. and Mrs. Brown own the stand. I've known them for a long time. So please be careful. If they've done nothing wrong, I'd like to continue my relationship."

Morris noted that Mr. and Mrs. Brown were basically one and the same person. Sometimes married couples looked and acted alike. This happened to be the truth with the Browns. In addition, they were so average-looking, he might not recognize them later in a lineup. But what he thought plain and average were marks of life. Something he and his friends lacked.

"I won't do anything to harm your reputation, I promise," he said.

Mr. Brown frowned when he saw them approaching. "Miss?" he said. He glanced at Morris from under his thick eyebrows.

"Evening, Mr. Brown," Agatha said.

Mrs. Brown had stopped sewing the deerskin, listening to them carefully.

"Evening, miss. Is everything all right with your order?" Mr. Brown asked. "Nothing rotten, I hope," he added.

Agatha shook her head. She opened her mouth to reply, but Morris interrupted her.

"Good evening, Mr. Brown. My name is Morris Reinhardt, and we were wondering where you acquired the meat you sold to Miss Wicks," Morris asked.

Mr. Brown didn't get a word out. His wife got up from her stool and laid the animal hide down.

"We had every given right to sell it. We did nothing wrong! And it was one of our best carpets we gave you," she said, her voice getting tense.

Mr. Brown stepped close to his wife. Morris couldn't tell if he did that to protect or to silence her. Mrs. Brown latched on to the hem of her gray skirt and squeezed it tight.

"I'm certain you did nothing wrong, but I'd like to know where you got that man's body. You see," Morris said and paused. Should he hold back the truth or get their immediate reaction? "You see, I am an acquaintance of the man inside your fine carpet and had no idea he had passed away. I would be grateful if you could tell us how this man came to be in your possession."

Mrs. Brown opened her mouth, but her husband silenced her by seizing her arm. "Missus and me found—"

"You shouldn't be telling him anything. We did nothing wrong, and who does he think he is? The king of the market? Who's this man, *miss*?" the woman snorted.

"I assure you, I am not here to harm you or pester you. I am here out of concern for the man and his family," Morris said. As far as he knew, Jeffrey Gilliam didn't have a family. Not the way the Browns would think.

"He's with Miss Wicks. He means no harm," Mr. Brown said, looking for confirmation from Agatha.

"We only want to know. That's all," Agatha said.

Mrs. Brown glared at Agatha. What goodwill there'd been in the past was gone.

"We found him at the Old Rainy Meadow Cemetery. People sometimes leave bodies there. Not everyone can bury their death or awaken them," Mr. Brown said. "We meant no harm. It's like tidying up the place," he added when he saw Agatha looking at him with disgust.

Morris saw no reason why she should be horrified. Hadn't she talked about roadkills before? This was in the same conceptual spectrum. What concerned him more was that if they'd found the man at the graveyard, then it meant someone else had been driving the coach to the bank. Presumably, the same someone who'd offed Jeremiah, and he'd missed that.

"Was he wounded?" he asked.

"Yes, stabbed. But missus here's good with the needle, and we didn't think it would do any harm," Mr. Brown said.

"Yes indeed, no harm," Morris said. "Thank you for your time. We better leave you to it and not scare any customers away."

Mrs. Brown snarled.

"Agatha, let's go," Morris said under his breath.

"But what about—" Agatha began, standing her ground.

"Not here."

They left the market booth. Behind them, Mr. and Mrs. Brown began to argue. It was a booming argument, but the farther they went, the more garbled it got, as all the other noises of the marketplace obscured their words. Agatha was about to say something. Morris shook his head.

"Not yet. We better get to the coach, and we can talk there."

"But you let them get away with it," Agatha said.

Agatha's voice irritated Morris. Not that it was whiny or high. It was because it sounded like she'd been disappointed not only with the Browns but with him as well.

"What could I have done? Seize them? I'm a banker. I have no authority over what they did."

She replied by turning her attention to the narrow paths between the booths and making her way back to the coach.

The marketplace had turned from wonder and glamour into a dirty, crowded place. Morris' cane tapped against the cobblestones out of sync, and every time it hit the ground, Agatha flinched. He was unsure how he could take back the words he'd said. They were only the facts.

It didn't take Morris and Agatha long to get back to the coach, which was miraculously still where they'd left it. The only reason it hadn't gotten stolen was that there'd been too many interested eyes, and those eyes hadn't come to an agreement about whose turn it was to steal. Morris and Agatha came back before there was a winner of the argument.

While walking, Morris had kept his mouth shut to avoid any add-ons. He'd pieced together that Agatha had expected him to express moral outrage. But what good would that do? Of course, he had a beating and bleeding heart despite what his clients and former dalliances would say. But his only crime was that he knew when not to exhaust it for something that was out of his hands.

Agatha crossed her arms. "We are here. Now, please explain," she said.

Morris could explain everything away. He was good at dancing around any subject and making anyone's head spin. He wasn't in the mood for that and didn't care to do it to Agatha. She was nice and didn't deserve him stringing her along.

"My associates and I," Morris began.

"You and Wilbur Sumner and Ignatius Vaughn. Do you think I can't remember?"

"Didn't expect anything else. There." He hesitated and searched for a clue on Agatha's face to tell him how she'd react. If she was morally outraged about one body, she would hate what he and his associates were doing and what'd gotten Jeffrey killed. "We better leave for your mistress' house and see what Wilbur wants to do."

"That wasn't what you were about to say, and I thought we were going to the police?"

Morris shook his head. "I'm not sure if that's wise. If anyone is going to go, I will go alone. I don't want to get you into trouble."

"How kind of you," Agatha said. She took her teeth out of her pocket and pushed them back in while watching Morris.

"I...never mind. Will you drive?" he asked.

"Yeshh," Agatha said.

17

HOW ABOUT IF WE WING IT?

he coach carrying Herbert, Mrs. Maybury, and Cruxh was heading for Mess. It rattled on after the driver got into his seat. Necropolitans thought Mess' name came from the place's despicable nature, but that would be an inaccurate characterization of the neighborhood. It got the name from the Raisin's Charitable Foundation's communal dinner they established under Oliver the Great's rule and against his wishes. The communal dinner, or as the locals liked to call it, Mess, was under constant attack from the man. It had to be moved around from house to house. Oliver the Great underestimated what people were willing to do for a good meal, especially in the sight of pickles.

Now Mess was a place that attracted misery. A place you could find in every city.

Herbert lived there and thought the place's reputation was exaggerated. He was more worried about what to do once he got into the ghouls' lair, while trying to ignore the pressure arising from Mrs. Maybury's special kind of silence. The undead woman wore the same look as Ona had whenever they'd disagreed. The ghoul sported the same expression as he had in those situations: a confused glare, stemming from guilt and from resentment over false accusations. Whatever had passed between those two had to be settled before they got to the lair, or else they'd put not only their lives in danger but his as well.

"After we get the tools, I want whatever is going on between you two to stop," Herbert said. He was sure he heard laughter, but neither of the others had opened their mouths.

"I presume you mean weapons?" Cruxh asked, ignoring the rest.

"Yes."

"I once again have to emphasize that I detest such contraptions. We do not need them. We have the warrant and our minds. We can simply ask the ghouls to come with us."

Mrs. Maybury puffed. She had clearly reached that stage of her and Cruxh's argument where there was a presumption that mute treatment was the best way to extort the desired outcome. Herbert wasn't sure if anyone knew what she hoped the outcome would be.

"You can do whatever you like, but I'm not going into ghoul lair without something longer than my arm," Herbert said.

Cruxh turned to face Herbert. There they were, his eyes again, doing most of the speaking.

"If you have to," Cruxh said. "But still, I think words are always a better way out of any predicament. I am confident that if I ask the ghouls to come with me, they will."

"Are you being serious? Confident? What if they won't? What if they attack us as they did with Mrs. Maybury?"

"That is always a possibility, but—"

"I won't put my faith in a hunch."

"Don't you trust words, Mr. Ringworm? Or can I call you Herbert?"

"Mr. Ringworm is fine," Herbert said. His old superstition about demons and names surfaced. "And not for a second. They seem to do all the lying."

"Ah, a cynic."

"No, a realist."

"Then, my dear realist, what will we do once we get

your equipment?"

"I'm not dear anything to you."

"Ah, I meant no offense."

"I doubt that."

"You do not seem to like us ghouls much."

Herbert's squinted his eyes and looked away. "How about we just do the job and refrain from speaking?"

"But mister, communication is the essence of success."

"Then we better keep it to a bare minimum so as not to ruin our chances," Herbert said.

Cruxh smiled, or more like his eyes sparkled. "You, sir, have a philosopher's soul."

"Very unlikely," he said and reverted back to silence. His attempt to mend the fences had gone sour. He should have known better. And yes, the ghoul had been right. He had no sympathy towards them. Then again, he had no sympathy for anyone. He had once, and that was for Ona, but otherwise, he'd rather be left alone. He should have just killed the necromancer when he had the chance, and none of this would matter.

Cruxh shifted his weight next to him. Herbert got the distinct impression that something bubbled inside the man. It might be something similar to what he was feeling: the restlessness from traveling inside. He needed to run. Sitting inside felt like a prison sentence. Would it be so wrong if he pushed the door open and let his head hang outside?

"Mr. Ringworm, I have the utmost respect for your expertise, but can I make one last attempt to appeal to your good nature and ask you not to get the weapons, or if not to your nature then to your reason. You have no use for weapons with us ghouls," Cruxh said.

Herbert laughed. It was a long time since he'd done that. "I—"

Cruxh interrupted him. "I respect your opinion, and you have a right to it. But can I show you something that might change your mind?"

"By all means, but I doubt there's anything you can say to make me change my mind, as you said."

"Alice, could I ask you to stop the coach," Cruxh said. His usual soft tone had a higher note.

"If I must," she said and knocked on the coach's wall.

Soon the coach stopped. It creaked to a halt and swayed as the driver got down from his seat.

"Madam?" the driver asked when he opened the door.

"The *gentlemen* have an *issue* they need to solve," Mrs. Maybury said. No one had any doubt what she meant.

The driver stepped aside, letting both Cruxh and Herbert out. Mrs. Maybury stayed in her seat.

"Will you join us?" Cruxh asked, holding out his hand, no, claw, to the woman.

Mrs. Maybury looked at the ghoul, and Herbert had a slight sting of sympathy towards Cruxh, who seemed to lose an inch from his height. He wanted to force the woman out both for the sake of the ghoul and to satisfy his own curiosity. He said nothing.

Mrs. Maybury lifted her chin but took the claw.

The coach was beside a narrow street. They were nowhere near Mess. They'd stopped on a street made for passing, not stopping, yet some had made the pitiful houses their home. Those some peered out of the windows, watching to see why a fancy coach had pulled up on their street. Herbert made a note of them and moved to look at Cruxh, who'd now helped Mrs. Maybury out.

"Mr. Ringworm, I know you find me offensive, and I can live with that. However, I have to show you why you have to reconsider the use of weapons not only for your own sake, but for my and Mrs. Maybury's sake and for the ghouls. We do not want this to blow out of proportion," Cruxh said. He pushed his feet onto the ground, and Herbert knew what he wanted. It was so clear that it was shameful how he'd missed it.

"You want to fight?" he asked, spitting out his words.

"No, I do not want to fight you. I would consider this a show of strength. If you do best me, then you are entitled to do whatever you want. My life is yours," Cruxh said. He took his top hat off and waited to see if Mrs. Maybury would take it. She did. Herbert noticed there was some elation in the way she moved. He wasn't sure, but thought he saw her mouth the words: "Finish him off." He felt his cheeks warm and his muscles tense. Had they been arguing about him?

Herbert rotated his shoulders, widened his stance, and reached his arms up to guard his face.

The ghoul nodded to him. "Mr. Ringworm, whatever comes from this, I did not mean it as an insult," Cruxh said.

Herbert wanted to laugh, to taunt the ghoul. Instead, he concentrated. This was a street fight, and there were no rules.

He felt all eyes on him. The opponents and the crowds. The inhabitants of the street were pressed against their windows, heckling and cheering. There was the familiar rush he got before going into the ring. He could win.

Herbert took Cruxh's need for speeches as an opportunity, pushing to his feet and sprinting forward. His leg muscles pulsed. He was light on his feet, as if he could fly. Herbert pushed his hand inside his jacket pocket, reaching for Jeremiah's vial. He saw Cruxh reacting and launching at him. That was about as much as he saw. His fingers closed around the vial, and he drew it out. Next thing he knew, Cruxh pressed his claw against his chest, and Herbert landed on his back, all the air leaving his body. After a moment of shock, he gasped. He didn't wait to regain his focus. Herbert swung the hand holding the vial against Cruxh, hoping the glass would break and the black liquid would kill the demon.

Cruxh seized Herbert's hand and twisted it into a lock with his free claw. With the other claw, he kept pinning Herbert down.

"Finish me off! What are you waiting for?" Herbert asked. He could taste blood in his mouth. His eyes had come into focus, and he saw the ghoul crouching over him.

From farther away, Mrs. Maybury said with an excited voice, "You heard the man. Finish him! We can always say the ghouls did it."

Cruxh let out a sad howl, the most ghoulish noise Herbert had heard him make.

Cruxh drew his claw off Herbert's chest and jumped away from him, still crouching down. The ghoul held the vial against his chest and looked at Herbert.

Herbert pushed himself into a sitting position.

"I only wanted to show you," Cruxh said. "Show that even a weakling like me can kill you in the blink of an eye. I needed you to understand." He looked at the vial in his claw and shook his head.

"You made your point. Clear enough," Herbert said. All his strength was gone. He stayed sitting, not able to stand up.

"No, I clearly did not, if you were willing to use this against me," Cruxh said, tangling the vial between his talons. "Pure Corruption, as your kind would say." Cruxh sighed. This was the first time Herbert had heard the ghoul refer to humans that way.

Herbert dragged his feet closer to him in case he needed to get up fast. He wasn't sure what the ghoul meant.

Were those tears?

"Alice, if you would be so kind as to give my hat back." Cruxh stood up.

Mrs. Maybury opened her mouth to protest.

"Not *now*, Alice," Cruxh said.

She shut her mouth and hurried to give him his hat.

Cruxh pocketed the vial in his waistcoat and took the hat from Mrs. Maybury. He said, "Mr. Ringworm, we better finish what we were doing and head to the lair."

Herbert nodded.

"Do you need my assistance getting up?" the ghoul asked. Herbert wanted to think he asked it to spite him, but there was no expression of malice on the ghoul's face. Just a deep sadness.

Herbert looked up at the windows. People were still observing them. Not as keenly as a moment before, yet there might be a chance for a rematch.

"No. I can get up," he said. He tested the weight of his feet before tipping his full balance onto them and standing up from the squat he'd gotten into. They'd hold for now. He hated what Cruxh had done, but in the back of his mind he respected the ghoul, who'd returned to his previous mild-mannered demeanor. There was no doubt who would kill who. But there was no doubt either that something fundamental had broken.

"Shall we go back inside the coach?" Cruxh asked.

Mrs. Maybury wavered. Herbert waited for her to explode any second, but she didn't. She surprised him by asking, "Will you escort me?" She gave her arm to Cruxh, and the ghoul more than eagerly took it.

Yes, don't mind me, Herbert thought. He dragged behind them. Words. Cruxh was wrong if he thought they would solve anything. But he had a point. Even if he brought all the weapons he could carry, they wouldn't amount to a victory. Dead and eaten.

◆

Minta half-slept behind her desk. Her eyes were heavy, and her pen wouldn't stay in her hand. She'd been going over her speech, or the tactical sketch, as she liked to think of it, for quite a while now. It wasn't getting any better. She knew that preparation was the key to everything, but she'd have to wing this one. That said, she knew how to influence the to-be-founded committee. It was not through arguing, demanding, or forcing them. It was through smiling, listening, and honey. If they liked her, they'd see her side. Minta grimaced. Getting people to like her was more work than barking orders. She had to listen to their concerns, relate to them while keeping a stupid constant smile on her face. All right, those were very effective ways, but still, she understood why some leaders just beat everyone into obedience. But those results melted away quicker. And terror was never a great cornerstone for society. It would collapse eventually. The irony in this was that it'd happen here in Necropolis as well when she was vanquished. Those not willing to continue playing nice were already picturing her as a corpse.

There was even a price on her head. Every time the amount rose, she knew she'd made the right decision. The sum was now at eighty thousand pure gold coins. It had started at the modest sum of a hundred gold pieces. It was all about supply and demand. The economy, what a funny thing.

She'd been thinking that the key to the current economic tangle was to make the bankers accept their own responsibilities for the risks they took. She couldn't give them money out of the citizens' pockets and postpone the economic collapse until a later date. It wouldn't be fair, although it'd balance the current situation and make the citizens love her again. Other committee members might go for an easy solution to gain popularity. But a popularity contest was a slippery slope to being paid off by anyone with enough money and influence to sway the public.

This living on borrowed money wasn't a sustainable system, and everyone knew it. The arrangement needed constant growth to keep up with the original loans before they were due. All the bankers' money and assets were tied up in those loans, and she was sure not many had a way to back up the credit, but it wasn't only that. If one of them crumbled, then the others would too, starting an avalanche.

To make the city bankers agree to an act of kindness of this magnitude was a one-in-a-trillion chance. They were the sort who lived by the philosophy "all for self and none for all." She couldn't deny that they needed them in the city, and every city, for that matter. Bankers created opportunities and made sure new innovations were possible. But now they'd grown too fat and too distant from common people, losing sight of things and causing more harm than good.

She'd have to make the committee members see eye to eye, and then force the bankers to cooperate with them, and hopefully save the city from ruins, and prevent loss of lives. No wonder her stomach ached.

"Ma'am," Dow said.

Minta tossed her plan into the wastebasket. "Is everything done?" she asked.

"I have contacted all those who you wanted to come. They will be here. I haven't been able to locate Mr. Worthwrite, but I am working on it," he replied. Minta saw him make a note of the papers she'd thrown away. He said nothing.

"Good. So, who did you get?" Minta asked.

"Frederick Kilborn, as you asked," Dow said.

You couldn't keep the man away even if you wanted to, Minta thought. "Mhm. And the bankers?"

"Albert Walker and Ida Mortician. Mrs. Mortician once worked for Mr. Worthwrite and now runs a moderately sized bank of her own. From what I have gathered, he has been gunning for her bank for a while now. And Mr. Walker has a slightly smaller bank than hers, but he has several holding companies all over the world and has a stake in key businesses in the city," Dow said.

"They'll have to do," Minta said. She knew both by reputation. If she'd done as Dow had asked her to do, she might know them better after attending the social events of the year. Such parties had always seemed like a waste of time.

"And the professor?"

"Chester Fen," Dow said.

"Ohh," Minta said. She knew him. He'd sent her letters over the years, demanding explanations for her decisions, and advising her how she could do better. She wanted to ask Dow, why him, but she already knew the answer. The man had a good reputation among the public. They thought of him as some kind of guru. She'd beg to differ.

"Ma'am," Dow said, "I know you plan to wing what you are going to do and say, but..." He opened his black jacket and took a square leather pouch in his hands. He opened it. There was a neatly folded paper stack. Minta knew the man didn't like it when she let her intuition guide her. Minta thought there was something creative and primal in it. Something very harmonious indeed. "...These would make things easier for you." Dow handed the papers to her.

Minta took them. She saw the committee members' names at the top of each page. She shut her eyes.

"I'm not sure if I want to know," Minta said. Whatever was written there would be very informative, knowing Dow.

"Minta," he said.

"Yes, Dow?" she replied, opening her eyes, wondering at his informality.

"You should read them. I have a feeling we'll need them to survive," Dow said.

Minta raised her eyebrows. "Kraken shit, Dow. A feeling?" she asked, instantly regretting her scorn.

"I know...but I have the same distinctive feeling I had before they tried to hang me. The city is sailing into deeper waters, and Kraken will swallow it whole if we can't stop this. I like my life too much. So will you please read them?"

"Hm," Minta said. Her first instinct was to dismiss him.

"I can feel it in my bones. It's the same shivering ache."

It could be just a draft, but Minta didn't say that aloud. "I'll read them."

"Good," Dow replied. "One more thing before I leave you to *prepare*. There is a rumor going around the town that they are setting up a monetary entity to control the markets and banks. Bertha Chaplain has already gathered her troops to advocate such a plan," Dow said.

"She wants more governmental control?"

"It seems like it."

"That had to come from the bankers," Minta said. Bertha didn't have an original thought in her body. The woman went with the flow set by others, finding ways to exploit them. She was far from clever, despite how she saw herself. Minta had always found her company tedious.

"I agree. And I think Mr. Ringworm was right about Mr. Worthwrite. This time around, he isn't joking."

"Yes, but why would he want control? He never seemed like the type."

Dow grinned, and when he saw her looking, he struggled to resume a straight face. "Think of the control like a huge block preventing entry to the city, but a block you can get around if you know how. That would explain why Mr. Reinhardt junior is with them."

"Okay, and the block would be against me as well?" Minta asked.

"I would think so... I better leave you to it then," Dow said, turning around.

Minta interrupted his exit. She asked, "Dow, do you ever think back to those days when we traveled the world?"

Dow turned back to face her and shook his head. "What would be the point?"

"They were good times. Don't you think?" Minta asked.

"Sure, we had fun back then, but we do now, too," Dow said. He laid out every single word carefully, not glancing towards Minta. They both knew she occasionally fell into nostalgia, remembering their past as being much better than it actually was. What Dow remembered was all the uncomfortable nights in a tent, trying to find a position on the ground that didn't cause his whole body to ache. Or the scorching hot sun or icy cold wind, or anything in between. Necropolis had perfectly fine moist air and an atmosphere of backstabbing that perfectly suited the man's tastes. Minta found it concerning that the man relished the fact he had to tiptoe around people and be ready to jump aside at the first sign of an attempted assault. Yes, he sometimes admitted to her late at night that their past life didn't lack monsters, but he'd rather battle with a sophisticated foe anytime over something feral.

"Do we?" Minta asked.

"Yes, we do. Look what you have done for the city. Its

inhabitants wouldn't have as swell of a time as they have now if it weren't for us. We have made it better," Dow said. Now he dared to take a glance towards her.

Minta sighed. Dow was right, as he always was. But she was starting to consider that the citizens had too swell of a time. The party had reached that point when one idiot[33] thought it was a good idea to crash and set the place on fire.

"Dow," Minta said.

"Yes?"

"I know what you did there," she said.

"I wouldn't presume any less," he said.

"But I'm not sure if I like this anymore," she confessed.

"The words of a true leader," Dow said, but there was a hint of concern in his voice.

"Your flattery won't help," Minta replied.

"We can talk about it after all this is over. You wouldn't want to leave in the middle of this mess," Dow stated.

Minta didn't reply. What could she say? Of course, I want to flee. Both of them would recognize such words were empty blather. He was right. She wouldn't leave, and any time the thought even crossed her mind, the horrible little man persuaded her to stay.

"So what are you going to say?" Dow asked before he left her alone.

"Nothing," she replied.

"I meant to the committee."

"So did I," Minta said.

"You can't just say nothing," Dow said.

"Of course I can. I make them talk, and I'll listen to their concerns. We can't push our opinions down their throats, as much as we would like to; it wouldn't get us far," she emphasized. That was one of Dow's problems. He didn't know how to put himself in another person's shoes.

"You have grown soft in your old age," Dow said.

Minta was sure she heard him snorting.

"I think I have," Minta said. She narrowed her eyes. "But don't think I won't crush them if necessary. It's just that there are better ways than shouting. Dow, too much hangs on

---

33   Okay, several idiots.

this. There's already too much that'll blow up in our faces by tomorrow morning. We have to be careful if *we* want to stay in the city."

"Maybe you are right," he said.

"I am, and it wouldn't hurt if you tried smiling," she said.

Dow frowned.

Minta didn't press the matter any further. He'd have to learn, and quick, if he wanted to continue doing this after her demise. Most likely after tomorrow. She hoped she wouldn't have to leave him alone. Dow was the most capable man there was, but he was also the most pitiful creature she'd come across. When she'd found him, he'd been accused of sorcery against his king. Hogwash, but sometimes it felt like what Dow did with bureaucracy was magic. She knew it was just his keen mind using the world around him, but others didn't.

Sometimes Minta wondered if the man had a longing to go back home, where his family was, as he hadn't made any ties here. He'd devoted his entire life to her. Minta had pushed him to make connections. Form a family. Anything other than stay loyally by her side, but he refused to leave her.

"And Minta, before I go. Whatever happens, I have deep respect towards you," Dow said.

"Are you being sentimental?"

"No; it had to be said."

Minta didn't pester him further. She opened the papers Dow had handed to her. They were as bad as she thought. She read past the infidelities. There were more dark deeds the committee members did behind the public veil. Minta's mildness turned into a grimace. She looked up from the papers and expected Dow to still be there with her, but he was gone.

"How do you expect me to face them now?" she asked the empty room.

If Dow was with her, he would say, "Much better."

Minta looked out of the window. Why was she even bothering with any of this? They, Dow and her, should hail a ship and sail away. The scenery outside was sickening, nothing like what she saw when she closed her eyes. She always found herself in the savanna, or occasionally just by the seashore next to a luscious, never-ending forest. Anything else but this dampness, this crude, filthy city with too many people in it. Where were the birds?

18

ANNOYINGLY IMPARTIAL

Petula and Ira had been wandering inside the tunnels for an eternity. Or so it felt, with Ira constantly shifting from brooding to verbal assaults. The target shifted from Morris to Petula to the soil underneath his feet and to everything he saw or cared to think of. All the tiny little choices the man had made tonight and before seemed to haunt him, and not in a good way. The way you realize the value of life and what matters. His brooding was far from any existential crisis. It was more his entitlement finding the world uncooperative. Petula kept glancing at her book, considering whether to clobber the man with it and see if that changed his tune.

"We're not getting anywhere, and I can't stand another second of staring at those murals. Can't you do something?" Ira asked.

They are reliefs, Petula thought. "I've said already thousands of times, I'm not the kind of caster you think. But if you like, I can make your mind shut down, so you don't have to see any more dirt, stones, the reliefs, my messy dress, my red book, your broken toe—"

"Oh, shut up."

She quite liked the art. It was the only thing keeping her company. The amount of work the ghouls had put into them was enormous, and she disagreed with Ira that they were primitive. What did he know about expressionism, when he only cared about the highest value? Which didn't necessarily mean skill or creativity.

Petula sighed. She took the book and opened it. She anchored her walking pattern to Ira's and let her body follow. It was wonderful what the mind could do if there was enough will. She could also use the will-o'-the-wisp, as she normally did, but they were capricious, as their nature dictated.

But her thoughts were scattered and skipping into the doom side of things. Petula found Ira's brooding infectious. She shut the book and listened to the absent sounds in the tunnel. Behind their own footsteps and the will-o'-the-wisp's crackle she heard water dripping and felt a gust of wind. They had to be going somewhere that would either lead out or to the ghoul city, as Ira wanted. But she also heard the echo of their own scuffling movements. A noise the ghouls would notice. They had to know she and Ira were there. Either they were ignoring Ira and Petula, knowing there were far worse creatures in the tunnels, or they were toying with them, wearing out their prey. Petula tucked the book under her armpit and looked around. Her mother always complained she let the world pass her by. Agatha had voiced the same concerns. They said that she should learn to seize the moment and be proactive. This was probably the time to be such a person. But how?

If her sister were here, she'd storm deeper into the tunnels in her size nine boots, demanding to be taken to their leader. She wouldn't care whose leader. The head ghoul or some coach-sized spider den mother. She'd get their respect either way. That was her sister. She, Petula, would sneer, leer, and jeer and wonder why she got served to the spiderlings. Petula looked at her own boots, her sensible black leather boots that would last her even in the afterlife. You could run in them, but her feet weren't running feet. They tiptoed around the library, carrying a body with a mouth made to shush people into silence. How could two sisters be so different? One climbing up trees and the other standing underneath, pointing out all the possible ways she could die.

Okay, so her strength wasn't running or climbing, but she had something else. She was in tune with the world. She could sense all the surrounding energy. The dead and the living. Petula shut her eyes and took a deep breath in. She stopped walking. In the background, she could hear Ira yelling at her, but she couldn't make out the words he said. It was like a murmur of little to no consequence. She lowered her barrier to sense those who always followed her. Her relatives and a selection of miscellaneous dead, and the hopeless souls with lost minds she couldn't help. But she couldn't sense them. They were absent for the first time. And there were no new voices whispering to her, lying, guiding, demanding, hating. She sensed only the soil, which was creating life out of decay.

This was all wrong.

Petula searched for anyone to guide them out of here, but Ira's agitated shouting hurt her concentration.

"Please shut up," she said in a controlled voice and shut her eyes again.

"I'm here if you need me," she said, trying to guide possible spirits towards her with compassion.

No one answered her call. She'd never seen a place where there was no residual dead energy.

"What are you doing? I demand to know. You can't ignore me. I'm your employer," Ira said.

"I'm trying to find a way home," she replied.

"No, you're not. We're going to that city."

"Or there." Anything but this. The absence of voices was getting unbearable.

"Have you lost your mind?"

"No, I'm trying to help us. We can't wander around these tunnels without a destination."

"We have a destination. We're going into that ghoul city," Ira said.

"Why do you want to go there? Once again, the ghouls couldn't have stolen anything from you."

"All this is under my bank. And I own the soil. So—"

"You can't be serious. I wouldn't say this place is under your bank. Even though your bank is a large building, it wouldn't cover all this area."

"A technicality. Nothing that will hold in court."

Petula could see it. Ira would get his way. Men like him were good at technicalities. They had to be, or they wouldn't get away with all they did.

"Your greed knows no bounds."

"Not greed, opportunities. That's what's wrong with most of you: you don't know how to seize the moments handed to you. You let arbitrary rules govern you."

"Someday they'll lynch you."

"Until then, I'll have fun."

His "until then" would be a short-lived notion, if the ghouls got to them. They had to know they were coming. If they didn't, it would be almost acceptable if Ira invaded the city, but only almost. People birthed the cities, and they should belong to the people. Then there were those who thought it was a good idea to sort out which kind of people were part of the city and which weren't. Such logic was a quick trip to a dystopia of pure homogeneity, where matching outfits never went out of style. But that wasn't what Ira was planning. He had an individualistic servitude in mind.

Petula glanced at the reliefs. The truth had to be there, but her encyclopedic knowledge of languages fell short. This was pissing her off.

"I think there's something wrong," she said.

"You don't say," Ira said. "You aren't that bright, are you?"

Petula heard her mother's voice: "*Count to ten.*" She ignored it. "What that's supposed to mean?"

"That you can't apply your book knowledge to a real-world situation. Life works differently. You should try to live a little," Ira said.

"I—" she began to reply, but then she knew what was wrong. It was the ghouls.

She shut her eyes and saw it. There was this great darkness in front of them and behind. Like a barrier.

"I know you are there. Come out of hiding," Petula said and opened her eyes.

It took a moment, but the ghouls descended from the walls and the ceiling. Petula and Ira followed their movements.

Petula glanced over her shoulder. There was an army of ghouls behind her.

A ghoul from the front infantry reluctantly parted

from his sisters and brothers as an emissary. No human would be as squeamish to face such an honor, but the ghoul who advanced one step at a time was intelligent enough to separate the necessary action from prestige.

"Sirr and missr, wouldr your ber sor krind arnd corme wirth urs?" He appeared almost ashamed by his plea. Behind him, the relief, lighted by the will-o'-the-wisp, added gravitas to the situation.

"Take me to your leader," Ira said and flashed a smile. He shouldn't have. The smile didn't suit him in the same way it didn't suit Petula. There was at least that one common factor they shared. It pretty much ended there. Okay, if Petula thought about it, she might admit she possessed the banker's calculative nature. But while she didn't care for humanity and rarely liked humans, she saw no reason to harm their freedom and dignity.

"If you would be so kind as to show me a way out, I would appreciate it," Petula said.

The ghoul hesitated. He glanced behind him. Some shook their heads. Only one ghoul seemed to nod while looking at Petula with a smile on her face. There was a creature who knew how to smile. It was warm and welcoming.

"Plearse, missr," the ghoul said.

"All right then. Take me to your leader," Petula said. She, unlike some, came in peace.

The ghoul showed them the way. The army followed a few feet behind. Too close for Petula's liking. Someone should teach the ghouls about personal space.

It took no time for Ira to find his stride.

"With proper backing from my bank, you could start a great trading empire here. If I'm right, you could do everything without taxation, as strictly speaking this isn't part of Necropolis' jurisdiction. So, there'd be an even greater profit for you. Also, it'd be lucrative to attract other potential businesses that struggle above. Yes," Ira said and trailed along with the ghouls.

Petula wasn't sure if he even cared if anyone was listening to him. The ghouls looked at each other in silence. Ira just radiated happiness. If he thought books weren't and shouldn't be the meaning of life, then Petula thought money, power, and the silly games the man played were a waste of humanity. She lived for acquiring reason. Not for something that fueled only the moment, leaving a bad taste in the mouth.

The tunnel sloped, taking them deeper underground.

Petula wasn't sure how long they'd walked. From the state of Ira's mouth and the awkwardness of the ghouls, she gathered it was long enough.

"If you follow the pattern I drew," Ira said, tapping a pen against a piece of paper he'd borrowed from Petula. He'd drawn diagrams on it laying out how the ghouls could turn the underground city into a profit machine by attracting investors like him and others to hide their assets here, and why not throw in gambling and other fun activities? "You could turn this place into a paradise. There'd be enough money for all of you to do whatever you wanted. You could make this little city of yours fatter—" He stopped mid-sentence. The ghoul city came into full view as the tunnel ended. It was bigger than they'd thought. The same aesthetic style they'd seen on the reliefs continued in the buildings in a grander way. Even Petula held her breath. "—than Necropolis." Ira finished his sentence. Somehow his belief in his words had dissipated before he reached the last syllable.

The ghouls guided Ira and Petula through the narrow streets. Eyes followed them from windows and doorways. Some of the ghouls hid behind other ghouls, and Petula felt like she was the huge scary monster they warned their children about. Her with her sinister ideas and outdated views. She felt ashamed for not seeing the ghouls as they were. Yes, she'd greeted those who cleaned the University or the streets and the one who maintained the building she lived in, but now she doubted her motives. Had she done it out of superiority or truly to greet another being? And in a way, Ira had seen ghouls more clearly than the rest all along, as equal and worthy economic participants.

They walked into a building that had to be the Town Hall. It was taller than the rest and more refined. To each side of its doors stood two statues. One might expect them to be things like ghouls, cats,[34] or even monkeys would do,[35] but instead, there were two bunnies. Bunnies that stood on their hind legs and wore suits of armor, granted, but you couldn't

---

34 Think lions or panthers, not furballs of pure cunning cuteness.

35 They can really throw their own weight.

mistake them, for the six-and-a-half-foot-tall, carrot-eating monstrosities had been based on the domesticated version of their ancestors.

Inside the building wasn't any better. Petula would never have guessed she'd find light in the darkest bottomless pit there was. She and Ira were taken inside a drawing room styled with the grand relief theme but full of smaller mockups of the bunny statues outside. The ghouls gave her a sandwich and a cup of coffee and left her alone with Ira and a couple of guards.

"This could be a true harbor for the free economy without the laws trying to smother what comes naturally for humans, and that is trade. Trade of favors, trade of commodities, trade of ideas," Ira shouted after the ghouls.

Petula sighed and took a sip of her coffee and was surprised. It was brewed to perfection. It was dark and bitter.

◆

Morris Reinhardt was a modern man. He had nothing against women working or taking the lead, as Agatha did by twisting her hands around the reins. Women were diligent and reliable, and someone else might add cheaper than men, but not he. That wasn't the point. Also, he was glad he didn't have to attempt to get another coach moving tonight. His joy of riding had been short-lived.

Agatha made it look easy to get the horses to obey her will. The usual traffic in the marketplace didn't cause her any alarm. She navigated with ease through the other carriages and coaches. Pedestrians, moreover, avoided her, giving them room.

Morris knew he had to mend fences.

"You and Petula are good friends. How long have you known each other?" he asked.

She wrinkled her nose. "Did Petula shay thath?" she asked.

"Oh, did I misunderstand something? She seemed to think highly and kindly of you," Morris replied.

"Shhe did?"

Morris coughed. "Maybe you are right," he said, trying to discover if he'd caused offense. "There don't seem to be any emotions going on inside that woman's head. If there are, it's a miracle."

There came an awkward silence.

Morris felt his chest tighten.

Then Agatha laughed. Not in the sweet giggling way, but a full-on horselaugh. He joined her. All the pent-up energy he'd experienced a moment before burst out. They both let their laughter wipe away any reservations. But when it died, the silence came back. He saw Agatha's face getting red.

"Shhe ish..." Agatha said. She paused and took the teeth out of her mouth, putting them back into her pocket.

Morris waited for her to continue on. Agatha didn't.

"She must be a great necromancer. She got Ira up just like that without candles or trinkets. I've never seen anyone do that." Morris moved his hand closer to her, laying it on the seat.

Agatha nodded. "She's the best. I don't think there's anyone like her in the city. Back in Uni, she used to torment the lecturers and senior professors. She locked on to their weak arguments and demanded explanations. You should have seen the pain on their faces. She got them, and bad. Whenever she didn't show up to the classes, there was a general sense of relief," she said and bit her lip while taking better hold of the reins.

A pedestrian saw the coach coming. The man withdrew back to the pavement and took no chances. Not that Agatha was a bad driver. Far from it. It was just that there was something in the way she held herself. Her impudence saying, "You better go around, or I won't be responsible for what happens." It was the necromancer in her. If he'd thought to observe the situation and not be so intrigued by Agatha, he might have noticed. Now he tried to come up with something to say. He was usually smoother than this.

"I'm sure you are as great as she is," Morris said.

Agatha laughed. It was full of scorn. "Not even close. I'm just better with people. That got me to be the class president and valedictorian. I have no grand illusions of what I can do and what I can't. But if she says we can do the transfer together, then she's right. She has always been a good judge of anything, really. Annoyingly precise and impartial."

"I'm sure—"

"Thank you, but I'm fine with what I am and what I'm not. Working at the church made me see that such comparisons are pointless when put in perspective," Agatha said. She seemed to loosen up.

Morris smiled.

"I get to help others," she added.

Morris wasn't sure what to think about her confession. He wasn't that big on the church. It was too bloody and narrow for his liking. But he liked their annual cookie competition. He believed Kraken existed and controlled Necropolis through the waves the god sent against their shoreline, but there were so many other powerful players on Necropolis' soil to devote his time to. But he guessed she was there for the community. There was no tighter group than the Kraken followers, with their dark robes and stuck-on tentacles.

"It must be nice," he said. The church had been there ever since the city was established. No other religion had gained such a strong footing in Necropolis. It might be because you could hear Kraken if you dipped your head under the water.

"Yes, it is. I get to work closely with Madam Sabine. You know of her?" Agatha asked.

Unfortunately, he did. Madam Sabine, formerly known as Mrs. Rosa Maupines, had seized his inner circle by storm. It'd started with his mate's girlfriend finding the church and Madam Sabine ensnaring her and spreading from there to those he thought to have more sense. Not him though. He'd sought every little detail he could find about the woman. Her humble past as a factory worker, her divorce, and then the reincarnation as madam of the church had surprised him, but not convinced him that she had some hidden wisdom. It saddened him how even the most notable persons in the city went to seek her guidance. Not that he thought her to be evil or a charlatan; he just didn't see the point. Not with his friends or with Agatha.

"Oh yes, I've heard of her," he said. He'd gone to see her once or twice. He could still see her approaching. Her short round figure swaying from side to side and her earrings clinking as she moved.

"I can get you a private session with her if you want," Agatha said.

"Too kind of you. I wouldn't want to put you out," Morris said carefully.

"You wouldn't. She would take you in as a favor to me." The thing with Agatha was that she'd been dissatisfied with the work she'd done and had sought refuge with the cult. Madam Sabine had been kind to her, guiding her to the right path. At first, the right path had been to polish all the church's doorknobs while Madam Sabine went to see the city's Housing Inspector.

"Do you know what clears my mind of all the questions?" the madam had asked. Agatha had shaken her head. "Doing chores." Since then, Agatha had gone to her with all of her troubles. Bertha wasn't happy about that, but Agatha snuck out as much as she could.

"Let's wait until this is sorted and then we can talk about it," Morris said.

"Oh, of course, you're right. How foolish of me," Agatha said and blushed.

Her reddened face made Morris' heart race. He kept his eyes forward, not knowing what to say.

They rode in uncomfortable silence, both of them trying to think about what to say to the other. Both thinking they'd made some mistake and offended the other somehow. Both eagerly wanting to mend what was not broken. Both opening and closing their mouths several times. Agatha kept her eyes on the reins, and Morris kept looking around, trying to find something to lock his gaze with, but the only things he saw were other people, the back side of the horses, and the occasional werewolf; nothing a proper gentleman should converse about. And he especially couldn't bring up how sweet and flowery Agatha smelled. But instead of him finding something to say, it was Agatha who surprised him.

"You know what Madam Sabine would say? She'd tell me to report the death. I've been thinking, and I'm sorry, but I don't agree with you. These matters aren't about you or me or about Mr. Sumner. The man is dead, and there should be an inquiry. The longer we stall, the easier it'll get for the killer to slip away. It's not a long walk from here to Miss Chaplain's house, and the police station is that way. You can walk from here. I'm going to the station with the body."

19

NECESSARY ALLIANCES AND THE RELIEF OF TALKING TO SOMEONE

inta had been going over the files Dow gave her for the last hour. She found it wrong on so many levels to go over the private lives of the committee members and the four bankers, whom Dow had thoughtfully included. What was private should stay private, as long as nothing illegal was done. Who was she to judge if someone preferred the company of a different species?

"Not my business," Minta snorted and shut the files.

"What isn't, ma'am?" the leader of the Necro Democratic Alliance asked. The man, Frederick Kilborn, stood at the office door.

"Mr. Kilborn," she said and stood up. He was early. She should have expected that from the man.

"Miss Mayor," he said with a solemn voice. Frederick Kilborn was a tall man with stern features obscured by a heavy beard. His dark brown eyes were set deep into his eye sockets. They made him look dead and haunting, even though the man was in the prime of his life: past the worries of youthful existential crises but not decrepit with old age. To make matters worse, he insisted on dressing like an undertaker.

The man lingered in the doorway, waiting for an invitation.

"Won't you have a seat," she said.

"I'd rather stand, if you don't mind," he said and came in.

Minta wasn't sure if she had any stamina left to deal with him tonight. He wasn't as bad and irritating as Mrs. Maybury or, for that matter, Bertha could be, but he had enough quirks to give her gray hairs.

"As you wish," she said and sat back down, forcing the man to come all the way in and stand next to the desk. He glanced at the spear over her head and then back at her.

"Can I get you something, coffee, tea, while we wait for the others?" she asked.

"I'm fine as I am. I don't drink after eight," Frederick Kilborn said. He laid his hand on the top of the chair in front of Minta's desk.

I bet you don't, Mr. Gremlin, she thought. "I do have to insist you sit down," Minta said.

The man hesitated but complied. "Is this meeting about what occurred tonight?" he asked.

"No, not exactly," she replied.

"Then what else, if not Mrs. Maybury's unfortunate incident?"

Minta was certain she'd used those exact words about the attack, but she now found them demeaning, downplaying Mrs. Maybury's experience.

"I have to insist you wait until the others get here. All will be revealed in due time. Are you sure you don't want any coffee?" Minta asked.

"No, but I want to know why you have summoned me here, and what you are going to do about the...the thing with Mrs. Maybury. All the racket that will follow from tonight's you-know-what will tear my alliance to pieces. The papers won't talk about anything else except *her*. I can't have that happen. You can't have that happen, not when we've been nothing but supportive of you, and you need all the good publicity there is," Frederick Kilborn said. His words sounded like a polite heads-up.

Yes, as nuts as Mrs. Maybury and Bertha. She had somehow expected more from Frederick Kilborn. He and she were the same. But he must have let his post as the head of the Necro Democratic Alliance change him, as no monster hunter behaved as he did. Least of all monster hunter royalty whose father and grandfather were decorated veterans.

She said, "The matter is being dealt with. The ghouls who attacked Mrs. Maybury are being retrieved as we speak. You don't need to worry about that. Dow and I have the best men on the job."

Frederick stared at Minta with his hollow eyes, which seemed to reach somewhere deep inside, trying to fish out any words kept back.

If there were any, she wouldn't let them out so easily. She didn't have to. There was a knock on the door. Dow stood there, frowning upon seeing Frederick.

"Ma'am, and good evening to you, Mr. Kilborn."

"Evening, Mr. Spurgeon."

"I came to say that your guests have arrived, and they are waiting for you in the audience chamber."

"Thank you, Dow," Minta said and stood up.

Frederick followed suit.

"Shall we join the others?" Minta asked.

Frederick nodded.

Dow led them down the stairs and to the audience chamber. The Town Hall had fallen quiet. Word of Mrs. Maybury's attack must have spread, and the ministers had left to plot to keep their positions if and when a power shift occurred. All of them were animals in a constructed habitat with socially agreed-upon rules, and all of them knew when to hide in their burrows.

Dow whispered to Minta as they made their way to the chamber, "You could have changed into something more presentable."

Minta pretended she didn't hear him. Yes, she could have put on something other than her comfortable trousers and wool coat that had worn thin in several places, and worn the black leather coat with the black fur collar. But all her fancy clothes made her feel like she was pretending to be something she wasn't. She preferred clothes that fit her like a second skin. Clothes in which she could run, crouch, crawl, and even dance if she was in the mood to.

Dow shook his head but didn't press the matter further. When they arrived at the audience chamber door, he held it open for them, letting Minta and Frederick in, leaving Minta to her committee.

Inside, Albert Walker, an undead banker, Ida Mortician, a human banker, and Chester Fen, a vampire and economics professor, had taken their seats. They sat far apart, eying each other and guessing the reason why they were summoned. They stood up when they saw Minta and Frederick enter.

"Good evening, everyone," Minta said. "And do sit back down. And Mr. Kilborn, won't you find a seat." The man obeyed, taking his usual place. Minta also walked to her own seat, which was miraculously empty.

"Thank you for coming tonight at such short notice. I wouldn't have asked you to join me if this wasn't important," Minta said. She familiarized herself with her new committee. Albert Walker was like any old undead: half-rotten, half-alive. He wore a stylish suit, and on the desk next to him lay a black bowler hat that usually hid the fact that he was almost bald if you didn't include the dried patches of hair here and there.

A little farther away from him sat Ida Mortician. She was as alive as they came. She was in her forties but didn't have a single gray in her long black hair. The woman was smartly dressed, going with a long black skirt and a short black coat. A style that Dow would most likely want Minta to follow. Minta gave the woman a small smile.

Lastly, Chester Fen had taken a seat near the door. The professor had silver-gray skin and looked anemic. He was an odd mixture of your basic vampire style, with black and red silk, but somehow he'd gotten his clothes to look like a tweed jacket and comfortable wool trousers. The more Minta looked at him, the more paradoxical the man appeared, and the more she was sure her eyesight was playing tricks on her.

"If you don't mind, I'll jump straight to the point," Minta said. Her audience agreed, nodding to her words. "As you may have noticed, the city's economic situation has declined rapidly over the past few years. The situation has become unbearable, and we need a solution to our problems now more than ever, as it has come to my attention that there has been a deliberate attempt to contort our economy for personal profit, or in this case, personal profits."

The two bankers looked at each other, trying to think who'd gone too far. Frederick was the only one who seemed to agree with her. The vampire, Chester Fen, leaned back in his seat, regarding Minta intently.

"That's why I've asked you to come. I need a highly skilled committee to aid me in steering the economy and helping me prevent Ira Worthwrite, Ignatius Vaughn, Wilbur Sumner, and the young Morris Reinhardt forming an alliance and attracting politicians to vote for a monitoring banking committee to oversee the banking practices and creation of money. A committee to regulate all the banks in the city."

"What do you want from us?" Frederick asked.

"I want you to give me viable options on how to proceed with Mr. Worthwrite and his associates and what to do with the economy. I'm asking you to tell me if there's a way to ease our citizens' troubles without the need to form a banking committee. Our citizens are struggling to make ends meet, struggling to pay their rent, buy food, and make enough money to live. We need to do something, but I don't know what," she stated. She had ideas, but she also knew that when Ira and his band of brothers were done with their campaign, everyone would see the banking committee as an attractive and sensible offer. Even Minta understood its usefulness, but when such an offer came from the four biggest banks in the city, from four men whom she knew to be ruthless and selfish in nature, there was something more going on that she couldn't condone. And no, she wasn't that willing to give the council members access to bankers and bankers access to the council members. There was too great a risk of corruption.

"If you gave people more money to solve their problems, there'd be more to go around," Albert Walker, the banker, said.

"But that would flood the markets," Chester Fen, the economics professor, replied.

"Yes, if we made money out of nothing. That'd be bad, as it'd make the prices go up and wouldn't put more money in circulation. But if it was their money to begin with, that'd be a different matter entirely," Albert said.

"None of this is the point of tonight," Ida Mortician, the other banker, said. "She's trying to get us to go against our own better judgment. To make us do something foolish like pardon the loans, or, or give extended time for repayment, or lower the interest rates. She's trying to make us into fools and go belly up. How does that serve my fellow bankers or me?"

Frederick interrupted before Minta had time to answer. "I thought we were here to find a solution, and not to accuse each other."

Ida crossed her arms.

Minta was oddly glad that Frederick was there. Sometimes the man knew how to surprise.

"Then what do you suggest?" Ida asked.

"I think Mr. Worthwrite is on the right track; we need governmental control—" Frederick said.

"You have to be kidding me," Ida interrupted him. "We don't need more control. That's the last thing we need."

"Then what?" Frederick asked.

"Maybe if the government takes a loan and begins a massive project that will put more money into circulation." Albert jumped back into the conversation.

Minta said nothing.

The others coughed.

"What?" Albert asked. "It's a sound proposition. Then it wouldn't be free money, and people will have worked to get it."

"Yeah, but that's just another payment on top of the existing one. The Town Hall would have to increase taxation, the amount of money in circulation wouldn't increase at all, and it would be the citizens paying the bill for reckless banking practices," Chester said in a tight voice, testing his place in the conversation.

"Not if the interest rates and payments were postponed until the economy is doing better." Albert had a comeback.

"That would thrust the problem onto the generations to come. When the payments came due, it would require the government to raise taxation so high it would suck any loose money from circulation, and it would destroy the economy then," Chester commented.

"Then how about a bailout for important businesses and banks," Albert said.

"That would lead to the same thing: taxation rising

and citizens paying for the risks bankers and business owners took," Chester said.

Albert snorted. "At least I'm trying to come up with a solution. I don't hear anyone else speaking."

"Of course not, we are thinking," Chester replied.

Minta wanted to laugh. She could already see everyone drawing their battle lines. This was going to be an interesting meeting. Something she wasn't likely to forget.

◆

Coordinating with differing motives, ideologies, and needs was as hard as herding cats. You could do it, but it took a spectacular amount of fish bites to get them to even lift their tails, let alone decide which direction to go in. Bertha found that one corpse wasn't as great a motivator as she'd thought. The guest whispered amongst themselves about her proposal and what it meant. William attempted to convince the whole dinner table full of politicians that what Bertha had said was horribly wrong. It'd ruin not only the city but them as well. Tempting William with a position in the committee had not panned out.

Bertha heard the whispers and listened to William's complaints, but her heart wasn't in it at the moment. What occupied her mind was Agatha's absence. She could always bully the room full of council members into obedience, but if something happened to Agatha, that'd be a catastrophe. She hated the fact that the necromancer was irreplaceable. Not only because it made her vulnerable but also because she didn't like Agatha that much. The nervous, agreeable woman sometimes made her want to blow her gasket. She could be so infuriating, always agreeing even with her absurd requests. More often than not, Bertha wanted to shake the woman and say: "Grow a backbone." But she couldn't do that. She didn't understand why the promising young necromancer she'd picked up from the University had to be so visibly afraid of life and words! Women, especially, in Agatha's position, who thought they could pass through life without causing ripples, made Bertha angry. Holy corpse worm, have a conviction about something! Anything! Bertha had made sure she'd lived her life both times without regrets. All her youthful mistakes warmed her.

Where the krak was the girl?!

Bertha let out a loud moan. Everyone looked at her guiltily. She collected herself and said, "Thank you for coming. We have had a fruitful conversation on how to fix this economic crisis that's troubling our citizens, and I'm glad we heard all sides and William brought up the possible downsides of forming a banking committee. We'll have a vote on the matter tomorrow. When we will hopefully have all our members present."

William lowered the hand he'd been chewing and looked at Bertha, ready for another round. But Bertha narrowed her eyes. The man said nothing.

"This has been a long day, what with all that has happened," Bertha said. "I'll go see Mrs. Maybury first thing tomorrow morning to see how she's doing, and we will convene at noon. Thank you and good night."

The party was over. Some of the undead moaned, as the body, their dinner, had a good many places left to sink their teeth into, but it was time to go home to form their opinions and search for necessary alliances. Yet, one politician tried to sneak the right earlobe. She put it down when she saw Bertha looking at her. She left the room mumbling about how she'd never eaten anything quite as tasty. There had to be a new spice involved.

Bertha shut the door after her guests and collapsed against it. She seldom looked at her hallway from this perspective. It was austere and impersonal. Agatha would have to do something about it when she found her. And she'd have to help her organize tomorrow's meeting. Before that, Bertha would have to visit some of the party members personally to convince them to take her side. William would surely already be making his rounds. Bertha pushed up from leaning against the door, but she didn't get far.

"Do you think he has gone potty?" a familiar voice asked behind her door.

"Who?" another familiar voice replied. Maybe some social gathering. An opera maybe, or those art openings that'd taken over the city's every petite corner house.

"Ira."

"He's the last guy who would go bananas."[36]

---

36 Not that the speaker was sure what bananas were. But they had to be something else to make people go cuckoo.

"Are you sure? He didn't seem like himself."

"Don't worry, Kitty will get him back to his old self in no time. So shut up. We are already here."

"Kitty is a sensible woman."

Someone snorted.

There was a knock on Bertha's front door. This had better be good, Bertha thought, and opened the door.

◆

Sometimes life feels like a cruel joke. Especially in those moments when everything you thought to be true is snatched away. Herbert knew exactly what it did to a man to lose all he loved and then be humiliated in the only thing he thought he was good at. If the soul leaves the body, there's nothing left but a formless mass with no value. Now he watched as the ghoul escorted the undead woman back to her coach. He was reminded of Ona. Tonight, he would die, die for her. That was the only thing he was still capable of.

There it was, the image again. Ona collapsed on her work desk at the bank. He could still see her looking up from her papers with a smile as she saw him coming to take her to lunch. She stood up and dropped and never got back up. The company necromancer told him her mind was too fatigued to be summoned. He felt her petite body in his arms, curled and motionless, as if she was still there. The pressure never left him. He'd carried her home for lack of a better plan and waited for her to move. Her parents blamed him for stalling and not doing what was proper. They insisted that this was why Ona had come back as a mindless zombie and was now locked in her parents' basement. They'd been right. What happened to Ona was his fault. It was because of him she'd worked tirelessly to be the best stockbroker the Worthwrite Bank of Necropolis Ltd had ever seen. He'd killed her.

"Ona," he muttered.

"What?" Cruxh asked.

"Nothing. Let's get this over with," Herbert said and stepped into the coach.

The ghoul didn't press the matter further. They rode in silence to the Library, where Cruxh had instructed the driver to go.

Whenever Herbert's glance brushed over Mrs.

Maybury, the undead woman seemed to gloat. She'd bested him. She saw him looking at her.

"I guess our Mayor's lackey is sulking," Mrs. Maybury said.

"Alice," Cruxh pleaded. He pressed his ears against his head, looking at Herbert with a puppy-dog expression. How could the ghoul be so docile? He appeared ready to apologize for his show of power. It wouldn't erase anything, least of all Cruxh's right to act as he had. Weapons would have been useless, and would have gotten them killed.

"I might have bruised my ego," Herbert said. "But I'm not sulking, nor am I anyone's lackey. I'm just reminding myself why I'm doing this. That justice prevails over pride." And it did. If Cruxh had to talk their way out of this for him to get Ona what she deserved, then no one would stand in the way of that, not him or Mrs. Maybury.

"You care about my justice? I thought you were here to keep me tamed and confined so as not to cause ripples for the Mayor?"

"To be frank, I care about justice, but not yours. I couldn't give a Kraken's ass what happens to you or between you and the Mayor. I only want to see Ira suffer."

"What does that silly banker have to do with any of this?"

"Just that we better find your ghouls."

"That's not an explanation!"

"Alice, I beg of you. Leave this be. He has no intent to harm you. You must see that," Cruxh said.

"Yes, why would I want to harm you when you are as irrelevant as the maggot that is crawling out of your ear?"

Mrs. Maybury was visibly appalled. And the fact that Herbert was right, and a maggot was indeed squirming out of her ear, didn't help the cause at all. It was downright rude to talk about the undead's parasites. It was like pointing out someone had crooked teeth. They couldn't help it.

Mrs. Maybury went on sulking.

After that, no one wanted to break the mood. They'd done their worst. You could say they rode to the Library in the deep stillness of life's troubled existence.

Soon enough, they arrived at their destination. Not that it'd ease their troubles. The magnificent building fought for their attention against the monstrous landscape. You could describe the place as a Gothic church of knowledge and frivolousness, as there were books of all genres. It was debatable which were the books of no substantial consequence whatsoever written purely to entertain; that would be a matter of where one put value: empathy and societal well-being or vigorous research to advance progress, awareness, or sometimes personal convictions. But to be honest, that would be a pointless argument. Why choose? Even now there were two older men sitting on the Library's steps, bickering about the subject. Herbert, Cruxh, and Mrs. Maybury passed them, having left the coach behind.

"You better lead," Herbert said. "But the undead woman stays between us in case your friends decide they aren't done with her."

"It will not come to that, but if that will please you, then it is a good solution."

They formed an unstructured line, and Cruxh led them up the steps to the tall building with gray walls, glass windows, and two heavy dark wooden doors reinforced with iron, as if they were there to keep at bay the darkest reaches of the human mind.

They stepped inside. The Library overwhelmed Herbert with awe every time he entered. After taking in the vastness of the space and the smallness of himself, Herbert saw the usual chandeliers, dark wooden bookshelves, red velvet carpet zigzagging between them, ornamental bannisters lining the stairs to the upper floors, the librarian's desk, and the filing cabinet there to keep order. And only then did he see the books. Tons of volumes, ranging from your garden variety necromantic literature to mythology to gardening to anatomy to stories about what it's like to be a human.

Cruxh guided them onward over the red carpet. Herbert could only guess where. Soon the ghoul stopped and pushed a finger against his blue lips.

Herbert wasn't sure whether to laugh or flee; instead, he whispered, "What?"

"The librarian," Cruxh said and pointed up.

Above them on the ceiling, a huge black cocoon made out of wings hung down, shaking a little every time they made a noise. When it stopped moving, Cruxh said, "Now we can advance, but slowly."

They tiptoed after the ghoul, occasionally stopping to

check if the librarian had woken. Mrs. Maybury tilted her head along with Cruxh's.

"Where we are going?" Herbert asked after another faint noise of rustling leathery wings had passed. It wasn't that the librarian was dangerous, at least not in the traditional sense of bloodsucking and converting virgins. No. It was far worse. The librarian was one of those who could make others think that they'd committed a mortal sin by making a noise. Not that the librarian was evil or anything, or did it out of spite; it was just that he, Nosh Feratu, had an acute sense of hearing, and any loud noise made him shriek. And there was nothing like the shrill cry of a vampire.

"There are two entries into the lair. One is behind a bookcase, but it is too far for our stomping feet. We do not want to draw too much attention. The other is just left of us," Cruxh said.

"Where's that?" Herbert asked.

Silence followed his question.

"You will not like it," Cruxh said.

"What does that matter? If it's the only option we have, then we go through there," Herbert stated.

"It is through the indoor privy," Cruxh said.

"All right," Herbert said. A privy was just perfect. He cursed himself for not killing the necromancer. He should have expected nothing else from the ghouls' devious minds than to use a shithouse as an entrance. But what did he care? There was no single ounce of dignity left in him. But he had to give it to the ghoul, he was a perplexing creature. Even though he hated Cruxh, on some level, he respected him. The ghoul chose humbleness even when he could dominate anyone with force. Also, his compliance wasn't a disguise for dominance.

Cruxh led them behind the privy door. He said, "You two better wait here while I have a look and check if it is empty." The ghoul didn't wait for an answer. He left Herbert and Mrs. Maybury alone.

"Do you think he'll be all right?" she asked.

"Who?" Herbert replied.

"Cruxh," she said.

"I think he can handle himself in a privy. Most men do. He's probably the most terrifying thing in there," Herbert added.

"He's not a thing. You should stop treating him so awfully," Mrs. Maybury said.

"I'm treating *him* as I would treat anyone else."

"Then you have dreadful manners," she said.

Back at you, Herbert thought. "Unfortunately, I do." The undead woman snarled.

"But I'm here. Doesn't that count for something?" Herbert asked.

At that moment, Cruxh pushed the door open. "There is no one in here."

Herbert found the privy to be way nicer than he expected. Someone had thought to paint pictures on the walls. There was a long wooden plank with five holes on each side of the room. There'd even been an attempt to curve the wood around the holes to make the whole business more comfortable. He'd never have put so much effort into such a place, but now, as he thought about it, a sculpture might brighten the privy. Not the usual kind, but maybe a woman in a flowy dress holding a vase. That would make the place look more relaxed, rather than a gargoyle watching over you while you were at it.

Cruxh crouched on the floor and lifted up a floor tile, revealing a man-sized entrance.

"You two better go first. There is a mechanism to the tile that needs special attention," Cruxh said.

"How do you suggest I go down?" he asked as he peered into the shaft.

"Use your claws," Cruxh said.

"I seem to be fresh out of claws," Herbert said.

"Then I must take you down. Alice, if you would hold this in this precise position?"

Mrs. Maybury complied. She bent over and held the tile.

"Now, Mr. Ringworm, I need to latch my claws around your waist, if you do not mind."

Herbert saw no way out of this. He complied. He let the ghoul, who came just under his chest, secure his claw around his waist and hoist him into his arms. The ghoul descended into the darkness, pushing his long fingernails into the soil and moving one swing at a time. It wasn't the fact he was being carried down that bothered Herbert, it was the fact that there was no way back up. That the death he'd thought would be in the distant future would soon be upon him.

The ghoul lowered him onto the ground.

"Stay here; I will get Alice." And from the sound of it, the ghoul was gone. He saw the faint light up in the cave ceiling, but that was about the only thing he saw. He tried to calm himself down as he did every time in the dressing room before heading out to meet his opponent. Herbert pictured a perfect storm. The sound of rain beating against the roof tiles, and the distant sound of thunder. He was at peace.

He was jerked from his thoughts when the ghoul thudded next to him, Mrs. Maybury on his lap. As the light from the ceiling vanished, a faint glow from the wall mushrooms illuminated the dark tunnels.

"Where are we?" the undead woman asked as the ghoul lowered her down from his embrace. She followed the mushrooms spreading farther into the unknown.

"Home," Cruxh said.

20

KILLING ISN'T PART OF A GOOD
GOVERNANCE

orris had two options: either he took a walk to Bertha's place or joined Agatha on her quest to the police station. A true gentleman or noblewoman would choose the latter. At least you could reason your way out of a station, if it came to that. But taking a walk never leaves a person. Some think walking is a mental state that offers a way out of society into nature, to your core self. And what gentleman would choose true nature over civilization? There behind the trees and hilltops lurks wildness, savagery, the most condemnable endeavor: self-reflection. Those who are most adventurous would add spirituality and intellectuality. But such things are dangerous and should be forbidden. Nature is no place for a gentleman.

Morris weighed the length of the road ahead and the inconvenience of walking with the inconvenience of going with Agatha to the station. To say it was an easy choice would be an underestimation of Morris' endurance for discomfort. Both paths would take him farther away from his little rebellion against Ira, but going with Agatha might reduce the distress Wilbur would suffer.

"I better come with you to the station," Morris said.

Agatha corrected her posture and said, "I hoped you would." She shook the reins, and the horses moved. It was the art of humans, how one push, one tug, one step shaped their existence, and still left no mark. The side of the street they'd been parked on was now empty, but there they'd ever be.

The city had stashed the station between the Town Hall and the shoreline. The previous ruler would have liked it if the whole law-upholding institution had been at the bottom of the sea, but he and his court at least had to pretend such an institution existed. Minta had brought it back, but it still had most of its wings cut off. The officer who'd stormed into Ira's office was part of the new wave of police who hadn't yet experienced the perks of being bought off and weren't yet jaded enough by the job to disregard the law.

The building they were looking for was in a dead-end alleyway. If buildings were sentient beings, this building had backed into a corner to protect its behind. It had been foolish enough to be made from flammable lumber instead of solid rock, but it'd started to reinforce itself, building from the basement up. But when it finished this undertaking, the question remained: was it the same building anymore, or was it something different, like the Ship of Theseus, an unfortunate man who had trouble with metaphysics.

This was the first time Morris had business in the Necropolitan Police Department. Somehow, until now, he'd avoided the place despite his study of law and occupation as a banker. There was always a subordinate willing to take care of the day-to-day business. As a matter of fact, he was rather interested in peeking inside the institution, which held terror to most, to see what the fuss was all about. Also, there might be an opportunity for him to flex his arguing powers. It'd been such a long time since he'd gone head-to-head with anyone, really. There was this rush he got when someone opposed him, giving him an opportunity to dispute their claims. He was sure Agatha could be such a person with enough encouragement.

Agatha had to circle around Northnekton Bay a few times to find a spot to park.

"Do you think we should take Mr. Jeffrey with us or leave him here?" she asked when she finally double-parked the coach, blocking anyone coming or going.

"I–" Morris said, but thought better than to criticize her. "I think it'd cause a stir to walk inside a police station carrying a corpse. We better leave him inside the coach."

"They'll want to see him," Agatha said, not pleased with Morris' tone.

"We'll lead them here when we have talked to someone," Morris said, wanting to appear reasonable.

"Oh, have it your way then." She let go of the reins.

They left the coach, heading into the station. Men and women in blue uniforms went in and out of the building. Morris expected one of them to come and demand Agatha move the vehicle. But no one paid any attention to the small infringement. If someone noticed, they changed their mind as soon as they saw the necromancer. Morris followed after Agatha. She took long strides, making Morris hurry to keep up with her. But when they were near the station door, he rushed to hold the door open for her, letting Agatha go in first.

Inside the station, time had ceased flowing through space. It looked like your grandmother's home, where all the pieces of furniture were from the prehistoric era, when they still made everything functional and long-lasting. But the station was well kept. There was nothing broken or too worn out, but—that was the thing, you could always add a but. The station looked like someone had forgotten it. Like someone had once tried to lift the mood by trying to paint the walls a light green, but that someone had abandoned the task midway when something more urgent had come up. Morris' automatic response was a twinge of guilt and an urge to find a brush. He soon forgot his reaction as a man in a blue uniform greeted them lethargically from behind a counter.

Why did the place smell like rat wee and mold?

"We're here to see the police chief," Agatha said, approaching the officer behind the counter, who was giving them his bare minimum attention.

The officer was what you would expect to find inside a place like this. Dark-haired, stocky, tall, and with a mustache to put all others to shame. He would be a complete insult with his somewhat stereotypical appearance, if he didn't look so at peace with who and what he was.

"And I want to be the Queen," the man who stood between the outside world and the gates into the heart of the police station said. He was superb at his job. That was why it was him who stood there greeting anyone adventurous enough to enter the place and not some other poor bastard.

Agatha looked at the man, stunned. She tried again.

"We're here to see Cuddy. My mistress knows him personally."

"So does my ma, and you don't see her barging in here," the man said.

Morris softly laid a hand on Agatha's arm, who looked like she was ready to give one of her speeches.

"Good evening," he said and flashed a smile at the officer.

"Sir," the man replied and kept his scowl in place, not willing to budge even a little.

"Could you assist us with a case of a missing person and possible murder," Morris said.

Before the man could reply, a head rose behind him, accompanied by the barking of dogs. The head, belonging to a body covered with a fur coat, said, "I know that voice. Is that you, young Reinhardt?"

Morris stared at Kitty Worthwrite. He wanted to yelp and take cover. The same thought passed over the officer's face. The man looked like he had been caught in the pantry with his hand deep in the cookie jar.

"Mrs. Worthwrite, it's always a pleasure to see you. How have you been?" Morris asked. He sounded like he'd eaten the officer's jar of cookies and was about to be sick.

"Yes, yes. Why do you insist on talking to that awful man? He has nothing to do with anything. Let them in," Kitty said.

The officer hesitated. Morris felt a twinge of sympathy towards the man, who complied with Kitty's order.

"Someone will be here to help you. Take a seat," the man said, opening the gates for them.

When they circled around the counter and passed through the gates, they found Kitty sitting on a bench behind the counter booth. Her two dogs lay on either side of her feet. She had her arms crossed. There were empty chairs next to her. The station's visitors had reasoned that a space between them and Kitty was the only healthy way to increase their life expectancy.

"Good evening, Mrs. Worthwrite," Morris said.

"Kitty," the woman replied, looking past him. "Is that the Wicks girl?"

"Agatha Wicks. Pleased to meet you, ma'am," Agatha said and curtsied. On the social ladder, Agatha was on a higher rung than Mrs. Worthwrite. She was nobler born, thus making it unnecessary for her to show the deep respect she had, but Kitty's age triumphed over the slight difference in the blueness of their blood, causing Agatha's curtsy to smooth any future interactions.

"That's what a proper necromancer acts and looks like, not like that horrible girl that has Ira hanging on for dear life and bringing the future of the bank to the brink of ruin. I barely escaped myself. I had to coax the gargoyle to let me out," Kitty said. "Both of you, take a seat."

Morris found himself automatically obeying her command.

"What's going on? Where are Ira and Petula?" Morris asked and sat down.

Agatha too sat down next to the woman. Kitty's two dogs must have smelled Agatha's blue blood, as they instantly considered her to be their new playmate, letting her pet them.

"Be careful, dear, they might bite," Kitty said, making Agatha draw her hand back just when the dogs had gotten used to being petted by a stranger.

"Mrs. Worthwrite, I need you to explain. What has happened to Ira and Petula?" Morris said.

"How should I know? Last thing I heard, they were going down the chute, and now my poor husband is trapped underneath the bank with that necromancer and in the clutches of ghouls! They took our gold, can you believe that? All I know is he could be dead by now, leaving me in ruins, and in the hands of these fools," Kitty said, letting her judgment land on every single officer in sight.

Morris couldn't understand a single word Kitty had said. He was afraid that if he asked her to repeat the whole story, it would make even less sense.

"Where are Nigel and the head of the bank's security?" he requested instead.

"Nigel is running around the city, trying to catch

Kraken only knows what, and Henry is helping his friend's wife, something about a missing husband and a cottage cleaning racket... What has that got to do with anything?" Kitty asked.

This answer made even less sense. Morris tried again. "Are you saying that Miss Upwood and Mr. Worthwrite are..." he searched for the word.

"They've been kidnapped by the ghouls, along with our gold. And these fine officers of the law aren't doing anything about it."

Morris finally gave in. "I have to confess, I'm not quite following what you're saying," he said. "Could you elaborate?"

"If I must. Ira went down the hole in the vault, and I had to push that necromancer in after him," she said.

Morris tensed up. "Is she all right?" he asked.

"Who?" Kitty asked.

Morris wasn't sure if she was toying with him or was so distraught she wasn't making any sense.

"Petula," he added.

Agatha coughed.

Morris glanced past Kitty towards the necromancer. Agatha gave him a shy smile.

"She must be. I sent her to my husband. But the thing is that the ghouls took our gold, and we need to get it back," Kitty said. It'd be easy to think of Kitty as callous and only caring about the money, but that was how she had been taught to speak. No one had ever taught her to show emotions or even told her what they were. She was only expected to be seen and not heard. Not that she'd succeeded in that, but she honestly didn't know how to interact with others.

"You say ghouls took gold from the vault and escaped down a tunnel and Ira followed after them?" Morris asked, finally following Kitty's scattered explanations.

"Yes! I have been saying that the whole time."

"And the kidnapping?"

"They must have taken Ira and Petula. Why else haven't they come back?"

◆

Under Necropolis, Petula sat in the odd room inside the ghouls' Town Hall. She was surrounded by all the mockups of the bunny statues outside. The mockups that seemed to follow her and smile at her situation. If she had any paranoid tendencies, she'd think there was an intelligence behind their expressions, but she didn't. She had to confess, she wasn't sure why anyone would care for bunnies enough to go to such lengths to build model after model to achieve perfect statues here underneath Necropolis. But she wasn't fascinated enough to ask. She had a cup of coffee in front of her, and she had opened the other book.

"I've been meaning to ask you. What is it with you Leporidae Lops? I can't seem to get a hold over your banks," Ira said, turning to face Petula. He sat on a bench nearer to the door.

Petula smiled. It was the kind of smile everyone from Leporidae Lop did when faced with such a question. Unlike the rest of the Leporidae Lops, Petula didn't lie.

She said, "Luck." Simple as that. That was the base of Leporidae Lop's economy. It should be kept far away from the undead man's devious mind.

Ira laughed. "I know a lot about business, and the right opportunities can make or break things. If you're saying people from Leporidae Lop rely on luck in their business decisions, then you've misunderstood the whole process of making money."

Petula shrugged. That was the thing with outsiders. She didn't have to lie about the secret of Leporidae Lop. They never believed what she said was true. Out here, away from the influence of her homeland's gods, she'd lost the connection to the whole force of luck, but if she concentrated, it hadn't gone away. It was all the dead energy and lack of faith. She didn't mind. Even when she'd been obligated to attend her family's secret luck rituals, she'd never cared for the whole thing. She'd rather listen to their old, dead relatives outside the ritual circles and make a note of what they said. Mostly unsolicited advice. Sometimes sexist and rude insinuations. But she'd known early on that death or growing old didn't necessarily mean becoming wise.

"You can't be serious?" Ira stood up.

Petula couldn't quite decide if he was restless because an opportunity was slipping away or because of all the pent-up energy inside him. The dead were like that. Always in motion, even the spirits. No one knew why. Some scholars theorized it was due to the fact that if they ever stopped moving, they ceased to be. Petula doubted the argument. She'd witnessed inanimate undead with light still in them. She had her own hypothesis, which had to do with the absence of restrictions. It was only a hypothesis, since there was no research. Research she would never get to do in Leporidae Lop.

"What does it matter if what I say is true or not?" She lowered the book enough to see Ira wasn't just making noise. The man was pacing around.

"You can't use luck to guide a monetary system. It'd be too whimsical to trust; it'd be like rolling dice with every decision you make," he replied.

"It could be as usable as the energy in your skull system, but what do I know. Money doesn't interest me that much. If I need it, I can always use a spade."

Petula wasn't kidding. She had the option of digging for her money, and not in the sense that she'd go into mining. Just that there were a lot of forgotten stashes left behind by those with paranoid personalities, those with the sense to hide their nuts from thieving relatives. Her grandmother had been one. She'd lined their flue with stacks of banknotes. The only trouble was that her father's brother had a habit of spending every dime he got his hands on, and he had a nose for other people's money. But he hadn't found all his mother's stashes. Petula knew where the rest was if she ever needed it.

"Can you use luck? You can't. Are you trying to mess with me?" Now he'd made a full circle around the table where Petula sat. The ghouls followed the man's movement with their eyes, staying otherwise stationary. One of them was Sirixh. That much Petula had deduced.

She had hoped there would be spirits around to ask what was going on beyond the room, but she was alone. Even the usual ones were still gone. So, Sirixh was her safest bet for an alliance, if necessary. Or Petula could try to possess her, but she wasn't that convinced it'd work on the ghoul, and altogether it was a nasty business, reserved as a last resort. Petula looked away from the ghoul back to Ira and said, "I'm not sure if it's such a bad thing to make investment decisions with a dice. It seems to be as accurate as most of the so-called professionals." Or more, but she left that thought out.

The door opened before Ira had time to reply. A smaller ghoul stepped in, accompanied by a group of taller and serious-looking ghouls. An armed escort. If they'd had a kinder and more approachable appearance, Petula would have snorted at the hyperbole. But she guessed there were those people among ghouls as well as humans who didn't see the funny side of life. She most often belonged to that group herself with her thirst for perfection.

The lead ghoul, the small female, if Petula was correct about her sex,[37] clicked her tongue.

"Welcome to our home," she said, after assessing both Petula and Ira. There was no telling what she thought about either of them. Petula brushed her fingers against the smooth cover of her book.

Ira made a noise, indicating he was about to start his economics speech again, but the ghoul silenced him with a mere glance. Ira swallowed. There was something to be said for natural predators and their power of bringing back to reality even the most gifted self-deluder. Not that it'd stall Ira for long.

But the lead ghoul turned her full attention to Petula instead. The skin on her back crawled. Petula guessed that the ghoul thought her to be the bigger threat. She wanted more than anything to use her necromantic powers to look inside the ghoul and decipher what she was made of. To see if she had a soul of some sort, and if not, then was she a demon, like some scholars would insist? Even a demon had to be fueled by something, but what? Pure intellect? There had to be a clue, a book somewhere that explained what the ghouls were. She just hadn't found it yet. How could she leave Necropolis and leave all this behind?

The truth was, there was such a book. It was the first and only thing the ghouls had ever stolen from humans. But Petula wouldn't find it here in Necropolis. It had been taken overseas to another ghoul colony for safekeeping. Here in Necropolis, there were too many nosy necromancers and demonologists wandering around. Who knew when they would find their way into the lair? Like Petula had.

---

37   It was sometimes hard to tell with ghouls, but what did it matter.

The head ghoul finally opened her mouth. She said, "I gather you followed some ghouls through the door in Mr. Worthwrite's bank."

"If I may..." Petula said, letting the ghoul fill in the rest.

"Gwerrusxh," she replied. How she said it sounded more complicated than its spelling might be.

"Gwer—rus—xh," Petula said, pronouncing every syllable.

"You have an ear for sounds," Gwerrusxh replied.

"One tries one's best."

"One must."

"We made a foolish error, thinking there was a threat to Mr. Worthwrite's vault, but as soon as we noticed this error of ours, we began looking for a way out."

"If you will let me interrupt, there's an opportunity here beneficial for—" Ira didn't get farther than that.

"I see," the ghoul said. There was a hint of extra gurgle in her voice. She'd hidden it thus far. "Which is it? Going home or coming down here to bargain for the rest of our lands?"

"Lands? These are my lands. I own the bank and everything underneath it."

"Isr thisr the only truth you see?" Gwerrusxh asked. Petula was sure she detected anger in the ghoul's broken speech.

"It's a fact—"

"Please ignore him. He doesn't know what he's talking about. And if I must, I can always wipe his memory." Petula interrupted Ira. She might be able to do that. She'd never tried the actual spell, but as far as she gathered, the suggestive power of hypnotism was the safest bet. "I think it's better for all of us if we weren't ever here? Let us leave, and you don't have to hear or see us afterward," Petula said softly. She nudged the ghoul a little in the way she'd nudge a spirit. If Ira said another word, they'd die. Usually, she'd have resorted to using a ghost to distract the ghoul so they could escape. Like she'd done several times when an ignorant Necropolitan had tried to rob her. But the place was still absent of spirits. It had to be the ghouls keeping them away.

"That isr alwaysr the case with your kind. You don't thinkr. You came here full of those maddening thoughtsr you are using on me. Do you thinkr I can't feel them? A proud necromancer, aren'tr you? But your skillsr don't affect me, nor did they affect our ancestorsr. There isr no truthr, there isr no control, and you won't leaver here until I say so—"

"Mother!" rang behind the ghoul's back. Petula couldn't see who'd said it, but the effect that word had was remarkable. The ghoul tensed up and looked almost guilty.

A smallish ghoul pushed his way in through the door and said, "You cannot threaten humans. You cannot keep them here against their will. And it is high time we stop hiding. Let us use this as an opportunity."

Petula wouldn't call her and Ira being there an opportunity; more like a catastrophe, if any of the banker's ideas got heard, but she was liking the part where the new ghoul declared their right to leave.

Petula said, "Then we are leaving."

◆

Minta Stopford listened to the experts quibble. Albert, the undead banker, continued arguing about a bailout being the only way to stop Necropolis from collapsing. If the banks failed, then everything else would fail and the savings of common people would be lost. There'd be a string of suicides and a wave of crime. Chester, the economics professor, continued arguing against the man, and so did Ida, who saw it as part of nature for the weak to fall. Frederick kept repeating that it was high time the government took over all the banks. No one listened to him. He only got side glances. Minta had a hard time keeping her mouth shut. But she had to rely on the fact that they'd eventually get where she wanted them to. If she intervened now, it'd only destroy the integrity of her request for their expertise.

"A bailout is our only option. You must see that. If we banks had more money to support the cost of all the failing loans, then we could go on, and the threat of the city going under is avoided," Albert said.

"You sound like a broken record, and I won't even demean myself by repeating my argument. But I have to ask, why should a government give the privately owned banks free money? It's clear the banks aren't willing to do the same thing in return for their clients who're being crushed under the weight of their loans, to the same citizens who are the government in spirit, at least, if not in heart."

"That's not the same thing!"

"It sounds to me like it's exactly the same. You continue forgetting that we don't have extra money lying around to bail you out. The only way to get such money is through implementing new taxes, like a tax for owning a chimney. That'll make the people revolt, or wither to death, or most likely cut off their chimneys, knowing Necropolitans," Chester said.

"I don't need bailing out. My bank is doing fine," Albert said, not listening to anything Chester had said.

"I doubt that, listening to your moronic views of the economy. You don't know anything about money," Chester said. Before the other man could come up with a response, Chester continued, "The only way I can condone a bailout is if the banks pardon their customers' loans."

Minta didn't like what she heard. Not the useless bickering or what Chester had said. The banks pardoning the citizens' and business owners' failed loans might not be the right road. It sounded like a fine and good solution if you didn't consider human nature. In the longer run, it'd hurt people if it was done blindly. Minta could condone debt counseling and both parties negotiating for fair compensation. There had to be hope for everyone. Without hope, everything turned into ashes. But wiping the slate clean would encourage even more adventurous risk taking. She couldn't let that happen.

The means to get out of this mess was to get extra money for people to use for their basic needs and extra money for companies to hire more people. The cost of everything had skyrocketed, along with the fear to take risks and invest. All right, it was the risk-taking that'd gotten the city into trouble, but it'd been based on lies and quick gains by giving bad loans hand over fist. Somehow, they'd gotten into a situation where the big picture and the fear of being punished had been lost. Somehow, bankers had secured their position to be free to act as they wished. Yes, of course she thought that the citizens should be free to act as they wished, but only as long as they didn't hurt others in the process.

The only question worth answering was how to find that extra money. The right solution depended on who you asked. Everyone was willing to fight to claim their truth was the right one. When it came to economics, people held their beliefs as tightly as a religion. They thought even looking at the other side of the argument was a great offense with damnable consequences.

One thing gave her solace: most of the bankers couldn't run away with their assets. Some could, if the situation got to the point of pitchforks and torches. Some like Ira and his buddies, but the rest would have to stay, as their assets were tied up in the bad loans or in their properties. They couldn't run out of the city carrying their houses on their backs. For that, they needed their homes to grow legs, but most bankers had studied the magic of numbers instead of the magic of animating objects. One extra curriculum lesson would have saved them from this embarrassment. But they'd rather take a parlor trick lesson: "How To Guide The Invisible Hand."

"Miss Mayor?" Ida asked, interrupting Chester's and Albert's staring contest.

"Yes, Mrs. Mortician, how can I help?" Minta asked, not knowing what to expect. The woman's unsavory nature had become painfully obvious from Dow's documents.

"If I have understood correctly, you need a satisfactory result by tonight?" she asked.

"Yes, if that's possible. I know it's not a lot of time to come up with an all-inclusive plan, but I'd be satisfied with an outline. Something we can start with," Minta said.

"And Ira's coalition makes this a pressing matter?" Ida asked.

"Y-es," Minta said, still not knowing what the woman was thinking. She was making the others restless as well; they were squirming in their seats, searching for a better position.

"Then the solution is simple. We hire a hitman to get Ira out of the way. We don't need to change anything. If he's the problem, then we remove him as we'd do with anything or anybody else," Ida said.

Minta coughed. That wasn't a solution she'd expected to hear. She should have.

"Yeah, you can't blame us if Ira accidentally loses his head," Albert said.

Frederick glanced towards Minta and raised his eyebrows. Minta wasn't sure if the former monster hunter approved the suggestion or morally opposed it.

"But I know Ira, and a severed head wouldn't stop him gabbling. It'd only fuel him. It's the necromancer's head we need to cut off," Ida said. It'd be her wish come true. Not only did she hate how Ira's mega-bank cut her bank's profits, but he'd said she'd never amount to anything. She'd publicly sworn revenge after being fired from her job at the Worthwrite Bank of Necropolis Ltd.

Now even Chester was glancing towards Minta.

"While I think your solution is a creative way to ease the government's troubles, I can't condone the assassination of Mr. Worthwrite or his necromancer. That's not part of good governance," Minta said. If Dow was here with them, he'd agree with the banker. Assassinations, torture chambers, and all the other dirty tricks were right up his alley. But if Dow had taught her how to rule and take command, then she'd taught the man an ounce of humanity.

"I think you are making a mistake. If we don't remove Ira from the equation, nothing we do will get us what we want. The man has a talent for getting his way," Ida persisted.

"How would killing Mr. Worthwrite help?" Minta asked. "He must have made sure, and I know for a fact he has made sure, that the idea of a finance committee has been put out there. There has even been a prelude to such an idea in the newspapers. Killing Ira would only take Ira out and leave us dealing with the matter."

"Yes, but we'd be dealing with it and not him. We'd be the ones choosing who'd sit in that committee and what they decided. If it's something the public feels is necessary, then why not give it to them?" Ida asked. "Then there wouldn't be a need for any banking reform; we substitute any threat with our own guy, and the matter is dealt with," she continued.

"What about his black book?" Albert asked.

Ida went one shade paler. "Light torture and then a quick kill. That usually does it," she said before she lost momentum.

Minta fought with all she had to keep any spite out of her voice. "Then what?" she asked with as warm a voice as she could. The monster hunter in her would have leaped over the table, seized the woman, tossed her out of the perfectly arched doors, and been done with all this business of murder. And the irony would be lost on her.

"We get rid of the rest of them. We can call it cleaning. I think the public will like it," Ida said.

"And what about your own banks?" Minta asked.

"What about them?"

"As far as I've gathered, they've had a rough time."

"Of course they have, but that's because Ira keeps pushing them, us, down. As soon as he's gone, we and the city will survive. I say we vote on hiring a hitman. Let's have a show of hands," Ida said.

Before Albert could lift his hand up, Chester jumped up from his seat. "No, I can't condone this. This is not about the economy; you're talking about murder. I won't have this," he said.

"Neither will I," Frederick said.

"I have to agree with both Mr. Fen and Mr. Kilborn; killing isn't on the table. There has to be another option that's staring us in the face," Minta said.

21

THE POETRY OF SURPRISE

Morris had a hard time following and understanding what Kitty Worthwrite said. The more she explained, the more the story sounded like an elaborate lie. Why would ghouls want to kidnap Petula, let alone Ira? Ghouls had never struck him as the types to do anything so drastic. The ghouls he'd hired worked tirelessly and never complained about anything. If you asked him, you'd have a hard time finding more law-abiding citizens in Necropolis. But if what Kitty said was true, he was gravely mistaken about their nature. Also, if they killed Ira, the bank would go to Kitty, because as far as he knew, Ira thought his children to be morons. His words, not Morris'.

"We have to get your husband and Petula out of there. We need to find someone who can handle this situation," he said. He had a few capable men in mind to prevent Kitty from rising to the head of the empire. Morris could handle Ira, but the woman scared him.

"What do you think I'm doing here?" Kitty asked.

"But these are the police," Morris said, leaning on his

cane.

"Haven't you been following? They say to contact them in case of emergency. That's what I'm doing. I'm being a good citizen and following what they say in the newspapers." She reached down to pet Bella and gave a warning glance to Agatha; if she insisted on hogging her dogs, there'd be far worse consequences than a bite.

Kitty was right. There'd been several advertisements in the newspapers throughout the year to uplift the image of the police force. It was part of the campaign the Town Hall council had started. Morris agreed with them to some extent that the city should have a working legal system, but he'd never had problems with his contractors. They'd always delivered results to his liking. Using the police for things like Jeffrey's murder was all right, but kidnapping and robbery of this magnitude needed the best money could buy.

His father would turn in his grave if he knew his son thought this way. He'd thought he brought Morris up better, but he was too busy being dead to care about the failings of the next generation's empathy or to understand the dangers of privately owned law.

"But how about the head of—" Morris began.

"The head of the bank's security is away. I told you that already. Don't you listen?" she asked.

"But—"

Agatha motioned for him to stop.

Morris complied. He had no reason to argue with Kitty. It was her right to do as she pleased.

"Then we better wait our turn," he said. But after all this was done and finished at the station, he'd do what was necessary to get Petula back home. And Ira too. He couldn't have Petula's death on his conscience.

Kitty responded with a superior sigh. What she thought was a mystery to him. She appeared worried about her husband, yet she was here. He'd spoken the truth about the police. As much as the Town Hall needed the city's finest to be functional and uphold the law, they clearly didn't. From the look of the station, the police would reach their potential in three to five years, and by that time Ira's flesh would be back feeding the maggots.

Agatha tried to make light conversation with Kitty, asking about the dogs. Morris let his mind drift. He watched as an officer marched a man with his hands cuffed behind his back to a desk, where an adequate punishment was put into motion. Soon the officer abandoned the man there to wait. More accurately, Morris thought, to forget the man's existence. Which proved Morris right that privatization of the government's core institutions was the proper path to make the city functional. Why not let people buy the services they needed?

The monetary entity he'd set up could force the city to sell its assets to the highest bidder, who'd make the city more efficient. Maybe a clause for efficiency could be made mandatory with a law, tying up the Town Hall council's hands. Morris searched for the right words for such a proposal, but a dispute snapped him out of his thoughts. The officer who'd charged into Ira's office stood near to them. An older officer shouted at her. The woman's face was red. Morris expected her to assert herself to the senior officer as she'd done to Ira, but her superior held a stronger power than the banker had. She kept her mouth shut, taking in the dressing-down. Morris was sure she'd given them her name. He prodded his mind, discovering he'd only registered the last name, Caster. Not a prominent family but an old name. There was a long line of kitchen maids, chimney sweepers, a few officers and other semi-skilled laborers like brick-makers, and one railway porter and several mudlarks. The one who he knew had been his mother's lady's maid. He watched the older officer point at a desk, and Caster collapsed behind it, not looking happy.

Morris had a feeling she was in trouble because of them.

"So why are you here?" Kitty asked, after growing bored with Agatha's attempts to please her.

He heard Kitty but waved his hand at the Caster woman, who was searching for an escape route from the misery she'd been assigned. Like Morris had intended, their eyes met. It took longer than Morris thought for the officer to have that necessary a-ha moment, but eventually, she did. Her expression turned from agony into a pleasant smile in slow motion.

"What are you doing?" Kitty asked and followed Morris' gaze. No gentlemen waved their hands in such a fashion. If they desired to be noticed, they'd make a slight nod or tip their hat. And Morris had a fine hat.

Morris didn't reply. He watched as the officer, Hortensia Caster, stood up and made her way to them. Her clothes still looked one size too big for her, but as she walked with a straight posture and an air of authority, there was nothing comical about her. Then again, no one could deny that appearance was part of the perceived power. Her clothing would hold her back, as her senile former police officer father would agree, even though he thought no women should enter the force.

"Good evening. My name is Hortensia Caster, and I will aid you. Would you be so kind as to follow me to my desk, so we can get your process started?" she asked.

Morris got up. He needed Kitty's matter to be dealt with, and soon. There was also the issue of the driver's killer being free, and based on the state of the station, this Caster woman was their safest bet to get any justice. Agatha and Kitty followed him, but he heard Kitty whisper, "But she's a woman."

"Yeah, but an officer willing to aid us," Agatha whispered back.

"I'm sorry about the chaos here; the upcoming protest is keeping us busy. If you take a seat, we can go over why you're here," Hortensia Caster said as they arrived at her desk.

Kitty sat down in the only seat available. The dogs circled around to take their places next to her.

"So how can I help you?" Hortensia asked.

Kitty glanced at Morris but began her story instantly, saying the same things she'd repeated to Morris but with a more coherent train of thought, adding a logical beginning and ending. Kitty had graciously forgotten to mention to him and Agatha, how they witnessed the robbery, and how she'd defended her husband by forcing Petula to go after him. She told the rest of the external circumstances and how from sheer determination she'd made the gargoyle tear the gate off its hinges and rescue her. The longer Kitty spoke, the more nervous the officer got. She kept glancing towards the stairs the senior officer had taken.

"I want my husband found! And those ghouls, they should be hanged! What are you going to do about it?" It was a good thing Kitty and Mrs. Maybury had nothing to do with each other, or the two forces combined could purge the city of ghouls and other creatures who irked them. Like cats.

Hortensia sat still and silent. Kitty peered into the poor officer's eyes, waiting for her to magically fix the situation. Morris wondered if Kitty intentionally tortured others. Most likely the torture was a somewhat pleasant side-effect of the way she dealt with other people.

"I... We need to form a search party and head to your bank's vault...and descend into the...tunnels," Hortensia said, trying to get her thoughts organized and sound professional.

"No, you won't!" Kitty said. "I won't have your kind trample inside the vault. It's a private place, and no one will break our clients' confidence."

Morris was relieved that Kitty had enough sense in her not to invite just anyone inside the inner sanctum of the bank. If Ira found out that Kitty let them in there, there'd be nothing left of the woman. From the kindness of the undead man's heart, he might have let her beg on the streets of Necropolis, but Morris was doubtful he'd be even that merciful.

"But—" the officer said.

"Find another way to find my husband and that necromancer of his."

"There isn't any other way," Hortensia said. "It's part of the normal procedure."

"Not where I come from. Where I come from, we respect our elders. So sit up straight and stop lounging. You are a tall girl; own up to it." At some point, the officer had turned back into an awkward, lanky girl who didn't know what to do with the extra reach of her limbs. She'd be relieved to know that such a decline was a normal side-effect of being around Kitty.

"I've been thinking, and I might be able to help," Agatha said, startling everyone. She didn't look pleased to have all eyes on her. Her posture collapsed. The Kitty effect had a habit of spreading.

"How?" Kitty asked.

"I've been wondering for a while, but I think that if I had something of your husband's or Petula's, I might be able to locate them on a map. It's really a simple finding spell, and I know not everyone believes in housewives' superstitions, but I'd say it has its merits. I've found several things I've lost that way. You wouldn't believe what funny places you can leave your teeth," she said and blushed when her bravery ran out.

Kitty opened her mouth to say her piece, but Morris interrupted her by saying, "I think that's a good idea. It won't hurt to try."

Kitty glanced at Morris and said nothing.

"Do you have anything of his or hers?" Agatha asked gingerly.

"Who do you think I am? Some magic Ira's-things dispenser? I'm his wife and...as a matter of fact, I do have something of his," Kitty said. She took her purse and rummaged through it, refraining from cursing as she tried to find the one thing she needed from the bottomless pit of chaos where all the missing items went to multiply, also known as her purse. She drew out a dried, gray piece of something. It took some time for Morris to realize what she held in her hands.

"Here you go," Kitty said and triumphantly thrust her husband's toe into Agatha's hand.

Agatha turned the toe around and smiled. "This will do. Now we need a string and a map."

Morris stared at the banker's toe and wondered if he saw bite marks on it. If he'd looked down at his feet, he might have witnessed a guilty expression on one of the dogs.

"I'll get you the map and the string," Hortensia said. She stood up and left the three of them alone. Before she was out of their view, she glanced back and paused, but went ahead nevertheless.

"What happens when and if we find my husband?" Kitty said, sending a meaningful look towards the way the officer had gone. "She doesn't appear capable of bringing Ira back."

"No, she doesn't. We hire someone or..."

"You two are as bad as each other. She's an officer of the law and will do everything in her power to help us. If you don't see that, then you know nothing of people. She's the first person here who has taken any interest in us, and she didn't even once interrupt, belittle, or doubt you. I think she's just the person we need," Agatha said. If it'd been any other person saying those words, she wouldn't have heard the end of it, but it was Agatha Wicks. Sometimes a title let you get away with murder, or in this case, with a small social infringement, which was in a way worse, as it was done with good intentions. Those things that pave the road to Hell.

The minutes it took for the officer to get back felt like an eternity in purgatory. It was the special way Kitty sat on the chair. All the unsaid things oozed out of her. A thick, tangible wall that only needed one word to unravel. Morris had never been as happy to see anyone in a blue uniform as he was to see Miss Caster, who circled back into sight behind the staircase. She was carrying a folded map in her hands and a bundle of what looked like pink ribbon.

When she got to the table, she spread the map over all the other things and handed the ribbon to Agatha, who'd been fiddling with Ira's toe all this time. Rather her than him. Dead flesh revolted Morris.

Agatha tied the pink ribbon around Ira's toe. She hung the contraption over the map and said, "All that's lost can be found. I call upon you to find Ira, whether he's lost or stolen. Seek him as this spell is spoken. All that's lost will be found." She repeated the mantra five times, keeping her eyes shut. On her second time through, the toe swirled over the map, to Morris' dislike. On the third time, the toe continued making wide arches. On the fourth, the circle narrowed and narrowed, and by the end of the fifth repeat, the toe came to a halt and pointed at the map like an accusing finger.

Morris, Kitty, and the officer bent over to see where it pointed.

"Hmmmm," Morris said.

"What?" Agatha asked and opened her eyes. She peered at the map and said, "Oh. Why are they at the Library?"

"It has to be that necromancer's fault," Kitty said.

◆

Some people handle pressure and stress better than others. They don't mind being in a tight spot or so high above that fear of falling has lost its meaning. Herbert had accepted his mortality, and that his death was minutes away, so the unknown and the ghouls didn't scare him. He only hoped that Minta would deliver justice by imprisoning Ira. While waiting, he occupied himself by examining the same reliefs Petula had marveled at. He was less interested in the incomprehensible footnotes and more interested in the technique used. They, whoever they were, had carved the reliefs into solid rock, but that wasn't the astonishing part. It was that all the refinements were so delicate, they'd break off after one wrong move from the artist. This was the first time he'd felt like he was looking at a true masterpiece. Whatever passed as art above ground level was crude and vulgar.

How could someone have made stone look light as a petal or a hand, so lifelike that he was sure there was a beating heart within it? The art even made him oblivious to the fact that the voice was gone.

"I," Herbert said.

"What?" Mrs. Maybury snapped.

He ignored Mrs. Maybury's tone and asked her, "Can't you see how that woman's hair is almost translucent?"

Mrs. Maybury's annoyance was quite understandable. Herbert had slowed their pace, as more than once he'd stopped to trace the lines of a ghoul, human, a building, anything that made his artistic heart elated.

"Stop ogling and concentrate on what we came here to do," she replied.

"But this is marvelous. These are beyond any talent you can see above. These are true art. Cruxh, who made *her*?" Herbert asked, examining a woman with delicate features. He'd been to every art opening in the city, searching for someone who could compose what he felt, but until now he'd seen no one who made him see the world like this. Pure joy.

Cruxh stopped in front of the woman Herbert had mentioned. She stood there in the middle of a group of ghouls. A disturbed mind would think the ghouls were trying to eat her, but an acute observer would see they embraced her. An even acuter mind would have seen how much the woman resembled a young Mrs. Maybury. But that was just a coincidence and not an omen.[38]

Cruxh frowned. "Several of us have contributed to the history of our people," he said.

"You made these?"

"No, not me personally. It is better if I stand in awe of the finished project, preferably from far away, rather than try to take part in the artistic flow. But I and books are great

---

38   Okay, maybe it was because the woman on the relief was Mrs. Maybury's great-aunt, who hadn't given Kraken's ass whom she associated with.

friends, if that is any solace?" Cruxh stated, looking embarrassed.

"But this was made by ghouls?" Herbert asked.

"I believe so. This woman, in particular, was made by a wonderful ghoul who I'm afraid passed away when her muse died. I know what you must think, but their connection was so strong that even her ghoulish essence couldn't bear the loss. But some other artists who've contributed to these still live, and if we have an opportunity, I can introduce you to them," Cruxh said.

Herbert hesitated. He needed Cruxh's words to be untrue. He couldn't find the lost poetry of his soul here amongst the ghouls, yet he felt inspired.

"This is all wonderful and informative, but we have better things to do than stand and stare at ladies. Let's go," Mrs. Maybury said. She had no soul for visual arts. She was like Cruxh: fonder of the written word. For her, it was poems that made her bloom, but only in secrecy.

Cruxh and Herbert complied. Herbert even picked up his pace, but made as many notes as he could.

Cruxh took them to the same ledge Petula and Ira had stood upon, looking at the city, but he left no time for Herbert and Mrs. Maybury to wonder, speak, or even think about what they saw.

"We will go down from here. Can you manage?" he asked, addressing Herbert.

Herbert stared at the city, his mouth hanging open slightly.

"Mr. Ringworm?" Cruxh asked.

No reply.

"Can you manage?" the ghoul asked again.

"Yes, I can manage," Herbert said. Not that he'd noticed what the ghoul meant. He couldn't take his eyes off the buildings.

"I am glad, as the other way would have been a longer route. Alice and I will go down first, and you will come behind. And Alice, I will carry you down," the ghoul said, offering his claw to Mrs. Maybury.

The undead woman stood on the ledge, and without a word, she propelled herself onto the stairs and climbed down. Cruxh hurried after her.

"Wait, let me aid you, the steps are dangerous," he

shouted, and his voice echoed in the huge cave.

If Mrs. Maybury replied, Herbert didn't hear her. If he'd paid any attention, he'd be proud of how the woman had handled Cruxh. However, the ghoul was right. Now, as he looked at the stairs, he saw there was no room for a misplaced hand or foot. Herbert didn't mind, but what made the climb almost impossible was that there was no grip. Someone had thought it was a good idea to polish the stone steps until they were smooth. He lowered his feet to the first step. Usually, he put all his weight on his feet, but now the uncertain grip of his soft leather shoes made him cling tighter with his hands, which his brain knew to be an error, but his body went ahead anyway.

Herbert's breathing got more laborious as he descended. The harder he fought not to slip off, the less control he had. He kept glancing down, trying to calculate how long he could go on and if the other two were alive. To his annoyance, both Cruxh and Mrs. Maybury seemed to handle the stairs with ease. There was only one option. Herbert shut his eyes and relaxed. He stopped squeezing for dear life, letting his body take the lead. After that, his movements were second nature. The gap between him and the two others got shorter, and he was down on the ground soon after them.

His legs shook when his feet hit the cave's floor. But he took no notice. Herbert gaped as the city opened up, inviting him in. The place was impressive. It was something he wished Necropolis to be: fluid and light. Almost every house had its own relief, mural, or a painting of the inner life of its inhabitants. Herbert kept swiveling his head, taking everything in. Cruxh didn't give him time to marvel. The ghoul hurried them into the city.

Herbert made note that even when there were corpses depicted on the houses, they were not there to appall. They celebrated life more than death. There had to be a great art school here; Herbert could only wish to attend.

Herbert was wrong. There was no school in the way he thought. The ghouls learned through an apprentice system. An older ghoul taught whoever sought their advice, and so the chain went on. The same opportunity they'd give to him, if he only thought to ask.

"We are here," Cruxh said and stopped at the steps of

the Town Hall, or at least it looked like one.

Herbert hadn't realized they were heading somewhere. He hadn't counted his steps or memorized every turn they'd taken. He'd even missed all the ghouls staring at him. But Herbert didn't hear a word Cruxh said or pay attention to his own failings. All the strength in his body left him. He was sure that any moment now his legs would give in, again.

"Why?" he asked.

"Mr. Ringworm, what is the matter?" Cruxh asked. He almost reached out to aid Herbert, but at the last minute he pulled his claws back.

"Those statues," Herbert said.

"For the parasites' sake, I know, they are hideous, but you don't have to be so melodramatic," Mrs. Maybury said.

Cruxh glanced at her, and if Herbert had given a damn about the woman and her words or her existence, he'd have seen a sign of her shame.

"I know they are not what you are used to in Necropolis, but I assure you, they are not an attempt to mock the fine culture of knighthood or cause offence to any type of guards. They are—" Cruxh said, looking at the two bunny statues.

"Where did you get them?" Herbert asked, cutting him off.

"The bunnies? I am not entirely sure how they came into our possession, but I assure you—"

"But they said they destroyed them. That they were an abomination," Herbert said. The power in his legs was gone. He'd have collapsed on the ground if Cruxh hadn't been there. The ghoul guided Herbert up the Town Hall's steps and made him sit down closer to the bunnies, forcing Herbert to see every mistake he'd made with them. Every time he'd lost his concentration while carving the bunnies, every time he'd gotten frustrated, every time Ona had distracted him was marked on the bunnies and their suits of armor.

"I am afraid you have lost me," Cruxh said, shaking his head at Mrs. Maybury, who was ready with her comeback.

"Those are mine. I made them," Herbert said.

"You did?"

"I'm a sculptor, or I was meant to be. But I was sure they destroyed those two."

"You are? How wonderful. Everyone in the city likes your statues. They, we, have seen nothing like them. There is a philosophical debate going on about their meaning, and if the fantastical element is a play on the hardship of modern life or a mockery of the spirit in the suit. Or, as I like to think, they are just bunnies in armor."

"But—"

"Enough. You two can reminisce about the past on your own time. I'm going to get my justice," Mrs. Maybury said. She wavered but stepped past them and into the Town Hall.

"I am sorry, Mr. Ringworm, I have to go. Alice, wait, you cannot just barge in," Cruxh said. He jumped up and rushed after Mrs. Maybury.

The bang of the door shutting behind Cruxh woke Herbert up. There was a group of ghouls staring at him. To make it clear, they'd heard the exchange between Herbert and Cruxh and were looking at Herbert weirdly.

Herbert stood up and backed away from the ghouls. His brain told him he'd survived this far, maybe there was hope. He'd never been that good with philosophical debates anyway. He went in through the doors and heard Cruxh say, "Mother!"

Even ghouls had to come into being somehow. The basic way was through natural birth. Then there's the option of splitting to multiply and fill the world, but complex creatures with complex plans tend to avoid such methods. Ghouls wanted to think of themselves as complicated beings with the ability to think about the present, mope over the past, and dream about the future, thus splitting hadn't been a valid choice; neither had traditional birth. But when your body is technically dead, creating life got a lot more complicated, and no, corpse worms weren't involved. How ghouls came into being was an enigma.[39] No one had ever witnessed the event. Like many, Herbert thought they came into being with a summoning. He was right to some extent. There was a ritual, but it didn't involve blood or chanting the name of an evil overlord. It was an event of one, two, or a group of ghouls coming together, agreeing to form a new life morphed from their essence and from a fellow ghoul's body

---

39   To humans.

whose mind had stopped functioning. Their philosophers had debated for centuries how this was possible, and which came first, the body or the essence, but they'd never reached a consensus. But how the word "mother" fitted into this picture was a mystery.

"You cannot threaten humans. You cannot keep them here against their will. And it is high time we stop hiding. Let us use this as an opportunity," Cruxh said.

"Then we are leaving," Herbert heard someone say.

"Cruxh," a shorter ghoul said, standing in a doorway, blocking him from seeing what was in the room.

"Hello, Mother," Cruxh replied.

Herbert had moved behind Cruxh and was thinking it might have been better to stay outside with the other ghouls and debate the meaning of his creations. As the creator, that was an awkward position to be in, even more so when the subjects had been created on a whim.

"I see you've brought humans with you," Cruxh's mother said. "I thought we agreed not to invite invading species into our home."

"Mother, I have brought them on a matter of great importance. It is time to introduce ourselves to humans and be part of Necropolis as neighbors and citizens. I want you to meet someone," Cruxh said.

Cruxh's mother turned around to face her son. She didn't look pleased, but that wasn't what caught Herbert's attention. It was the necromancer sitting in the room and staring straight into his eyes. She tilted her head, and Herbert was sure the tight line between her lips curled a little. This would change everything. That was the same thought Petula had at that precise moment.

"And who might that be?" Cruxh's mother asked.

"Mrs. Maybury, this is my mother, Gwerrusxh. She is our leader. And Mother, this is Mrs. Maybury, a council member," Cruxh said, stepping out of the way so the women could see each other.

Herbert ignored the exchange and the fact that Gwerrusxh had bared her teeth. He kept looking at the necromancer and the newly revealed undead banker.

His hands squeezed into fists.

22

A BITE MIGHT CHANGE EVERYTHING

eldom did you want to find bankers standing on your doorstep. Even someone like Bertha went over the deeds of her house, the balance of her bank account, and the debts she owed to reassure herself that she stood on firm ground before she greeted the two bankers. Ignatius and Wilbur were there for some other reason, and she had her suspicions what that was. Either they were working with Morris and Ira, which was doubtful, as the four men hated each other, or they'd come to the same conclusion as the other two bankers and were here to sway her to their side against Reinhardt and Worthwrite. What she didn't quite get was how they'd heard. She'd kept her mouth shut. Not that Morris' proposal was novel. But they'd mentioned Ira and Kitty.

"Good evening, gentlemen. To what do I owe this honor?" Bertha asked.

"Evening, Mrs. Chaplain, may we come in and have a moment of your time?" Wilbur asked.

"Have you two finally found Kraken? If you have,

I'm not interested," she said and hoped that the curl of her lips spoke on her behalf as she stepped aside.

"What on earth is she talking about? I have nothing to do with that institution. What gives them the right to tax my income? What does a bloated octopus need money for?" Ignatius asked, not looking happy at all.

"I think it was meant as a joke," Wilbur said.

"Joke? Ugh," Ignatius said.

"Yes, a bad one, but do come in," Bertha said. Sometimes the clostridium botulinum combined with formaldehyde and silicon dioxide stopped her brain from working. Not that she needed a brain. It was all about the spirit. But the joke had come from her past street-self. She'd gone to lengths to make that girl disappear, but the two bankers had brought back unpleasant memories she'd suffocated and packaged into a neat box. A box that was never to be opened.

Bertha let the bankers in and took a glance outside the house before shutting the door. There was no sign of her coach or Agatha. Just the bankers' transportation. She guided them to the drawing room, or parlor, as it was more commonly known.

"Do sit down," Bertha said, showing the bankers to chairs near the fireplace. She chose an armchair and slumped down. She had to correct herself to appear to have a working spine.

"How may I help you?" she asked.

"We are here because of your assistant," Ignatius began.

"Is she all right?" Bertha asked, letting out a low moan.

"She's fine. We are here to borrow her to resurrect Mr. Worthwrite," Ignatius said and leaned farther away from the undead woman.

Wilbur shook his head. "What Mr. Vaughn means is that we were sent here by Miss Wicks while she aids Morris Reinhardt with an unfortunate incident, but they'll be here soon. In the meanwhile, we'd like to ask your permission to allow Miss Wicks to take over the possession of Mr. Worthwrite's soul. As you may have already gathered, there's a connection here, and your assistant would secure the situation," he said.

Bertha frowned, or she tried to frown. Her face didn't quite follow her inner thoughts.

"Hm. I'm not sure what you're talking about, but what Miss Wicks does is her own choice. I might employ her, but she has the freedom to choose her clients," she said.

They all knew that wasn't true. Such a charade was expected from her. If word got out that she restricted Agatha's freedom to choose, Bertha would not only anger the labor union; in addition, she'd have the Necromantic Alliance's lawyers all over her. That was something a dead person should avoid at any cost.

"Of course, but would you think of helping Mr. Worthwrite as a favorable decision?" Ignatius asked.

"Certainly I would. As a prominent member of the community, I have to see to it that we don't lose any pillars of our society, and the head of the biggest bank dying would have an everlasting impact on Necropolis. But if I may ask, where are Miss Wicks and young Reinhardt?" Bertha asked. She quite liked the younger Reinhardt. He was modest and bendable, despite his flair for social validation, unlike his father, who had weird views about money and duty.

"They are at the marketplace and should be coming here soon," Ignatius said.

"And she is fine?" Bertha asked, searching for any extra emotions going through her.

"Should be. But as we are now here, I think we have more vital business to discuss. I want to know how you have been fulfilling your part of the deal," Ignatius said.

"Ignatius," Wilbur said.

"Mrs. Chaplain is a highly intelligent woman, and she has already figured out our involvement. The question is, does she want to hold her position and rise higher with our aid or not?" the man stated. He reached for a red wine decanter on the table between him and Wilbur and poured a glass for himself and then, after careful consideration, poured one for Wilbur as well. It was pointless to offer one to Bertha.

"Asking has never hurt anyone, and I like a man who gets straight to the point. Yes, I'm willing to work with you to secure a position beneficial to all of us. But as you know, my loyalties lie with the public, and I'll conduct my affairs accordingly," Bertha said, knowing it was never wise to come off too eager.

"That goes without saying," Ignatius said, shooting a glance towards Wilbur, who slurped his wine. The color, which had been gone from the man's face, came back.

"I'm glad we are in agreement, yet I have to say that instead of concealing your involvement, I'd have preferred you to be upfront, as I've always appreciated your and Mr. Sumner's involvement in the city's prosperity," she said.

"There was no attempt to deceive or hide our part from you. But there would be...how shall I put it, dangers, if it was widely known that the five of us were working together," Ignatius said.

Wilbur's posture told another tale. So did Ignatius'. They were uncomfortable at the thought of coming out of hiding. Bertha couldn't blame them. But she didn't like to be thought of as a stooge. If and when Agatha got hold of Ira's soul, she'd make sure that she was never kept out of the loop.

"I couldn't agree more. One should never reveal something lightly."

A sense of apathy washed over Bertha. Her body wanted to double over, but she couldn't let it. She had to push back against the emotion. Darn that girl and her melancholic tendencies, she thought. It had to be that young Reinhardt fellow, making matters worse.

Agatha's and Bertha's connection was unnatural and dangerous. Originally, raising the dead had been a source of cheap labor. But the early necromancers soon found it wasn't that easy to separate the mind and the body. Not, at least, with the fresh corpses. You could say the mind came back like a stowaway. The mindless were difficult to work with. They were clumsy, for starters. So, the mind had to stay. But every time you try to bind conscious creatures into servitude, there are problems. They begin to think things like unions and employment regulations are a good idea. Soon, the first rule of necromancy, to be the master, was forgotten. It was hard to assert dominance over someone who argues back and has seen the great beyond.

"Are you all right, Mrs. Chaplain?" Wilbur asked. He'd gotten up and moved to her side.

Bertha snarled before she faced the round man. "Perfectly fine, Mr. Sumner. I better get you something to accompany the wine while we wait for Miss Wicks and young Reinhardt," she said. Bertha was done sitting. Her bones were getting stiff.

"You looked...never mind. The wine is enough," Wilbur said and moved back to his chair when Bertha gave a low moan. A moan that would make any prey flee.

Wilbur stumbled back to his chair, and Bertha's primal urge to launch and bite into him rose. She didn't. Bertha had standards.

Even Ignatius gasped for breath.

She shouldn't have done that, not with these men, but Agatha's emotion had been so strong.

"You asked me what I've done to secure our plans going forward. The Union of the Undead is having a vote on forming the committee tomorrow, and they'll vote yes," Bertha said with a soft voice, trying to defuse the situation. To make her statement true, she needed tonight, or more like this morning, to secure those yays.

Not that things ever went according to plan, even with someone like Bertha.

There was a knock on her front door. Bertha got up and shambled to the door, picturing all the possible ways Agatha was hurt, as the knocking didn't sound like the polite, almost apologetic knock of the necromancer.

The two bankers followed her out of the drawing room to the doorway, peering out to see who'd knocked.

There on her doorsteps were three men who looked serious enough to be able to cut her head off before she got to their windpipes.

"Good evening, gentlemen," she said.

"We have come to get Wilbur Sumner and Ignatius Vaughn," a tall man said. He was the biggest of the bunch. He looked like a man who could demolish homes just by banging his fist against the walls. What made him appear even nastier was the fact that he didn't have that dumb, dull light in his eyes. There was a tiny sparkle, making Bertha guess whose men these were. The two others didn't have that usual law-enforcement way about them either. To be precise, these men had that other kind of presence. The one that sneaks in through windows, cuts your throat, and steals your valuables—and your organs.

"I'm afraid you have the wrong address. This is the residence of the head of the Union of the Undead, and that's me, Bertha Chaplain. So, you better leave and look for them somewhere else."

"Ma'am, with all due respect—"

"That's Party Leader Chaplain to you," Bertha interrupted.

Without blinking, the man said, "Party Leader Chaplain, we know the men in question are inside your building. I have direct orders to take them with us, and I have the authority to do that by any means necessary."

"And if I may ask, where are you planning to take *my* guests?"

"To the Town Hall." And there was nothing funny about the way he said it.

◆

Life is a complicated symphony with ups and downs. At one moment, it seems like you go along with the tune, and at other times you swim against the current, hitting every low note there is. It would be easier if you could be the sole composer, but right next to you, other symphonies are made: beautiful songs or disturbing melodies.

Petula had always watched and listened to what went on around her, only intervening if others' lives got too close to her piece, pushing them away. The driver, the man who'd tried to kill her earlier tonight, was a destructive note. She calculated the odds of the man using his fists against her. Based on the whiteness of his knuckles, he was foolish enough to ignore the ghouls.

She was the only one paying attention to him. The others watched the exchange between the mother and the son and his undead companion. Matters of the heart were something Petula stayed away from. They were something she'd never come to terms with. If you asked Petula, she was in control, no matter what emotion and thought passed through her.

The driver kept his eyes on her after glancing at Ira. Petula shook her head. It'd be moronic for him to try anything. Okay, there was a possibility that the ghouls would let him kill her, and Ira in the process, removing the annoying problem. But Ira's death would cause huge ramifications. A missing mega-bank owner would shake Necropolis' economics and social structure.

Petula lowered her book and got up, making the driver flinch. He hesitated.

"Excuse me," she said. That didn't have the effect she had hoped for. She cleared her throat and used the voice she'd been given. The kind of voice you use when you're not messing around.

"Excuse me," she said. This time she got the attention she wanted, and more.

The driver reacted when everyone looked at her. He pushed the undead woman out of his way, took the nearest statue mockup, and threw it.

To Petula, the bunny, the mockup, was coming at her in slow motion. Her mind told her to step to her right, and the unpleasantness could be avoided, but her body stayed put. Only the Leporidae Lops would understand the irony of her death. To be killed by a bunny.

But her death never came.

Sirixh, the guarding ghoul, leaped into action, snatching the statue before it reached Petula. But that wasn't surprising. What was more surprising was that Ira had launched himself at the driver and knocked him over. The undead man's mouth was wide open, and he was about to bite into the driver's hand, which the man had lifted up in protection. It was a myth that an undead bite turned you into a zombie. The infected wound might kill you, and in Necropolis that meant you had a high chance of ending up as an awakened undead, but it wasn't a symptom per se.

The driver screamed as Ira bit into his flesh. He didn't get much further, as Cruxh knocked Ira off the man, pinning him down. There was a distinctive sound of Cruxh's jaw clicking open. But this time there was no bite. The ghoul jumped off the banker and went back to the driver, helping the man up.

"As much fun as this has been, along with your family reunion and the morbid courtship, the fact is, my client and I are leaving. You've entered into my client's private property without permission, you're holding us against our will because of your own mistakes, and now you've brought a man here who has attempted to murder my client," Petula said, keeping tight control of her emotions. But if she was honest, her hands were shaking.

Her words didn't cause the reaction she'd intended.

But it wasn't her words that failed to deliver; it was Ira dominating the room, and not with his views this time. He hadn't calmed down. The man was angling to get his next attack through and finish the intruder. Ira toyed with the driver, making false launches.

Sirixh lowered the bunny mockup onto the desk.

"Mother? Shall I?" she asked.

"No, he's not ourrrs," Gwerrusxh replied.

"Then what?" Sirixh asked.

The head ghoul turned her dreary eyes to Petula.

Petula crossed her arms and stared back.

"Control him, or you leave me no choice but to order him to be taken down. And if you go down that road, you'll never leave here," Gwerrusxh said.

Petula bit her cheeks, hating that the ghoul was probably right.

Ira made another attempt to launch, but the ghouls and the driver stepped aside, as the undead was still feinting. Even though the man had regressed to basic instincts, he still comprehended that they outmatched him.

"If I command him, in exchange, I want to know what you are and where you come from, and to leave in one piece," Petula said.

The head ghoul laughed. It was a high, yelping sound, making Petula's ears ring. "You're in no position to bargain. Like I said, call him off, or I will."

"You wouldn't dare. He's the head of one of the biggest banks in Necropolis, and if he goes missing and is found dead because of you, what do you think the humans will do? It's already highly volatile up there, and they need only one reason to explode."

"Cruxh, is this true?"

Ira made another attempt. Cruxh had to pull the driver behind him.

"Yes, the necromancer is right. The city is in a state of chaos, and while many would celebrate Ira's death, he's one of them, and it might cause backlash. More so now, as our kind attacked Mrs. Maybury."

Gwerrusxh groaned. "Call him off, and I'll let you leave."

"That's one out of three," Petula said.

"That's the only offerrr you'll get. Take it orrr leave

it."

Petula hesitated. She wanted to know. No, she needed to know what the ghouls were, but she also needed to leave and go home.

"Ira," she said.

The undead man relaxed. His shoulders hunched, and the animalistic rage turned into a dull light in his eyes.

Petula took a step towards the door and said, "We are leaving."

"Please, miss. Stay for a while. There is a lot to sort out," Cruxh said.

"There's nothing to sort out. That man is a murderer. I gather that even down here you have moral laws against taking a life," Petula said.

Ira was getting livelier. He was coming back to his former self, which you could argue was not that great to begin with.

"Ha, I knew it. The Mayor sent him to kill us," Mrs. Maybury said. The woman reminded Petula of her Aunt Essie. It was the way she spoke. Even when she was clearly agitated, her self-assurance and ability to dominate others seeped out. All this time she was looking for the next target to latch on to, the same way Aunt Essie did whenever entering a new room. There always had to be a target.

"I'm not here to kill anyone," the driver said.

"That's rich," Petula said.

"Except him," the man said.

"Mr. Ringworm," Cruxh pleaded.

"I have a right to kill that man. He murdered Ona," Mr. Ringworm stated.

"And my life is collateral damage?" Petula asked.

"You should never have gotten involved. You should know better than to open your door to strangers and go with them."

"And how do you know that?"

"I've killed no one," Ira protested, his consciousness lagging a few seconds behind the reality happening around him.

"Yes, you did! You worked her to exhaustion until she was nothing but a shadow. When she got home, she just collapsed into bed, not even having the stamina to sleep or eat, just staring without seeing. You did that every time you said what she did wasn't enough. Every time you demanded more profits. And that was always."

"I did no such thing. What we do demands a lot from a person. She should have told Human Resources she needed a lighter workload or a leave of absence. She should have just asked. And if she wasn't able to handle the pressure, then she should never have gone into banking," Ira said.

"You are a monster. Of course, she couldn't go and ask. What you do inside that bank of yours is pure torture. People compete against each other, never achieving your approval, never able to show weakness, and never able to be humane. You destroy people and rebuild them in your image: corrupted souls who do anything to win." The driver was visibly shaking.

Ira laughed. "What would you have us do? We are a bank. The entire purpose of our business is to make a profit."

"No, you have misunderstood. You were originally made to store and guard money. You turned into a profit machine where you feed on your own clients and anyone who gets in your way," Herbert said.

"We provide loans to build up the city, to fuel the economy, and to give opportunities to invent, to think, to make. You're the one who's mistaken about what we do."

"Do you even remember her?"

"Of course I do," Ira said.

"You are lying," Herbert barked.

"I remember all my high-performing employees. Your Ona was on her way to becoming the best broker in the bank before she collapsed at her desk. And I gather you're the young man who came to get her. Herbert Ringworm," Ira said.

The driver staggered backward, almost stepping on Mrs. Maybury's toes.

"I'm sorry for your loss, but I would prefer if we could have kept her as well. I hired the best necromancer there was to get her back ASAP, but she was gone. She's gone, and I can't buy her back," Ira said.

Herbert just stared at the man.

Mrs. Maybury pushed past him. "You came here to get your own justice, not mine!" she said.

"Alice," Cruxh said, lowering his claw to the woman's arm.

"What does it matter whose justice?" Herbert said. The will to fight had left his voice.

Before Aunt Essie, no, she meant before Mrs. Maybury could snap back, Petula said, "You should do something about that wound." Trying to defuse the situation, she nodded towards the driver's arm. "It could get infected."

"Sirixh," Gwerrusxh said.

"Yes, Mother?"

"Get that man's wound cleaned."

"Yes, Mother." Sirixh rushed to Herbert, begging him to come with her. At first, he protested, glaring at the banker. But something had calmed in him. He went with the ghoul.

When they were gone, Gwerrusxh said, "Now, I need an explanation."

Ira opened his mouth to speak, but the ghoul lifted her claw. "From my son," she said.

Cruxh watched them from under his eyebrows and said, "Mrs. Maybury was attacked at the Town Hall meeting by three of ours."

"The ones who led the necromancer and that man here?" Gwerrusxh asked.

"Presumably."

"And they stole several ounces of gold from me, and who knows what else," Ira added.

The head ghoul glared at the man. Ira retreated from the front of the room to stand next to Petula.

"I think we better talk outside," Gwerrusxh said.

"But—" Cruxh began.

The older ghoul silenced him with a glance and turned around to head out.

"Come along," she said.

"Yes, Mother," Cruxh said. He looked at Mrs. Maybury and said, "Wait here. I will sort this out." And he hobbled after his mother.

"So, Mr. Worthwrite chose you. Are you any good, girl?" Mrs. Maybury asked, walking away from the door, passing a remaining guard.

"Leave her be," Ira said. Ira learned quickly. There was always a market for scouting out possible necromancers.

"There's no need to be hostile. I was making light conversation," Mrs. Maybury said. Somehow light conversation and Mrs. Maybury didn't seem to belong in the

271

same realm. If those two ever mixed, there might be serious ramifications for the fabric of reality.

"I'm the best," Petula said, looking at the door. She had a distinct feeling that her opportunity to leave here in one piece just walked away after his mother.

"I can work with the best," Mrs. Maybury said.

23

IN A DIFFERENT LIFE, I'D CHOOSE OPTION B

inta leaned back in her chair. Killing Ira wouldn't have been a valid option even before, when it was ruled a permissible way to get rid of an opponent. There were still laws from those days that were open for interpretation. There'd been cases where killing a rival had been considered as freedom of speech. Of course, these had involved good lawyers. Minta had considered the option for a microsecond. But while presumably Dow and Ida, the banker, would think it a good way to solve their problems, Minta didn't think a civilized society should take that road.

Yes, the laws and her own rule had failed to stop Ira growing this big, but they couldn't blame Ira or his associates for everything. It wasn't the greed of one. It was the greed of all.

"If I may say, I think there's a reasonable solution that doesn't involve killing, bailouts, or loans," Chester, the economics professor, said.

He got a side glance from Albert, the banker.

"I'm open to all suggestions," Minta replied.

"New laws for banking," Chester said.

Albert groaned unintentionally.

"What do you mean?" Minta asked, leaving no time for Albert to form his thoughts. If there was anyone in the room who might bring new ideas to the table, it was Chester.

"We need tighter rules to regulate what's permissible and what isn't. We need to prosecute those who've broken the law or even the spirit of the law. The government should have an active role in monitoring what's happening. Now, you've let the bankers run free, and it's no wonder they've taken risks with money they don't have so that a single calamity will bring the shaky house of cards down," Chester said.

"Mr. Fen is right. The government should seize the banks and nationalize them," Frederick said.

"Oh no, that's not what I mean. I still think a free economy is the right path, but the government is in charge of laws and prosecution, and they should use that power more. Investigate even little rumors of wr—"

"Loans aren't as bad as you all think." Albert spoke over Chester. He looked like he was ready to launch at the professor, who, in his opinion, liked his own voice too much. Then again, Minta could be mistaken, and a parasite was just passing through the man's intestines.

"There are other ways to get a loan than from us. There are other banks and countries. A loan from another nation might solve everything. We could call them government bonds and only pay the interest rates, leaving us, I mean you, with extra money to target different areas of the economy, speeding up the process of recovery," Albert continued.

Minta wasn't sure. Money always came with strings attached. Sure, there was nothing bad about loans it they were for a good cause, for developing something, but taking a loan to cover one's expenditures was out of the question. Okay, it might ease the situation. Then there was what Chester had said about the new laws and regulations. That would make the bankers revolt.

Albert seemed to read her mind. He continued, "Money for developmental targets. Something that would stimulate the economy. Something we export."

"Hmm," Minta said.

"I don't know. There's something dirty about taking a loan from another country. It's like giving up," Ida said, crossing her arms. She did not look happy that her suggestion had been pushed aside so easily. She'd gotten used to being the one kid in the room everyone admired and pampered.

"You can't be serious?" Albert spat out.

"Yes," Ida insisted.

"But all we do is give loans," he said.

"Yes, but that's different. This should be kept inside our own borders, as such loans will welcome interference from outsiders, and it'll only turn against us in the end. Also, if this has to be done now, before Ira gets his hands on the heart of the city, there won't be enough time to negotiate a reasonable loan. I, as a reasonable person and a banker, can't condone a carelessly drawn-up solution with volatile tendencies," she said.

"Then what to do you suggest?" Albert asked. That parasite still continued its journey.

"We beat Ira at his own game. We form a committee before he does and sell it as a divine solution for the public. If we are the ones in control, then Ira is the one who has to bend over and do our bidding. As Mr. Fen said, we can sell this to the public with new laws and regulations, and a campaign prosecuting those who've blatantly broken the law," Ida said, entangling her arms and reverting back to her former arrogant self, taking pleasure from every pair of eyes on her.

Minta hated that the woman had a point, even though she clearly didn't believe a single word she uttered. Ida was, and had always been, against any regulations, but Minta guessed that her need to triumph over Ira trumped everything else. But if they made the committee first, on their own terms, it'd allow them to deal with the threat from Ira later, giving her enough time to react. It was still a patch-up, postponing the problem and hiccups for a later date. However, it'd give economic power to the committee. When there was power, it was rarely left unused.

"Hmm," Minta said.

"But a loan—" Albert said.

"Of course, all of us here would be on that committee, representing the academics, politics, and us, banks." Ida interrupted Albert and smiled.

Chester didn't look happy. Minta could only guess it was because Ida had stolen his momentum. Neither did Frederick, but the man never looked happy. In this case, he should. This would get him more power over Necropolis than Bertha. What Albert was thinking was hard to figure out. Either he'd smelled an opportunity, or he was contemplating lashing out at Ida.

"So, what do you think?" Ida asked. "It would work as a peace offering between...everyone, really. We could call it the Stopford Committee, or something like that," she added when it took a long time for the others to answer.

Minta fought down the urge to snarl. Not because of the proposal, but the name.

"You really cannot tell me that you're against this. It's the best we can offer on such short notice. It's something we can draw up in one night and implement tomorrow. In the spirit of goodwill, we could offer some leniency for the loans due. A little nudge to get the public on our side," Ida said when no one replied.

Minta hated to admit that this was the best they could do for now. She'd thought along the same lines, but not exactly this. She'd never planned to be tied to these people for the foreseeable future. Then again, she could have ended up with worse people. At least she knew their secrets.

"You are right. This is the best solution for now. I will ask Dow to construct the committee's schedule and our work order, but of course, I have to ask if all of you agree to be involved in planning Necropolis' economics and banking?"

That wiped the smirk off Ida's face. If she'd thought she could come into the committee licking the cream off the cake and walk away richer, she had another think coming; involving Dow would make sure of that.

"I'm not sure about this," Chester said. "This is, of course, a great opportunity, but..." He sucked air in between his teeth.

Minta wasn't sure whether to jump in and convince the man. He would be a pain in the ass.

"I understand if your work keeps you engaged, but Mrs. Mortician is right: we need someone with your academic background and expertise. It'd be a shame to have to go with someone else," she said, keeping a smile on her face while she spoke, making sure even her eyes smiled. During her years in power, she'd learned this tiny trick to make her seem genuinely delighted in any circumstances. It was a simple mind switch she did. She thought about the most positive thing in the situation and smiled at that. Now she smiled at the fact she'd soon get out of the room and away from these horrible people.

She continued, "We can get over this hurdle with true cooperation. After tomorrow and after we've gained the blessing of the public, together we can turn the economy around, making sure a similar situation will never happen again. Not on our watch. And the committee will be an opportunity for something new to happen. It might even be the key we have been looking for to make Necropolis an even better place to live, and all this is thanks to your group effort." She took a breath in, and asked, "Mr. Fen, Mr. Kilborn, and Mr. Walker, will you join myself and Mrs. Mortician to form an economics committee that will shape the core of Necropolis?"

Frederick coughed, and said, "It'd be my honor to serve this city to the best of my abilities."

Minta translated the man's words to their true meaning: "Of course, I'm in whenever I can stick it to Bertha."

"Thank you, I'm glad to hear that," she said. "Albert? Chester?"

"I think I must join. You'll need my expertise," Chester said.

Minta had known he would join. He just needed his ego to be smoothed and buttered. But this was something the man had waited for all his life. Why else had he sent all those letters to her?

"It seems like I can't decline. But I want us to go over the loan options once more, and the bailouts," Albert said.

Minta sighed. "We'll calculate and research all the possible options that will bring the most well-being to all our citizens in the long run. Bailouts and loans included," she said, wanting to add that knowing Chester and Frederick, not a single option would be left unturned. "Now, lady and gentlemen, if I'm correct, a reporter and photographer are waiting for us, ready to immortalize this moment and put us in the history books."

That seemed to cheer everyone up. Vanity was so easy to sell, even to those with keen minds. Something to do with the basic need to feel important and valuable. A picture in the paper was more worthwhile than a good deed done in secrecy.

Minta was glad they'd arrived at a solution, but there was one fallacy in her logic. She thought that the economy was a wild horse with rational motives and objectives, to be tamed and understood, but in truth, the economy was more like Kraken itself, with numerous tentacles that seemed to have a mind of their own. And she could only control one tentacle at a time, and even that tentacle had the power to pull her under the water.

◆

Herbert followed the ghoul. Everything was painted in endless gray. The pain in his arm throbbed, reminding him of the fact he was still alive. He shouldn't be. Ira should have killed him. He had failed even at dying for Ona. Herbert ignored the hyper-realistic ink drawings on the walls, which wouldn't be invented by humans for another century. He only wanted this moment to end.

It was bad enough to be trailing after some ghoul, again. And this one seemed like a happy, deranged doll with an ax. Mind you, the ax was her huge claws.

Why was she constantly smiling? Maybe it was some strange ghoul thing, even though scholars insisted that smiling was a universal language shared by all sentient beings. But what did scholars know?

"What do you humans need for healing?" Sirixh asked behind her warm expression.

"Alcohol," he said.

"I know you humans like to consume alcohol when things look abysmal, but I advise against impairing your mental state in your current situation. Maybe you can do that later, when we have settled all the accusations?" the ghoul asked.

"For the wound," Herbert said. How would a ghoul know anything about killing germs? Not when bacteria were the building blocks of their life, keeping them animated with nutrition and composition.

"Oh, forgive me. I thought...never mind," the ghoul

said and began sulking. If Herbert had been a better judge of ghoulish character, or in any way interested in others around him, he'd have noticed Sirixh beating her head against an invisible wall and cursing her stupid assumptions. But because Herbert had not truly seen or heard other people since Ona's death, or even before it, he was only concentrating on the blackness of his own heart.

"We might have alcohol in one of the storage rooms. Sometimes your discarded items find their way here," Sirixh said.

Herbert didn't reply. What was there to say? Herbert didn't care what found its way here. The world was full of lost pennies, purses, and grannies. He had enough of those. Not that he'd seen his grandparents in ages. As far as he knew, they were happy being undead and tormenting his parents.

"I'm sorry for what happened to you," Sirixh said after they turned a corner.

"Sorry about what? What do you know about anything? You don't know a werewolf's ass about what happened to me and what it's been like."

"I didn't mean to offend. I only—"

"No one ever does, yet they do."

Sirixh hung her head. She pushed open a lovely red door leading into a storage room. It should have been painted black.

Everything that'd ever been discarded had come here. There were unmatching shoes, hats, gloves, umbrellas, books, and lots of socks, along with the meaning of life, packaged in a neat box marked with the text "do not open." What Herbert missed was a bunch of lost arks of the covenant. There might even be a crown or two. But he only had eyes for the pile of weapons in the corner, or to be precise, a long, narrow dagger lying on top of the pile. It was a dull-looking thing, but its blade glinted. He turned his back on the weapons, watching the ghoul look for a way into the pile of discarded wooden crates in search of one marked "alcohol."

"I know I've seen a crate here. You remember the shipwreck from last year?" Sirixh asked, continuing to scan the room and rearranging her memories so the storage room's contents were present.

Herbert shook his head. Of course he did. It'd been a devastating blow to the city's economy and supplies. Not only had they lost a massive amount of luxury goods, but food as well.

"Some of the cargo washed into the tunnels."

"Okay," Herbert said.

"Can I ask? Why do you use alcohol? I know it's not made for wounds."

Herbert took a small step back. "To make us forget ourselves."

"Why would you want to do that?" Sirixh asked. She lifted a heavy box filled with golden and wooden grails and put it away.

He took another step backward.

"Sometimes who we are gets in the way of what we want to be...or do," Herbert replied. He knelt down when the ghoul leaned to lift another box, her back to him.

"If you want to sit down, there are better boxes away from the weapons," Sirixh said, making Herbert freeze. The ghoul looked over her shoulder, and Herbert complied. He took a long step away from the weapons and sat on top of a wooden box.

The ghoul turned her head away and soon said, "I found it."

Sirixh came over to him without making a sound. There was something odd in the world when a creature that barely came up to his chest could hold such terror. He'd been told all his life that size doesn't matter, not being the tallest of the bunch. But ghouls made a mockery out of those kind words. Yes, he'd been able to function in the ring despite being heads shorter than the werewolves or any other opponent, but he'd never inspired terror in them. Not like Sirixh did.

"How do you want me to administer this?" the ghoul asked.

"I have to roll up my sleeve, and you pour it on the wound," he said. He could already feel the burning sensation from the whiskey she'd found. It would have been better if he'd advised using water on the wound, but that seemed too mild a solution for a zombie bite.

Herbert pushed his sleeve up and saw the damage Ira had done. The bite had broken his skin, and the wound was oozing blood from deep puncture marks. Before Herbert had time to prepare himself for what was about to come and ask the ghoul to administer the cure, Sirixh had poured the whiskey on his arm.

Herbert screamed.

"I'm sorry, I'm so, so, so sorry. I'll take it away!" Sirixh reached for Herbert's arm.

He snatched it back. "It's okay. It just burns."

"Are you sure? That scream. I have never heard anything like it," Sirixh said, and she hadn't. Not even when she and the pack had beaten Cruxh to a pulp, or when the pack had beaten her before that. Their rite of passage had been silent. She'd only heard something similar when she'd released a fox from the iron jaws of a human contraption, but even the fox had sounded mild compared to the noise Herbert had made.

"I'm fine. Now get me a piece of cloth to wrap around the wound," Herbert said.

The ghoul stood up and went back to where she'd found the whiskey. From the same shipwreck had come yards of fabric. Fine silk, heavy velvet, and your common hemp for everyday use.

Herbert cursed the throbbing pain. The burning had subsided, but the cuts ached. He needed a bandage badly, but that wasn't the reason he had to send the ghoul away. In the box next to him, under a pile of old books, lay a stack of letters that had caught his eye. But no, he wasn't interested in writing an angry reply to the ghoul; he was interested in the letter opener neatly packed in with the stylish papers. He reached for the set, opened it, and before the ghoul came back, he pushed the knife inside the sleeve of his good hand. He also took a green bottle marked "polish" out of the box and tucked it inside his jacket pocket.

The ghoul had found the hemp fabric. She tore a piece and tied it a few times around his arm.

Herbert twisted in agony as the pressure brought both relief and pain. Another scream wanted to come out, but he bit it back.

"Is it too tight?" Sirixh asked, seeing his discomfort.

"It's fine," he breathed out between his lips, not sounding convincing.

"If it's too tight, tell me," she said.

"It is fine."

"Are you sure? Do you need anything else?" she

asked.

"Laudanum," Herbert replied. He sometimes used it after he got unlucky in the ring, barely getting out of the way of mauling teeth. The only problem with it was that it made him not quite himself, but that didn't sound like a bad choice. Not now.

"What is that?"

"A painkiller."

"I don't think we have one, but if you like I can look?" Sirixh asked, looking at the piles and piles of boxes.

"Don't bother," Herbert said.

"Then we better get you back to Cruxh," Sirixh replied.

"If we must," Herbert said, and got up from the box. He wasn't convinced that he wanted to see Cruxh, or anyone else for that matter. But at least there was hope now. He bent his arm so that the letter opener stayed in place and followed the ghoul out of the room. Herbert took one last look and knew that in a different story, this place would have been his goal, his dream come true, but now he didn't give a rat's, werewolf's, or even Kraken's ass if all the treasures and secrets of the world were left behind.

He shut the door.

24

EMOTIONAL BASIS OF DECISION
MAKING

Petula could usually take judgmental eyes. She'd gotten used to them during her childhood from her aunts, grandmothers, and uncles, not to mention the dead, watching and nitpicking everything she did and was. And in Necropolis, every person she came across measured her worth based on exterior and status. So it was. So it went. But how Mrs. Maybury looked at Petula was different. There was more behind her soulless eyes than the usual judgment. There were plans.

Mrs. Maybury and Ira had taken their places on opposite sides of the table after exchanging a few pleasantries. Ira had reverted to inspecting the attempted murder weapon, or the so-called bunny statue. Mrs. Maybury had turned to observe Petula, of which she was now painfully aware.

Petula lowered *Philosophiæ Naturalis Principia Necromantiae* onto her lap and locked eyes with the undead woman.

"Spit it out," she said after it became clear the woman could hold her own.

Before Mrs. Maybury answered, Ira said without raising his voice, "Forget it, Mrs. Maybury. She's mine."

Petula was about to object that she was not anyone's, but Mrs. Maybury got ahead of her.

"I have a perfectly adequate necromancer," she replied. She had, but unlike Ira, Bertha, or anyone who'd hired Jeremiah Black, Mrs. Maybury had gone with obscurity. She'd reasoned that any basic necromancer with moderate talent and healthy habits was fine. Anyone who called themselves the best or amazing attracted too much attention and risk. Life was already hazardous enough, without adding to it with one's own stupidity. Even if she ate right, exercised, and got her eight hours of beauty sleep, or the equivalent of those actions as an undead, she could fall victim to calamity. And calamity and stupidity went hand in hand. Of course, you could say she was the calamity to most. And of course, Mrs. Maybury didn't think of Agatha, Jeremiah, or most of all Petula as vacuous. It was just that someone plain and common worked fine. She'd stayed alive this long without losing her mind worrying. At least not about her necromancer. It was reading the newspapers that made her mad.

"Then what do you want?" Petula asked.

"Aren't you a straight shooter," Mrs. Maybury said, smiling.

"Why would you say that?" Petula asked, but the conversation ended there, as Herbert charged into the room.

He pushed the door forcefully against the wall. Behind him, Sirixh jumped up and down on her feet. Her face was covered with a green liquid, and she was trying to rub her eyes clean. A bottle was smashed next to her. Herbert ignored the guarding ghoul, Ira, and Mrs. Maybury. He dashed forward, sliding the letter opener from his sleeve, and reached for Petula. He pushed the blade against her throat, forcing her up from her seat.

No one, not even Petula, had time to react as Herbert used the body he'd fine-tuned to perfection. The guarding ghoul was the only one who'd moved halfway from its post. The ghoul halted when the knife found its way against Petula's skin.

"Don't move," Herbert said.

The ghoul yelped.

"Or that!"

The sound made Petula's fingernails curl.

"Let her go." Ira smacked his hands against the table, making it slide a few inches. Mrs. Maybury scooted away before the table hit her.

"I'm faster than you. Test me," Herbert said.

The banker bared his teeth but made no move.

"We are leaving," Herbert said, keeping Petula close to him, making sure no one could get in the way or get between them.

Leaving, Petula wondered. That suited her, but had something cracked inside the man after the conversation with Ira? He'd seemed beaten. She took a step forward but stopped.

"My book and my bag," she said.

"You won't need them," he replied.

"I'm not leaving without my things," Petula said. By things, she mainly meant her books. She planted her feet, putting all her weight on her heels.

Herbert responded by bringing the blade closer to her skin. The letter opener was surprisingly sharp.

"Move. You don't want to test me. Not after the night I've had."

Petula did as she was told. She searched her memory for a command to use against the living man. But there were no ghosts to possess him. She could command Ira to attack, but the driver would be quicker than the undead man. The only option was a distraction. But how?

He guided her out of the room. Sirixh, who'd recovered, stepped aside, along with the other ghouls who'd responded to the alarm.

"But I thought he was a philosopher," Petula heard a ghoul whisper.

"I guess they can be radical as well," someone replied.

Herbert played their retreat smart. He kept his back to the wall, and he kept Petula and the knife between him and the ghouls. They almost made it out of the door without interruptions. Ira and Mrs. Maybury trailed after them despite Herbert's warnings, but it was Cruxh's voice that made the man hesitate.

"My friend, what are you doing?" the ghoul asked.

Herbert's breathing got heavier. "One more time, you are not my friend," he replied.

"We can work this out. Let me help you. This is not the way to solve anything," Cruxh said, ignoring Herbert's comment.

"Help, how novel. I've gotten all I want," the man said. He kicked the door open with his heel and maneuvered them out. There were more ghouls there, but they gave room to Herbert and Petula.

Petula couldn't help but notice, despite her current predicament, that the air inside the ghoul city was fresher than on ground level. She could smell the saltiness of the sea air. Petula pondered if it was normal to pay attention to foolish little things in moments like this.

Cruxh, along with Ira and the rest, emerged out of the same doors they'd used. Even Cruxh's mother had come to the steps, but Gwerrusxh shook her head and went back inside.

"Humans," Petula heard her say.

Mrs. Maybury looked alarmed. If a stare could have killed, Herbert wouldn't only be dead. He would be incinerated.

Herbert moved backward. He cursed, trying to keep an eye on where he was going, and on the ghouls and Cruxh. He took them the opposite way to where Petula had entered the city and where the stairs were.

"You don't have a plan, do you?" she asked.

The man groaned.

"How do you suppose we get out?" she asked, making her voice high enough for the ghouls to hear. Her throat pushed against the blade as she did that, making the blade draw its first blood.

"What are you doing?" Herbert asked.

"I want to get out of here as much as you do. So instead of you acting like an idiot, let's help each other out for both of our sakes," she replied.

Cruxh pointed his claw to their right. There was a slope leading up through the buildings.

Herbert dragged them towards the street. "What makes you think I won't kill you?"

"Because not only Mr. Worthwrite's family and Cruxh would hunt you down, my sister would make sure you regretted the day you were born," Petula said. Larissa would track the man down, but Petula had lied about the regret part. Larissa wasn't one to torture anyone. She liked to blow things up, but only inanimate objects that had gotten in her way. Larissa had even rescued their father and her husband, along with a grumpy old bookshop owner from the Leporidae Lop prison, with her explosive cocktails. Nevertheless, Larissa would make sure justice was served. Most likely with some kind of re-education. But Herbert didn't need to know that.

"I wouldn't have done this if I cared what happened to me," he replied.

"If that was true, then I would be dead," she said. Self-preservation, what a thing. It made humans endure even the most excruciating pain in the hope of survival. Even if that hope was taken away, the mind might break and move into dreamland, but the body endured.

He stopped and pushed the blade harder against her throat.

"Thank you for reminding me," he said.

The ghouls and the undead stopped as well. They'd taken steps as Herbert took steps. Cruxh had pleaded several times to Herbert to reconsider; he could speak on his behalf to the Mayor and ask her to have mercy on him. Ira had shouted the opposite, not helping Petula at all. But that was the banker for you. He thought bullying others into his way of thinking was the ideal way to live his life.

"Back away," he said. "Or I'll kill her."

This was getting repetitive, and Petula already missed her books. Either he killed her now or let her go. She needed him to decide.

Cruxh yelped, and most of the ghouls shrank back, disappearing from view. Petula followed them with her gaze, but it was impossible to make out where they'd gone. She was sure she could still feel their pressure.

The only ones who stayed near them were Cruxh and the undead. Ira tried to control his rage as best he could. He struggled not to launch himself at Herbert, but there was a chance he might turn back into a mindless thing. The Necromantic Council gave two options in such a situation: to soothe the spirit back into control or, if that failed, to put him down. Then again, if Petula got all technical, she didn't have a legal right to resurrect him in the first place. When all this got out, her life would get messy. Her only hope was to slip out of town and hope the Council sent no one after her. Which was unlikely. They knew how to hold a grudge.

"Be reasonable," Cruxh said.

"Yes, ask for an escort out," Petula whispered.

"Stop helping me," Herbert groaned. Petula felt the blade shake. She wondered why the man hadn't killed her already.

"I want to help you," Cruxh said. "You are my friend."

Herbert's whole body tensed again.

"How many times do I have to tell you we are not friends?"

"If not for the sake of friendship, then for the sake of reason. You must see this won't lead to anything good. One false move and the banker next to me will rip you apart. You must let her go and surrender," Cruxh said.

"Ask about the exit," Petula pressed. By now she was sure he wasn't going to kill her. Ira's words had broken his will. He needed to get out of here alive. But emotional stability was clearly a delicate subject for him.

"Shut up," Herbert said, wavering.

"Please, miss, stop messing with his head," Cruxh said. "I can hear your whispers. They are not helping. I will help you leave if you let me save him. You must see that his heart is misguided," the ghoul said.

"If he lets me go, you promise to let me leave?" Petula asked.

Simultaneously, Herbert said, "Getting justice is not misguided. If our government won't do anything about a man of Ira Worthwrite's status, then they leave people no other choice than to take justice into our own hands." He tightened his grip on the letter opener.

"Promise?" Petula asked over Herbert.

The ghoul nodded.

Petula shut her eyes, blocking Cruxh, Herbert, and everyone else out except Ira. She concentrated on the man, pulling and pushing him, making his soul tender. Herbert's knife hand shook. She felt his other hand clutch harder, pressing her against his body, but she ignored it.

She focused all her efforts on Ira's scattered mind. Inside the man, contradictory impulses warred against each other: the need to take a bug out of his ear, the need to silence the ghoul once and for all, the need to taste Herbert's flesh, the need for Petula to be subdued to his will, the need for her to marry Morris Reinhardt and forget about leaving. Petula could get lost in there. She coaxed his wants out of his body and whispered his name, urging him to follow her voice.

Ira's body fought against her, keeping his soul inside.

"Ira," she whispered. "Veni ad me. Sequitur vocem meam."

He forgot the bug and his loose knee. "Yes," Ira said.

"You know what to do," she said.

Petula heard Cruxh give a high-pitched yelp.

She had to hurry.

"Ira," she said and pushed the man's consciousness inside Hebert's body.

Petula opened her eyes when Herbert squeezed her harder, pushing the blade against her throat, but the final jerk never came. He released her, and at the same time, Cruxh rushed to Petula, pulling her away from the man.

Herbert collapsed onto his knees, screaming uncontrollably.

"You did not!" Cruxh screamed at her.

Petula just looked past the man at Ira.

"Clever girl," she heard Mrs. Maybury say.

Ira's body crumpled to the ground like a useless old thing.

"Now I want to leave," Petula said.

Herbert continued screaming as Ira's soul and mind continued invading his body. Petula didn't feel bad for him, not when the man had an impulse to kill. Petula couldn't quite respect anyone who thought they could solve their problems with violence. She condoned self-defense, but this was about justice, and justice should happen in a courtroom.

◆

Bertha, against all protests, followed Wilbur and Ignatius to the cart with the men who'd come to take them to the Town Hall. None of them had been happy to leave Chaplain's residence, but Dow's men[40] had allowed Bertha to alert her butler and trust him with the details of where they were going. The man promised to tell Agatha and Morris as soon as they arrived.

Riding on an open cart brought back memories Bertha didn't care to remember. She shifted her weight on her seat. The morning sun had risen, and those citizens who preferred day to night had gotten up and driven away the children of the night. The two bankers looked miserable. Wilbur kept mumbling something about his daughter giving birth. Ignatius kept shooting glances at the man to silence him, but Wilbur took no notice.

"I hope it's a boy," Wilbur muttered.

"Can't you think about anything else?" Ignatius said.

"No, not really," Wilbur replied.

"Can you think why Mr. Spurgeon or Miss Stopford want to see you?" Bertha interrupted before Ignatius could start an argument. She'd presumed Minta and Dow were behind this.

"As far as I know, nothing," Ignatius replied. He took his pocket watch out. He opened the lid and closed it without thinking.

The nearest of Dow's men chuckled. A weaselly-looking one with long, dark, greasy brown hair. He'd be the first one to attest that when he and his men got involved, they'd always done something. Most often something that got them sent to the gallows. He had personally delivered several someones to the other side, where eternal silence was guaranteed.

"Then they must know," Bertha said. "Or at least suspect," she added.

Ignatius squirmed. "It was bound to happen, but my and Wilbur's involvement should never have come out," he said, glancing at the weaselly-looking man, who pretended to look at the scenery with great interest. It was an achievement, as there was not much to marvel at. One house was identical to the next. The city planners had thrown out innovation and courage when Engel and Nutterbird had canonized their aesthetics.

"This could be about something else. It might have

---

40   Or so she presumed.

been better if you'd stayed behind to wait for Miss Wicks and Morris," Wilbur said.

Now the weasel man pressed down his laughter. Denial was a powerful force in the universe, along with emotions, which were often the basis of decisions, however much reasonable people argued otherwise. But there was something beautiful about denial. It made the world more interesting. You could say the most absurd conversation the weasel man had ever had was when he'd escorted a man to the guillotine. It went something like this:

"Beautiful day, isn't it?"

"Uh-huh."

"Do you think I can take a stroll after we have gotten this all over with?"

"I hope not."

"But my dear sir, such a day shouldn't be wasted. One must always seize a moment of idleness and replenish one's soul."

"One must."

Afterward, he'd taken that stroll, carrying the man's head from the city's center to the designated pit. The man had been right. It'd been a lovely day.

"What does your master want from us?" Bertha asked, turning to face the man. She'd had it with the constant chuckling.

The man coughed and looked towards the huge man who'd delivered the request on her front steps. The huge man greeted his glance with a stare. If Bertha was correct about the gesture, the huge man meant, "You have dug your own grave, you can dig your way out as well." The huge man turned his attention back to the man guiding the cart.

"What my master wants from Mr. Sumner and Mr. Vaughn is above my pay grade. You need to ask that when we get to the Town Hall," he said, and went back to looking at the buildings. This time he was not pretending.

"I demand to know. I'm the—"

"Head of the Union of the Undead. I know who you are, Miss Chaplain, of Driftwood Rise 186, Ocean District. Never married, came from—"

"That's enough. How dare you threaten me?!" she hissed.

"I wasn't threatening you, Miss Chaplain. I only

answered your question," the weaselly-looking man said.

Someone sighed at the front of the cart.

"I'm sure Mr. Spurgeon won't look kindly on how you handle yourself," Bertha said. There was something about the man that reminded her of her past.

"I apologize if I've offended you in any way, madam," the man said, tipping his head, yet not wiping the smirk from his lips.

"Don't worry, I'll see that you apologize. Now, if you'd stop listening in to a private conversation."

"*Of course*, madam," the man said, and slid farther into the back of the cart, still sitting hearing distance away.

"Whatever happens inside the Town Hall, let me handle it," Bertha said. She was already building up her defense against any accusations Minta or Dow could sling at her. There was a way to destroy their claims of impropriety. Desperate times called for desperate measures. She, with the aid of her friends, had tried to solve the mess. Yes, that was what she'd done, and so nobly.

"With all due respect, I can speak on my own behalf," Ignatius said.

"You two are jumping ahead of yourselves. I think it's better to hear what Miss Stopford wants before making hasty accusations or actions. She's the ruler of Necropolis, and she has power over our fate," Wilbur said, pleasing neither Ignatius nor Bertha. Soft, modest points were never that popular in politics or in business. Radical, out-there, aggressive, and controversial ideas were the way to get attention. What Wilbur proposed was docile. It was a wonder the man had gotten to his position without more initiative.

What Bertha didn't know was that Wilbur had been lucky. He'd been in the right place at the right time and had known how to use those opportunities to his advantage. There was also the fact that his family had been rich, making those opportunities more common than, say, for any Joe from the street. At first, Wilbur had gone down the same path as Reinhardt Senior, but then he'd gotten lost in the jungle of gold, power, and esteem.

Their conversation was cut short. The cart stopped next to the Town Hall. In the distance, there came the muffled voices of people. But what was happening elsewhere held no interest for them. Except for the weaselly-looking man, who shuddered. He offered his hand to Bertha to help her get down. She took it grudgingly.

"What is your name?" she asked.

"Just describe my appearance; he'll know me," the man said and stepped aside to let the bankers get off the cart.

Bertha chuckled. She had to admit, the man was amusing and full of charm with his odd features and sharp wit. Just the kind of man she'd have lost her mind and heart to when alive, until the familiarity crept in. Too bad the man lacked status. Oh well, her body was dead, so it was a moot point anyway.

The men led them into the building.

The weaselly-looking man opened the door for her, and before she went in, he winked at her. Maybe Agatha could have a dalliance with the man. It was a shame to throw away a good character. It might cheer up the sulking necromancer and get her away from Madam Sabine's bosom.

"Let me speak on our behalf," Bertha reminded the bankers when they stepped in. She was kidding herself. She might be able to bully most of her fellow Union members into obedience,[41] but Ignatius and Wilbur were a different breed. They knew their worth, unless Ira was around.

They also knew when to keep their mouths shut.

"Sir," the towering figure of a man boomed behind Bertha.

Only then did she note who he'd spoken to. Dow stood in the shadows of a gargoyle statue.[42] He stepped out. He wore a loose black jacket that reached to the ground, looking like the leader of some horrific cult sacrificing the souls of good people.

"Good evening, madam and gentlemen," Dow said. "It was nice of you to join us. Now, if you would be so kind as to follow me."

"What's this about, Mr. Spurgeon? And who's 'us'?" Bertha asked.

"All in due time." Dow spun around and made his way towards the Town Hall's audience chamber. He forced Bertha and the bankers to hurry after him. Their previous escort headed back outside.

---

41   Even Mrs. Maybury, once in a blue moon.

42   Or the real thing. It was hard to tell with their kind.

Dow took them up the stairs next to the audience chamber, leading them to the upper floors. To a huge open area that was occupied by Minta Stopford, Frederick Kilborn, Chester Fen, and two others Bertha didn't recognize. R. Porter and his photographer stood in front of them. The reporter wrote on his pad as Minta spoke. Minta's committee, group, whatever, beamed with pride, making Bertha curse under her breath. This was not about a public rebuke. This was Minta playing her first move, forcing Bertha's actions out into the open.

She boiled with rage.

"Now, if you don't mind waiting here until the Mayor is ready, I will go and collect the rest of our guests," he said. Dow left them, giving them no time to object.

25

SPENDING AN ETERNITY IN THE LIBRARY DOESN'T SOUND THAT BAD

 erbert screamed. Not from the existential crisis of whether he was or wasn't. He screamed because he was suddenly posed with the question of whether one being could simultaneously be two. His body was sure "there can be only one," pushing them both out.

Some in Necropolis believe the soul is in the heart, others think it's in the gut, and the rest believe that there's no soul and self-awareness is the product of the brain's neurotransmitters carrying messages here and there. But that argument is easily dismissed, as the thinkers were sure no one could fit a postal system inside a head. Let alone a functional one.

Herbert didn't care what anyone thought or where his soul was ejected from. He fought to keep his body and soul intact. But so did Ira. Herbert had gotten glimpses of the man's intentions as their consciousnesses intersected. Ira had found a new life, and he wasn't going to let go.

"You get him out of there," Herbert heard Cruxh say.

"Why?" Petula asked.

He wanted to kill her. Ira didn't.

"I did what you asked. I made him let me go. Now I expect you to hold up your end of the bargain."

"I am a man of honor, and I will escort you out, but you have to separate those two. They will destroy each other. You must see he is hurting," Cruxh said.

The ghoul was right. Herbert's whole body ached with a feverish ache, as if it was fighting off a virus.

"Hm," Petula said.

"Does that mean what I think?"

"I'm afraid so. I don't think I can put Ira back into his old body. Not at least in the mood either of them is in right now, and not here," Petula said.

"You..." Cruxh said, cutting his own words short. Herbert couldn't believe the man and his need to be correct and polite. He doubled over as Ira tried to gain control through his gut.

"It wasn't like I had another choice. He was planning to kill me..." Petula let her words trail off.

"You—" Herbert said, but Ira tackled his larynx.

"If I get home, I might be able to find a way to undo all this without anything getting too complicated. But I need Agatha for that," Petula said.

Cruxh's eyes shone with a sad light. He sighed as he looked at Herbert and then at the necromancer.

"Then we must get you home. Are you sure you can help him there?" Cruxh asked.

How dare they decide his fate for him? Herbert pushed his weight into his hands. He almost got up. He would have, if it hadn't been for Ira's attempt to command his feet, making him drop back onto the ground. Cruxh dashed to his aid, helping him up. The feet were wobbly, yet, with the help of the ghoul, he could stand.

"I'll have you—" Herbert said. Again, Ira interrupted him.

"Yes, I think there's a way," Petula said. Herbert didn't like the way she said it. "We better take Ira's body with us," she added.

Cruxh yelped. A ghoul, Sirixh to be precise, came to his aid, holding Herbert up. If Herbert had had more control over his body, he'd have shaken loose from her touch. Now he had to take whatever got him to the necromancer's home.

Cruxh moved to take Ira's body. When he touched it, Herbert shrieked. Not voluntarily.

Cruxh let go of the undead and shot a glance towards him.

Ira tried to speak through his mouth, but Herbert didn't let him. He spoke over the man. What came out was gibberish, as the two men fought for control of the body.

Cruxh touched Ira again and hoisted him over his shoulders, looking at Herbert with concern. He kept nodding as his mouth kept babbling on.

"That's going to be annoying," Petula said, regarding Herbert. He wanted to shrink, hide, do anything else but be the center of her attention.

"Oh well. Ira, shut up!" she said.

Ira stopped.

"I want him out of me. I don't care how. Just do it." Herbert spat out the words, to his own surprise.

"Are you all right?" Cruxh asked.

"What do you think?" he replied, and his arm jerked.

"I... We better hurry then," Cruxh said. "Mrs. Maybury, would you care to follow us?"

"And what about my justice and my needs?" Mrs. Maybury asked.

Cruxh howled. The ghouls who'd attacked Mrs. Maybury came next to Cruxh. They refused to look towards Mrs. Maybury.

"Now we can leave," Cruxh said.

"What about my books?" Petula asked.

"I assure you, you will get them later. Now, we better leave before anything catastrophic happens. He cannot hold Ira off for long," Cruxh said.

Sadly, Herbert agreed. Shivers moved all over his body, and his hands were cold and clammy. He took a step forward. His feet were made from jelly. The necromancer had shown him his place, making him lose himself to the banker, whose thoughts leaked in.

Cruxh had them follow him up the slope he'd told Herbert to use. They walked across the city, back to the tunnels, past the buildings the ghouls had made to symbolize their ideas. Herbert paid no attention. However, he noted the tunnels were empty of the reliefs. In their place, mushrooms and other underground vegetation grew from the damp wall.

"Cruxh?" Petula asked after they'd walked in the tunnel for a while. Her voice seemed to rouse Ira. The man became alert and ready to act on any word she said.

"Yes?" Cruxh replied.

"What are you?" she asked.

"That is a difficult question that depends on the moment. At one moment, I can be—"

"The question wasn't existential. I want to know what you ghouls are and why the spirits stay away," Petula interrupted.

"But miss, that is two separate questions."

Two questions too many, Herbert thought. If he had more energy to make a snide comment, he would, but Ira pressed on him.

"So? Am I only allowed one question? Is this like with three wishes, except I don't even get that? And I wonder if those two are as separated as you would like me to believe?" Petula pressed on.

"Oh, a sharp eye. Are you a philosopher like Mr. Ringworm?" Cruxh asked.

"Is that what you are? A philosopher? But no, Mr. Cruxh, I'm not a philosopher. I'm a scholar," Petula said.

"Aren't they one and the same? Both attempt to understand the world through observation." The ghoul smiled as he spoke. Not that he ever stopped smiling. He was one of those annoying fellows.

Herbert groaned, and so did Ira at that precise moment. There was a moment of awkwardness. Those two didn't want to share anything, even a single thought.

"You are trying to avoid my questions," Petula said.

"On the contrary, I'm trying to understand where your questions are coming from. Is this an attempt to understand me and my kind, or are you asking for control?" Cruxh replied.

"Why would I want to control you?" Petula sounded astonished.

Cruxh looked towards Herbert. So did Petula. Neither Herbert nor Ira liked that. Herbert wasn't sure if he saw a glimpse of remorse or guilt, but the necromancer looked away.

"Could you two please stop? You're giving me a

headache," Mrs. Maybury said. "And tell the poor creature what you are and stop tormenting her."

Cruxh grinned. "She will figure it out on her own if she truly wants to know. We are out of time." They'd arrived at a metallic door built into the cave's wall. Cruxh let out a quiet yelp, and one of the ghouls who'd attacked Mrs. Maybury hurried to open the door. The undead woman flinched at the sudden movement.

Behind the door was a steep staircase that led up a narrow path. The steps weren't as steep as those Herbert, Cruxh, and Mrs. Maybury had used to get into the city. Still, they looked just as unwelcoming. Herbert, at the moment, did not trust his legs or his body to follow even the simplest commands.

Cruxh went in first, carrying Ira's carcass. Herbert followed after, helped by the ghoul Sirixh. Then Mrs. Maybury and Petula came. Lastly, the three ghouls who'd started all this misfortune hobbled patiently from one step to another, as if they were capable of moving at the speed of light and now time had come to a halt.

Herbert and Ira found a rhythm after the first twenty steps. They tried to shake the ghoul off, but Sirixh only latched on tighter. She communicated with Cruxh using quiet yelps, surely making up for the mistake she had made earlier, letting Herbert attack. But that was just a possibility. Maybe she'd tagged along to aid Herbert for altruistic reasons. Some would beg to differ, saying there are no actions without self-serving motives. Those who thought so were assholes thinking that the value of an act came from pureness of heart, and not because it was the right thing to do.

Anyway, above the staircase was another metallic door. Cruxh balanced Ira against his shoulders and pushed the door open, leading them through a bookshelf to the Library. Or at least, both Herbert and Ira thought it to be the Library. They soon got a confirmation.

Petula shut her eyes and let the familiarity wash over her. If she turned her head to her right, she would find *The Handbook for Necrocreature Symbiotes*. Actually, she wouldn't. She had it back at home. But next to the empty space would be *The Handbook for Parasite of Vertebrate Uses in Necromantic Rituals*. She'd read that already. On the shelf above, she would find

Infectious Diseases Emitted by the Dead written by Floriane Lith. She knew there was an interesting chapter about burial soil and how to use it as a poison. Her feelings were so strong and vivid that they seeped into Herbert's consciousness through the connection between the undead and the necromancer. He was sure he could even hear a quiet whisper of voices, of spirits. Herbert didn't like the feeling at all. Neither did Ira.

Ira didn't care for the place. It was full of dusty old tomes and took a huge chunk out of the city's budget, the common fund. The least they could do was start charging money for the loans.

Whoever thought a shared connection was a good thing was a fool. There had to be privacy. There had to be an individual and not just many parts of some super-organism. Then again, maybe it was individualism that caused the pain of desire and all the wars.

"Why don't you enter through here rather than Ira's bank?" Petula asked, bringing everyone back to reality.

"The librarian," Cruxh said, as if that should explain everything. It did. Even now, you could sense the librarian looming over you in the shadows. You could hear his breathing and judgment in the pressured silence. If you could bottle the atmosphere, what the librarian emitted, you would win awards at a creep festival.

Herbert shuddered. But that might be because, for a split second, Ira and he had been one.

"But wouldn't entering through Ira's vault be more difficult?" Petula asked.

"Not at all. Not with all the built-in secret passages," Cruxh replied.

"But still," Petula insisted.

"Our main entrance was there long before Mr. Worthwrite commissioned his building," Cruxh said.

They didn't get any farther with the conversation. Dow interrupted them.

"Good evening, ladies and gentlemen," he said, stepping into view from behind a bookshelf, startling everyone, including Cruxh.

"It is nice of you to finally arrive. I have been waiting for you, and you know how it is in here. But nevertheless, you are present. Now, if I may ask you to join the others at the Town Hall? I think Miss Stopford has a few issues she needs to address," Dow said, tipping his black top hat to the onlookers.

"And it is nice to finally make your acquaintance, Miss Upwood. My name is Dow Spurgeon, and I am the Mayor's secretary. I truly enjoyed your presentation on the uses of the soul in modern necromancy. It was very eye-opening and made me think about the state of the business as a whole. Not to mention my own mortality. But that is a discussion we can leave for another time. Right now, you need to follow me. Transportation is waiting for us," Dow concluded.

"I do have to insist."

◆

Morris watched Ira's toe pointing at the Library on the map. He couldn't understand why the man was there. Ira never struck him as someone with a taste for literature. Others might point out, Petula being one, that knowledge was power, but they'd be wrong. Ira had no need to read every single book ever printed. It was enough to be able to read human nature, and as a last resort, he could always employ those who had spent their lives in the pursuit of knowledge. So the only reasonable explanation for Ira being in the Library was the necromancer, as Kitty had said. She had a bigger hold on him than Morris had thought.

"Still, why would they go there?" he wondered aloud.

"It's that awful necromancer. She kept reading nonstop," Kitty declared.

"Petula?" Agatha asked.

"Yes," Kitty said, daring the necromancer to let out another word.

Agatha didn't care. She continued, "She's quite pleasant when she's around books or solving a problem. Back in the—"

"What's that got to do with anything? Can't you see, she's in cahoots with the ghouls, holding my husband against his will in the Library and tormenting him to get to his money or the book. Morris, is she in it?" Kitty interrupted Agatha, which in some bizarre way could be seen as righteous, as when anyone started their sentence with "back in the day," they should hold their peace forever.

"I'm sorry, I don't quite follow," Hortensia, the officer, said. Neither did Morris, for that matter.

"I didn't ask you," Kitty snapped.

"How should I know what is in your husband's black book? And I'm sure there's a reasonable explanation for all this that does not involve any plot against you or Ira. But we better head there and find out what's going on," Morris said.

"I'll alert my supervisor and the lead detective. They can summon the apartment's hostage negotiator," Hortensia said. And when she said "summon," it was precisely the correct word.

"Are you a fool?" Kitty shrieked, making the whole room look in their direction.

Morris wanted to hide. Kitty's tactlessness was too much, yet she survived in Necropolis' high society with ease.

"I'm sorry, Mrs. Worthwrite," Hortensia replied automatically. She corrected her uniform.

"What good would a negotiator do? We need an army. I want this station mobilized to arrest my husband's kidnappers!"

Kitty's demands were worse than Morris had expected.

"What I suggest is finesse," he interrupted before the officer hurried to fulfil Kitty's wishes. He gently laid his hand on Kitty's arm.

"What do you have in mind?" Kitty asked. Her voice was back to its normal volume.

"That instead of rushing in there with a negotiator or with the whole station, four of us go and have a look. And if there's a reason for alarm, then Miss Caster will alert the whole police station and see to it that Mr. Worthwrite is safely returned to you," he said.

"But what if—" Kitty asked.

He moved his thumb against her arm to calm her down. In the past, it'd worked on all his women. Kitty was no different. She laid her hand over his and patted it twice.

"I'm sure there's no better negotiator in this place than you," Morris said. With someone else in mind that might have been smarmy, but with Kitty it was the truth. The woman had a way of making others see her side of things, and not always by bullying others into accepting her opinion. The whole city dressed according to Kitty's taste. Morris remembered the time he'd thought going back to three-quarter-length trousers and flashy vests was just what one needed in life, but soon he and the rest of the Necropolitians forgot such a notion, as Kitty had commented on the fashion at a dinner party, bankrupting those who'd stocked such items without asking Kitty first. In addition, Morris knew she'd been the best debater back in her school days. There were many legends about how she'd crushed her opponents.

"We do it your way. But if we fail, my husband's death is on your hands," Kitty said, freeing herself from his touch.

"But sir and Mrs. Worthwrite, I can't just leave my desk unattended. I do have to go to my supervisor and let her know what's going on," Hortensia said.

"And what about Jeffrey?" Agatha asked.

Morris had already forgotten Jeffrey and his body.

"He can wait until we've solved this. It's not like he's going anywhere," he said.

"Are you sure?" Agatha asked. She'd let go of the pink ribbon and was fiddling with her false teeth. Morris hated the sight of them.

"I have a feeling that this will all sort itself out when we find Ira and Petula," he said.

Agatha nodded. "I think I know about the feeling you are talking about. I hope Petula is all right," she said.

To Morris' surprise, Kitty said nothing. She was fixated on the officer.

"This is an opportunity for you to wipe away the mistake you made," Kitty said.

That was playing dirty, Morris thought. But it was so like the woman to sense the problem and home in on it. She was more like Ira than Morris had thought. Or as bad as Ira.

"I can't," the officer replied.

"Yes, you can. It's your duty to protect and serve, or do I have a misconception about the oath you swore?"

The officer squirmed. Morris, on some level, felt bad for her, yet he made no effort to step in and stop Kitty before she got her clutches on the officer's inner voice and corrupted it with doubt.

"Okay, but I do have to inform my supervisor where I'm going." She lowered her head. "I'm a trainee, you see, and I can't go out without a partner. I already did that once today. I went without her and I put both of us in danger."

"Hogwash. This is a place for you to show initiative and do what's right. I'm sure there's an article somewhere that states you have to help in case of an emergency. So write a note and come with us," Kitty said.

"There is. Article two-three-nine-Y states I have to act swiftly in an emergency to secure the public's safety."

"There you go."

"But—"

"You are slouching again. Stand up straight, and go ahead and write that note so we can do our duty to save my husband and Agatha's friend Petula," Kitty said.

The officer wrote a note, pinning it to the map next to the Library.

"Do you want this back?" she asked, lifting Ira's toe from the string.

"Keep it," Kitty said.

"It can be re-attached," Agatha said.

"It's a piece of evidence, and as a citizen, I won't tamper with police procedures," Kitty replied.

Morris clenched his bad leg so as not to let out a laugh. The twinge of pain always worked. He eased the pressure and leaned against his cane.

"If this is settled, then we better leave."

Hortensia took a wooden baton from next to the table and pushed it under her armpit.

Morris saw Kitty searching for words. He shook his head, and thankfully, she kept her words to herself. Hortensia let them out of the police side of the fence.

"Going out?" the man behind the welcoming desk asked.

"Yes, Carl. They need my assistance," Hortensia said.

Carl, or Mustache Man, as he would be forever known to Morris, said, "Good luck," after noting with whom the officer was heading out. The two dogs made him uneasy. They seemed to be an extension of their master. Morris could imagine his thoughts. They went like this: "Rather you than me." He could relate to him. Actually, he would love to stay behind and finish painting the walls. This place needed to be elevated to the next level.

They headed out. Hortensia looked like she was ready to march across the city to the scene of the crime, judging by the way she was going down the station's steps.

"We'll take my coach," Kitty said, showing them to one parked next to the police station, blocking anyone who had an urgent need to access the place. She did not wait for an answer. Her driver jumped down from the seat as soon as she saw Kitty coming. The woman held a door open for them.

"Madam?" she asked.

"To the Library, Cherry," Kitty said.

They went in, and the two dogs nestled on Kitty's lap and, to Morris' dislike, partly on his as well. He could smell their musky, yeasty odor. He looked away. Tonight, or morning, as the day was already well in process, had moved from one sticky situation to another. It would have been simpler if Morris had never gotten out of Wilbur's coach when they arrived to collect Jeremiah. Maybe then everything would have gone differently. First of all, no dogs would be drooling and rubbing their stench on his best suit.

The coach tugged into motion. It made back-and-forth movements as it turned around at the end of the street. Then it moved again but soon stopped.

Kitty pushed her head out of the window and asked angrily, "Cherry?"

"Someone has parked their horses in the middle of the street," came the reply.

"Who would do that?" Kitty asked.

"Madam, I don't have the faintest idea."

"I can get up and move them," Hortensia volunteered.

"No, you stay put. I won't have you running off on foolish errands," Kitty replied.

Morris looked at Agatha, who sat there, indifferent.

"No need to get up. We are going to go around it," Cherry said.

"Good," Kitty said and leaned back in her seat and stroked Lugosa. "The whole city is going down the drain. People don't have any manners."

"No, madam," Agatha said and looked out of the window as they circled around the double-parked coach. She smiled.

Or Morris was sure she had smiled.

He was glad to leave the police station behind and, to

be honest, Jeffrey's body. Maybe someone would find it and take it off his hands? Wilbur wouldn't like that though. Oh well, he'd get back to it later, along with the proposal and getting on with his life. This whole committee debacle had taken a lot more time than he'd initially thought, making him neglect his duties to his father's bank, to his friends, and to his own health. He let his eyes rest on the officer's notepad, which she'd taken out a moment ago.

"When we get there, I'll go in first," Hortensia said. "Then Mrs. Worthwrite will follow close behind to aid me in talking to the kidnappers. Miss Wicks will follow her. And Mr. Reinhardt, can you come in last to protect our backs from any surprises?"

"I'm happy to do that," Morris said. When deciding which was the most dangerous place in a line, the front or the back, the front won. At least if he was the last, he could run away, the Library being roomy and all. But then there was the librarian. But a more relevant question than front or back was why the coach had slowed down when there was at least half the distance still to go.

The vehicle came to a sudden halt, making everyone sway back and forth. The officer's baton rolled to Kitty's feet, making the woman bite her tongue on a shout so the dogs didn't jump off her lap. Agatha looked for her teeth, which she'd taken out again to fiddle with. They'd dropped next to Morris' feet. He pushed them farther under the bench next to Kitty's dress hem to hide them.

"Cherry?!" Kitty asked, distracting Agatha.

"Sorry, madam, but we can't go forward. We have to wait," Cherry said. Her round head appeared in the window for everyone to see.

"Why not?"

"I think it is the protest, madam."

"What?"

"The protest against the Mayor. The streets are packed with people. And they are heading to the Town Hall."

"Can't you make them move?"

"I could if there were fewer people, but madam, when I say the streets are packed, I mean it," Cherry said.

They all got out of the coach. Cherry hadn't been lying. There was a huge assembly of people drifting away from them, blocking their way to the Library.

"What now then?" Kitty asked.

"We go on foot. It's faster," Hortensia said and beamed.

26

ENOUGH! I'M GETTING
CLAUSTROPHOBIC

There's something peaceful about the written word. Maybe it's twisted and all wrong, and happiness shouldn't be bound between covers, but for Petula, it was. All around her, bookshelves held promising titles. And lately, she'd been drawn to the medical and biological side of necromancy. There was so much she didn't know. There was even a great possibility that parasites and bacteria were the true source of life. That they held the key to emotions, moods, and everything. That they were the reason why humans, alive or dead, existed.[43] There was a possibility that we are merely a vessel for breeding and spreading. That would be something. Petula thought it was high time humans stopped thinking so highly of themselves. If she could only get her hands on the books, but no, they expected her to interact. To be part of this mess others had created. She'd done to Herbert what anyone would do, to persevere.

---

43   Not excluding animals.

But she worried about leaving the will-o'-the-wisp locked inside her pack for an unknown duration with the knife. Spirit lights were essentially evil,[44] and with a knife, hers could turn homicidal. Though, she expected the ghouls to manage.

She felt the small man who had come to get them observing her. Petula glanced towards him. He didn't even look away like most people would. He didn't have to. There was something in the way he carried himself. That same thing that had made everyone obey him instantly, even Mrs. Maybury. If the woman was truly like her Aunt Essie, she wouldn't have complied without a good reason. Petula frowned.

There came a faint hissing sound above her. Without glancing up, she knew who was making the noise. She didn't care. Not now. They had already trailed after the man to the librarian's desk and his filing cabinets, which guarded the place with their ultimate rule. If she wanted to leave, now was the time to speak up or forever hold her peace.

"Whatever this is about, it doesn't concern me. I'll go home to pack, and when and if Mr. Ringworm and Mr. Worthwrite want to go back to their former selves, you can bring them to my place, but well ahead of my four o'clock ship, or I won't be there to meet you," she said, despite knowing her leaving wasn't going to happen. Not from the Library and not from Necropolis. Nevertheless, she entertained the hope as long as she could. It was her only hope for normality. Or her equivalent of normality, which was beyond what others thought life or a day should look like. First of all, no one wanted to spend hours upon hours dissecting and analyzing corpses, not even in Necropolis. Secondly, why couldn't she socialize like normal people did? It couldn't be healthy to stay cooped up inside with her subjects and books. It was a sure road into a padded room. Not that this was abnormal in Necropolis, where madness was a required job qualification.

Dow glanced up before answering. Then he looked at her intensely and replied, "I would prefer you to come to the Town Hall to see the Mayor. As soon as you awakened Mr. Worthwrite, you got involved. And now that I see he isn't

---

44   Or at least according to the humans, but evil isn't that black and white.

doing so well, it would be good for you to explain yourself to the Mayor. I am sure she isn't the only one who is interested in Mr. Worthwrite's condition. We wouldn't want any unfounded rumors circulating around."

Petula clenched her teeth. She'd done nothing wrong, and the Town Hall should have nothing to do with the Necromantic Council. And what she'd done to Herbert and Ira was self-defense.

The Library was again filled with the hissing sound, making everyone hasten their steps.

Petula glanced up, and the Librarian's cocoon moved as he shifted his weight. The man could be so melodramatic, but what did she care. He always found the books she wanted, going the extra mile to satisfy her every need. He knew as much about books as she did, and he was so nice and helpful. Petula was the only one who thought that way. Others found the man's service rude, slow, and painful.[45]

They walked past the Librarian's desk. Petula tried to find a way to reason her way out of this. In a sense, there were more of them than Dow. They could take him, but she had a feeling that she might be the only one unwilling to go with Dow, except maybe for Cruxh, who was concerned for Herbert. Herbert himself followed the man without any sign of distress.

Dow pushed the Library's doors open, letting them out. Petula took a last look at the place. She felt a twinge of pain in her chest, not sure if the pain was because of the unknowable future or leaving all these books behind. If she had to guess, she would think the latter. She went out.

A carriage waited for them at the foot of the Library's steps, surrounded by three unsavory men with enough character to start their own band. One of them, a weaselly-looking man, flashed a smile as they approached. Petula should have assumed Dow wouldn't come alone without

---

45 Even now, Petula got special treatment from him; the Librarian left them alone because of her. Otherwise, he would have come swooping down and driven out the horrible, noise-making creatures. Not that it was a favor that Petula asked for. Actually, she quite hoped for the opposite. She would have preferred the Librarian to shoo the others away, giving her an opportunity to be alone amongst the books and escape this social mess that was happening now. But that was it. People, or in this case a vampire, often enough think they are mind readers. They rarely are. Asking would help.

muscle.

"I—" Petula said.

Dow stood next to her and said, "Miss Upwood, all will be revealed at the Town Hall. I have to wonder, doesn't a curious person like yourself want to know how this all ends? You have been involved thus far, and maybe you should think of this as a learning opportunity."

Was that another threat? It didn't feel like it. The man was trying to appeal to the only side of her that'd comply, and it worked. Petula headed to the carriage. The weaselly-looking man offered her his hand to help her up the steps, but she just walked past him.

The man chuckled. She heard him say to Dow, "Not a party I would like to attend. You have your work cut out, sir."

If Dow replied, it wasn't with words.

One by one, they all entered the carriage, taking their seats. The carriage lurched into motion when Dow's men took their positions, but they didn't get far.

A man shouted, "Petula?!"

Dow held his hand up, and the carriage stopped abruptly, making Petula grab her seat so as not to be flung forward against Mrs. Maybury.

"Aah, good of you to join us, Mr. Reinhardt. You saved me the trouble of finding you," Dow said.

"I..." Morris said and looked towards Petula.

Petula looked away. She'd seen Agatha behind the man. He'd managed to find her, then. Good, Petula thought. Not that her good sounded that pleased.

"Won't you all join us, even you, Miss...Caster, is it?" Dow asked.

"Hortensia Caster, sir," the officer said. "But I'm afraid we are in pursuit of—"

"Ira?" Kitty asked, cutting the officer short. Cruxh had laid the corpse next to him on a seat. The man's head was leaning on the ghoul's shoulder, looking cozy, if you asked Petula.

"What have you done to my husband?" the woman screeched, trying to stare Petula down.

Petula smiled. She hadn't meant to.

"I'm here, darling," Herbert said, or Ira, whichever way you wanted to see the matter.

Kitty looked startled. Almost ready to faint.

"Ahh, now that everything is settled, won't you all get on, and we will make sense of this at the Town Hall. I am afraid time is of the essence," Dow said.

"But—" Kitty began to say. Morris took the woman by her arm and steadied her.

"I have to insist," Dow said. "But of course, only if Mrs. Worthwrite can manage."

"I'll help her up," Morris said. With his help, Kitty got on the carriage, the two dogs following close by. Agatha and Hortensia followed after. The officer instantly took her rulebook out and began to flip through it, a confused look on her face.

Morris headed Petula's way when he'd gotten Kitty seated behind her husband.

Kitty's hands shook.

"Agatha," Petula said, looking past the banker. "Sit next to me." Agatha hesitated but complied.

Morris frowned and took a seat behind them. "What's going on?" he whispered as he sat down.

"Your guess is as good as mine," Petula replied.

"What has happened to Ira?" he asked and looked towards the banker's corpse.

Petula bit her lip when she saw Kitty's still shaking hands. "A possession," she said, wanting to look away.

"Petula, you didn't?" Agatha said.

Petula bit her cheek, drawing blood, as the other necromancer looked at her with her big eyes.

"I had no other choice," she said, tasting the iron in her mouth.

The carriage moved again. This time there were no interruptions.

◆

Minta pictured a huge green forest opening up in front of her as she spoke to the reporter about the newly formed monetary committee and how it would prevent another catastrophe of this magnitude from happening. She should warn the reporter about the wolf that moved silently in the midst of the trees. Minta shook the image off and tried to concentrate on the man immortalizing her, Ida, Albert, Chester, and

Frederick in his paper. But she couldn't get the image of the forest to go away. Every time she closed her eyes, every time she doubted the sincerity of her own words, every time she knew nothing would change as long as there were humans and their self-serving motives, she saw the forest and the wolf.

"The committee will be there for the citizens, holding the banks liable for their actions and seeing that their books are open to the public, and to aid the city in getting the spending right. These fine men and woman behind me are the first line of banks, politicians, and researchers to aid the Town Hall in securing a stable economy," Minta said, knowing that the words were merely decorative until they were fulfilled. The question was when and if they would ever be accomplished. It would be a long and difficult road ahead to get her new committee to agree on anything concrete.

The reporter wrote her words down, searching for ways to use Minta's words against her. He could and should do that. But all this was an interlude for later, when she tied everything into a neat package for the man to report. Which would either cost her everything or secure her many more years in office, and if she was being honest, she wasn't sure which was worse.

Her plans were being set in motion sooner than she'd thought. Minta watched Dow escorting Ignatius, Wilbur, and, to her horror, Bertha into the building. The woman could make this impossible. But Minta could let her shine in all her own glory and doom. She turned her head back to face the camera obscura, going against the convention and smiling.

There was a bright flash, erasing the picture of the forest, drawing an unpleasant image of dark, looming characters. The banker variety.

"Ah, Miss Chaplain and Mr. Vaughn and Mr. Sumner. Nice of you to come," Minta said when she got her vision back. She stepped out of the focus of the lens. Dow left them before she could recap what'd happened between her and the committee members, who now murmured behind her, baffled as to why the bankers and Miss Chaplain—the enemy—were there.

"Mayor," Bertha said.

The two bankers tipped their top hats.

"Miss Stopford," Ignatius said.

"Now, if you would be so kind as to take a seat and

wait for the others to join us," Minta said.

Bertha narrowed her eyes and got ready to chew Minta's head off. Figuratively...of course.

Minta smiled and continued on before Bertha had time to collect her thoughts.

"We'll have to wait for all your associates, Miss Chaplain. I think young Reinhardt is missing, and of course Mr. Worthwrite. I hope his transition into his new life was a pleasant and easy one," she said, making Ignatius and Wilbur squirm in the way only gentlemen can.[46] Bertha looked confused, and before she had time to recover, Minta laid more cards on the table. "In the meantime, let me introduce you to the trust that helped me to put together a monetary committee to aid the city's economic situation, and to Mr. Porter, who has graciously come to note this historic event. But you already know him, if my memory serves me right. He interviewed you earlier this year."

"What is this about?" Bertha asked, finally getting her words out. Not with the tenacity she usually had. She looked a shade ghostlier, but still retained that unfriendly aura of hers.

A smile wouldn't hurt anyone, Minta thought. But you couldn't help some people. They didn't understand that if you put a pen between your lips, happy thoughts were sure to come. If not from your inner life or muscles, then at least from the laughs received. But to some, the world was a depressive place without beauty, sympathy, or helping pens. They preferred to see the dark side of everything.

Ignatius stepped past the undead woman. "Miss Stopford, I think we have a right to know why we've been summoned here to be paraded in front of *them* and Mr. Porter." He glared at the committee members. There was another fellow who preferred the dark side. It might be the whole Necropolis effect. If Minta wanted to find someone with a healthy sense of optimism, she better look elsewhere.

"As do we," Ida said, moving away from the stairs. "Was this a ruse? You get us to come up with a solution and obey you, and then you switch to the major leagues after the convenient photo op? I won't have it. We won't obey. I won't

---

46 Invisibly, with their buttocks clenched, stiffening their backs, and shuddering their whiskers. No, scratch that, their mustaches, despite having none.

let Mr. Worthwrite waltz in and take over something that could be a good thing for the city and morph it to suit his own needs."

Minta heard the reporter chuckle. The gloomy man had finally laughed. There was something here.

"I wish it was that simple," Minta said. "I genuinely —"

The reporter laughed out loud, cutting Minta short, which was a good thing. Starting a sentence with "genuinely" didn't sound very convincing. There might be times when someone honestly meant it when they said "I am genuinely interested in what you are saying," but those moments were damn rare to find.

"Are you making fun of us?" Ida asked. Her "us" sounded more like "me" to Minta's ears.

Minta wanted to laugh at the absurdity, laugh at the night and morning she'd had, and finally go to bed and be done with these people and with this whole sordid affair. But unlike the reporter, who was halfway to the floor, ready to roll, she had to try to make sense of these humans and try to fix the situation.

The reporter continued roaring. Either she'd made the man mad because he'd realized what Minta was trying to do or he thought she'd gone cuckoo. Which she was sure she had. At least, she'd lost sight of who she was during all these years in office. She wasn't even a shadow of her past self, who'd been content and happy about what she did and where she was. Now she had constant heartburn.

"There's no intent to ridicule you or anyone else, and I promise we'll have a satisfying conclusion if you would be so kind as to wait for the others to join us. Then all will become clear," Minta said. She wasn't sure if even she found her words compelling. The long day was getting to her.

At this point, Porter's laughter had turned into hysteria. His photographer held him up to stop him convulsing too much. He was making others uncomfortable by causing doubt, and his mood was infectious. Laughter in general was. Though not this kind.

"Mr. Porter, are you all right? Can I help you? Can we help you?" Minta left Ignatius and the others standing there, gasping for breath. She laid her hand on the reporter's upper back when he didn't stop laughing. That seemed to jolt the man back to the moment.

He blinked several times and then adjusted his suit and got a better grip on his notebook.

"I'm perfectly fine. I had something caught in my throat," the reporter said.

"That's what I thought. I'm glad to hear you are doing better. But I have to address you all before anyone gets any wild ideas, and I would like you to be fully present," Minta said. She detached from the reporter and moved away from everyone to form her own island. It was time to stop stalling. She only wished Dow was already here with her, but she was forced to do this on her own.

A few of the Town Hall's visitors and ministers had gathered to watch what was happening with their Mayor and the rest of the notable people. Minta didn't drive them away, as whatever happened here tonight had to be heard and spread around.

"I've brought you all here because of the current, unbearable situation in the city. The economic downturn has not only ruined businesses but the lives of our citizens, driving them to desperate actions. As I mentioned to Mr. Porter, things have to change. That's why I asked Albert Walker, Chester Fen, Frederick Kilborn, and Ida Mortician to help me find a solution to ease our citizens' troubles. They suggested a monetary committee, and I've agreed that this is the best course of action. But it won't solve anything if we don't address the issues on a general level, and there Mr. Porter comes to our rescue. He's going to report what occurs here tonight, giving the public an honest view of how policies are made and how their troubles are addressed."

R. Porter straightened his back, and asked, "Then you don't mind if I ask: why have you created this divide between the Union of the Undead and the Necro Democratic Alliance? You are including one party leader and excluding another from this new so-called monetary committee. Or should I ask: is it just a new bureaucratic entity to make our lives yet more complicated?" The man looked alert, and whatever he'd experienced before was gone. Maybe he had finally understood that this was a great opportunity to go back to real reporting, and not just be a lapdog for the news Ira and his associates wanted to hear. Not that bashing Minta was far from their wishes.

Bertha eagerly jumped in. "Finally the real questions are being asked. Creating a gulf between the parties isn't good for citizens. If we want to achieve a better Necropolis, and as you, Miss Stopford, put it, to solve the current distress, then we should work together and not segregate our political entities."

Frederick snorted, which was unlike the restrained man. "I would like to see you build bridges between our two parties," he said.

"Maybe this is a great opportunity to put down our swords and work together. Maybe both Mr. Porter and Bertha Chaplain are right..." Minta didn't get any further. She watched as Dow approached them. "Ah, Mr. Spurgeon, good of you to join us, and...Mrs. Maybury, what a surprise."

Everyone present stiffened when she mentioned those names, the onlookers included. The reputation of Mrs. Maybury extended beyond politics and beyond the shop of her late husband. In addition, Dow's name was whispered in the darkness like that of a bogeyman who comes to take you if you misbehave.

"Ma'am," Dow said and nodded, his word sounding more like an apology than a greeting. Minta understood why. It was bad enough that Mrs. Maybury was there, despite her having a positive effect on Bertha, who looked like she had seen a ghost, her eyes wide and her face a shade bluer. But it wasn't only Mrs. Maybury who would cause indignation. There was also Herbert, whose involvement was shaky at best. And Ira seemed to hang from the polite ghoul's shoulder, bringing two additional variables into the equation. The unconscious devil wasn't quite what Minta had in mind when she thought to bring everything out into the open, but neither was a ghoulish angel who couldn't see the value of doing something the wrong way. Then there was Ira's necromancer, whom she knew nothing about. Minta let herself get familiar with the girl. She stared back. There was a distinct feeling of her body and mind being weighed while being given a thorough poking. Minta pictured the spear in her hand. The necromancer glanced at the spear, and for a fraction of a second, Minta felt confused, looking at her own hand as if the weapon really was there. It wasn't.

"Hm," she said.

Whenever two necromancers occupied the same

space, there was an instant assessment. It might look entirely pleasant. Lots of smiling. Kind words. But underneath the surface, the other one held a threat. It was a wonder that Necropolis' University could function. It only managed because of heavy regulation and the promise of punishment here and hereafter. In the Town Hall, outside the University's compounds, there were no such rules. The Necromantic Council frowned upon turf wars. However, it didn't forbid them.

To add on to the complication, Bertha cried out, "Agatha." To have three necromancers in the same room was inviting calamity.

Behind Bertha's necromancer came Morris, Kitty, an officer of the law, and four more ghouls. Minta started to doubt her own plans. There were too many volatile parties in the room, which made the conclusion unpredictable and raised the number of possible casualties. She didn't even count the ghouls who'd attacked Mrs. Maybury, who now stood looking docile.

She sighed.

Herbert's hand jerked. Minta shot a glance towards him. He did it again, making little out-of-place movements. Only ever so slightly, so that a careless viewer would have missed them. Minta took a deep breath in and pushed past the barrier the five ghouls in the room created between this world and the spirit world. It wasn't a barrier exactly. The ghouls were spirit repellent. Not shooing spirits off for peeing on the lawn, but keeping them away for fear of being used as energy sources. Ghouls weren't only corpse eaters. They ate the whole thing. But here in the Town Hall, the dead's presence was greater. They gravitated towards power and action, towards life-force in its rawest form.

Minta mumbled an incantation, pushing out the living's demands and Dow's gentle cough. Then she saw it, what Ira's necromancer had done, or so she presumed, as spirits didn't tend to move from one body to another of their own accord. Something to do with the mind-body connection. Who knew if that became possible when the scientists in the University learned to tamper with something called quantum.

Minta squeezed her invisible spear. Such incantations weren't exactly forbidden, but it was something you didn't do. Mr. Ringworm had to be in pure agony.

"Hm," Minta said with such emphasis that all the murmurs died out. All eyes were on her.

"I guess we can start. It seems we have everyone we need here, even Mr. Worthwrite," she added.

"Yes, I'm here," Ira said through Herbert. If Herbert's voice had been depressing and melodic, now it sounded as if it came from beyond this world. Heavy and lifeless.

◆

Petula didn't care for the way the other necromancer looked at her. Or the Mayor, as she called herself. In her opinion, no practicing necromancer should ever call themselves that. Also, there was no reason to keep imposing her authority over her, flexing and clenching her right arm as if she carried something imaginary there. Petula just wished the woman would spit out whatever she wanted and be done with her, with them. These theatrics were pointless. People went on doing what they did, not giving a hoot what she thought about how they should act.

Behind the woman, a photographer turned the camera obscura, aiming it in Petula's direction. She moved aside, unwilling to leave any evidence she was there. She noticed that the man, Dow, who'd come to get them, did the same. Their movements angered the photographer, who swung her hand to make them move back into the picture. Neither of them obeyed.

"Good to hear that you're doing fine, Mr. Worthwrite, but I do hope that Mr. Ringworm is still in there and alive," Minta said.

"He's around," Ira said. His words were beyond eerie. A beat without substance.

"Now then. I've asked you to come here in order to clear the air and lay the ground rules for how we proceed from here on—" Minta said.

Bertha interrupted her. "Who are you to order us to come here? This goes against the constitution and the guidelines on how a member of the Town Hall council should act. Nothing about this is legal, and it has no effect on the future," she said. "You should have put this on the agenda if you wanted to address some issue."

"For once I agree with Bertha. Acting behind our backs goes against everything you are meant to do. It's high time we weigh your leadership skills and see if there's someone more suitable for the job," Mrs. Maybury said.

Not that changing leaders ever truly helped. Someone similar was always willing to take their place. But it was easier to blame one person than to admit that the problem was in all of us, in the culture that fed the system that preyed on the weak and valued money and winning over people and empathy. Minta had been a good leader, but a good leader can only go so far without running against the general atmosphere. The opposite holds true, as well. A bad leader can't get far if the society is functional and protects its citizens from tyranny and madness. Like those with bad hairdos.

"Alice!" Cruxh said.

"I mean it. It's high time this city sees something new and stops going on and on with the same tired old style. Don't you want to come out of hiding?" Mrs. Maybury asked.

"Alice!" Cruxh let out.

"You yourself argued that a moment ago with your mother. Now is your opportunity to step up and demand what is rightfully yours," Mrs. Maybury stated.

"Cruxh, what is this about?" Minta demanded, sounding more confused than assertive or friendly, as she'd done earlier. Petula noted that the woman had a habit of saying her words softly. Almost as if every word she said was more like a question than a statement of facts.

"Equal standing for ghouls," Cruxh said.

A few humans, including Ignatius, snorted.

Petula shook her head. Tonight kept escalating from one event to another. People were too immersed in their drama, thinking it serious and important. But when you looked at it, this was just another story among many. May it would be a story with consequences, but a story nevertheless.

"I thought we had that. We treat all undead according to the laws shared by all inhabitants of the city," Minta said.

Cruxh spoke first, before Bertha or Mrs. Maybury could address the travesty of the laws for the undead.

"First of all, the misconception of us being undead should be changed. None of us has died and come back. I understand why we were put in such a category at first, and we gave our blessing for it, but I think it has done more harm to us than helped us to be part of Necropolis. We are a distinctive entity separated from the living and the undead. Some would like to call us demons, but such a word has bad connotations. We are not here to tempt anyone. We are ghouls, and that should be enough," he said.

"If we create a new category, would that satisfy you?" Minta asked.

Petula guessed this wasn't why they were here.

"I think dividing anyone into categories, undead or living or anything else, is restrictive. It separates us from each other and makes us compete without a good reason to do so. We are all Necropolitans and should be thought of as such," Cruxh said.

"That still doesn't tell me what to argue," Minta said, sounding somewhat desperate.

Petula watched the older necromancer in disbelief. How could she have ever thought to control them all? Even Petula, who had a great disinterest towards others, knew these people who the Mayor had summoned here were beyond manageable. They had too much to lose if they didn't get their way.

"Why should there be an argument of any kind?" Cruxh asked.

"There should be," Bertha interrupted, cutting Ira, who'd been about to say something, short, but only because there had been a power struggle between him and Herbert. "But the argument isn't about a category or whether ghouls should be fully-fledged citizens. The argument is about the fact that our Mayor is working behind our backs, forming committees to undermine the power of the selected political entity. That's a case for treason. I oppose any monetary committees. We should create no such thing, as they'll become corrupt in time and cause more harm than good. And who knows if this economic downturn will pass on its own. We cannot be sure if our actions and new laws will lead to more harm than good. I agree with Mrs. Maybury that it's high time we see if there are any other options."

The reporter was about to have a new bout of hysterics. His photographer helped him control it. Petula was the only one paying attention to them, and only because she was noting her surroundings and wondering how easily she could just walk away.

"Of course, I'm right. I've been saying that for a while, that we need a new necromancer to take over the government. Someone new and young, with enough stamina to battle against the banks, for example. This committee of yours is too little too late," Mrs. Maybury said.

Minta opened her mouth to argue back. This time she had a lot to say. Most likely leading up to an unhappy ending.

"This is absurd—"

"If I may interject," Dow said, jolting everyone around him. Not Petula though. She hadn't heard about the man and his reputation. She had always seen politics as irrelevant. It had nothing to do with science. Okay, maybe occasionally the University had to go begging for money, but that was a job for managers, not scientists. And of course, there were laws restricting what they could and could not do. But now, as she saw these so-called policies being made, she was appalled.

"Dow?" Minta asked, sounding relieved.

He looked away. "Maybe Mrs. Maybury is right. We need other options," Dow sighed.

The Mayor clutched her right hand. Petula could again see her holding something, but what, she wasn't sure. She looked around and saw others looking bewildered. The only ones who seemed content were Mrs. Maybury and the dual Herbert Ringworm.

"The only natural option is Miss Upwood," Ira said, cutting the delicate balance in the room with his words. "She's an excellent necromancer and has enough character to lead this city." Which could be translated as his vested interest in her made Petula alluring despite her attitude defects.

"Petula?" a woman asked. It was Agatha. She stood near Bertha, shoulder to shoulder with Morris, and behind them loomed Kitty and Hortensia. However, Hortensia didn't loom. She took a law book out of her pocket and opened it.

Petula's head spun. She wasn't sure what was worse, seeing Agatha close to Morris or the words Ira had uttered.

You need oxygen. Breathe, she reminded herself. She breathed in. Still, nothing made sense.

"Miss Upwood? You have to be kidding me," Ignatius

spat, and only then noticed it was Ira who had spoken.

"No, it has to be her," Ira said. "She will solve all..." Ira swallowed the rest of his words. His legs thumped down as he tried to move forward. He swayed and stopped in an odd position while everyone stared at him.

"Dow? Why?" Minta asked, taking this as an opportunity to get a word in.

The man took his time answering. Petula could hear the silence. It sounded like millions of thoughts being processed at once.

"A chance for a new start..." he finally said. "Mr. Worthwrite could be right. The girl is a good option. She is one of the best in the city, and she is young," he said, meeting the Mayor's gaze.

"No!" Petula said. The room was spinning. It wasn't supposed to go this way.

"Miss Upwood," Cruxh pleaded.

"Not you too. I have had it with this day. I won't be Mr. Spurgeon's puppet, nor Mr. Worthwrite's, nor Mrs. Maybury's, nor yours," Petula said. She was getting claustrophobic. She could feel the Town Hall's walls closing in and the time slipping away. "I have been patient, but this is enough. I'm going home."

"Petula," Agatha whispered.

To Petula, Agatha saying her name was like a shout from the rooftops. She wasn't her Petula.

"If anyone is going to take the Mayor's place, it's my Agatha," Bertha commanded.

If Petula thought she was having a miserable time, she should think again. The Mayor was about to snap. There was a heavy pressure building up, and the once translucent spear was becoming more solid. However, it was not made from steel but from the dead spirits around them. Then Petula remembered that the only way to exchange leaders in Necropolis was to kill the former one.

"I won't let you kill me," Minta said.

Petula heard Ira chuckle. Herbert had to be losing the battle against the banker.

27

DOING THE RIGHT THING IS A BUGGER

he dead won't stay dead if you don't let them rest. If you keep feeding them, giving them reasons to come back, they do. They hunger for life. Life that's so precious that the living ignore it when they are alive. The living who waste it on frivolous animosities and take it away for minor incidences of hatred, sometimes on a mass scale. The living who're so blinded by what they see that they forget what matters. It's a wonder that humanity has survived thus far. To this point, where the dead inside the Town Hall saw an opportunity to live, to seize the concentration of raw energy formed by greed, lust, and pride. The first dead to come out of hiding was Jeremiah Black. He'd been waiting the entire night to be whole again. To be seen and heard. The bankers had ignored him and so had the necromancer who'd replaced him.

He pushed past his fear of the ghouls, finding his way to the Mayor, whose panic was as alluring as a pot of gold at the end of the rainbow. If there was someone who he could use, it was her. Of course, she was dangerous and powerful, but she'd let herself get weak. Sheer exhaustion oozed out of the woman. With his help, they could command the room and make this masquerade come to an end.

The Mayor had divided her attention between the necromancers and her other opponents, but that wasn't his way in. It was the sadness and betrayal she felt towards Dow. It was what'd shattered her mind. Jeremiah pushed past her barriers. The woman released her grip on the spear she'd accidentally formed. She struggled against him, trying to drive him away.

"*You need me,*" he whispered to her. "*You cannot take them all without my help. Let me in, and you walk out of here as a winner.*"

Jeremiah had never felt this alive and alert before. It was as if finally someone had opened up all his senses, which his former body had restricted. The body that'd craved booze to make his life bearable. There was no longer any need to numb himself or his fear of the disorder that was life. He got the spirit and the feeling just right to once and for all take control over his own actions.

He would start an avalanche. Those spirits who had slumbered were beginning to rouse. Those who'd been active, he made hungry. Those who'd been hungry, he made ravenous. This was his opportunity to get payback, and he took it.

◆

Petula's head spun. All around them spirits were awakening, and Ira kept whispering into her ear to seize power from the Mayor by killing her. Occasionally, Herbert groaned, trying to fight back to stop Ira using him like a puppet. Petula glanced at the man or men and then to Agatha, who stood opposite her. Their eyes met. She looked distressed, and it was no wonder. Behind her, Bertha chatted away, cajoling and pushing Agatha the same way Ira was doing her.

"Kill her! We can make this city a better place, you and me, Agatha. This is our only opportunity to make a change," Bertha said, echoing almost word for word what Ira was saying to her.

Petula shook her head.

Agatha stared back with a blank expression, looking more colorless than before against her painted black hair. She might crack. Her high morals, which Petula knew her to have, and her stupid need to please others were clearly fighting each other for dominance. Petula wasn't sure which one would win.

She mouthed the word no, without letting out a sound. If Agatha understood what she said, she didn't reciprocate. She continued staring at Petula with a blank expression.

There was a loud screech. Petula spun her head around, seeing the ghoul, Sirixh, covered with spirits.

The other ghoul, Cruxh, yelped and dashed to aid his sister. He shooed the spirits away but didn't devour them, even though he could.

The dead had awakened, and they were hungry. Hungrier than Petula had ever seen them. There among them were those who'd attached themselves to the living and the undead present in the room, as well as those who'd latched on to her ever since she stepped onto Necropolis' soil. You could say necromancers were like catnip to the spirits, who needed their wants to be heard. Now the spirits had gained enough strength to knock down the statues, vases, and paintings. They could interact with anything that wasn't nailed down. The pieces of furniture whined, moments from bursting from their frames as the dead's raw energy swept over them. The lights kept flickering, and the prey, the unfortunate bystanders, dashed to take cover as the spirits swooped to tug their hair and pull on their clothes.

Petula ignored the noises and the other people. She took off her coat, letting it rest on her left arm while she rolled up her sleeves, revealing complicated patterns tattooed on her arms. She unbuttoned a few of the collar buttons, baring more tattoos on her chest with ancient runes, symbols, and mantras she'd found in the books to be used as a guard against evil. Those spirits who'd thought her to be an easy target stopped in midair. Even Ira ceased to chat and took a step back, letting out a whine.

Farther away from Petula, the Mayor struggled against the invading necromancer, Jeremiah Black. Minta had her eyes wide open, and she mumbled something. Most likely a spell to control the man, who Petula had seen entering her.

She wasn't sure if the woman could fight him off. What she'd heard about the man was that he was stubborn and proud. That was an unfortunate, volatile cocktail.

"Go on, girl. Do what is asked of you," Bertha encouraged Agatha.

Petula watched Agatha twisting her face into a deep look of concern. She wavered.

Petula, on some level, liked and respected her, but she was a second-grade necromancer despite her high marks. Grades that she'd gotten simply by being nice and socially agreeable. Yet, if this chaos continued and Jeremiah kept the Mayor occupied, Agatha might have a chance. But most likely, she'd get herself hurt. If the Mayor took any notice of the living necromancer, she didn't show it. She continued mumbling.

Agatha let out an incantation as well, pacifying the spirits around her. Unquestionably, she was saying all the wrong words; Petula was sure of that.

She hated all this commotion and social interaction. Why should she care about Agatha or the Mayor or anyone else? Whatever was happening now was an opportunity to walk away and leave Necropolis for good. No one except Ira paid her any attention.

She was wrong, however. Dow kept a watchful eye on her from the shadows, where the man had retreated to watch the spectacle unfold. She didn't notice. Either way, no one would stop her.

Petula looked at Agatha one more time, then at the Mayor. Minta had shrugged off her coat and revealed the same kind of tattoos as those that decorated Petula's arms. They were older ink than hers. Clearly, the Mayor was fighting the spirit off with more skill than she'd thought, but the dead necromancer was still coming at her, pushed outside but attacking. There might not be a need to intervene.

But as soon as Petula started to walk to the front door, the room felt like morning porridge. The gooey kind. The spirits kept trying to restrict her movements. She mumbled an incantation and shook free of their touch. Her tattoos handled the rest. But there was another patch of spirits, and another. She kept pushing them away as she walked onward. The spirits tried to secure their hold on her and ride her like a wild animal. Some of them tried to find

their way in, doing to her the same thing she'd done to
Herbert. None of them succeeded. Yet, her walking slowed.
There were too many of them. More than there should be.

Petula stopped. Someone was doing this. This wasn't
usual behavior for spirits. They wanted to be alive, but a
coordinated attack on their part was not right. She took a
deep breath in. It would have been too good to be true if she
could have just walked away. Not that her conscience would
have let her open the door and leave. She grimaced. Living in
isolation had been a lot easier than this.

Petula watched as Jeremiah kept attacking the Mayor
and goading the other spirits to follow his example. Oh well,
she thought and faced the necromancer.

"What is wrong with you?" she asked. Okay, not the
best question to ask from someone clearly on their last nerve.

Jeremiah laughed, sounding manic.

Yep, Petula thought. His imploded ego was what she
hated about Necropolis. There seemed to be no end to the
supply. It could be Necropolis' fast pace of life, overcrowding,
and the concentration on superficial pursuits combined with
an obsession with death and dying, or more like eternal life
and youth, messing with their heads, combined with the
thought that the world owed them. Ha, no one owed them
anything.

It seemed like she had to do the right thing. She
hated doing the right thing. To trap the spirits and bring
back control. Okay, it was a game she could play, unlike what
Ira and Bertha had proposed. Killing for power was a waste of
time and humanity. She, they, could do better. That was the
thing. The insignificant reason seemed to gain more ground
than the big ones. Other people concentrated their efforts on
money and prestige while there were bigger questions to
answer, like why the Kraken shit were we here at all? Was the
universe never-ending, or was there an edge somewhere, and if
there was, how was it even possible? But no, glittering gold, a
penny, was more important and interesting to most than the
ultimate questions about life and the universe and everything
between those two buggers.

Petula snorted and concentrated her attention on
another spirit, which had enough life force to rally the others
to cooperate. It was the spirit that she'd seen following the
driver, Herbert. Petula had had a glimpse of her on the coach

and again as soon as they'd emerged from the ghoul city. She searched for the woman's name.

"Ona," she said aloud.

The spirit materialized in front of her. Herbert gasped behind her.

"Ona," she heard him repeat.

The spirit of the woman wavered. Her edges fluctuated between solid and hazy, fused into the background.

"I need you to be fully present here," Petula said.

The air stirred again. Another spirit pushed through Ona's body. Petula lifted her hand and said, "No." The spirit recoiled and fled.

"*Why?*" Ona wailed, becoming more solid.

"What are you doing to her?!" Herbert shouted. He tried to rush towards Petula and tackle her, but Ira once again took control of the body.

"Leave her be," Ira whispered.

"Help me, and I'll help you," Petula said, ignoring Herbert and Ira.

"*Can you give me life as you did for him?*" Ona asked, pointing her finger at her paramour. "*I want her,*" she added and turned her attention to Agatha.

"It doesn't work that way," Petula said.

"*Why?*"

"It is her life to keep," Petula said, looking at Agatha. She was surrounded by spirits, who drew back as Agatha whispered her incantations. Her eyes had turned milky white as she tried to soothe the spirits back to the afterlife. She was exhausting herself at a rapid speed. Her hair turned ash-white after each word she uttered. She would kill herself if she continued tapping into her own life-force that way. But at least she wasn't foolish enough to attempt to kill the Mayor.

"*Don't lie to me. You did it to him. You can do it for me. It's so cold here, please,*" Ona wailed.

"I cannot. It was a mistake," Petula said, squeezing her coat harder. It might be too late to help Agatha. To save her. But she had to try. There had to be something else she could bargain with. Something Ona valued more than her hunger. Oh well, Petula thought.

"He'll die if you don't help me," she sighed and strengthened Ona's memories, tugging her, making her remember Herbert's every touch, every word, every look.

"*That's not fair. I deserve to be alive,*" Ona whimpered.

"There's no such thing as 'I deserve.' Not here. I could say the same and walk away, but I don't. You died. Face it. That's the truth. But you can make something out of it, instead of complaining. It's time to let go and let the living go on living. I promise, I'll get Ira out of Herbert's body and give him a chance to live his life, but you have to help me first, or there won't be anyone left to save," Petula said. This saving business was hard work. No wonder people often opted out.

Ona was silent. She fluctuated between this world and the beyond.

"*What do you want?*" she finally asked.

"We'll take hold of the room together and push the spirits back to where they belong. I'll show you how, and you'll use everything you have to command them," Petula said.

Ona flickered.

She took that as a yes. She instantly began to channel her thoughts through the spirit, lending energy and strength to Ona, taking full control of her.

Jeremiah noticed what she was doing. So did Minta. The Mayor nodded to Petula and once more started to mumble her spells. Jeremiah instead surged towards her. A wave of anger and hatred washed over Petula and, for a second, she was sure it was her fault he was suffering. She should have helped him as soon as she saw him the first time. She hadn't, and now this was all happening because of her. Petula forced the sensation away. She could take it as true, as there was a sliver of accuracy, or as an unfounded accusation with self-serving motives. She took it as the latter. She continued coaching Ona, who was getting hold of the spirits, easing their hatred and hunger and other nasty emotions Jeremiah had coaxed out. Together they helped the spirits let go of this world and transition to their afterlife. Wherever and whatever that was.

Jeremiah attacked again with the same lousy results. Petula channeled his angst and needs away.

The screeches and the dead energy that had been present in the room, feeling and smelling like raw electricity, began to die down. But not only because of Petula's and

Ona's efforts. Minta had regained control of her emotions, and she was working the room the same way as Petula. So was Agatha, whose hair had turned as white as snow. Her rosy cheeks and lips were pale, and she looked like a shadow of her former self. Petula wasn't the only one to notice the changed appearance. Jeremiah made a sharp turn in the air and dashed towards the necromancer, pushing in easily. For a while, Agatha's posture collapsed, but when she came back, she looked broken, with heavy arms and a glazed expression.

"Do you think I'll go away that easily?" Jeremiah asked, using Agatha. "The answer is no, not when my killer walks among you and you do nothing to stop him. I want to have my dues."

"And this helps how?" Petula asked, raising her eyebrow.

Jeremiah hesitated. Petula had that effect on people. You could say that her somewhat impudent, strong attitude made others reconsider if their words were sane and logical. Most of the time, they weren't. The thing was, people are seldom textbook sane or logical. If they were, that would be insane.

"I want—"

"We have already established that. You want. But how about what you are doing? How does this serve anything? The Mayor was having a nice chat with her..." she said, searching for the right word. Somehow enemies didn't seem fitting in this situation. "...Colleagues," Petula said, and continued on, "then you came along and disrupted new policies being made. Policies that affect hundreds and thousands, and not only you. So let me ask again: what does this have to do with anything?"

There was a peal of laughter, but it didn't come from Jeremiah. It was Dow. His laughter was hollow, filling the room, making everyone doubt if they heard the laugh, thinking it must have been a mistake, yet still shivering.

Petula took the distraction as an opportunity to poke around Agatha's and Jeremiah's head. The man had twisted his mind around hers, making it difficult to separate the two without losing Agatha completely.

"Ona," Petula commanded. The spirit snapped to attention.

"If you think your little friend scares me, you are a

fool," Jeremiah said, recovering from Petula's unusual treatment of other people.

"I have no intention to scare you. You just need to step out of my friend, and everyone can go away happy," Petula said.

"What makes you think I will do that? She's mine now," Jeremiah said.

"No. Agatha!" Morris cried out, after recovering from all the weirdness. Morris tried to touch Agatha, but her hand slapped his away.

"Could you please keep out of this? Can't you see you are agitating him? I'm trying to do something here," Petula said.

"Then do something! Now you are just chatting with him," Bertha snapped before Morris could say anything.

"Generally, a nice chat goes a long way," Petula said. It was true. If people just talked and listened, most of their troubles could be avoided. And it was the listening part that made a huge difference, but most people seemed to forget that. Even Petula, who often enough thought she knew better. She did. But that was beside the point. You had to give room to other opinions and emotions, or so her mother insisted.

Jeremiah laughed, sounding unlike Agatha. More cold and calculating.

"Then what do you want to talk about? How about we do what Miss Chaplain wants? How about if I aid her to take over the city?" he said.

Bertha moaned.

"Why would you want to do that?" Petula interrupted the undead woman before she could jump on the offer. She was genuinely interested. Petula couldn't understand why anyone would want to take responsibility for a whole city. It was bad enough trying to take care of her own life, let alone the lives of thousands of miserable bastards.

The room had turned quiet. The spirits were gone, except for Ona and Jeremiah. Minta had sent the rest on their way, whether they wanted to go or not. Okay, there was a gentle munching sound from a few of the ghouls who'd attacked Mrs. Maybury, who were eating a couple of nasty spirits, but they would swear by Kraken that they were truly a bad lot and deserved all they got. Also, in the corner where R. Porter had huddled down came the almost inaudible sound of a pen scratching against paper. But otherwise, the room was silent. Then again, if you listened carefully, you could hear the suppressed silence of people trying not to breathe.

"He doesn't. He only thinks he does, because that's what is taught to us," Minta said, barely getting her words out past her sheer tiredness. "But tell me, who killed you?" she asked. Minta knew the art of listening and understood it was the cornerstone of necromancy.

"That man," Jeremiah said, pointing his finger at Herbert.

Mrs. Maybury's "hah" echoed in the room.

"Alice," Cruxh pleaded.

Petula used the distraction as a chance and pushed Ona inside Agatha's body. She went in willingly, causing a three-soul problem. Unlike a two-soul problem, no closed-form solution for all possible sets of initial conditions existed for the three-soul problem. No one had calculated what would happen to a body if there were three distinct forces pulling it towards them. Two was somewhat computable, but three was a guessing game. There were too many variables interfering with the result.

Petula tilted her head and looked at Agatha, who'd collapsed to her knees. Petula was sure she could calculate this subtraction so that the initial person was left.

"Hmm, this is interesting," she said.

"Girl, what did you do?" Minta stuttered.

When Petula didn't answer, Minta said with an angry voice, "Get them out of her this instant!"

"I think I can solve this," she said. "There has to be a way that souls can nullify each other without destroying the initial host, in this case Agatha. But I think I can use Ira's empty body to move things around."

That was it, Petula thought. She could solve this. She laughed. Her bright voice sounded like a melodic note. Petula began to move the souls around, persuading the spirits to do her bidding. Jeremiah would be a difficult one to budge, but she had her ways.

Petula shut her eyes and let out an incantation.

Ira's body jolted upright.

28

IS IT TOO EARLY FOR CONFESSIONS AND PROTESTS BEFORE A CUP OF TEA?

inta watched as Petula worked. She kept juggling the souls from one body to another, using Ira's rotten corpse as storage. Minta couldn't help but be fascinated by the woman and her work. She'd put Ira's soul into the mix, freeing Herbert from the freeloading parasite, or as others wanted to see, from the banker's clutches. Afterward, Herbert had to be subdued by Cruxh before he got to Petula and killed her. Petula continued her work, ignoring what was happening around her, using Ira as a pacifier between Agatha and the soul she had to leave behind. To Minta's amazement, the words the necromancer used didn't sound like any language she knew, and after carefully listening, she realized that the woman spoke in numbers and mathematical formulas, yet the spirits followed her command. Ira most of all. Even when she muttered something about pies.

Petula was unlike any other necromancer Minta had ever seen. She just smiled and shuffled the souls with ease.

This all had to look bizarre to the other onlookers, who couldn't see the spirit world, but the tension in the room told her they perceived something huge and important happening. At least, the constant jerking of Ira's corpse made sure of that.

"Let the Mj be the soul of the body coordinated at Xi and Yi moved from the body A," Petula said and let out a chuckle when she was finally able to confuse Jeremiah enough to move him inside Ira's body.

Jeremiah let out a scream but couldn't do much else, as Petula had somehow bound him to her and to Ira.

Minta stared at the corpse in disbelief.

"Now I need a vessel. Preferably two," Petula said hoarsely, her voice rasping her throat.

When no one replied, she added, "Anything will do." She looked around, bewildered, as if she saw for the first time everyone looking at her, horrified. If she said "boo," Minta was sure over half of the room would piss themselves, and the rest would flee in panic, leaving behind Dow, making friends with his new pet.

"Would one of the statues do?" Minta asked, nodding towards the floor, where the spirits had knocked the artwork over.

"Oh, yes. Those are perfect," Petula said, beginning to mumble her formulas again. She really didn't have to whisper; Minta could never have copied a single incantation she said tonight.

Soon enough, she'd moved the spirits around, putting Ona inside an octopus statue.

Next, she shifted Ira inside his own body, finally liberating Agatha from all the spirits. The woman slumped down, fatigued and out of this world. The young Reinhardt rushed to her aid, drawing Agatha into his lap. Bertha looked disorientated, as if she wasn't sure which way was up or who she was. But Minta didn't pay any attention to them. She watched as Petula moved Jeremiah out of Ira and into a small horned statue with six eyes and a huge belly.

"Now, I think, I could use a drink," Petula said and sat on the ground. "Then one of you will take me home. I'm pretty sure I deserve a nap."

It took no time for Dow to appear from the shadows, carrying a pitcher and a glass, pouring water for Petula. He stayed near her, observing the room.

Minta felt numb as she watched her assistant and the necromancer. All she could think was along the same lines as Petula, to have a lie-down. But she knew she had to address the questions that hung in the air: "What the Kraken shit just happened? And what now?" She just didn't know how.

"I think..." she started, searching for the rest of the words. "This has been enough for tonight. Go home, and we'll all convene here tomorrow and finish what we started," Minta continued, despite not wanting to see any of them again. She would prefer a long rest somewhere far away, and alone.

"She's right. Nothing good can happen tonight. The matter is dealt with, and we better head home to have a good night's sleep," Frederick said, crawling up from behind one of the knocked-over tables. His words were accompanied by loud shouting coming from outside. Muffled voices cheered the name Ernest Shivers and derided Minta's rule.

By all means, Minta thought. If the citizens wanted Ernest Shivers, the man whose tragedy had spread like wildfire in the newspapers, then he should sit on the Town Hall council. There was no harm. And the people had a right to choose. But she wasn't sure if she cared any longer. Minta clutched her pocket, where her notebook was nestled.

"No, I'm not leaving here without justice." A woman's voice echoed in the Town Hall. Minta lifted her case up and expected to see Bertha or Mrs. Maybury, but she was met with the stern face of Mrs. Worthwrite. "My husband was kidnapped and brutally attacked by that necromancer," Kitty continued, pointing at Petula. "I want that addressed tonight. I've brought an officer of the law with me, and I, we, have a right to have her arrested, along with the ghouls who stole our gold and degraded Ira."

Minta lifted her fingers to her eyelids and massaged them. Oh, good Kraken, she thought. Let me survive this day.

Just when she thought the worst had already happened, some of the protesters pushed in with their signs, chanting her name, and not in a good way.

◆

Morris couldn't believe his own eyes. He saw the spirits for the first time. He'd sensed their presence in the past but never actually seen one. This was nothing like what he'd expected. Jeremiah Black moving from one body to another was weird and gave him the creeps. He still had nightmares about his own possession. Also, he was sure this was his fault somehow, and now Agatha lay on the floor in his lap, unconscious. He'd watched the spirits sway against the woman and had done nothing. He pulled her closer and observed Petula, who sat on the floor, looking small and powerless.

Soon Kitty's demand for justice filled the space, and something inside him broke. He looked at the towering woman and the mob behind her, holding signs like: "Grandma is hungry"—one that could be interpreted on so many levels in Necropolis—and "Down with the Queen!"— again, clearly not thought through—and the sad, almost unnoticeable sign: "I'm not a number."

No, you are not, he thought. Neither is Agatha, nor Petula. He was the number here. Morris laid Agatha on the floor carefully. She whined as he did so. Morris brushed her white hair off her face, but when she didn't react, he eased her the rest of the way down.

Morris stood up, searching for Hortensia, and begged her to come with him.

"Sir?" Hortensia asked and glanced at Mrs. Worthwrite, who looked at Morris with a gaping mouth.

"I'll need your help. I need you to do the right thing despite what's been thrown at you," Morris whispered, not wanting his secret to come out. Not yet. "I've seen you writing in your notebook all night, and there's more to add," he continued after a slight hesitation. This would end badly for him, but it had to be done. This had to end.

"Sir, I'm not sure what you're asking of me," Hortensia stated.

"All will become clear soon. I only want to know if you are someone who'll uphold the law despite status, power, and money," he asked.

"Sir?" Hortensia replied. She gently touched his shoulder.

Her touch disarmed him, making all the strength leave his body. He almost changed his mind, but those genuine, huge, honest eyes convinced him otherwise.

"I take that as a yes. Do your duty and nothing less or more. All this is my fault, and I need to pay," he said, removing himself from the woman's touch.

Hortensia looked at him, searching for sincerity. She nodded, but before letting him go, she asked, "You won't do anything illegal?"

"No."

"You promise?"

"You have my word," Morris said.

"Okay," she replied.

"Hold this," he said, handing her his cane and the sword along with it.

Morris limped away from Hortensia to the center of the crowd. In the background, he saw Ignatius and Wilbur make their way through the onlookers towards the exit, wearing polite smiles on their faces and saying, "pardon me, excuse me, don't mind me." You could say they knew when the pitchforks and torches had been taken out from their pasture.

"If someone could stop them," Morris said, raising his voice and pointing at his associates. Ignatius strode onward, but Wilbur had halted in his tracks when he'd spoken. The members of the crowd stepped in, blocking their exit, smelling a rat when they saw one.

"Thank you," he said. Morris could feel Ira's eyes upon him, disapproving, yet not saying a word. He wished he hadn't forgone his weapon. There might come a moment when he'd have to rely on it to stop the man from getting to his jugular.

But what had to be done had to be done, and now.

"I have wronged you all. Write this down, Miss Caster, word for word. The same goes for you, Mr. Porter. I beg of you. This has to be remembered," Morris said, darting a glance towards the reporter. He saw the man flip open a new page. Good, he thought and turned his attention back to Ira and Hortensia.

"Morris, what are you doing?" Mrs. Worthwrite demanded.

"Let him, darling. He's only going to make an ass out of himself," Ira said.

Morris wasn't sure if that was a warning or not, but he didn't care about his little black book of secrets any longer.

"I, Ira Worthwrite, Ignatius Vaughn, and..." Morris

hesitated. He could still save one person from this, who had asked silly questions the entire time, like "is this right or wrong?" or "what is going to happen if we succeed?" But then again, Wilbur had never stopped them or walked away. "And...Mr. Sumner have worked against the public's and the Mayor's best interests behind their backs. With the aid of Bertha Chaplain, we've been preparing to bring a monetary entity into the city to make it easier for the four of us to take control of the markets. We've tightened our grip on the money and ceased any leniency towards our debtors, bringing about bankruptcies to increase discontent and thus push our solution as the only plan against the rogue banks, including us. But we would be able to take the hit, as we as individuals have more capital than anyone in the room combined.

"In our defense, the situation had become unbearable. We had to do something to stop the other banks giving loans without collateral and destroying us all. The competition had gotten to the point where all of us were lying about our assets, giving more money out than there was to be given, and without caring where we gave it or if it was ever going to be paid back. We hid the risk by selling them onward as bonds to be invested in. But that's not an excuse. Those are the facts.

"So I think the right thing to do is not to strip the power of Miss Stopford, who has put the citizens' needs before her own, but to arrest those who are the cause and not the symptom. Miss Caster, that's your cue. You are the embodiment of the law. Arrest us."

Hortensia looked bewildered.

"I..." she said and slumped her shoulders. Morris had feared this, that she was like the others he'd seen back at the police station. No backbone, no dignity, and no sense of justice.

Frederick laughed, but soon he cleared his throat and said, "Go on, arrest Miss Chaplain and her conspirators!"

Hortensia still hesitated.

Cruxh came to her rescue. He got off Herbert's back, who'd lost his will to fight, and approached Hortensia. She flinched.

"May I assist you?" Cruxh asked.

Morris wasn't sure what was happening, but he wished they'd hurry up. Both the crowd and Ira were getting restless. Not to mention the Mayor and the rest of the politicians. If they stepped in, there was no telling how this might end. That was the thing with politicians: most of the time they acted at the wrong time, after the fact. What followed was often enough more confusion and disorder rather than a fix.

"This is official—" Hortensia said.

Cruxh cut in and said, "But milady, I have been deputized and am an officer of the law. I hold the law in utmost respect and know every page of the book *The Rules and Laws of Necropolis*, which you are holding in your hand. Here is my identification." He handed over the document Dow had given him for Hortensia to inspect.

"Hmm," she said and glanced around. Morris hoped she had the stamina to dole out justice with the help of the smallish ghoul. "I think there has been more than one infringement. More than what Mr. Reinhardt said. And we should—"

"Arrest everyone who has broken the law," Cruxh finished her sentence.

"We need—"

"More hands."

"Yes," Hortensia said and frowned. Not because of the eager and honest eyes of the ghoul, but because she would like to finally be in charge. The overly helpful ghoul undermined that. She pushed Morris' cane underneath her armpit, trying to balance it there while flipping open her notebook.

"I can help you with that," Cruxh said, not meaning the cane, which Hortensia was handing to him. He pretended he didn't notice. Cruxh let out a loud yelp. All around them, a twenty-fold group of ghouls came out of hiding. Sirixh was the first to stand next to Cruxh and offer a salute to Miss Caster.

Morris was startled, to put it mildly. So was Hortensia, who took a step back, looking at her new troops who had appeared out of nowhere.

The thing with ghouls is that while you'd think everyone would notice them, what with them being somewhat terrifying, they were actually unobtrusive and easy to overlook, like a cleaning lady. It took a special mind to notice such people. A mind that treated everyone as human beings and did not judge them by their status and jobs. However, much as Morris liked to think he was the kind of person who'd notice, he wasn't. He'd missed the ghouls following them from the Library and hiding behind staircases, statues, and whatnots. He'd been too occupied with himself and his own discomfort.

Cruxh continued, "Miss Caster, you have the authority to deputize in case of emergency. It's written on page thirty-six. I advise you to use that power. My brothers and sisters are happy to aid you and arrest anyone you tell them to." He saluted, lifting his claw against his forehead.

"I... You will now act under me according to the law," Hortensia stammered. There was a moment of silence as she rearranged her thoughts. "Arrest everyone except Mr. Porter and his photographer, Agatha Wicks, and the crowd. Everyone else is involved in incitement to murder and public disorder. Arrest Mr. and Mrs. Worthwrite, who have to be charged as instigators. Also, arrest those who have plotted against the Town Hall council for conspiracy to overthrow the government. Which means Bertha Chaplain, Mr. Worthwrite, Mr. Vaughn, and Mr. Sumner," she said with a stern voice.

Cruxh barked, and four ghouls sped into action.

"And while I'm not well versed in blue-collar crime, I think we should extend our arrest outside these walls to all the bankers, if, as Mr. Reinhardt says, they have indeed falsified their books and conspired to cause this calamity in our city. That should be investigated. Also, I think we have to take Miss Stopford and the other necromancer into custody to be questioned about the public disorder and the trapping of another person inside someone else's body. Also, Miss Stopford has acted behind the Town Hall council's back and might have violated the constitution... Who am I forgetting? Oh yes, arrest Herbert Ringworm for murder, attempted assault, and breaking and entering into a bank. Take the statues that contain the two spirits as evidence of the crimes committed, and also as perpetrators of an assault. And who else?" Hortensia said, drawing in a deep breath.

"My attackers," Mrs. Maybury said.

"Yes, the ghouls who attacked you. I think I have that here in my notebook somewhere," Hortensia said, glancing at Cruxh, who only nodded in agreement. Worry seemed to melt from Hortensia's face. "And we should take Mr. Spurgeon in to be questioned about his involvement, and Mrs. Maybury for the same reasons. And you, Morris Reinhardt, you are charged with conspiracy against Necropolis and its people," Hortensia said, sighing when she said Morris' name.

As Hortensia spoke, Cruxh deployed his ghouls to seize the assailants. The last ghoul next to Cruxh took hold of Morris, and Morris was relieved. Finally, he could rest.

"You have the right to remain silent and refuse to answer questions. Anything you say may be used against you in a court of law. You have the right to an..." echoed in the Town Hall.

◆

Petula was escorted out of the Town Hall by the ghouls. They carried the two statues after her, communicating in quiet yelps. She'd give almost anything to understand what they were saying, especially now, as she knew there was more to them than met the eye, and they were some of the oldest creatures on the continent. They had to know some of the terrific historic secrets of the necromancers long forgotten by humans. If only she could spend time alone with Cruxh... But now she was somewhat busy being arrested and walked through the crowd, who looked at her and the politicians with gaping mouths.

The mob had come here to get justice, to be heard, but this was going too far. Ghouls arresting their leaders and being commanded by a lanky girl in a too-big uniform didn't seem right. What they'd expected was to have a nice shout and an opportunity to shake their signs, then go home and have a nice cup of tea, feeling like they'd done their part. But this, to see actual change happening, was wrong. Due to the sheer confusion, they made room for the convoy to pass. Not that anyone dared to oppose a twenty-fold group of ghouls.

Ira pushed past the others and hurried next to Petula, his captor trying to keep up. He sucked his teeth when he got to her.

"What is it?" she asked, without having to tap into his inner thoughts. His agitation was visible for all to see.

"You should have killed her when you had the

chance and none of this would have happened. You'd be the leader and they'd have to bow to you," Ira said. His "you" sounded a lot like *me*.

"Let it go," Petula said, and she couldn't help but laugh. It was obvious by now that she wasn't going home. The ship would sail before they found her innocent, or at least noticed they couldn't charge her with anything. Yet, she felt relieved. Her family would be critting disappointed and angry at her for a while for not appearing, but they'd recover. She couldn't leave. This conversation with Ira was something she'd never experience in Leporidae Lop. No one would think of urging her to kill someone as a sane or even viable option there. But here, in Necropolis, anything was possible. Death didn't stop you from living your life to the fullest, as was the case with Ira, who frowned as she laughed.

Petula silenced him when he was about to argue back.

She said, "Enough with the killing. It's not the way to practice politics, and what right do you have to intervene in such matters? You are a banker. So stick with what you know, run for Town Hall as an independent party, or forever hold your peace."

If Ira had something on his mind, he didn't say it. Petula turned her attention away from him and concentrated on walking through the city, feeling the crowd's eyes upon her as she moved. People had emerged from their homes and businesses to observe what was happening. Some of the mob at the Town Hall had trailed after them, and the arrests had become a spectacle; a symbol of purification. Someone with a nervous tendency might be agitated and feel like the world was coming to an end, but not Petula. She knew life would go on, some way or another, that it would take a meteorite to bring the world to its end,[47] but even then things like cockroaches and termites might survive and waddle on without a second thought for humans. They would merely think "good riddance." Then again, the cockroaches might miss humans and free lunches.

Petula decided to enjoy the journey to the Metropolitan Police Station, watching the streets and houses curiously. She'd never had a reason to come to this neighborhood, which was older than most of the city and

---

47   Which was a much nicer way than, say, nuclear war.

poorly kept. The houses needed a heavy coat of paint to make them presentable. Still, she savored the atmosphere. This was Petula's equivalent of a stroll in the woods. Her mind and spirit were at peace. She belonged here.

They were marched into the police station, greeted by confused and terrified officers of the law. She had a slight moment of hesitation as she stepped in, when she thought they might summon the Necromantic Council to judge her misdeeds. She pushed the fear away. Whatever waited for her, she could take it. She'd done something tonight she'd never thought to be possible. She'd juggled spirits from one body to another, even a living soul. What others might have missed was her moving Agatha inside her own body for safekeeping, when Jeremiah Black had been at his worst. Otherwise, he would have destroyed her, and Petula couldn't have lived with that. Not when she thought she was responsible. And losing Agatha would have been... She couldn't even think about it.

"Dow?" Petula heard Minta ask.

"Yes," he replied.

"How does the wording go?"

"What wording?"

"Is it 'best' or 'kill'?"

"Aah...one necromancer has to best the other."

"Good," Minta said.

The station's door shut behind them, leaving the mob outside, waiting for something new to happen, like the building blowing up or the dead rising from their graves.

29

I THINK I WOKE UP IN THE WRONG
UNIVERSE

ow sat on a bench. He tapped his fingers against his leg and barely listened to the party leader. He thought about the other Dows in the alternate universes. Did they also get what they wanted and yet feel unsatisfied? Or were his jitters just about a new beginning? He should know better, as being satisfied was beside the point. All this was for feeding the city. It needed energy, innovation, and new blood, otherwise it'd wither away and die. One person was irrelevant and could be sacrificed. The city came first.

"I demand to—" Frederick said, getting angrier by the minute as Dow refused to engage.

"Sir, with all due respect, you not being charged with anything doesn't mean you are free of guilt and blame," Dow finally said.

The man clearly had "how dare you" on his lips, but instead, he said, "All I want is access to the Mayor."

"That is not possible for now. The government is

under construction. When systems have been restored to their usual function, we will be in touch, and a new committee might or might not be formed."

"You can't do this, Dow! This goes against—"

"We are acting according to our constitution. I know this is a difficult process, but I ask you, as I asked Mrs. Maybury, the new head of the Union of the Undead, to have patience. Now, I think, this meeting has come to an end."

"I won't go silently. Don't think for a second I'll let you get away with this. She's—"

"I wouldn't dream of thinking otherwise, but you won't be seeing her today," Dow interrupted him. His words came out in a growl.

Frederick stiffened. He looked over Dow's shoulder, searching for the invisible dog.

Dow could put the man at ease and let him in on the secret, but why would he extend such a courtesy?

"Good day, Mr. Kilborn."

"Mr. Spurgeon," the man said and hurried out.

The man left him alone in his office. Dow glanced at the dog bed. After the arrest, he had wanted to lie there for days, exhausted, but in his line of work, there was no rest. To be honest, he liked it that way. The idle days made him restless anyway. Dow stood up and made his way out as soon as he was sure Mr. Kilborn was gone. He had business with the Mayor.

Dow was back to being the secretary. He hadn't been charged with anything, as he had had a given right to state his opinion. The same had gone for Mrs. Maybury. She had gotten what she had wanted, and he had gone back to being Dow Spurgeon. The rest weren't as lucky.

He smiled. It wasn't a smile you would show to others.

There was nothing better than being Dow Spurgeon here in Necropolis. He thrived in the moistness, pollution, and rotten air and atmosphere of the city. He wouldn't be seen dead living in some godforsaken forest with massive ancient trees, steep green hills, and a waterfall. Those weren't for him. He would get frustrated with the clean, fresh air, healthy habits, and the peace and quiet.

The Town Hall staff hurried away at the sight of him. So did the Ministers of Education, Defense, and Agriculture, who were unsure about their function after the regime change and had gotten together every night since to make sense of what was happening. Dow had a good idea of what was said in those meetings. He flashed a smile before they scurried away.

Minta was right; a smile worked perfectly.

The men fled in terror.

Dow knocked on the Mayor's door.

"Come in."

"Mayor," Dow said.

"I wish you wouldn't call me that."

"Then what do you prefer?"

"Petula is fine."

"If I must."

"You must."

As impudent as the previous one. "The coach is waiting at your request," Dow said instead.

"My request? I thought I had no option," Petula said, yet she had gotten up from behind the desk, where the two statues kept her company. Along with an orange tabby, who sat on the desk, licking itself and glaring Dow ever so often.

Dow ignored the cat and couldn't help but glance behind Petula at the missing spear. There was a twinge of nostalgia. But this was better, he reminded himself. He still had Minta's memoir to write, so there was no forgetting her.

The change of leader had quieted down most of the tumult among the citizens. Minta's declaration of her defeat by Petula at the police station had stunned everyone. Dow could still remember the look on Bertha's face. Not to mention the rest of the lot. R. Porter had had a field day after that night. He had let loose with his news pieces, not sparing anyone. Not even Petula, but it was hard to take a shot at someone who shied away from social interaction. She, in some bizarre way, was morally pure.

Minta had used the constitution to her advantage, saying that the wording "best" didn't necessarily mean kill; that it could also mean a show of strength that was beyond the abilities of the current leader, and Petula had shown just that. She had argued that Petula was thusly the rightful leader of Necropolis. The only one who had argued back had been Petula. The others had been too bemused to say anything, and when the thought of changing leaders had settled in, Petula's objections had been overruled by the whole room. Some had thought to make a puppet out of her, for example Ira, but that wasn't going to happen. Not on his, Dow's, watch.

He helped the Mayor into a thick gray wool jacket. That was another annoyingly similar feature in the two women. A hint of flair wouldn't hurt anyone. You had to have character as a leader, or you were a faceless bureaucrat, and that was his job. Also, she didn't seem too happy about his assistance, constantly complaining and saying she could do it on her own. In the beginning, Minta had been the same. They learned. Eventually.

But everything was changing. Not that Minta's retirement to the countryside to paint watercolors and write had been a miracle cure for the city. Neither had the imprisonment of Ignatius, Wilbur, Morris, the Worthwrites, and the other bankers. Not that the economy went away. It ticked on like a parasite of the human mind, serving no master. So did politics. At least they had forced Bertha to retire. He would rather have seen her behind bars, but she had good lawyers. The best. The same ones who had successfully claimed that murder was part of free speech.

Dow guided Petula out of her office. The kitchen maid, Ann, passed them as they made their way down the stairs. She gave a shy smile and a curtsy.

"Ann," Petula greeted her.

"Good evening, miss," Ann said and hurried off.

There was another thing Petula and Minta had in common. Always so polite. But with Petula, only to those she wanted to, which during her few days in power totaled the kitchen and cleaning staff. To the politicians and her other subordinates, not so much.

They were soon out of the Town Hall. Dow held the door open for the new Mayor as she stepped into the coach. She had her arms crossed, and she didn't look happy. Not that the woman ever looked *happy*. And she complained, a lot.

She manifested a book to read out of her coat pocket as she took her seat. It was the same book Cruxh had returned to her, along with her bag, the angered will-o'-the-wisp, and the murder weapon. He familiarized himself with her while they drove to the Old Rainy Meadow, wanting to solve the mystery of how the woman's mind worked. He had gathered that she would be difficult to control. Even when she appeared to be absent, she was fully present, seeing and hearing every move Dow made and didn't make. Sometimes Dow was sure Petula knew what he thought and more. He would have to work hard to keep his inner wishes and fears to himself.

They were going to the graveyard to pay their respects to the newly deceased Mr. Worthwrite. Ira had been buried today. As far as he knew, it had been a family affair. The press and curious onlookers had been kept away.

Ira's family had accused Petula of murder, but such accusations were quickly muffled, as any trial would have put everything that happened that night out in the open for the public to gawk at. The Worthwrites knew when to be smart. They would get their revenge later.

Dow would protect her. Petula had great potential, if she would only follow his suggestions. He had his ways to motivate her. If he kept supplying her with rare books, she would stay contented, making everything easier this time around.

The horrendous night had worked out perfectly. Not that he had exactly planned it to go like it had, yet when opportunities presented themselves, you had to seize them. For a long time, he had battled with the idea of how to replace Minta with someone new, younger, and with enough power to go on. Every year that had gone by had made Minta ever so restless and tired, jeopardizing all the work Dow had put into Necropolis. Now he didn't need to stop. With Petula, he had at least forty years or more, if he played his cards right. He got out of the coach when it stopped, letting the Mayor out.

"I'll go on my own from here," Petula said.

"I can't let you do that," Dow said.

She stared at him.

He persisted despite the scowl.

He heard her sigh.

They walked through the cemetery. The mist was thick, as always. Some things never changed. Sometimes he thought that he and the mist would be the last men standing when all the people were gone and the city was nothing but a memory of what it was. So be it.

When they got to the grave, they weren't the only ones there. Agatha had arrived before them. A will-o'-the-wisp hovered over her head, casting a light over the freshly dug ground and Ira's new headstone.

"Petula." The necromancer turned to face them before she could possibly have seen or heard them. And the seeing part was unlikely. Agatha's eyes had stayed milky-white.

"Agatha," Petula said.

"Have you come to—" Agatha asked.

"I have. It's the least I can do to make sure, if there's anything left of him, he won't come back. And, of course, to give him a peaceful passing," Petula interrupted her.

"Can I stay and listen?" Agatha asked.

"If you want."

Petula moved closer to the grave and started her liturgy. For anyone listening without knowledge, it would have sounded like a haunted and sorrowful song of a daughter's or a lover's loss, but such was the power of perception. Petula soothed Ira's spirit, making sure he would never return.

Dow watched Agatha and her wisp companion. He was ready to act if there was any attempt on Petula's life. He doubted that there would be, but these were delicate times. Everything was raw, making the city ready for another change. Not that Agatha was one to rock the boat. That was why she wasn't in Petula's place. Also, there seemed to be an affection between the two women.

When Petula was done, Agatha said, "I'm sorry, I didn't mean to mess it up." The wisp flickered restlessly above the woman. After Petula had been freed from prison and had taken on her mayoral role, Agatha and Petula had tried to transfer Ira's possession over from one to the other, with bad results. Dow had been there monitoring the whole process and keeping an eye on Petula. She was still a bit flaky. She might try to flee or do something foolish. Altogether, Dow was glad that Ira had died. He had suggested an assassination in the first place. If Minta had listened to him, things might have turned out different.

"Don't worry about it. This is for the best. And it could have been me saying a wrong word," Petula said.

Agatha smiled. "That's very kind of you, but we both know that isn't true," she said.

"There is a chance," Petula insisted. "But anyway, why are you here?"

"Madam Sabine said it would be all right for me to bless Ira's passing even while I'm a novice," Agatha said. There had been rumors that Agatha had left necromancy and joined the Church of Kraken as a full-time priestess, or priestess-in-training, in this case. Such a shame, Dow thought.

"That is nice of you," Petula said.

"Thank you," Agatha said. "And I'm truly sorry. I never meant it—"

"I'm the one who should be sorry. Will your eyes ever heal?"

"No," Agatha said. This time the softness in her words was gone.

"Hm," Petula said. "How is Morris?"

"Fine," Agatha said.

"Fine?"

"Okay, he's not happy at all. The house arrest has made him moody, and you know," Agatha said.[48]

"Your visits must cheer him up," Petula replied, not sounding sincere.

"If only. After every visit, he gets even more restless, and I don't know what to do with him," Agatha said, not noticing her tone.

"You can always stop seeing him," Petula said.

Dow shook his head. He had a lot to teach her about diplomacy.

"I can't do that," Agatha said, appalled.

"Then you'll have to endure his moods," Petula replied.

"Then I must," Agatha agreed.

"You can always visit me if you like," Petula said after a long silence. Dow was sure those words didn't come easily for her.

"As a priestess, or...?"

"As yourself; and we might find a way to recover your sight," Petula said, laying her hand on the woman's arm.

Agatha startled but let Petula's hand stay there.

Dow didn't like the sound of that.

"Mayor—Petula—we must go. Mr. Cruxh and Mr.

---

48   Morris would disagree. He wasn't moody. It was just that the reality of his actions had caught up with him, and while he accepted whatever verdict the court would give him, he wasn't that keen on the punishment itself. But he didn't regret his confession. Not one bit.

Ringworm are waiting for you at the prison," he said.

Agatha looked towards Dow for the first time, and he wondered if she saw more than she admitted.

"Don't let me keep you. I'll say my prayers and be on my way to church," Agatha murmured.

"Will you be fine alone?" Petula asked.

"I manage. I haven't forgotten everything I know, and I have my wisp."

Petula smiled. "Will you visit?"

"Sure," Agatha replied.

Petula parted with the woman, leaving Agatha there by the grave with her wisp.

"Do you think that was wise?" Dow asked as they walked back to the coach.

"Wiser than going to see Herbert."

Dow coughed. "Yes, he has requested to see you."

"Why?"

"To be pardoned. I guess he wants to explain."

"Why should I care about his explanations? They don't concern me. And I'm not going to pardon a known murderer. He killed that poor driver, and, of course, Jeremiah, and who knows who else."

"Cruxh set this up," Dow replied.

"Oh, I see. Him," Petula said.

◆

Cruxh waited for the Mayor and her secretary outside the prison's visiting room. He had submitted a request to see Herbert, but he had refused, again. He had sent countless letters to the man. The only reply he had gotten was: "if you want to help, get me a meeting with that necromancer." Cruxh hoped that after this, he would be allowed to see him. It was imperative.

He straightened his uniform. This one fit, unlike Miss Caster's. Cruxh was now a junior police officer in training. For the first time in his life, he felt like he had come home. There was right and wrong, and it was his job to guard it. The police chief hadn't been happy about the new addition of ghouls to his force, but Cruxh had a distinct feeling that the chief wouldn't be a chief for long. Hortensia Caster showed promise, and maybe one day he himself would sit behind that big desk.

When Cruxh heard the footsteps of Dow and Petula, he straightened the nightstick on his hip.

One set of footsteps sounded like someone trying to walk without leaving a mark, and the other was rigid, as if the body was only a vessel for the mind. He more than anyone understood what it was like to be trapped inside his own body. He was first and foremost a ghoul, and only after years was he Cruxh to some. But he was good at wearing people down. And he had something that would lighten up the necromancer's mood.

The visitors soon appeared, and Cruxh greeted them with a smile. It was always heartbreaking to see the initial reaction, but he had learned that people were more than their impulses. Not that Dow was people in the traditional sense.

"Good evening!" he said.

"Officer," Dow said.

"Evening," Petula said. "Is this necessary?"

Cruxh paused to decipher the question. The new Mayor was unlike the other in manners, but there was so much that was the same. He hadn't been pleased about the change and hadn't agreed that Minta had lost the fight. She should still be here, but the change of power had seemed to satisfy everyone, even Minta herself.

"I assure you, this is essential for his recovery and..." He hesitated, but added, "You owe him this much."

"Owe is such a strong word," Petula said.

"But, Mayor, an accurate one," Cruxh replied.

"We are here," Dow warned.

"Yes, thank you," he said.

"I think we better go in. We have a busy night ahead," Dow said.

"Could I have a moment of the Mayor's time before you meet Mr. Ringworm?" he asked.

"I don't—" Dow said.

"If I'm to be the Mayor, as you all seem to insist, then I think it's my duty to hear out the keepers of the peace," Petula said.

Cruxh watched Dow flinch. It was a small gesture, and if Cruxh didn't know his kind, he would have missed it.

"I will stay close by," Dow said.

"You do that," Petula replied.

Cruxh took Petula farther away. He reached for the chest pocket of his uniform.

"I have this for you," he said, keeping his back to Dow, blocking his sight.

He handed her the vial with the black liquid he had taken from Herbert.

"Hm," Petula said and took the vial into her hand. "What is it?" she asked.

"You wanted to know what we are. We are that," he said, nodding towards the vial. "It is pure corruption. It is our essence. I need you to find out if that is true or not."

"What do you hope it to be?" Petula asked. Her usual monotone had turned livelier.

"What I hope holds no sway. I, we, need the truth. And I think you are the right person to discover it."

The necromancer paused, shook the bottle, and watched the liquid swirl inside.

"I think I can help you," she eventually said.

"Thank you," Cruxh replied.

"I might someday need help and..." Petula let the rest of her words hang in the air.

"Of course," he replied, thinking she had learned fast.

Petula pocketed the vial, and they made their way back to Dow.

"I'll leave you to it," Cruxh said.

"You are not coming in?" Petula asked.

"He wants nothing to do with me," Cruxh said. "But before I go, Mr. Spurgeon, Mother said she does not want to see any wolves, half or not, lurking in her tunnels. This was a one-time deal. Next time such a person is caught spying, there will be consequences." He left them, not wanting to hear the response. He had delivered it as he had promised and kept his word despite how painful it might be.

He heard the necromancer laugh.

Cruxh left. He went home. He had wanted to stay and eavesdrop on what was said, but that would have been unethical. Cruxh slumped in the armchair that stood nearest to the door in the sitting room. He took a deep breath in.

"Is that you?" Mrs. Maybury's voice came from somewhere in the house.

"Yes, dear," Cruxh said.

It was a perfectly nice house in the middle of

Necropolis. Mrs. Maybury had sold her family home to one of her living sons, and they had bought this one together. Cruxh dared not tell Mrs. Maybury that he knew nothing of owning, managing, or maintaining a house. That all this comfort made him uneasy. Humans liked all things soft and formless. He only needed a place to lay his book and have a moment to himself. Any hole would suffice. But he had to admit, there were some advantages to living as others did. It was easier to invite colleagues over.

"Good," she said, coming into the sitting room, carrying a stack of papers.

Cruxh instantly felt better after seeing her.

"Busy day?" he asked.

"You might say that. Your sister's party keeps signing new applicants, and I'll have to find an assistant to go over all these people," she said, dropping the papers on the desk next to the armchair.

Cruxh saw no point in most of the furniture in the room, with its bleak, superior, and overcrowded style, but Mrs. Maybury seemed to think the tables, the armchairs, and the rest of it were somehow important. That the wretched table he kept hitting his knee against conveyed some social status. How could a table or a chair do that? he wondered. Okay, it was different to sink into the armchair than to sit on a beautifully carved stone, but the action was the same. It never altered. What altered was the perception of the perceiver. However, he conceded that it was nice to be inside the house, in this precise armchair, so close to Mrs. Maybury.

Cruxh sniffed the air and smelled her formaldehyde-coated skin with a hint of rot.

"I can help you with them. Sirixh should not have asked you," he said, looking at the application forms she had laid next to him.

"Don't be silly. You have your duties," she said.

"But you are my duty," he said cheesily.

Mrs. Maybury moaned. Either it was a natural reflex of her dead body or she actually liked what he had said.

"You know, your sister's party has achieved so much in no time. I know I should see her as an enemy of my party, but I have to say, the new addition to the tired, old two-party system is a welcome distraction, as nothing is as dualistic as we like to think," Mrs. Maybury said, sitting on the armrest.

"Everything is so different now. I keep waiting to wake up and find out it was just a distorted dream."

"But dear, you do not sleep," he said.

"You know what I mean," she replied in a somewhat tight voice.

"Yes, I know what you mean, but if we do wake up and this is all taken away, the only thing we can do is advance our causes until then."

"You have to see that all our enemies are already lining up. They hate her, you, and me, and how you let the ghouls loose in the legal system."

"I know, but they have a right up to a point to pursue those notions. We are a democratic sovereignty, and our constitution gives them a right to their opinion and assembly, but as soon as they cross that line, I and my pack will be there waiting."

"But—"

"You cannot prevent it. Politics are about creating a good life, and we all hold different ideas of what that might be. There is no escaping our backgrounds and their influence on what we find valuable and important. One side finds it unnecessary to provide health care to others, as they have the money needed for that in contrast to those who do not. What that side might need is a stable, cheap workforce, and thus they pursue policies along those lines. Then there are those who see other people's interests as detracting from their own, taking away their freedom, pride, or value. All of this is just a game of who gets what from the shared pie. What is troubling is the general lack of understanding of how interconnected we all are. Even the rise of magic cannot take that away."

"That might be. But not everyone is dependent on others."

"No, and there lies the true power."

"All very well. Still, there will be a time when we are not as independent as we would like to be, and my fears will come true," she said.

"Yes, you are right. Even our new leader is finding out she cannot sit alone on the throne. You have to network, or you will find your head on a plate."

Mrs. Maybury groaned. "Cruxh, you are too trusting, optimistic, and open. People will walk all over you if you let them."

"You will be there to stop them," he said and scooped Mrs. Maybury into his lap and gave her a soft peck on her cheek.

"You bet I will."

"The hearing for your attackers is the day after tomorrow," Cruxh said.

"How helpful of them."

"Alice?"

"Yes?"

"Did you mean all this to happen? Us and all?"

"Some of it, yes."

"And the ghouls?"

"All of this worked out in the end."

"But—"

"Don't overthink things. Everything is good—for now."

30

A FRIEND OF ALL, A SERVANT OF NONE

Herbert lay on a straw mattress, reading a book. He'd been lucky with the prison they'd sent him to. The other ones used the prisoners for hard labor and were generally unhygienic and overcrowded. This one had a different sort of warden, with modern thoughts about how to turn prisoners into well-behaved members of society and how torture and punishment only demoralized the prisoners, making their lives brutish and short. You could say Necropolis' Reformatory for the Criminally Insane and Other Offenders was bursting with new ideas.

The warden, or as he wanted to be called, the Chief Officer, or more accurately James, cherished the rise of his prison population, thinking it was due to his reputation, ignoring the fact that there were more offenders because petty theft of food and other essential goods had increased. Usually, such offenders were sent abroad or to the workhouses, along with their families, but the workhouses were full, and foreign nations wanted nothing to do with prisoners from Necropolis. They had some concerns about the prisoners' habits, like their fascination with the dead.

All in all, James Hardrick was a decent man, but a disgrace to his family; going around seeing prisoners as humans and thinking exercise in undergarments was good for your morals was plain embarrassing. Not that Herbert had any problems with exercise. It was more to do with the man's choice of clothing.

Also, what was all this fuss about seeing a shrink? All the demands to talk about his feelings and about Ona were messing with his head. The fact that she was trapped inside a statue made him want to scream. Then there was the fact that Ira refused to go away. If Herbert shifted his attention up from the book, he'd see the banker sitting on the mattress, waiting for him to engage. He was out of his body, there was that, but the necromancers had messed up. They'd let the banker slip between their fingers, and here he was, tormenting him.

"Leave me be," Herbert said.

"Shut up, mate," said his cellmate, who used the general reading time as his napping time.

Herbert tried to smother his anger. But the deep wells of hatred had to come out at some point. He squeezed the mattress.

"I wouldn't try it, mate," his cellmate said. The man was as big as a raving, mad bear, and his inner demons were even larger.

Ira shook his head at the foot of the bed.

"Is everything all right?" a soft voice asked from the cell door. It was James Hardrick, peering inside the room. The little bugger was resilient. He seemed to manifest himself without a word of warning, wearing a friendly face, as if Herbert was his greatest pal. What made matters worse was that this would go on for years to come. He'd gotten a long sentence for the two murders.

"He's seeing things again," Herbert's cellmate, Nevin Shaw, said.

"Oh dear, oh dear... Our inner thoughts can manifest themselves. Breathe in and imagine a calmness wash over you. Count to four as you inhale and count to six as you exhale. There's a soothing, blue ocean waiting to meet you," James said, breathing along with Herbert.

"There, that's better," he said when Herbert's hands

relaxed.

Nevin had sat up and was eyeing them both.

"Mr. Ringworm, you have a visitor, or should I say, visitors," James said in a joyous tone.

Herbert's cellmate puffed but went back to lying on the bed.

Herbert stood up and followed James out of his cell and along the prison corridors. While they walked, the man made a point to nod, greet, and wave at every member of the staff and even to the prisoners. He looked like a king. Herbert had a deep-seated distrust of anyone so gleeful, especially in Necropolis.

Ira agreed with him. He said, "*What a brick.*"

That brick had turned an old castle into a prison. A prison with two-person cells and craft areas. He had even planned to install wood paneling on the walls to make the place feel less dismal, but James had run out of money. The workhouse had needed the proper equipment for the prisoners' crafts so they could sell them at the market, getting a fair price. Another one of James' ideas that embarrassed his wife. Herbert refused to take part in any prison programs. His hands itched to carve, but on principle, he didn't. Also, he refused to accept that the prison had better food than outside. And he refused to engage with Ira. But he wondered who'd come to see him. Was this another pitiful attempt from Cruxh, or had his mother come back to tell him once more that she'd disowned him?

Herbert looked at Mr. Hardrick's back and wondered for a moment if he should strangle the man and flee. It would be so easy.

He shook his head. Cruxh would hunt him down.

"Here we are," James said. He stopped next to a light green door. The man held the door open, leading Herbert into a bare room.

"Your visitors will be in soon," the man said. "Do you need anything while we wait?"

"No," Herbert said. Freedom, he wanted to say, but what was the point. "If it's Cruxh, you better send me back to my cell."

"Eh, it's not him. You have an appointment with the Mayor and Mr. Spurgeon."

Herbert grunted. They had finally come. He glanced

over his shoulder in Ira's direction. There was no emotion coming from the ghost in the usual sense, but Herbert had spent enough time with the man to know he wasn't pleased.

"*They'll never let you go,*" Ira said.

"If you don't shut up and leave, I'll tell her you are still around."

"I can't leave you alone, Mr. Ringworm," James said and frowned.

The man was a lunatic.

Herbert kept his mouth shut, but for once, Ira had disappeared.

"Would you like to visit the therapist today? It might do you some good," the man said.

"No," he replied, as silence would only provoke the man.

There was a knock at the door. James opened it, letting Dow and Petula in.

The necromancer looked past Herbert to the spot where Ira had been. She squinted her eyes.

"Do sit down," James said, indicating the two chairs in front of Herbert.

"Would you leave us?" Dow asked and looked at the warden from under his eyebrows.

"I should—"

"Mr. Hardrick," Dow said.

"Yes, of course, sir," the man said and hurried out.

"So, Mr. Ringworm. What's this about?" Dow asked, standing at the door, refusing to sit. The necromancer followed his example.

"I asked to see the Mayor alone," Herbert said.

"I think we have had this conversation before, about universes and everything," Dow replied.

"Suit yourself. Pe—Mayor, I demand to be released. I was wrongly imprisoned. Yes, I may have killed them, but I was provoked," Herbert said.

When no one replied, he continued, "I've been thinking, as I've had some extra time on my hands. All this was too convenient for Dow. When I look back, I'm sure he toyed with my emotions to push me to act the way I did. He wanted this to happen. I can't be—"

"So what if he did?" Petula interrupted, surprising not only Herbert but also Dow.

"He's not the man you think him to be. He'll toss you aside as he did to the former Mayor when you've served your purpose," Herbert said.

"I wouldn't expect any less of him. You're wasting my time," Petula said.

"But—"

"You still hold a grudge, slinging accusations without taking responsibility. I remember you saying our reactions are our own, and now you want me to believe otherwise. No, Mr. Ringworm, you'll serve your sentence. It is of your own making. Good day," Petula said and stepped towards the door.

"Wait! I can give you something else," Herbert shrieked.

"A knife or a bunny statue?" Petula asked.

Dow chuckled.

"My cellmate, he's a smuggler. He's running the operation from here. I can give you information," Herbert said. He sounded desperate even to himself. He had to get out of here. He needed to be free. To climb. This place was suffocating him.

"Why should I care about a smuggler?" Petula asked.

"You are the Mayor!"

"Yes, how unfortunate," Petula said and pushed the door open.

"Wait, you can't leave me. This is not how this should go," Herbert pleaded, hating how pathetic he sounded.

"I thought you asked me here to apologize, but as always, you are all about yourself and your needs. I can't help you. We are leaving. Dow, are you coming?" Petula concluded.

"Yes," Dow said and left Herbert there without saying a word.

Herbert slumped against the back of the chair.

"*I told you she wouldn't care about you,*" Ira said.

"Go away," Herbert said.

"*I need you to contact Kitty for me. She'll get you out of here in no time,*" Ira said.

"Why would she do that? I thought she had her own troubles with the law."

"*She has the best lawyers. And I'll help you to make her see your value,*" Ira said.

"Why would you want me out of here?"

"*We could do great things together,*" Ira said.

Herbert snorted.

"*Think about it.*"

◆

If only the world was fair, if only bad things happened to bad people, and if only there was a simple, unifiable truth, then maybe life wouldn't seem odd and random, and then maybe humans would learn how to be good and nice to each other and the soil they walked on. If only.

It wasn't as if Petula Upwood didn't care about her fellow men, and in particular Herbert. She just didn't know how to show empathy. Not when there were so many to be empathetic towards. Of course, she felt awful about what'd happened to the man, not only with Ona but also with him being kicked out of the University, his parents, and everything. She'd made Dow cough up. But he'd murdered people. There was no getting past that. She couldn't pardon him. She couldn't let him walk the streets, allowing people to fear whether he'd solve his next problem by killing. In Necropolis, you at least had to pretend to do it for free speech or for some mad experiment. And yes, Petula had no doubt that Dow had toyed with him for personal gains, but that didn't take away the pain of Jeremiah's or Jeffrey's families. She had to remember them.

Petula had visited both of the men's families when the courts had asked her opinion for the sentencing. That was another thing wrong here in Necropolis. Her power should be separated from judicial power. They had to uphold the law on their own, even against her and the Town Hall council. All this business with politics was horrible, and Mrs. Maybury always seemed to be there.

She couldn't help but wonder who in their right mind would think she, Petula, would be a suitable Mayor.

Yes, she'd bested the former Mayor, as Minta had put it. She could do it again in a heartbeat, but this shouldn't be the consequence of her laborious study and self-preservation. She should be heading home instead of seeing people with a yard-long list of demands. She'd naively believed that the demands went the other way around. What an idiot.

Petula pushed her hand inside the coat's silk pocket and held the vial between her fingers. At least there was some hope for being stuck in Necropolis. Petula was doubtful that her rule would do any good for the city, but she could help the ghouls. Not that she didn't love Necropolis. This was where her heart would always be. Like Dow, Petula liked the hardened soul of the place, but as a necromancer and not as a mad woman, running around the city while trying to put out fires. Fires others had started. Also, Dow was constantly there. Never letting her out of his sight. When he wasn't, it was one of his goons instead. The weaselly-looking man, mostly.

"So, are you happy now?"

"Ma'am?" Dow asked.

"It's Petula," she said.

"I forgot."

"My name?"

The man gritted his teeth.

"Answer my question. You got me here, you pushed Minta into her retirement, and now things can go on until one of us dies. Are you happy?"

"Happiness is overrated."

"And Mrs. Maybury?"

Her question made the secretary uncomfortable. He took his time to reply. "A necessary evil."

Yes, evil. The evil he forced her to spend her time with. She would rather be in prison than in the same room as Mrs. Maybury, but Petula's misgivings had been swept under the rug when she swore the Mayor's oath. Her illegal awakening, her connection to the bankers accused of treason, and the mishap with Herbert had been forgotten just like that. The Necromantic Council glorified her. The University wanted her to come back to give lectures. The citizens were just happy to see the back of Minta and gain another idiot to compromise. Her.

"Why me? Why couldn't you go with Agatha?" she asked.

"Do I have to demean myself by answering that question?"

"I guess not."

"Are you done?" Dow asked.

"Two more," Petula said.

"Then will you lay this to rest and get on with the program?" Dow asked, or more like demanded.

"Was Mrs. Maybury in on this? The ghouls? How about Minta?"

"Why do you keep on insisting on talking about Mrs. Maybury?"

"Just answer the question."

"She is a force of will, and I think she saw a way to bring chaos. Who knows? But no, there was no plot. Just opportunities to be seized in the right place and at the right time."

"You would do this to Minta?"

"That is a third question, but I will indulge you. She needed a way out. This was the best one I could come up with that held enough dignity to allow her to leave in peace without regrets to taint her other pursuits."

"But if there had been a fight, I could have killed her," Petula said.

Dow led her out of the prison and into the night air of Necropolis. "That is always a possibility. We all have to die one day," he said.

Petula squeezed the vial.

◆

Minta lay her hands behind her head on the soft ground. She had finished painting for today, and she watched as the robins swooped over the nearby lake. Birds were magnificent creatures. They symbolized all that it meant to be human. Joy, renewal, death, knowledge, creativity, freedom, cunningness, trickery, luck, life, and happiness. They were beautiful. Minta shut her eyes and listened to the world around her thrumming with life. This was what life should be like. The chirping, the wind, the warmth of the sunlight, the smell of freshly cut grass, and the intoxicating scent of the trees.

She had escaped.

She was free.

AUTHOR'S NOTE

Penny for Your Soul started from a single idea. I got this vision of undead bankers, and soon after necromancers invaded the story. You had to have something fueling the undead. There were a dozen different versions of how the plot would go and who the characters would be before what you read transpired. But the story was defined when the three bankers marched into poor mister Jeremiah Black's death scene and there on it wrote itself, bringing in characters like Agatha and Bertha, and one of my favorites, Cruxh.

After every revision, the book and the city of Necropolis came stronger. It might not be the city I would love to live in with all the macabre and ruthlessness, but it's not a city so unlike ours. You can see it as a parallel to our cities if greed and power were all that is important. But luckily in the real world, there are people like Hortensia, Cruxh, and Minta who believe in the good of others and see their duty to bring justice.

But what kept me writing was Petula and her somewhat unwilling quest to find her destiny. I had to see there was a crack to her hard exterior. Something to make her step into the real world and engage with others. I'm glad she found Agatha and the tabby, but I'm also excited Dow will challenge her, or otherwise, she would get bored, and with a mind like hers that would be catastrophic.

Thank you for reading my book. The reason I wrote it was you. Something to entertain you, characters to get caught with, and maybe found an appreciation to creatures like Cruxh and take pity on people like Herbert who we all are. We all try to scrape by in this mad world which doesn't ask questions and can take away what we love too easily.

Sincerely,
K.A. Ashcomb

ABOUT THE AUTHOR

K.A. Ashcomb grew up reading books by Terry Pratchett and other comical fantasy authors. After acquiring her MA in Comparative Religion, spiced with Social Psychology and Sociology, she found herself working behind a bookshop's counter. With tons of free time on her hands, she began to create stories about gods, unfortunate heroes, and other jerks to amuse herself. The stories grew bigger and bigger, and she had to put them on paper, and so her first book Worth Of Luck was born, and now Penny for Your Soul.

When she isn't writing books or playing video games, you can find her in the local forest reservation, roaming there while trying to find her way back to her keyboard, beloved books, her two mischievous cats, and her husband.

COMING NEXT FROM K.A. ASHCOMB

Sigourney is back! Luck is driving her to her home town with a locomotive. Accompanied by Siarl and the Rabbit god of luck, she has to confront her past and let it free. She comes to face to face with her brother, and the only way out is to save the industrializing city from his clutch or else...